D1407802

Penny Jordan, one of Harlequin's most popular authors, unfortunately passed away on December 31, 2011. She leaves an outstanding legacy, having sold over 100 million books around the world. Penny wrote a total of 187 novels for Harlequin, including the phenomenally successful *A Perfect Family*, *To Love, Honor and Betray*, *The Perfect Sinner* and *Power Play*, which hit the *New York Times* bestseller list. Loved for her distinctive voice, she was successful in part because she continually broke boundaries and evolved her writing to keep up with readers' changing tastes. *Publishers Weekly* said about Jordan, "Women everywhere will find pieces of themselves in Jordan's characters." It is perhaps this gift for sympathetic characterization that helps to explain her enduring appeal.

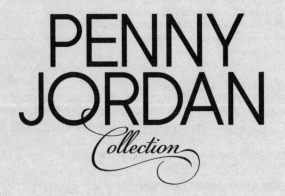

PENNY JORDAN
Collection

A LITTLE SEDUCTION

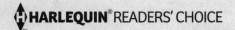

HARLEQUIN® READERS' CHOICE

Recycling programs for this product may not exist in your area.

ISBN-13: 978-0-373-24986-2

A LITTLE SEDUCTION

Copyright © 2013 by Harlequin Books S.A.

The publisher acknowledges the copyright holder of the individual works as follows:

A TREACHEROUS SEDUCTION
Copyright © 1999 by Penny Jordan

THE MARRIAGE RESOLUTION
Copyright © 1999 by Penny Jordan

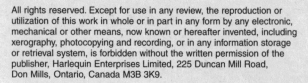

Printed in U.S.A.

www.Harlequin.com

CONTENTS

A TREACHEROUS SEDUCTION

CHAPTER ONE

BETH GAVE AN involuntary gasp of horrified disbelief as she stared white-faced at the contents of the crate she had just opened.

'Oh, no! *No!*' she protested in despair as she picked up the wine glass she had just removed from its packaging, one of a suite of matching stemware she had ordered on her buying trip to Prague.

Beth closed her eyes; her face had gone deathly pale and she felt rather sick.

She had invested so much in this Czech order, and not just in terms of money.

Her fingers trembling, she opened another box, biting her bottom lip hard as the decorative water jug she had in her hand confirmed all her growing anxiety.

Three hours later, with the storeroom at the back of the small shop she ran in partnership with her best friend Kelly Frobisher strewn with packages and stemware, all Beth's worst fears were realised.

These…these abominations against good taste and style were most certainly not the deliciously pretty reproduction antique items *she* had ordered with such excitement and pleasure all those months ago in the Czech Republic. No way. *This* order, the order she had received but most certainly never placed, might equate in terms of numbers and suites to what she had bought, but in every other way it was horrendous, horrible, a parody of the beautiful, elegant, covetable top-quality stemware she had seen and paid for.

No, there was no way she would ever have ordered anything like this, and no way could she ever sell it either. Her customers were very discriminating, and Beth's stomach churned as she recalled how enthusiastically and confidently she had titillated their interest by describing her order to them and promising them that it would turn their Christmas dinner tables into wonderful facsimiles of a bygone age, an age of Venetian baroque, Byzantine beauty.

Sickly she stared at the glass she was holding, a glass she remembered as being a richly gorgeous Christmassy cranberry-red with a depth of colour one could almost eat.

Was it really for this that she had put the small shop, her reputation and her personal finances into jeopardy? Was it for *this* that she had telephoned her bank manager from Prague to persuade him to extend her credit facilities? No, of course it wasn't. The glassware she had been shown had been nothing like this. Nothing at all!

Feverishly she examined another piece, and then another, hoping against hope that what she had already seen had simply been a slight mistake. But there was no mistake. Everything she unpacked possessed the same hallmarks of poor workmanship, inferior glass and crude colouring. The blue she remembered as being the same deep, wonderful colour as a Renaissance painter's Madonna's robes, as having the same depth when held up to the light as the most beautiful of antique stained-glass windows, the green she recalled as possessing the depth and fire of a high-quality emerald, and the gold which had had gilding as subtle as anything to come out of an expert gilder's workshop were, in reality, like comparing the colours in a child's paintbox to those used by a true artist.

There had to have been a mistake. Beth stood up. She would have to ring the suppliers and advise them of their error.

Her brain went into frantic overdrive as she tried to grapple with the enormity of the problem now confronting her. After being delayed well beyond its original delivery date, the order had just barely arrived in time for their Christmas market.

In fact, she had planned this very afternoon to clear the shelves of their current stock and restock them with the Czech stemware.

What on earth was she going to do?

Normally this would have been a problem she would immediately have shared with her partner, Kelly, but these were not normal circumstances. For one thing, she had been in Prague on her own when she had taken the initiative to order the stemware. For a second, Kelly was quite rightly far more preoccupied with her new husband and the life they were establishing together than she was with the shop at the moment, and they had mutually agreed that for the time being Kelly would take a back seat in the business they had started up together in the small town of Rye-on-Averton, where the girls had originally been encouraged to come by Beth's godmother, Anna Trewayne.

And for a third…

Beth closed her eyes. She knew that if she were to tell her godmother, Anna, or Kelly, her best friend, or even Dee Lawson, her landlady, of the financial and professional mess she was now in all three of them would immediately rush to her aid, full of understanding and sympathy for her plight. But Beth was sharply conscious of the fact that, out of the four of them, she was the only one who always seemed to get things wrong, who always seemed to make bad judgements, who always seemed to end up being duped…cheated…hurt. Who always seemed to be a loser…a victim…

Beth shuddered with a mixture of anger and anguish. What was the *matter* with her? *Why* was she constantly involving herself with people who ultimately let her down? She might, as other people were constantly reminding her, be placid, and perhaps a little too on the accommodating side, but that didn't mean that she didn't have any pride, that she didn't need to be treated with respect.

None of the other three would have got themselves in this situation, she was sure. Dee, for instance, would most certainly not have done. No, she couldn't imagine anyone ever managing to dupe or cheat Dee, with her confident, businesslike manner, nor Kelly, with her vibrant, positive personality, nor even Anna, with her quiet gentleness.

No, *she* was the vulnerable one, the fool, the idiot, who had 'cheat me' written all over her.

It had to be her own fault. Look at the way she had fallen for Julian Cox's lies; look how gullible she had been, believing that he loved her when all the time what he had really been interested in had been the money he had believed she would inherit.

She had been stricken with shame when Julian had left her, claiming that he had never told her that he wanted to marry her, accusing her of running after him, pursuing him, of imagining that he had ever felt something for her.

Beth's face started to burn. Not because she still loved him—she most certainly didn't, and she doubted deep in her heart that she ever had; she had simply allowed him to persuade her that she had, because she had been flattered by the assiduous attentions he had paid her, and by his constant declarations of love, his insistence that they were soul mates. Well, she had certainly learned her lesson there. Never, ever again would she trust a man who treated her like that, who claimed to have fallen crazily and instantly in love with her as Julian had done, and she had stuck to that private vow even when…

Beth could feel her heart starting to thud heavily as she fought to suppress certain dangerous memories.

At least she hadn't made the *same* mistake twice. No, she agreed mentally with herself, she'd just gone on to make fresh ones.

A failed romance and the public humiliation of other people knowing about it, painful though it had been, had at least only damaged her own life. What had happened now had the potential to humiliate not just her but Kelly as well.

They had built up a very good reputation in the town since opening their crystal and china shop. Because they were a small outlet they concentrated on matching their customers' needs and, where they could, innovatively anticipating them.

Kelly had already told her enthusiastically that they had several very good customers, with celebrations of one sort or another coming up, to whom she had mentioned the fact that the purchase of some very special and individual stemware might be an excellent idea.

One customer in particular had been talking excitedly to Beth only the previous week about purchasing three dozen of the crimson Czech champagne flutes.

'It's our silver wedding this year—two days before Christmas—the whole family will be coming to us and it would be wonderful to have the glasses for then. I'm having a large family dinner party and we could use them for the champagne cocktails I'm planning to do, and for the toasts…'

'Oh, yes, they would be perfect,' Beth had enthused, already in her mind's eye seeing them on her customer's antique dining table, the delicacy of the fragile glass and the richness of the colour emphasised by the candlelight.

There was no way Candida Lewis-Benton would want to order what she, Beth, had just unpacked. No way at all.

Valiantly Beth fought the temptation to burst into tears. She was a woman, not a girl, and, as she had thought she had proved when she was in Prague, she could be determined and self-reliant and, yes, proud too. She could earn her *own* self-respect, and never mind what certain other people thought of her—certain other not-to-be-thought-of, or thought *about*, arrogant, overbearing men who thought they knew her better than she knew herself. Who wanted to take over her life and her, who thought they could lie to her and get her to acquiesce to whatever they wanted for her by claiming that they loved her. And she had known, of course, just what it was *he* had wanted. Well, she had at least shown him just how easily she had seen through his duplicitous behaviour.

'Beth, I know it's probably too soon to tell you this, but I…I've fallen in love with you,' he had told her that afternoon in the pouring rain on the Charles Bridge.

'No, that's not possible,' she had replied hardily.

'If that wasn't love, then just exactly what was it?' he had demanded on another occasion, and he had touched his fingertips to her lips, still swollen and soft from the passion they had just exchanged.

She had answered boldly, 'It was just lust—just sex, that's all…' And she had gone on to prove it to him.

'Don't be tempted into falling for the promises these

street traders make to you,' he had warned her more than once. 'They're simply pawns being used by organised crime to dupe tourists.'

She knew quite well what he'd been after. What *he'd* been after was exactly what Julian had been after—her money. Only Alex Andrews had wanted her body thrown in as well.

At least sexually Julian had done the decent thing, so to speak.

'I don't want us to be lovers…not yet…not until you're wearing my ring,' Julian had whispered passionately to her the night he had declared his love—a love he had not felt for her at all, as it later transpired.

It seemed almost laughable now that she had ever agonised so much over his perfidy. Perhaps the acute sense of self-loathing she had experienced over his betrayal and accusations had had more to do with the humiliation he had made her suffer rather than a genuinely broken heart.

Certainly, whenever she thought about him now, which was rarely, it was without any emotion whatsoever other than a distant sense of amazement that she could ever have considered him attractive. She had gone to Prague determined to prove to herself that she was not the emotional fool Julian had painted her as being, vowing that never again would she let herself be conned into believing that when a man told her he loved her he meant it.

She had come back from Prague feeling extremely proud of herself, and equally proud of the new, hard-headed, hard-hearted Beth she had turned herself into. If men wanted to lie to her and betray her, then she would learn to play them at their own game. She was an adult woman, with all that that encompassed. Mistrusting men as emotional partners didn't mean that she had to deny herself the pleasure of finding them sexually desirable.

The days were gone when a woman had to deny the sexual side of her nature. The days had gone, too, when a woman had to convince herself that she loved a man and that, even more important, he loved and respected her before she could give herself to him physically.

She had been living in the Dark Ages, Beth had told herself—living her life by an outdated set of rules and an even more outdated set of moral beliefs. An outdated and far too idealistic set of moral beliefs. Well, all that was over now. Now she had finally joined the real world, the world of harsh realities. Now she was a fully paid-up member of modern society, and if men, or rather a certain man, did not like the things she did or the things she said, then tough. The right to enjoy sex for sex's sake was no longer a purely male province, and if Alex Andrews didn't like that fact then it was just too bad.

Had he really thought she was going to fall for those lies he had told her? All those ridiculous claims he had made about falling in love with her the moment he first saw her?

Prague had been surprisingly full of people like him. British- and American-born in the main, students, most of them, or so they'd claimed, taking a year out to 'do' areas previously off limits to them. Some had family connections in the Czech Republic, some not, but all of them had possessed a common ingredient; all of them, to some extent, had been living off their wits, using their skills as linguists, charming a living out of gullible tourists. In Beth's newly cynical opinion they'd been only one step removed from the high-pressure-sales types hawking time-share apartments, who had made certain holiday areas of the continent notorious until their governments had taken steps to control their activities.

True, Alex Andrews had alluded to the very different

lifestyle he claimed to lead in Britain. According to his own description of himself he was a university lecturer in Modern History at a prestigious university college who was taking a sabbatical to spend some time with the Czech side of his family, but Beth hadn't believed him. Why should she have? Julian Cox had claimed to have a highly profitable and respectable financial empire—he had turned out to be little more than a fraudster who had somehow managed to keep himself one step in front of actually breaking the law. It had been plain to Beth from the first moment she had met him that Alex Andrews was very much the same type.

Too good-looking, too self-confident…too sure that she'd been going to fall into his arms just because he claimed he was desperate to have her there. She wasn't *that* much of a fool. She might have fallen for that kind of line once, but she certainly hadn't been about to fall for it a second time.

Oh, yes, she had escaped making a fool of herself over Alex Andrews, but she hadn't been able to prevent herself from…

Numbly Beth studied the stemware she had unpacked. There was a sick, shaky feeling in her stomach, a sensation of mingled panic and dread. It had to be a mistake… It *had* to be.

She simply couldn't face telling Dee, Anna and Kelly that she had made a spectacularly bad error of judgement—again.

And she certainly couldn't face telling her bank manager. She had really gone out on a limb with the loan she had persuaded him to give her—and she it.

Anxiously she got to her feet. The first thing she needed to do was to ring the factory.

She was just about to dial the number on her invoice

when the telephone rang. Picking up the receiver, she heard her partner Kelly's voice.

'Beth, you're going to hate me for this…' Kelly paused. 'Brough is having to go to Singapore on business and he wants me to go with him. It could mean us being away for over a month—he says that since we would be almost halfway there anyway we might as well also fly on to Australia and spend a couple of weeks with my cousin and her family.

'I know what you must be thinking. We're coming up for our busiest time and I've only been working a couple of days a week lately anyway. If you'd rather I didn't go I'll understand… After all, the business…'

Beth thought quickly. It was true that she *would* find it hard to manage for what sounded as though it was going to be close on five or six weeks without her partner, but if Kelly was away then at least it meant that Beth wouldn't have to tell her about the stemware. Cravenly Beth admitted to herself that, given the opportunity to do so, she would much rather sort out everything discreetly and privately without involving anyone else—even if that meant getting someone in part-time to help with the shop whilst Kelly was away.

'Beth? Are you still there?' she heard Kelly asking her anxiously.

'Yes. Yes, I'm here,' Beth confirmed.

Taking a deep breath, she told her friend and partner as cheerfully as she could, 'Of course you must go, Kelly. It would be silly to miss out on that kind of opportunity.'

'Mmm…and I would miss Brough dreadfully. But I do feel guilty about leaving you, Beth, especially at this time of the year. I know how busy you're going to be, what with the new stemware… Oh…did it arrive? Is it as wonderful as you remembered? Perhaps I could come down…?'

'No. No…there's no need for that,' Beth assured her quickly.

'Well, if you really don't mind,' Kelly said gratefully. 'Brough did say that we could drive over to Farrow today. I've been given the address of someone who works there who makes the most wonderful traditional hand-crafted furniture. He's got one of those purpose-built workshops in the Old Hall Stables there. It's been turned into a small craft village. But if you need me at the shop…'

'No. I'm fine,' Beth assured her.

'When are you putting the new stemware stuff out?' Kelly asked enthusiastically. 'I'm dying to see it…'

Beth tensed.

'Er…I haven't decided yet…'

'Oh. I thought you said you were going to do it as soon as it arrived,' Kelly protested, plainly confused.

'Yes. I was. But…but I want to get a few more ideas yet; we've still got nearly a fortnight before the town's Christmas lights and decorations are in place, and I thought it would be a good idea to time the window to fit in with that…'

'Oh, yes, that's a wonderful idea,' Kelly enthused. 'We could even have a small wine and nibbles do for our customers…perhaps have the food and the drinks the same colour as the glass…'

'Er…yes. Yes…that would be wonderful,' Beth agreed, hoping that her voice didn't sound as lacking in enthusiasm to her friend as it did to herself.

'Oh, but I've just realised; we'll be leaving at the end of the week so I shall miss it,' Kelly complained. 'Still, we'll definitely be back for Christmas; that's something I have insisted on to Brough, and fortunately he agrees with me that our first Christmas should be spent here at home…together… Which reminds me. Please save me a set of those wonderful glasses, Beth.'

'Er, yes, I shall,' Beth confirmed.

With luck, she would be able to get the mistake in her order reversed and the correct stemware sent out to her whilst Kelly was away. Whilst Kelly was away, yes, but would she get it in time for the all-important Christmas market? When selecting the pieces for her order she had deliberately focused on the colours she deemed to be the most saleable for the Christmas season; deep red, rich blue, fir-tree green, all in the lavishly baroque style and decorated with gold leaf. Beautiful though the pieces were, she doubted that they would have the same sales appeal in the spring and summer months.

One hour and five unanswered telephone calls after she had finished speaking with Kelly, Beth sat back on her heels and stared helplessly around her chaotic storeroom.

The horror and the anger she had initially felt at having received the wrong order were giving way even more to frantic unease and suspicion.

The factory she had visited had been a large one, and the sales director she had spoken with suave and business-suited. The cabinets which had lined the walls of his plush office had been filled with the almost mouth-wateringly beautiful stemware from which he had invited Beth to take her choice for her order.

His secretary's office, which she had glimpsed through an open door as he had escorted her from the reception foyer and into his own office, had been crammed with the most up-to-the-minute modern technology, and it was just not feasible that such an organisation would not, during office hours, have its telephone system fully manned and its faxes working.

But every time Beth had punched the numbers into her own telephone she had been met with a blank silence, an emptiness humming along the wire. Even if the factory had been closed for the Czech Republic version of a Bank Holiday, the telephone would still have rung.

The most horrible suspicion, the most awful possibility, was beginning to edge its way into Beth's thoughts.

'Don't be taken in by what you've been shown,' Alex Andrews had warned her. 'Some gypsies are thought to be used as pawns in organised crime. Their aim is to sell non-existent goods to gullible foreign tourists in order to bring into the organisation foreign currency.'

'I don't believe you. You're just trying to frighten me,' Beth had told him furiously. 'To frighten me and to make sure that I give my order to your cousins,' she had added sharply. '*That's* what all this is really about, isn't it? Telling me you've fallen in love with me…claiming to care about me… I *would* be gullible if I had fallen for your lies, Alex…'

Beth didn't want to remember Alex's reaction to her accusations. She didn't want to remember anything about Alex Andrews at all. She wasn't going to allow herself to remember *anything* about him.

No? Then how come she had dreamed about him virtually every night since her return from the Czech Republic? a small inner voice taunted her.

She had dreamed about him simply out of the relief of knowing she had stood by her own promises to herself and not fallen for his lies, his claims to love her, Beth told her unwanted internal critic crossly.

She looked at her watch. It was almost four o'clock.

No point in trying the Czech suppliers again today. Instead she would repack her incorrect order.

Dee, their landlady for the shop and the comfortable accommodation that went with it, who had now become a good friend, had invited her over for supper this evening.

Dispiritedly she started to repack the stemware, shuddering a little as she did so. The crystal was more suitable for jam jars than stemware, Beth decided with a grimace of distaste.

'Haven't I heard,' Dee had queried gently a few weeks ago, 'that some of the processes through which their china and glassware are made are a little crude when compared to ours…?'

'At the lower end of the market perhaps they are,' Beth had defended. 'But this factory I found originally actually made things for the Royal House of Russia. The sales director showed me the most exquisite pieces of a dinner service they'd had made for one of the Romanian Princes. It reminded me very much of a Sèvres service, and the translucency of the china was quite breathtaking. The Czech people are very proud of their tradition of making high-quality crystal,' Beth had added.

She had Alex Andrews to thank for *that* little piece of information. It had been something he had thrown furiously at her when she had accused him of trying to persuade her to buy his cousins' goods, and the cause of yet another quarrel between them.

Beth had never met anyone who infuriated her as much as he had done. He had brought out in her a streak of anger and passion she had never previously known she possessed.

Anger and passion. Two very dangerous emotions.

Quickly Beth got back to repacking the open crates.

Remember, she told herself sternly, you aren't going to think about him. *Or* about what...what happened...

To her chagrin, Beth could feel her face starting to heat and then burn.

'God, but you're wonderful. So sweet and gentle on the outside and so hot and wild in private, so very hot and wild...'

Furious with herself, Beth jumped up.

'You weren't going to think about him,' she told herself fiercely. 'You *aren't* going to think about him.'

CHAPTER TWO

'MORE COFFEE, BETH...?'

'Mmm...'

'You seem rather preoccupied. Is anything wrong?' Dee asked Beth in concern as she put down the coffee pot she had been holding.

They had finished eating and were now sitting in Dee's sitting room, where several furnishing and decorating catalogues were spread open around them. Dee was planning to redecorate the room, and had been asking Beth for her opinion of the choices she had made.

'No. No...I like the cream brocade very much,' Beth told Dee quickly. 'And if you opt for the cream carpet as well, that will allow you to bring in some richer, stronger colours in the form of cushions and throws...'

'Yes, that was what I was thinking. I've seen a wonderful fabric that I've really fallen for, and I've managed to track down the manufacturer, but it's a very small company. They've told me that they can only accept my order if I pay for it up front, and of course I'm reluctant to do that, just in case they can't or don't deliver.

'I've asked my bank to run a financial check on them and let me have the results. It will be a pity if the report isn't favourable. The fabric is wonderful, and I've really set my heart on it. But of course one has to be cautious in these matters, as no doubt you know.

'You must have really been keeping your fingers crossed in Prague whilst you waited for your bank to verify that the Czech company was financially sound enough for you to do business with.'

'Er…yes. Yes, I was…'

Beth took a quick gulp of her coffee.

What would Dee say if Beth were to admit to her that she had done no such thing, that she had quite simply been so excited at the thought of selling the wonderful stemware she had seen that every principle of financial caution she had ever learnt had flown right out of her head?

'Kelly rang me today. She was telling me that she and Brough are hoping to make an extended trip to Singapore and Australia…'

'Mmm…they are,' Beth agreed.

She *ought* to have asked her bank to make proper enquiries over the Czech factory. She knew that, of course. Not just to ensure that they were financially sound, but also to find out how good they were at meeting their order dates. She could even remember her bank manager advising that she do so when she had telephoned him to ask him for extra credit facilities. And no doubt if he hadn't been on the point of departing for his annual leave on the very afternoon she had rung *he* would have made sure that she had done so.

But he had and she hadn't and the small, nagging little seed of doubt planted earlier by her inability to make telephone or fax contact with the factory was now throwing out shoots and roots of increasingly strong suspicion and dread with frightening speed.

'How will you manage whilst Kelly's away? You'll have to get someone in part-time to help you…'

'Yes. Yes, I shall,' Beth agreed distractedly, wondering half hysterically what on earth Dee would say if she admitted to her that, if her worst fears were confirmed and her incorrect order had not been a mistake but a deliberate and cynical ploy to take advantage of her there was no way she would *need* any extra sales staff because, quite simply, there would be virtually nothing in the shop to sell.

Another fear sprang into Beth's thoughts. If she had nothing to sell then how was she going to pay her rent on the shop and the living accommodation above it?

She had absolutely nothing to fall back on, not now that she had over-extended herself so dangerously to purchase the Czech glass.

Her parents would always help her out, she knew that, and so, too, she suspected, would Anna, her godmother. But how could she go to any of them and admit how foolish she had been?

No, she had got herself into this mess, and somehow she would get herself out of it.

And her first step in doing that was to locate her supplier and insist that the factory take back her incorrect order and supply her with the goods she had actually ordered.

'Beth, are you *sure* you're all right…?'

Guiltily she realised that Dee had been speaking to her and that she hadn't registered a single word that the older woman had been saying.

'Er…yes…I'm fine…'

'Well, if it would be any help I could always come and relieve you at the shop for the odd half-day.'

'*You!*' Beth stared at Dee in astonishment, surprised to see that Dee was actually flushing.

'You needn't sound quite so surprised,' Dee told Beth slightly defensively. 'I *did* actually work in a shop while I was at university.'

Had she hurt Dee's feelings? Beth tried not to show her surprise. Dee always seemed so armoured and self-contained, but there was quite definitely a decidedly hurt look in her eyes.

'If I sounded surprised it was just because I know how busy you already are,' Beth assured her truthfully.

Dee's late father had had an extensive business empire which Dee had taken over following his death, managing not only the large amounts of money her father had built up through shrewd investment but also administering the various charity accounts he had set up to help those in need in the town.

Dee's father had been the old-fashioned kind of philanthropist, very much in the Victorian vein, wanting to benefit his neighbours and fellow townspeople.

He had been a traditionalist in many other ways as well, from what Beth had heard about him—a regular churchgoer throughout his life and a loving father who had brought Dee up on his own after his wife's premature death.

Dee was passionately devoted to preserving her father's memory, and whenever anyone praised her for the good work she did via the charities she helped to fund she was always quick to point out that she was simply acting as her father's representative.

When Beth and Kelly had first moved to the town they had wondered curiously why Dee had never married. She had to be about thirty, and surprisingly for such

a businesslike and shrewd woman she had a very strong
maternal streak. She was also very attractive.

'Perhaps she just hasn't found the right man,' Beth had
suggested to Kelly. That had been in the days when she
herself had believed that she had very much found the
right man, in the shape of Julian Cox, and had therefore
been disposed to feel extremely sorry for anyone who
was not so similarly blessed.

'Mmm…or maybe no man can compare in her eyes to
her father,' Kelly had guessed, more shrewdly.

Whatever the truth, one thing was certain: Dee was
simply not the kind of person whose private life one could
pry into uninvited. And yet tonight she seemed unfamiliarly vulnerable; she even looked softer, and somehow
younger as well, Beth noticed. Perhaps because she had
left her hair down out of its normal stylish coil.

Certainly it would be impossible to overlook her, even
in a crowd. She had the kind of looks, the kind of manner that immediately commanded other people's attention—unlike *her*, Beth decided with wry self-disdain.

Her soft mousy-blonde hair would never attract a second look, not even when the sun had left it, as it had done
last summer, with these lighter delicate streaks in it.

As a teenager she had passionately longed to grow
taller. At five feet four she was undeniably short… 'Petite', Julian had once infamously called her. Petite and
as prettily delicate as a fragile porcelain doll. And she
had thought he was *complimenting* her. Yuck. She was
short. But she was very slender, and she did have a softness about her, an air which had once unforgettably and
almost unforgivably led Kelly to say that she could almost have modelled for the book *Little Women*'s Beth.

On impulse, before going to Prague, she had had her
long hair shaped and cut. The chopped, blunt-edged bob

suited her, even if sometimes she did find it irritating, and had to tuck the stray ends behind her ears to stop them from falling over her face when she was working.

'You are beautiful,' Alex Andrews had told her extravagantly when he had held her in his arms. 'The most beautiful woman in the whole world.'

She had known that he was lying, of course, and why, and she hadn't been deceived—no, not for one minute—despite the sharp, twisting knife-like pain she had felt as she had listened to him in the full knowledge of his duplicity.

Why would he possibly think she was beautiful? After all, he was a man who any woman could see was quite extraordinarily handsome in a way that was far more classical Greek god than modern-day film star. Tall, with a body that possessed a steely whipcord-fit muscular strength, he'd seemed to radiate a fierce and very high-charged air of sensual magnetism that had almost been like some kind of personal force field. Impossible to ignore it—or him. Beth had felt at times as though he was draining the will-power out of her, as though he was somehow subtly overpowering her with the intensity of his sexual aura.

He also had the most remarkably hypnotic silver-grey eyes. She could see them now, feel their heat burning her. She could...

'Beth...?'

'I'm sorry Dee,' she apologised guiltily.

'It's all right,' Dee assured her, with her unexpectedly wide and warm smile. 'Kelly told me that you'd collected your stemware from the airport and that you were unpacking it. I must say that I'm looking forward to seeing it. I've got some spare time tomorrow. Perhaps if I called round...?'

Beth could feel herself starting to panic.

'Er…I don't want anyone to see it until the town's Christmas lights go on officially,' she told Dee quickly. 'I haven't got it on the shelves yet, and—'

'You want to surprise everyone by making a wonderful display with it,' Dee guessed, her smile broadening.

'Well, whatever you decide to do with it, to display it, I know it's going to look wonderful. You really do have a very creative and artistic eye,' she complimented Beth truthfully, adding ruefully, 'And I most certainly do not. Which is why I needed your advice on the refurbishment of my sitting room.'

'Your eye is actually very good,' Beth assured her. 'It's just when it comes to those extra details that you need a bit of help. That crimson damask trimmed with the dull gold fringing would make a wonderful throw…'

'It'll be very rich,' Dee commented doubtfully.

'Yes, it will,' Beth agreed. 'Perfect for winter, and then for spring and summer you could switch to something softer. Your sitting room French windows open out onto the garden, and a throw which picks up the colours in that bed you've got within view of the window would be a perfect way to bring the garden and the sitting room into harmony with one another.'

Beth glanced at her watch and stood up. It was time for her to leave.

'Don't forget,' Dee urged her, 'if you *do* need some help in the shop, let me know. I realise that Anna sometimes stands in, when either you or Kelly aren't available, but…'

She stopped as Beth was already shaking her head.

'There's no way that Ward will allow Anna to spend several hours on her feet right now. Anna says that you'd think no woman had ever had a baby before. Apparently it doesn't matter how often she tells him that being pregnant is a perfectly natural state, that she's happy and there's absolutely nothing for him to worry about; he still treats her as though she's too fragile to draw breath.'

Dee laughed ruefully.

'He's certainly very protective of her. He was most disapproving the other day when he found out she and I'd been to the garden centre and that I'd let her carry a box of plants. But then I suspect he still hasn't completely forgiven me for sending him away when he came to look for Anna before they were married.'

'You were only trying to protect her,' Beth protested. She liked Ward, and was pleased that her godmother had found happiness with him after being widowed for so long, but she could well understand how two such strong characters as Dee and Ward would clash occasionally.

Only a very, very fine line separated a strong, determined man from being a bossy, domineering one, as she had good cause to know. Ward, fortunately, knew which side of the line to be on; Alex Andrews did not.

Alex Andrews.

He would certainly have enjoyed her present predicament, *and* he would have enjoyed even more saying 'I told you so' to her.

Alex Andrews!

Beth parked her small car outside the shop and let herself into the separate rear door which led upstairs to the living accommodation she had originally shared with Kelly.

Alex Andrews!

She was *still* thinking about him as she made herself a cup of tea and headed for her bedroom.

Alex Andrews—or, more correctly, Alex Charles Andrews.

'I was named for this bridge,' he had told her quietly the day they had stood together on Prague's fabled Charles Bridge. 'A reminder, my grandfather always used to say, of the fact that I was half Czech.'

'Is that why you're here?' Beth had asked him, curious despite her determination to remain aloof from him— aloof *from* him and suspicious *of* him.

'Yes,' he acknowledged simply. 'My parents came here in the early days after the Velvet Revolution in 1993.' His eyes had grown sombre. 'Unfortunately my grandfather died too soon to see the city he had always loved freed.

'He left Prague in 1946 with my grandmother and my mother, who was a child of two at the time. She can barely remember anything at all about living here, but my grandfather...' He stopped and shook his head, and Beth felt her own throat close up as she saw the glitter of tears in his eyes.

'He longed to come back here so much. It was his home, after all, and no matter how well he had settled in England, how *glad* he was to be able to bring up his daughter, my mother, in freedom, Prague always remained the home of his heart.

'I remember once when I was at Cambridge he came to see me and I took him punting on the Cam. "It's beautiful," he told me. "But it isn't anywhere near as beautiful as the river which flows through Prague. Not until you have stood on the Charles Bridge and seen it for yourself will you understand what I mean..."'

'And did you?' Beth asked him softly. 'Did you understand what he meant?'

'Yes,' Alex told her quietly. 'Until I came here I had thought of myself as wholly British. I knew of my Czech heritage of course, but only in the form of the stories my grandfather had told me.

'They had no substance, no reality for me other than *as* stories. The tales he told me of the castle his family had once owned and the land that went with it, the beautiful treasures and the fine furniture...' Alex gave a small shrug. 'I felt no sense of personal loss. How could I? And neither did I feel any personal sense of missing a part of myself. But once I came here—then...then...yes... I knew that there *was* a piece of me missing. Then I knew that subconsciously I had been searching for that missing piece of myself.'

'Will you stay here?' Beth asked him, drawn into the emotional intensity of what he was telling her in spite of herself.

'No,' Alex told her. 'I can't—not now.'

It was then that the heavens well and truly opened, causing him to grab her by the arm and run with her to the shelter of a small, dangerously private alcove tucked into a span of the bridge. And then that he had declared his love for her.

Immediately Beth panicked—it was too much, too soon, too impossible to believe. He must have some ulterior motive for saying such a thing to her. How could he be in love with *her*? Why should he be?

'*No!* No, that's not possible. I don't want to hear this, Alex,' she told him shortly, pulling away from him and out of the shelter of the alcove, leaving him to follow her.

Beth had first come across Alex at her hotel. The staff there, when she had asked for the services of an interpreter, had prevaricated and then informed Beth that, due to the fact that the city was currently hosting several large business conventions, all the reputable agencies were fully booked for days ahead. Beth's heart had sunk. There was no way she could do what she had come to the Czech Republic to do without the services of an interpreter, and she had said as much to the young man behind the hotel's reception desk.

'I am so very sorry,' the man apologised, spreading his hands helplessly. 'But there are no interpreters.'

No interpreters. Beth was perilously close to tears; her emotions, still raw in the aftermath of discovering how badly Julian Cox had deceived her, were inclined to fluctuate from the easy weepiness of someone still in shock to a numb blankness which, if anything, was even more frightening. Today was a weepy day, and as Beth fought to blink away her unwanted emotions through the watery haze of her tears she saw the man who had been standing several feet away from her at the counter turn towards her.

'I couldn't help overhearing what you were just saying,' he told Beth as she turned to walk away from the desk. 'And, although I know it's rather unorthodox, I was wondering if *I* could possibly be of any help to you...'

His English was so fluent that Beth knew immediately that it had to be his first language.

'You're English, aren't you?' she challenged him dubiously.

'By birth,' he agreed immediately, giving her a smile which could have disarmed a nuclear warhead.

Beth, though, as she firmly reminded herself, was made of sterner stuff. There was no way *she* was going to let any man, never mind one who possessed enough charisma to make him worthy of having a 'danger' sign posted across his forehead, wheedle his way into her life.

'I speak English myself,' Beth told him pleasantly and, of course, unnecessarily.

'Indeed, and with just a hint of a very pretty Cornish accent, if I may say so,' he astounded Beth by commenting with a grin. 'However,' he added, before she could fire back, 'it seems that you do *not* speak Czech, whereas I do...'

'Really?' Beth gave him a coolly dismissive smile and began to walk away from him. She had been warned about the dangers of employing one of the self-proclaimed guides and interpreters who offered their services on Prague's streets, approaching tourists and offering to help them.

'Mmm...I learned it from my grandfather. He came originally from Prague.'

Beth tensed as he fell into step beside her.

'Ah, I see what it is. You don't trust me. Very wise,' he approved, with astounding aplomb. 'A beautiful young woman like you, on her own in a strange city, should always be suspicious of men who approach her.'

Beth glowered at him. Just how gullible did he think she was?

'I am not...' Beautiful, she had been about to say, but, recognising her danger, she quickly changed it. 'I am not interested.'

'No? But you told the receptionist that you were *desperately* in need of an interpreter,' he reminded her softly. 'The hotel manager will, I am sure, vouch for me...'

Beth paused.

He was right about one thing: she *was* desperately in need of an interpreter. She had come to Prague partially to recover from the damage inflicted on her emotions by Julian Cox and, more importantly in her eyes at least, in order to buy some good-quality Czech stemware for her shop.

Via Dee she had obtained from their local Board of Trade some addresses and contacts, but she had been told that the best way to find what she was looking for was to make her own enquiries once she was in Prague, and there was no way she was going to be able to do that without some help. It wasn't just an interpreter she needed, she acknowledged; she needed a guide as well. Someone who could drive her to the various factories she needed to visit as well as translating for her once she was there.

'Why should *you* offer to help me?' she asked suspiciously.

'Perhaps I simply don't have any choice,' he responded with an enigmatic smile.

The smile Beth dismissed. As for his comment—perhaps he hoped to make her feel sorry for him by insinuating that he was short of money.

Whilst she was still wondering just what she ought to do a very elegant dark-haired woman in her early fifties came hurrying down the corridor towards them.

'Ah, Alex, there you are!' she exclaimed, addressing Beth's companion. 'If you're ready to leave, the car's here...'

She gave Beth a coolly assessing look which made Beth feel acutely conscious of her own casual clothes and the older woman's immaculate elegance. She had the chicness of a Parisian, from the tips of her immaculately manicured fingernails to the top of her shiningly groomed chignon. Pearls, large enough to have been fake but which Beth felt pretty sure were anything but, were clipped to her ears, and the gold necklace she was wearing looked equally expensive.

Whoever she was, the woman was obviously very wealthy. If this man was acting as an interpreter for her he *must* be trustworthy, Beth acknowledged, because one look at the older woman's face made it abundantly clear that she was not the sort of person to be duped by anyone—no matter how handsome their face or how sexy their body.

'You don't have to make up your mind right now,' the man was telling Beth calmly. 'Here is my name and a number where you can reach me.' Reaching into his jacket, he removed a pen and a piece of paper on which he quickly wrote something before handing it to Beth. 'I shall be here in the hotel tomorrow morning. You can let me know your decision then.'

She wasn't going to accept his offer, of course, Beth assured herself once he and his companion had gone. Even if he had been an accredited interpreter provided by a reputable agency she would still have had her doubts.

Because he's too sexy...too...too disturbingly male, and you're too vulnerable, an inner voice taunted her. I thought you were supposed to be immune to men like him now. You said that Julian Cox had cured you of ever falling in love again.

No. That will never happen, she answered her sharp-tongued inner critic swiftly. There's no way I could ever be in danger of falling for a man like him, a man who's far too good-looking for his own good. Heavens, he must have women swarming all over him. Why on earth should he be interested in someone like me?

Perhaps for the same reason that Julian Cox was interested in you, her inner critic taunted. To him you probably seem to be an easy meal ticket. A woman on her own, vulnerable. Remember what you were told before you left home.

Beth was determined not to accept Alex's offer, but in the morning, when she presented herself at the hotel's reception desk again, insisting that she desperately needed an accredited interpreter, the man behind the counter shook his head regretfully, repeating what Beth had been told the previous day.

'I am sorry, but we simply cannot. There are conventions,' he told Beth.

It crossed Beth's mind that she might have to abandon her plans to make this a business trip and simply do some sightseeing instead. But that would mean going home, having to admit to another failure… She had come to Prague to look for crystal, and she was not going to go home until she had found some.

Even if that meant accepting the services of a man like Alex Andrews?

Even if it meant accepting that—*yes!* Beth told herself sternly.

She had eaten her breakfast alone in her room; the hotel was busy, and, despite all the stern admonishments she had made to herself, she still didn't feel confident enough to eat in the dining room—alone. Now she ordered herself a coffee and removed the guidebook she had bought on her arrival in Prague from her handbag. For all she knew Alex Andrews might not even turn up. Well, if he didn't there were plenty of other foreign students looking for work, she reminded herself stoically.

She went and sat down in a corner of the hotel lobby, not exactly hiding herself away out of sight, but certainly not making herself very obvious either, she recognised with a small stab of irritated despair. Why was she so lacking in confidence, so insecure, so…so vulnerable? It was not as though she had any reason to be. She was part of a very loving and closely knit family; she had parents who had always supported and protected her. Perhaps that was what it was. Perhaps they had protected her a little too much, she decided ruefully. Certainly Kelly, her friend, seemed to think so.

'The waiter couldn't remember what you'd ordered, so I've brought you a cappuccino...'

Beth nearly jumped out of her skin as she heard Alex's husky, sensual voice.

How had he found her here in this quiet corner? And, more importantly, how had he known she'd ordered coffee in the first place? And then, as he placed the tray he was carrying down on the table in front of her, Beth guessed what he had done. There were two cups of coffee on it and a croissant. No doubt all of them charged to her room!

'I actually ordered my coffee black,' she told him curtly, and not quite truthfully.

'Oh.' He gave her an oblique, smiling look. 'That's odd; I could have sworn you were a cappuccino girl. In fact I can almost see you with just a hint of a creamy chocolatey moustache.'

Beth stared at him in angry disbelief. He was taking far too many liberties, behaving far too personally. She gave him a ferociously frosty look and informed him arctically, 'As a woman, I hardly find that a flattering allusion. *Men* have moustaches.'

'Not the kind I mean,' he returned promptly as he sat down beside her, a wicked smile dancing in his eyes as he leaned forward. His lips were so close to her ear that she could actually feel the warmth of his breath as he whispered provocatively, 'The kind I meant is kissed off, not shaved...'

Beth's eyes widened in outraged fury.

He was actually pretending to flirt with her, pretending to find her *attractive*.

She started to get up, too furious to even bother telling him that she was not going to need his services, when, out of the corner of her eye, she caught sight of the beautiful crystal lustres the salesgirl was placing on the display shelves of the hotel's gift shop. Beth caught her breath. They were just so beautiful. The lustres moved gently, catching the light, their delicacy and beauty so immediately covetable that Beth ached to buy them.

A friend of her mother's had some antique Venetian ones which she had inherited from her grandmother, and Beth had always loved them.

'What is it?' she heard Alex asking her curiously at her side.

'The lustres...the wall-lights,' Beth explained. 'They're so beautiful.'

'Very beautiful and I'm afraid very expensive,' Alex told her. 'Were you thinking of buying them as a gift, or for yourself?'

'For my shop,' Beth told him absently, her attention concentrated on the lustres.

'You own a shop? Where? What kind?' His voice was less soft now, sharp with interest and something which Beth told herself was almost avaricious—too avaricious to be mere polite curiosity.

'Yes. I do...in a small town you won't have heard of. It's called Rye-on-Averton. I...we sell good-quality china and pottery ornaments and glassware. That's why I've come to Prague. I'm looking for new suppliers here, but the quality has to be right, and the price...'

'Well, you won't beat those pieces for quality,' Alex told her positively.

Beth looked at him, but before she could say anything he was telling her, 'Your coffee's going cold. You had better drink it and I had better introduce myself to you properly. As you know, I'm Alex Andrews.'

He held out his hand. A little reluctantly Beth took it. She had no idea why she felt so reluctant to touch him, or to have any kind of physical contact with him. Any other woman would have been more than eager to do so, she was quite sure. So what did that make her? A frightened little rabbit...too scared to touch such a good-looking and sexy man because she was afraid of the effect he might have on her? Of course not.

Quickly she shook his hand, and just as quickly released it, uncomfortably aware of the way her pulse-rate had quickened and her face become flushed.

'Beth Russell,' she responded.

'Yes, I know,' Alex told her, confessing, 'I asked them on Reception. What's it short for?'

'Bethany,' Beth told him.

'Bethany...I like that; it suits you. My grandmother was a Beth as well. Her actual name was Alžběta, which she anglicised when she and my grandfather fled to Britain. She died before I was born—of a broken heart, my grandfather used to say, mourning the country and the family she had to leave behind.

'When my parents finally visited Prague, after the Revolution, my mother said that she found it incredibly moving to hear her family talking about her. She said it made her mother come alive for her. She died when my mother was eight...'

Beth made an involuntary sound of distress.

'Yes,' Alex agreed, confirming that he had heard and understood it. 'I feel the same way too. My mother missed out on so much—the loving presence of her mother *and* the comfort of being part of the large, extended family which she would have known had she grown up here in Prague. But then, of course, as my grandfather used to say, the opposite and darker side of that was the fact that because of his political beliefs he would have been persecuted and maybe even killed.

'The rest of the family certainly didn't escape un-scathed. My grandfather was a younger son. His eldest brother would, in the normal course of events, have inherited both lands and a title from his father, but the Regime took all that away from the family.

'Now, of course, it has been restored. There are some families living in the Czech Republic today who have regained so many draughty castles that they're at a loss to know what to do with them all.

'Fortunately, in the case of my family, there is only the one. I shall take you to see it. It is very beautiful, but not so beautiful as you.'

Beth stared at him, completely lost for words. British he might claim to be, British his passport might *declare* him to be, but there was quite obviously a very strong Czech streak in him. Beth had done her homework before coming to Prague; she knew how the Czech people prided themselves on being artistic and sensitive, great poets and writers, idealists and romantics. Alex was certainly romantic. At least in the sense that he obviously enjoyed embroidering reality and the truth. There was no way *she* came anywhere near deserving to be described as beautiful, and it infuriated her that he should think her stupid enough to believe that she might be. Why was he doing it?

She was about to ask him when the lustres caught her eye again. Alex was right; they would be expensive on sale in a hotel like this one, but there must be other factories that made the same kind of thing—factories that did not charge expensive hotel prices to tourists. Without an interpreter, though, she would have no chance of finding them.

Beth turned to Alex Andrews.

'I know exactly what the going rate for interpreters is,'

she warned him fiercely, 'and you will have to be able to drive. *And* I intend to check that the hotel management is prepared to vouch for you…'

The smile he was giving her was doing crazy things to her heart, making it flip over and then flop heavily against her chest wall like a stranded salmon.

'What are you *doing*?' she protested, panicking as Alex reached for her hand.

'Sealing our bargain with a kiss,' he told her softly as he lifted her nerveless fingers to his lips. And then, before they got there, he stopped and told her thoughtfully, 'Although perhaps on second thought…'

Beth went limp with relief. But it was a relief that came a little bit too soon, for, as she started to pull away, Alex leaned closer to her and swiftly captured her mouth with his own, kissing it firmly.

Beth was too shocked to move.

'You…you kissed me,' she gasped in a squeaky voice. 'But…'

'I've been wanting to do that from the first moment I saw you,' Alex told her huskily.

Beth stared at him.

Common sense, not to mention a sense of self-preservation, screamed to her that there was no way she could employ him as her interpreter, not after what he had just done, but his mesmeric grey eyes were hypnotising her, making it impossible for her to say what she knew ought to be said.

'We'll need a hire car,' he was telling her, just as though what he had done was the most natural thing in the world. 'I'll organise one.'

CHAPTER THREE

BETH GAVE A small sigh as she replaced the lustres on the glass shelves of the hotel's gift shop.

The previous day, after Alex Andrews had dropped her off following their visit to the first of the factories on her list, she had come into the shop and asked the price of the lustres they had on display.

As she had expected, they were expensive—*very* expensive.

'This piece is from one of our foremost crystal factories,' the salesgirl had explained to Beth. 'The lady whose family owns and runs the factory would never normally allow their things to be displayed in such a way, but she is a friend of the owner of the hotel. Normally they work only to order. Those wishing to buy their glassware have to visit the factory and speak with the people there themselves. The factory has been with the family for many, many generations, although it was taken away from them for a time during the Regime...'

'The lustre is very beautiful,' Beth had sighed.

Yes, it *was* very beautiful, she thought now as she left the gift shop.

The factories she had already visited today produced nothing even approaching the quality of the piece in the gift shop. The people she had met there had been friendly and helpful, eager to do business with her, but Beth had known the moment she saw their glassware range that it was not right for her shop—they specialised in highly individual pieces, highly covetable pieces. But it had not been her disappointment over the quality of what she had seen that had caused her to storm back to the car several paces ahead of Alex Andrews, her lips pressed together in a tight, angry line.

Still, at least this evening she would be seeing the stall holder in Wenceslas Square, who had promised her that she would bring her samples of the kind of glass she wanted to buy.

Yesterday, after Alex Andrews had left her to go and organise a hire car, Beth had spent an anxious hour restlessly walking by the river, trying to convince herself that she had not been as reckless as she feared in accepting his offer of help. For some reason, although technically she was the more senior 'partner' in their 'relationship', and she therefore held the power, the control, she couldn't quite escape the feeling that Alex had manoeuvred her into employing him, and that he was deliberately trying to manipulate her.

She'd known that she was going to have to be on her guard with him, and that she couldn't trust him. He was a man, after all, just like Julian. Another charmer...another chancer...

By the time he had returned she had told herself that she was fully armoured against him.

She'd deliberately had her lunch early, so that he wouldn't suggest they could eat together, thus ensuring that she wouldn't be tricked into paying for his meal. But even then he had *nearly* caught her out.

Eating so early had meant that she hadn't been particularly hungry, and so she had left the hotel dining room having barely touched her meal. Just as she had done so, Alex had walked into the hotel foyer. The warmth of the smile he had given her could quite easily have turned another woman's head, and Beth had certainly been conscious of the envious looks she'd attracted from the three female tourists who'd been watching them.

'We still haven't discussed exactly what you want to do,' Alex told her as he reached her. 'I thought we would have lunch together so that we can do so. There's a very good traditional restaurant not far from here that I know you'd enjoy...'

What she would not give for just one tenth of his impressive self-confidence, Beth thought enviously as she started to tell him curtly, 'No, I've already...'

'And these are the factories you want to visit,' Alex was saying as he picked up her list.

'Yes,' she agreed tersely.

'Mmm... Well, they certainly produce reasonable-quality crystal, but if what you're looking for is more along the lines of the pieces you were looking at in the gift shop then I would recommend...'

Alarm bells began to ring in Beth's brain. She had been warned at home to be wary of the touts paid by some of the more dubious manufacturers whose aim was to sell inferior-quality goods to the unwary at inflated prices.

'None of the reputable manufacturers would want to tarnish their reputations by becoming involved in that sort of thing,' she'd been told by a friend. 'The Czechs are a very artistic and a very proud people, but unfortunately, like any other nation, they have their less honest citizens. But that shouldn't af-fect you.'

'I don't want or need your recommendations, thank you,' she interrupted Alex abruptly. 'I am paying you to act as an interpreter and a driver. Whilst you were gone

I've been looking at my maps. Since we're already half-way through the day, I think that today we should visit the closest of the factories, which will be this one here…'

As she spoke Beth held out the map to show him where she meant.

Immediately he began to frown.

'I wouldn't advise that you visit that particular factory,' he told her quietly. 'And as for it being the closest… As the crow flies, it may indeed seem so, but it can only be reached by a very circuitous route, and some recent storms in the area have resulted in heavy floods which have left some of the roads virtually impassable. And besides, I rather think if we did go there you'd be disappointed in what they produce.'

Beth could scarcely believe her ears. She had anticipated that she might have problems with him, and quite definitely had serious doubts about the wisdom of employing him, but she had scarcely expected him to start arguing with her right from the word go. His previous manner towards her had suggested quite the opposite, and it came as rather a shock to her to see him in such a decisive and, yes, dominant role. Where were the compliments he had given her earlier? Where was the easy charm and teasing warmth?

'I hadn't realised you were such an expert on crystal,' she told him tightly.

He gave a brief shrug and told her lightly, 'I should be; it's in the blood.'

Beth was slightly confused. What did he mean? That because he was half-Czech he must automatically know about crystal? For sheer effrontery he had to be without equal, she decided angrily.

'Well, it may not be in *my* blood, but so far as I'm concerned I am still the best judge of what will and won't sell in *my* shop,' she told him assertively. 'And the only way I can decide whether or not any manufacturer produces the quality of crystal I want to sell is by seeing it for myself...'

'It's certainly one way of doing it,' Alex agreed. 'But you have to remember that the Czech Republic manufactures a very wide range of glass to suit all pockets and all tastes, and therefore, to my mind at least, it makes sense to eliminate those factories and manufacturers which are not going...which do not produce the type of goods you want.'

'Yes, it does,' Beth concurred, gritting her teeth as she told him, 'Which is why I was very specific about my requirements when I discussed them with our local Board of Trade representative before I left.'

'Perhaps you weren't specific enough,' Alex told her challengingly. 'Certainly, from my knowledge of them, at least half the factories on your list make either novelty or everyday glassware of a type I doubt you would be interested in.'

'Oh? I see. And you would know about that, of course. Tell me, Alex, don't you think it's rather stretching the arm of coincidence a little too far that miraculously, just as I should need an interpreter and guide, one turns up who purports to be an expert not just in the manufacture of crystal but also in knowing exactly what type of goods I want?'

There was a brief pause before Alex responded with unexpected dryness, 'Not really. After all, crystal is one of the country's most famous exports. Naturally I suspect that any guide you would have employed would have known something about its manufacture...'

'But not so much as you?' Beth suggested cynically.

'No, not so much as me,' he agreed gravely. 'But I

can see that you're determined not to take my advice and so...' he glanced at his watch '...the sooner we leave the better, if you really want to visit this specific factory this afternoon.'

Later, as they drove in an uncomfortable silence over roads which Beth was forced to acknowledge were not the best she had ever ridden on, she admitted inwardly to herself that had it been another guide, an accredited guide, who had suggested to her that she might find it more difficult to reach her destination than she had envisaged she would probably have listened and accepted such advice, but because it had been Alex...

But then, hadn't she every reason to suspect him? she asked herself defensively. Look at the way he had introduced himself to her and flirted with her. Not that he was flirting with her *now*... Far from it. She glanced briefly at him as he sat beside her, concentrating on his driving.

Even dressed in a pair of faded jeans and a polo shirt he still possessed a very powerful presence, a very potent maleness, she acknowledged reluctantly.

It was plain, too, that she had offended him earlier by rejecting his advice—his *unwanted* advice, she reminded herself—because there was quite definitely a very stern and remote set to his mouth. And, whilst he had been polite, and careful to describe to her the historical nature of the countryside they had been driving through, he had done so in a way that had very definitely kept a distance between them. Which, of course, was exactly what she had wanted—wasn't it? Of course it was. She was simply not the sort of person, the sort of *woman*, who got any sort of pleasure or...or...anything else out of challenging people and creating an atmosphere of tension and sexual aggression between herself and a man. No, she didn't find that sort of thing exciting or…or stimulating in any possible kind of way.

It turned out that the factory which was their destination could only be reached by a cobbled road with a teeth-jarringly uneven camber, so much so that when they finally drew up in front of it Beth had to stop herself from exhaling a pent-up breath of relief.

It would never do to allow Alex Andrews to think that she regretted not listening to his advice, but cravenly, as they started to walk towards the factory, Beth prayed that the glassware she had come to see would vindicate her decision and make their trip worthwhile.

Picturesquely the factory was housed in what seemed an almost fortress-like building-cum-castle, but when Beth couldn't help remarking on this Alex told her grimly, 'Until recently it was used as a prison.'

A prison. Beth shivered and took a few steps backwards just at the moment when a dilapidated lorry came roaring into the small courtyard.

She heard the screech of its brakes as its driver reacted to her presence but for some reason she found it impossible to move, even though she could see the lorry bearing down on her.

A few feet away from her she heard Alex curse as he moved like lightning, turning and grabbing hold of her, lifting her bodily off her feet as he swung her out of the lorry's path.

The whole incident had lasted less than a handful of seconds but it left Beth badly shaken. So much so that she could actually feel herself trembling violently as Alex continued to hold her.

'It's all right…it's all right,' she could hear him saying gruffly to her. 'You're safe…'

Safe!

Beth raised her head to look at him, the politely formal words of thanks she had intended to utter forgotten as her glance meshed with his.

How could eyes that were such a cool pale grey look so...so hot, like molten mercury?

'Alex...'

She could feel the heat in his gaze as it shifted from her eyes to her mouth. Her lips started to tremble—and soften. Involuntarily she could feel them starting to part...to open in an age-old signal of female recognition—and invitation.

This couldn't be happening, she told herself hazily. She *couldn't* be standing here in the courtyard of this dilapidated building knowing that Alex Andrews intended to kiss her, knowing it and not doing the slightest thing to prevent him from doing so other than to utter a token 'no' as the downward descent of his head blotted out the daylight and she felt the warm, sure pressure of his mouth against hers.

If she was completely honest, when Julian had kissed her she had never truly enjoyed the too wet, too soft sensation of his mouth on hers, and had, on many occasions, actively tried to avoid it.

Some women were just not particularly highly sexed, she had assured herself, and she quite obviously was one of them—which made it all the more extraordinary that she should feel, the moment Alex Andrews' mouth touched hers, as though her whole body was engulfed in a heat even greater than that generated by the blast furnaces used to heat silica.

Was it possible that somehow Alex Andrews had the power to convert her raw anger and dislike, her suspicion of him, into something else, a very different kind of emotion, just as the heat the furnaces used on the raw ingredients of the silica sand could turn it into the molten liquid which ultimately could be converted into the most beautiful crystal glass? But of course it wasn't. How could the negative, self-defensive emotions she felt towards Alex ever be converted into something else, especially since she herself didn't want them to be? So then why was she melting so into his arms, into his body; why was *her* body becoming molten liquid with the white heat of her own desire?

'Do you believe in love at first sight?' Alex asked hoarsely against her lips. His hands were cupping her face, his thumbs gently stroking the hot flesh of her flushed cheeks.

'Oh, yes,' Beth sighed mistily.

Hadn't it always been one of her most cherished private dreams that one day she would meet a man, *the* man, and from the very first second of setting eyes on him, she would just know that *he* was *the* one?

But of course that was a silly, almost adolescent fantasy, a daydream that, now she was a grown woman, life and reality had forced her to abandon.

The mistiness in her eyes gave way to a grave sadness that told Alex far more than her silence and the abrupt, fierce denial which followed it.

'No. No, of *course* I don't. Love at first sight, it's a fiction, a fantasy,' Beth objected angrily. 'It's…it's *impossible.*'

'No, not impossible,' Alex corrected her gently. 'Incomprehensible from a logical point of view, perhaps, but not impossible. Ask any poet…'

'Oh, poets,' Beth denounced dismissively, but the sharp tone of her voice was still at odds with the betraying expression in her eyes.

Someone, somewhere in her past, had hurt her—

and badly, Alex recognised. Someone at some time had robbed her of her faith and her trust, had forced her to retreat into the prickly thicket she had built around her emotions, but *he* could see what lay beyond that thicket; *he* could see in her eyes the woman that she actually was—a tender, loving, *lovable* woman, a woman who—
'Oh, no...look over there,' Beth commanded, her voice suddenly as filled with emotion as her eyes as she pointed in the direction where a cat was stalking an unaware bird.

'Oh, no. *No.* It's going to catch it...'

As he heard the urgency and the anxiety in her voice Alex reacted instinctively, clapping his hands loudly together to distract the cat and alert its potential victim.

As the bird flew away, and the cat gave him a baleful glare, Beth turned to him, her eyes shining with relief.

'Oh, that was good,' she praised him involuntarily. 'I'm glad you didn't hurt the cat, like some people might have done...I wouldn't have wanted it to be hurt. After all, it's only obeying nature...'

Such a soft, tender heart, Alex marvelled, but apparently there was no softness or tenderness in it for him... apparently... When he had kissed her her kisses had been honey-sweet, but the words she spoke to him were vinegar-sharp and they were not, he felt sure, the words of her heart.

How long was she going to be here in Prague?

Somehow he would find a way of persuading her to drop her guard and allow him into her life...her heart... her love... Somehow.

Seeing the look in his eyes, Beth went cold with the icy sweat of misery that swamped her. What was it about her that gave Alex the idea that she was so desperate to be loved, so vulnerable to his patently false flattery that she would be deceived by him? Did she really come across as so needy, so…so…helpless? How many times before had Alex used the same ploy on other gullible female tourists? Beth's teeth started to chatter, the icy cold shivers racking her nothing to do with the cool mountain air. In Prague it had been a warm, sunny day when they had left, but here it was much cooler, the sun obscured by mist.

'You're cold,' Alex was telling her. 'Here, take this…'

Before she could stop him he was removing his own jacket and wrapping it around her.

She wanted to refuse. The jacket smelled tormentingly of him, a subtle, sensually male scent that she could have sworn she would not normally have noticed, but which for some reason she suddenly seemed to have become acutely responsive to—far too acutely—if the heat that was now flooding her body was anything to go by.

Quickly she moved away from Alex and deliberately removed the notebook she had brought with her from her handbag. According to the details she had been given at home, the factory they were about to visit produced an extensive range of modestly priced goods.

What she was looking for, in addition to the kind of crystal she could sell in the shop, were some artistic and unusual little pieces that would make an eye-catching window display and tempt people in to buy, something along the lines of the pretty, delicately tinted glass sweets she had seen displayed to good effect in an exclusive shop she had once visited in the Cotswolds.

With one eye on the Christmas market, Beth was thinking in terms of some pretty and delicate glass Christmas tree ornaments, or even possibly some novelty, but still attractive, glass swizzle sticks.

However, once they had presented themselves in the factory's main office, and she had introduced herself to the factory manager, Beth's heart started to sink as he proceeded to show her some samples of the type of article they made.

The manager's English was good enough for her not to have needed the services of an interpreter, which, when she realised that all Alex's warnings about the unsuitability of the factory's goods for her market had been more than justified, made her chagrin increase.

The things she was being shown were simply not of the high standard required by her customers, and far too mass market for her one-off select gift shop. With a heavy heart Beth wondered how on earth she was going to get out of accepting the offer of a tour of the factory which the manager was enthusiastically offering her. She had no wish to hurt his feelings, but…

Behind her she could hear Alex saying something to the factory manager in Czech. Enquiringly she looked at him.

'I was just explaining to him that since you have other factories to visit there won't be time for you to accept his very kind offer,' Alex told her smoothly.

Illogically, instead of feeling grateful to him for his timely rescue, Beth discovered as they headed back to the car that what she was actually experiencing was a seething, impotent, smouldering, resentful anger.

'Is something wrong?' Alex asked her in what she knew had to be pseudo-concern as he unlocked the passenger door of the car for her.

'You could say that,' Beth snapped acidly back at him in response. 'In future, I'd prefer it if you allowed me to make my *own* decisions instead of making them for me.'

As she spoke she wrenched impatiently at the car door handle, and then gave a small, involuntary yelp of frustrated anger when it refused to yield.

Imperturbably Alex reached past her and opened it for her.

'And will you please stop treating me as though I'm totally incapable of doing anything for myself?' Beth told him sharply.

'I'm sorry if I'm offending you, but I was brought up in the old-fashioned way—where good manners were important and where it was expected that a man should exhibit them.'

'Yes, I can see that. I suppose your mother stayed at home and obeyed your father's every whim…'

Beth knew even as she spoke that what she was saying was unforgivably rude. No matter what her personal opinion was of men who treated women as second-class citizens, she still had no right to criticise Alex's home life. Alex, though, far from being offended, was actually throwing back his head and laughing, a warm, unfettered sound of obvious amusement which strangely, instead of reassuring her, made her feel even more angry than before.

'I'm sorry,' he apologised. 'I shouldn't laugh, but if you knew my mother—*when* you get to know my mother,' he amended with a very meaningful look, 'you'll understand why I did. My mother is a highly qualified senior consultant, specialising in heart disorders. She worked all through my childhood and still continues to do so. The old-fashioned influence in my life actually came from my grandfather, who lived with us.'

Immediately Beth felt remorseful and ashamed. Her own grandparents, who lived in the same small Cornish village as her parents, were similarly old-fashioned and insistent on the necessity of good manners.

'I apologise if you thought I was trying to patronise you,' Alex added once they were both in the car. 'That

certainly wasn't my intention.' He paused and looked
straight at her, and then told her softly, 'Has anyone ever
told you that you have the most sexily kissable mouth?
Especially when you're trying hard not to smile…'

Beth gave him a frosty look.

'I'd really prefer it if you didn't try to flirt with me,'
she told him primly.

She tried to look away, but discovered that she
couldn't; there was something dangerously and powerfully mesmeric about the intent look in Alex's eyes.

'What makes you think I'm flirting?' he challenged
her silkily. 'And don't try to pretend to me that you aren't
just as aware of what's happening between us as I am…I
felt it in the way you reacted when I kissed you…'

Reduced to a mortified, tongue-tied silence, Beth
could only manage to turn away from him and drag her
gaze from his.

He was certainly persistent; she had to give him that.
Personally, she didn't know why he was bothering. She
must have made it plain to him by now that she was no
push-over, and that his dubious talents could be put to
far more profitable use on another and more gullible female tourist.

It was tempting to tell him just why she was so immune to his practised flattery, but to do so would undoubtedly involve her in some more of the kind of
dialogue at which, she was beginning to discover, he
was more adept than she—and there was no way she
was going to allow him to get the upper hand in their
'relationship' again.

CHAPTER FOUR

'HAVE YOU MADE any plans for this evening?'

Beth tensed as she listened to Alex's question. They had just walked into the hotel foyer, following their abortive visit to the factory. The journey had left her feeling tired and a little stiff, and she was looking forward to having a hot bath and an early night—on her own.

'I've got some paperwork I need to deal with,' she answered quickly, and not entirely untruthfully. Well, she did have some postcards she could write, and then she wanted to make a few notes on the factory she had visited and to read up on those she still had to see.

'I would have asked you to join me for dinner,' Alex continued, 'only I'm already committed this evening— a family celebration; we're going to the opera and—'

'I hope you enjoy it,' Beth told him politely, wondering why, when by rights she ought to have been both relieved and pleased to learn that she was not going to be pressured into spending the evening with him, what she actually felt was an uncomfortable and indigestible sense of abandonment and disappointment.

'Do you?' Alex challenged her gently, stepping forward as he did so.

Panicking that he might be going to kiss her again, Beth immediately stepped back from him, and then saw

from the amused twinkle in his eyes that he had realised
what she was thinking.

'You're safe here,' he told her teasingly. 'It's far, far
too public for what *I've* got in mind.'

The lift doors opened, disgorging half a dozen hotel
guests, and Alex nodded towards them, telling her softly,
'Now, had we been in *there* it might have been a different thing. There's something very, very erotic about the
thought of making love, wanting one another so much
that it's impossible to wait until one reaches the security
of one's room—of *needing* one another so immediately
that one's prepared to take the risk of being discovered,
of having one's passionate surge towards fulfilment interrupted...'

Beth stared at him, her face starting to flush, her body
hot with reaction to the soft sensuality of his slowly spoken words and to the mental images he was conjuring up
in her own suddenly fevered imagination.

'I wouldn't know. I do not have those kind of thoughts,'
she told him distancingly and defensively.

For the second time that day Alex threw back his head
and laughed.

'Somehow I don't believe you,' he told her wickedly.
'I think that in secret, in private, *you* are a very sexy,
very sensual woman indeed. But you prefer to keep the
secret, the sweetness of that sensuality hidden from all
but your chosen lover. And who can blame you for that?
Or him for wanting to explore that private sweetness and
possess it...possess you...?'

Beth didn't know what to say or do. The way he was
behaving—the things he was saying, the intimacy he
was creating between them—was so totally outside her
own experience that she simply didn't know how to deal
with it.

'What time do you want me?' Alex was asking her huskily. Beth stared at him, involuntarily licking her suddenly dry lips. 'After breakfast…about nine?' he was adding.

He meant what time did she want him to meet her in the morning, Beth realised. For one moment she had actually thought…

After Beth had left him Alex did not leave the hotel straight away. Instead he walked over to the gift shop, thoughtfully studying the lustres that Beth had admired.

In some ways the glass reminded him of Beth. Like her it was delicate, and yet surprisingly resilient. Like her its purity and beauty made one catch one's breath, inspired and moved the human soul. Beth certainly inspired and moved his soul, not to mention certain far less ethereal parts of his body, he reflected ruefully. He had never known himself to be so dangerously at the mercy of his own emotions.

Perhaps it had something to do with the fact that he was in Prague. Perhaps being here released a hitherto unsuspected and very deeply emotional part of his personality, enabled him, empowered him to react instinctively and immediately to those emotions instead of behaving with caution and logic as he would have done at home. Classic symptoms of a holiday romance? Alex grimaced to himself. In many ways he wished that were the case, but he knew himself too well to accept such a definition of his feelings.

Love at first sight.

How did you account for the unexpectedness of such feelings? How did you evaluate or analyse them? You couldn't…you simply had to acknowledge that they were too strong, too powerful, too overwhelming for mere mortal logic to deal with.

Beth.

Bethany...

Alex closed his eyes, trying to blot out how the sound of her name as it left his lips would make a possessive male litany of love and desire against her skin as he held and caressed her. In the morning light her skin would be as flawless and perfect as the crystal teardrops on the lustres.

No. This was no mere holiday romance, no mere giving in to the mood and magic of the city, even if Prague was a city that was a part of his heritage and his blood. Perhaps the intensity, the impetuosity driving him on now was a previously unfamiliar part of the British side of his personality.

Perhaps if he was honest he was a little bemused by what was happening to him. Bemused, but still instinctively and automatically convinced that his love was the love of his lifetime, a love that would last a lifetime.

Convincing Beth, though, he suspected, was not going to be easy. She was suspicious of him, and perhaps rightly so, and he could see, oh, so clearly, how much her outward antagonism towards him, her animosity, masked an inner fragility and fear. Somehow he would find a way to show her that she had no need of those protective barriers against him. Somehow he would find a way...

After Alex had gone—unexpectedly without asking her to pay him for the day—Beth went upstairs to her room, intending to spend the rest of the evening there. But once she had bathed and eaten she suddenly got an unexpected surge of energy. From her bedroom window she had an excellent view of the river. The sky had cleared and was now washed with a tempting evening palette of colours;

soft blue, pale yellow and a heavenly indescribable silvery pink.

Down below her in the square she could see people strolling around, or sitting at the pavement cafés.

She was, she reminded herself, here to enjoy herself, and to explore Prague and its historical beauty, as well as on a buying trip.

Before she could change her mind she dressed in comfortably casual chinos and a soft shirt and, picking up her jacket and bag, made her way down to the hotel foyer.

Her guidebook had an excellent street map; she could hardly get lost. Wenceslas Square was her ultimate destination. It featured largely in all the articles she had read about the city and, to judge from the photographs, with good reason.

As she walked in the Square's direction her attention was distracted by the plethora of shops selling crystal and china. At each one she stopped to examine the contents of their windows. All of the goods displayed were breathtakingly good value, but, to her disappointment, none of them had on show the same quality of glass she had seen in the hotel gift shop. She was just re-examining the display in one window when a young man approached her.

Only eighteen or so, he gave her a winning smile and introduced himself in broken English, asking her if she would like a guide to show her the city.

Firmly Beth refused, relieved when he immediately accepted her refusal and walked away. The Square was only a few yards away now, right at the end of the street she was on, but even though she had seen the photographs, and read the enthusiastic descriptive guide to it, she was still not totally prepared for its magnificence, nor for the sense of stepping back into history that walking into it gave her.

Here, surrounded by the stall holders displaying their wares, it was almost possible to feel that she had stepped back into the medieval age... A juggler juggling brightly painted balls winked at her as she walked past him; in the centre of the Square a quartet were vigorously playing classical music. A little boy clung nervously to his mother as a fire-eater leant backwards to swallow the licking flames of fire he was holding. A few feet away acrobats tumbled, reminding Beth that the Czech Republic was famed for its highly skilled circus acts.

But it was the stalls that gripped her real attention, taking her back to her childhood and the wonder of visiting antiques fairs with her grandparents. Here it was once again possible to capture that age-old magic. At one stall a man was actually making sets of armour as his customers waited. At another a dark gypsy woman was displaying hand-made jewellery. But it was the stalls selling glassware that predictably drew Beth like a magnet.

Slowly she wandered from one to another, trying not to feel too desperately disappointed when she realised that there was nothing for her to buy.

'You are looking for something special?' one stall holder asked her encouragingly. 'A gift, perhaps...?'

Beth shook her head.

'No. No, not a gift,' she told her. 'Actually, I'm here on business. I have a shop at home in England and I want...'

She paused, not sure just why she was confiding in this dark-eyed gypsy woman with her insistent manner.

'I have seen a piece of glass in the gift shop of my hotel—very Venetian...baroque, crimson, painted... gilded...

'Ah, yes, I know just what you mean,' the woman told her enthusiastically. 'We do not sell such pieces here, but I know where to get them. If you would be interested in seeing some I could get some for you to look at, say for this time tomorrow...'

Beth stared at her, hardly daring to believe her luck.

'Are you sure we're talking about the same thing?' she began doubtfully. 'All the glass I have seen so far...'

'Is like this. No...' The woman finished for her, rummaging in a large box and triumphantly producing a book which she handed to Beth.

Beth stared at the photograph the woman was showing her, scarcely able to contain her excitement. The goblets depicted in it were exactly what she was looking for: heavy, antique, made in richly coloured glass.

'Yes...yes, that's *exactly* what I want,' she agreed.

But Beth was no fool.

'But these here in this photograph are genuine antiques,' she felt bound to point out.

'These are, yes,' the woman agreed after a small pause. 'However, there is a factory where they specialise in making such glass—but only to special orders, you understand.'

Special orders. Beth looked doubtfully at her, remembering the price she had been quoted for the lustre in the gift shop.

'But surely that means they will be very expensive...'

'Maybe...maybe not,' the woman replied mysteriously. 'It all depends on the size of the order, no? I shall bring some for you to see,' she announced, closing the book. 'If you will be here at this time tomorrow evening I shall show you what a good bargain we can make...'

Half an hour later, as she hurried back to the hotel, Beth asked herself what she had to lose by returning to the stall tomorrow evening.

Nothing...

After all, she hadn't made any kind of commitment to buy anything. She was simply going to look, that was all.

Caught up in her excitement, she suddenly realised that she had lost her way a little, and that she was now in a part of the city that was unfamiliar to her. There was an imposing building in front of her which she was sure must feature in her guidebook. All she had to do was to check the name of the square she was now in and redirect herself to her hotel.

As she delved into her bag for her guidebook a large crowd of people suddenly started to emerge from the building she had been studying, all of them dressed in evening clothes. Idly watching them, Beth suddenly froze as she recognised Alex Andrews amongst them. If he had looked toughly masculine earlier in the day, dressed in jeans and a polo shirt, that was nothing to the way he looked now, wearing a dinner suit. Taller than most of the other men in the crowd, he would have stood out even without his strikingly handsome good looks, simply on account of the way he held himself, Beth recognised.

As Beth watched him she suddenly realised that not only was he not alone but that the woman who was with him was the same soignée, elegant older woman she had seen him talking with in the hotel foyer the previous day.

Alex was patently oblivious to *her* presence, and as Beth observed them from the shadows she saw him put a very protective arm around the older woman whilst she, in turn, moved closer to him, lifting her face towards his with such a luminous look of love in her expression that Beth felt her throat start to close up and she was swamped by a mixture of contempt and anger. So much for his comments to *her*. It was quite plain that his companion believed that she had a *very* special and intimate relationship with him. Beth only had to witness the way he lifted her hand to his face, gently touching his cheek, to see that.

Her stomach churned with nauseating disgust. Not for the older woman, who plainly believed that Alex returned the feelings Beth could see so clearly revealed on her face, but for Alex, who quite obviously had no compunction whatsoever about what he was doing.

So much for the family gathering he had told her he was attending. But why was she so shocked—and so upset? Surely what she had just witnessed only confirmed what she already knew—that, quite simply, he was not to be trusted. Instead of feeling this helpless, anguished sense of loss and betrayal, she ought to be feeling pleased that her suspicions were vindicated.

She *was* pleased that they had been vindicated, Beth assured herself doggedly. She was more than pleased— she was delighted. *Delighted.*

'Have you seen the Charles Bridge yet?'

Beth shook her head, not wanting to allow Alex to engage her in any unnecessary conversation. After what she had seen last night she had made herself a vow that she would make it plain to him that there was no way she was going to fall for his cynical manipulation of her feelings.

In fact just as soon as she had had her breakfast she had approached the hotel manager to ask if there was any chance that another interpreter might now be free, but once again she had met with the same response. The conventions taking place in the city meant that it was impossible for them to provide her with this service.

Tempted though Beth had been to tell Alex that she simply no longer required his help, common sense had forced her to acknowledge that this would be cutting off her nose to spite her face. Although it was true that most

Czechs could either speak or understand English, Beth needed to be very sure of exactly what was being said if she should decide to give any of the factories an order, and she also needed someone to help her negotiate the best possible price she could for whatever she might decide to order, and that meant having someone with her who had a proper grasp of the Czech language.

However, there was one thing she could do, and that was make sure that she spent as little time as possible with Alex Andrews, and to that end Beth had decided that today, instead of only visiting two factories, she would insist that they manage to visit three, which meant that would leave her with only another half a dozen on her list.

'No? Then *I* shall take you to see it,' Alex was announcing, ignoring Beth's steely silence. 'I expect you already know that it was the first permanent bridge to be built in Northern Europe and—'

'Yes, I *have* read the guidebooks,' Beth interrupted him shortly. 'But as for seeing it…' She shook her head and told him briskly, 'I'm here on business, and that has to take priority over everything else…'

As she spoke she couldn't resist looking towards the gift shop. The lustres were still there, tantalisingly.

She gave a sigh.

'I have been thinking,' Alex told her quietly. 'If good-quality reproduction Venetian baroque crystal *is* what you are looking for then my cousins' factory is most definitely somewhere you should visit. If you should wish to visit I'm sure I could arrange something.'

'Yes, I'm sure you could,' Beth agreed sarcastically. Just how stupid did he think she was?

'Is your cousins' factory mentioned on my list?' she asked him, already knowing what the answer would be.

As she had known he would, Alex shook his head as she held her list out to him.

'These factories were originally state-owned, and though they are now back in private hands they do not... My cousins' factory is not like them. It does not cater to the mass market. Until the Revolution they mainly supplied the Russian hierarchy.'

'Fascinating though the history of your family undoubtedly is—to you,' she told him coolly, 'I'm afraid that I simply don't have time to listen to it.' She glanced at her watch. 'There are three factories I want to see today, so I suggest that we make a start...'

She could see that Alex was starting to frown.

'Beth,' he began, reaching out to catch hold of her arm. Unable to move in time to prevent him, Beth went rigid as she felt his fingers circle her wrist.

'What is it? What's wrong?' he asked her huskily. His thumb was resting on the pulse in her wrist and she could feel it starting to hammer frantically against his touch. He could obviously feel it as well, because his thumb started to move against her skin in a rhythmic, circular stroking movement that should have been soothing but for some reason had quite the opposite effect on her hypersensitive nervous system.

'Nothing's wrong,' she lied jerkily, willing herself not to allow the deep tremor she could feel beginning deep within her body like some subterranean force to manifest itself in open shivers and shudders of reaction.

And then, to her own self-contempt, she heard herself asking him sharply, 'Did you enjoy yourself last night—with your family?'

The appraising look he gave her made her wish she had kept silent.

'Yes, I did,' he agreed calmly, 'but nowhere near so

much as I would have had you been with us, and certainly nowhere near so much as I would had we been alone...'

Beth's gasp was, she assured herself, one of furious female outrage. How dared he have the barefaced cheek to stand there and say such a thing to her when she knew, when she had seen with her own eyes, just how he had spent his evening and with whom?

'Tonight, I want you to have dinner with me,' he was continuing. 'Tonight, I want you,' he added, underlining the sensuality of his message and his desire.

But that desire was faked, flawed, a lie, and Beth knew it.

'I can't. I've already made arrangements for this evening,' she told him coolly.

Ridiculous to feel that *she* was at fault just because of the way he managed to fake those dark shadows in his eyes and that male look of hurt withdrawal in the tightness of his mouth. *She* was the one who was being badly treated, not him.

'You're not going to find what you're looking for at any of the factories on your list,' Alex informed Beth as they left the third factory.

'No. I'm coming to realise that,' Beth said testily. She felt both tired and disappointed, but that was not the real cause of her defensive anger and she knew it. Five hours of being cooped up in a small car with Alex was beginning to have its effect on her equilibrium—and her emotions.

She had done everything she could to hold him at a distance, but to her chagrin, instead of recognising that she had guessed what he was up to, he'd seemed to think that she wasn't very well, anxiously asking her in some concern several times if she was suffering from a headache or feeling unwell. Only her own cautious nature had prevented her from telling him that if she *was* suffering from any kind of malaise then he was its cause. But there was more to what she was experiencing than that, she was forced to acknowledge honestly.

Had she simply been able to feel for him the contempt and disdain she knew he deserved then there would have been no need for her defensive and protective anger. But against all logic, and certainly against any cerebral desire on her part, she was unable to deny her body's physical reaction, her body's physical *response* to him; that was why she was getting so uptight and angry.

Every time he made some comment about wanting her, every time he alluded to how much he desired her, she could feel herself starting to react to him. And she had even, at one morale-lowering point, found herself wishing that he *would* put his softly suggestive comment about longing to silence her sharp tongue with his mouth into action.

'You're so prickly that a man can't help but feel tempted to wonder what it would take to make you purr,' he'd informed her outrageously when she had refused his suggestion that they find somewhere to have lunch.

'You're right,' he had agreed, when she had told him shortly that she didn't want to eat, his eyes suddenly dark and hot. '*My* appetite isn't for food either. What I really want to taste is the sweet softness of your flesh. Its juices will be like nectar, honey to my lips, whilst—'

'Stop it,' Beth had demanded frantically, unable to screen out the mental images his erotic words had provoked for her. How could she dislike him so much, distrust him so much, and yet, at the same time, *want* him so much?

It was just sex, she told herself fiercely. That was all.

For some reason he had aroused within her a hitherto unexperienced need, a desire she had never suspected herself capable of feeling. The hesitant and awkward experiments of her teenage years had simply not prepared her for what she was feeling now—and that was all it was, a quirky build-up of the sexual desire she should perhaps have felt at a younger age but which, for some reason, she had not, and which was now manifesting itself in this totally unacceptable reaction to Alex Andrews.

Yes, *that* was what it was, she decided in relief. It was just sex…just an itch that needed scratching… Shocked by the unfamiliar directness of her own thoughts, Beth tried to concentrate on the countryside they were driving through. Just because she now knew the cause of her disturbing reaction to Alex, that didn't mean she had to give in to it, she warned herself. And at least it meant she no longer had to worry about it, she told herself in relief.

'Look…I'm sorry if I seem to be crowding you or rushing you,' Alex was saying gruffly at her side. 'All this is new territory for me, you know. I've never actually felt like this before, experienced anything like this before. I always knew that one day I would fall in love just as passionately and permanently as my grandfather fell in love with my grandmother, but I have to confess I didn't expect it to be so…'

Heavens, but he was quick, clever… Beth acknowledged as she forced herself to be detached and step outside her own feelings to admire the adroit way he was handling not just the situation but her as well.

First the advance, now the back-off. No doubt he expected her to feel chagrin and to start pursuing *him*. And as for that schmaltzy comment about his grandparents…!

CHAPTER FIVE

'I'M SORRY THAT none of the factories we visited today came up to your expectations.' Alex joined her in the hotel's gift shop and looked at his watch. 'It's too late for me to organise anything now, but why don't I give my cousins a ring and arrange for you to visit their factory? We could...'

They moved back into the hotel foyer, which was very busy with business-suited people who Beth assumed must be attending one of the conferences in the hotel the manager had told her about. She felt tired and disappointed, but those feelings weren't the real cause of the desire she felt to snap sharply at Alex.

Why, when she knew exactly what kind of man he was and exactly what he was after, was she experiencing this sense of new panic and fear that her self-control might not prove strong enough for her to hold him at bay? What was the matter with her? Surely she had enough intelligence to know that once one had been struck by lightning a first time one did not return to the same tree in a thunderstorm and stand there waiting for it to happen again. Not unless one was a very peculiar sort of person who thrived on suffering pain.

Was she that kind of person, the kind of person who only attracted the sort of relationship, the sort of *man* who would hurt and humiliate her? Beth knew from the strength of her own inner abhorrence that she wasn't.

So why, then, did she feel the way she did?

She felt the way she did because she was sexually attracted to Alex, she told herself brutally; she was chemically and hormonally responsive to him. That was all... It crossed her mind as the movement of the crowd pushed her up against him and he reached out automatically to hold her that it might almost be worthwhile actually giving in to what she was feeling, what she was *wanting*, and simply having sex with him. Perhaps once she had done so, once he had realised that she was able to separate her feelings of sexual desire for him from her emotions, that just because she went to bed with him it didn't mean she was going to allow him to persuade her to give his cousins her business or him her money, he might stop trying to pressurise her. After all, she already knew that the only real interest he had in her was a financial one, despite the attention he was paying her and the compliments he was giving her.

'It's too crowded in here. We could talk more easily in your room.'

Alex's words, whispered so temptingly against her ear, mirroring so closely the intimate sensuality of her own thoughts, threw Beth into feminine panic.

'No. No...' she denied quickly, frantically trying to make some space between them. Could Alex feel the tumultuous, uneven thudding of her heartbeat as clearly as she could feel the deep male pounding of his? And, if he could, was it having the same intense effect upon his senses as his was upon hers? Beth closed her eyes, struggling to break free of the tide of hungry need she could feel welling up inside her. All day long she had been fighting against this; all day long she had been struggling to hold both Alex and her own unfamiliar responsiveness to him at bay.

Now, pressed up against him in the airless atmosphere of the hotel lobby, she was terrifyingly aware of how readily her senses responded to him, of how great the temptation was not to move away from him but to move *closer*.

'I could ring my cousins from your room,' Alex was telling her persuasively. 'I promise you you won't be disappointed, Beth.'

Was it just her imagination, or was he subtly implying that her expectations of pleasure would not merely be satisfied by the quality of his cousins' glass? Beth could feel her face starting to burn with hectic hormone-driven colour.

The warmth of his breath as he spoke to her was so tantalisingly like a caress that she had to grit her teeth to stop herself from moving closer to it, to stop herself from imagining how it would feel to have the soft caress of his mouth moving against the tender, vulnerable pleasure spot just behind her ear, to move from there to...

Beneath her clothes Beth could feel her nipples peaking and thrusting eagerly against their protective covering, flaunting their availability and their need.

Frantically Beth decided that she had to do something, anything, to put a stop to what was happening.

'From the way you're talking, anyone would think that your cousins are the *only* manufacturers who produce high-quality reproduction antique glass,' she told Alex challengingly, gritting her teeth as she deliberately pushed herself away from him and looked into his face.

'Well, they aren't the *only* ones, but they do have a reputation for being the best. Of the only other two I know, one has order books going right into the millennium—mainly from its American customers—and the other is presently in negotiation with an Italian company that wants to go into partnership with them.'

'How very convenient,' Beth told him sarcastically. 'But as it happens I've actually found my own source…'

'You have?' Alex was frowning slightly. 'May I ask where? None of the factories you've got listed…'

'It isn't somewhere on my list,' Beth told him, too infuriated by his patronising manner to be guarded or cautious. 'I've been told by one of the gypsy stall holders in Wenceslas Square that she can supply me with an introduction to a factory that makes the quality of glass I want.'

'A stall holder in the Square?' Alex looked patently unimpressed. 'And you believed her?' he derided, before asking her hardily, 'You didn't give her any money, did you?'

'No, I didn't. Not that it's any of your business,' Beth defended herself sharply. She felt like a naughty child, called up before her head teacher to explain herself, and it wasn't a sensation she was enjoying. What right, after all, did Alex have to question any of her decisions? And as for his comment about her not parting with any money…!

'She's going to get some samples of the glass for me to look at…'

'You've told her where you're staying?'

If anything he was looking even more disapproving, and a belated sense of caution warned Beth not to tell him that she had actually arranged to go down to the Square to meet with the stall holder that evening.

'She knows how to get in touch with me,' was all she permitted herself to say.

'You do know the reputations some of these gypsies have, don't you?' Alex demanded. 'You must have been warned. A lot of them are illegal immigrants into the country. They are well known to be in the pay of organised criminals...'

'What, *all* of them?' Beth derided him, parodying his tone of voice to her minutes earlier.

'This is not a situation you should take lightly,' Alex told her sternly. 'These are potentially very dangerous people.'

Beth couldn't help herself. Childish though she knew it was, she gave a heavy, theatrically bored sigh that stopped Alex speaking immediately and caused his mouth to harden into an implacably tight line.

'Very well,' he told her curtly. 'If you won't listen to my advice then at least, for your own safety and my peace of mind, let me be there when you see these people.'

Let him be there... Knowing what she did, and knowing now just how determined he was to push her in the direction of his family's business—no way.

The crowd which had thronged the lobby was thinning out now. The girl behind the reception desk, catching sight of Alex, signalled to him.

'Excuse me,' he said to Beth quickly, walking towards the desk. Beth could hear the girl saying something to him in Czech—telling him what? she wondered, her curiosity aroused by the girl's unexpectedly respectful manner towards him, rather as though she considered Alex to be someone important.

From what she had seen of them, Beth knew that the Czechs were a very polite and courteous nation, treating one another with courtly good manners which seemed to have gone rather out of fashion in other Western countries, but the clerk behind the desk wasn't merely treating Alex courteously; whilst her behaviour wasn't exactly obsequious, it was very definitely deferential.

Frowning a little over this perplexing insight into someone else's opinion of Alex, Beth quickly warned herself against encouraging herself to see hitherto unnoticed good points about him. She had made *that* mistake with Julian Cox, determinedly supporting him and even defending him to her closest friends when they had tried gently to warn her what kind of man he was.

She had even ignored the fact that her own best friend, Kelly, had had to reject his advances at the same time that she was actually seeing him, letting Julian persuade her that Kelly was just jealous.

Beth could hardly bear now to reflect on her own wilful foolishness. She knew that Kelly and her friends, most especially those closest to her—Anna and Dee—all believed that Julian's perfidy had broken her heart. And it was true that she had believed that he loved her, that she had allowed herself to be carried away by the fantasy he had created around them both, the romantic deception he had woven. She was, as Beth was the first to admit, someone who was inclined to be a little over-idealistic, to believe that all her geese were potential swans, so to speak. However, even whilst Julian had been pressuring her to make plans for an elaborate engagement party, even whilst he had been swearing undying love to her, a tiny part of her had been just that little bit concerned, just that little bit wary that he was rushing things too much, that she wasn't being given time to assimilate her own feelings properly.

All her life there had been fond, loving people there to make her most important decisions for her, to relieve her of the burden of having to do so for herself. Her parents, her grandparents, even her friends, all of them loving and caring, all of them protective, all of them acting from the best possible motives. But Beth could see now that their love and their protection had taken from her the right to make her own decisions *and* her own mistakes. It wasn't their fault. It was her own. She ought to have been more assertive, less passive, less eager to be the beloved, adored child and more eager to be the respected woman. Well, all that was behind her now. For practical reasons she needed the services of an interpreter and a guide, but that was all. There was no way she needed anyone else's support or anyone else's advice in deciding what she wanted to buy for her shop.

Alex was still speaking with the girl behind the reception desk. Beth came to a quick decision. Whilst he was busy she had the perfect opportunity to get away from him. Quickly she headed towards the lift, only realising how anxious she had been that he would come after her once she was safely inside it and it was moving.

She had the lift to herself. Briefly she closed her eyes, her face burning as, without meaning to, she suddenly found herself remembering what Alex had said to her about being in a lift with her the previous day.

Angry with herself for the wayward and highly personal nature of her thoughts, she told herself determinedly that she had far better and more important things to think about than Alex Andrews.

Once inside her room, she rang down to the reception desk and informed them that she didn't want to be disturbed—under any circumstances or by anyone.

She doubted that Alex would genuinely be concerned at not being able to make contact with her. After all, she wasn't his only woman 'client', was she?

Beth frowned as she tried to analyse the feelings tensing her body when she recalled the very elegant, if undeniably older woman she had seen him with the previous evening—the evening he had told her he intended to spend with his family. She hadn't looked the sort of person who would be taken in by the attentions of a flirtatious interpreter, but then perhaps, like her, she'd recognised Alex for exactly what he was and had decided to… There had certainly been a good deal of intimacy in the closeness of their bodies as they had stood together.

Beth wrapped her arms protectively around her own body. The distasteful suspicions flooding her mind should surely have the effect of totally destroying the physical desire she had begun to feel for Alex, not feeding the unexpected jealousy she could actually feel.

Annoyed with herself, she paced the floor of her room. It was too early for her to go back to the Square, where she had seen the gypsy, and she felt too restless to remain here in her room—as well as much too aware of the growing danger of wanting to remain alone with her own seriously undermining, intimate thoughts.

Perhaps a guided tour of the city would help to pass some of the time. Besides which, she genuinely wanted to see more of the place which had such a wonderful reputation.

Three hours later, at the end of her chosen tour, Beth had to acknowledge that she hadn't realised the breadth of Prague's varied history. She had been shown the Jewish Cemetery, and had marvelled at its antiquity. She had stood on the hillside and looked down at Prague's pretty rooftops, admiring their copper cupolas and the soft warm reds of its tiles and bricks. She had seen the castle, with its many courtyards, and wandered with the other eager members of her group along the narrow streets lined with tiny, fascinating gift shops.

Having thanked her guide for her stimulating talk, Beth excused herself, slowly making her way back towards Wenceslas Square, stopping at one point to order a sandwich and a pot of coffee at a small attractive café where she could sit outside and watch the world go by.

If anything the Square was even more crowded this evening than it had been the evening before when she had first visited it, Beth decided as she made her way through the groups of other sightseers thronging the large cobbled area. The armour-making stall, the fire-eater and the acrobats were all there, and familiar to her, barely meriting more than a second interested look as she hurried to the stall where she had met the gypsy. Not only was the Square more crowded with tourists, there also seemed to be more stalls as well, Beth recognised, and at first she thought that her stall wasn't there.

Anxiously she searched for it, her attention momentarily caught by the pathetic sight of two young children huddled in a doorway clutching a grey-faced, ominously quiet baby. She had heard that sometimes the gypsy mothers, in order to pursue their begging more easily, sedated their children by whatever means they could, including the use of drink and—appallingly, to Beth's mind—drugs.

Poor child, and poor mother too, Beth's tender heart couldn't help feeling. Whatever the rights and wrongs of their political situation—and Beth was the first to admit that she was in no position to be any judge of that—she couldn't help but feel sad for the plight of her fellow humans.

Even though she knew she was probably doing the wrong thing, she couldn't stop herself from giving the grubby child who approached her a handful of small change.

As she firmly shooed the children away, shaking her head to show that there was no more money, she saw the stall she had been looking for tucked away to one side of a larger one. Relieved, she hurried towards it.

The woman she had seen the previous evening recognised her immediately, beckoning her over with a wide smile.

'I have here the glass for you to see,' she told Beth in a conspiratorial whisper, drawing her into the canvas-covered rear of her stall.

Its canvas covering obscured the light and smelt strongly, causing Beth's throat to close up uncomfortably. There was a heavy odor in the air that might have been incense, or perhaps something a little less innocuous. Beth really didn't want to know.

'See…here it is…' the woman was telling Beth, touching her on the arm as she directed her attention to several pieces of glass she had placed on a makeshift table formed from an old box. Beth had to kneel down to see the glass properly, but once she did so she caught her breath in awed delight, instinctively reaching out to take hold of the beautifully crafted items the woman was showing her.

Only now, in the relief of having her judgement vindicated, was she able to admit to herself how very, very important it was to her to be able to tell Alex Andrews that she had managed to find her glassware without his help.

'Oh, but these are wonderful, *perfect*,' she told the woman huskily.

As she inspected them and held them, examining them carefully and holding them up to the light, despite the gypsy woman's fierce protest and the way she shielded them from the sight of anyone else by standing in front of them, Beth found it hard to believe that they were not actually genuine antiques.

But of course they couldn't possibly be. Glassware

such as this, *had* it been antique, would have been locked away in a museum somewhere. To have owned glass like this in the seventeenth century one would have had to have been a very wealthy person indeed. It was, no doubt, something in the traditional manufacturing process that gave the gloss an 'antique' look.

The more she studied the pieces the gypsy woman was showing her, the more Beth's excitement grew. To be able to display glassware such as this in her shop would indeed be a wonderful coup. So far as she knew, no one had ever seen anything like it, other than in private collections or locked away behind glass doors in a handful of very expensive and up-market specialist stores. The gilding alone...

In all, the gypsy woman had brought half a dozen pieces for Beth to examine, in three slightly different styles of stemware, in cranberry, the deepest, richest blue Beth had ever seen, gold and emerald. There was a very ornate pedestal bowl, with an intricately faceted stem that caught the light as brilliantly as a flawless diamond, a breathtakingly beautiful water jug, with flowers cut into its handle and lavishly embellished with gilt, two wine glasses and, last of all, a pair of lustres even more beautiful than the ones Beth had seen in the gift shop. She wanted it all, knew she could *sell* it all if, and it was a very big if, the price was right.

There were, here and there in Europe, she knew, small factories with dedicated craftsmen that still made such articles, but at a cost that put them way, way out of the means of most people. A wealthy oil sheikh, a millionaire pop star, royal houses—*they* might be able to afford whole suites of such stemware, but her customers, even the most comfortably off of them, could not.

All Beth's original plans to purchase good-quality but

relatively inexpensive plain glass crystal stemware, perhaps embellished with a discreet amount of gold, flew out
of her head—and her heart—as she studied the pieces
the gypsy woman displayed to her.

Her budget was relatively small, and she had no doubt
that these pieces would be expensive, but Beth knew she
just had to have them. Already she could see them displayed in the shop. Already she could hear the delighted
gasps of their customers, the flood of sales. Her excited
thoughts ran on and on whilst Beth tried as sedately as
she could to elicit from the gypsy what exactly the factory *did* manufacture.

'Do these come in suites of stemware?' she asked her,
picking up one of the glasses. 'A full set, or just these
wine glasses?'

'A full set could be made if that was what you wanted,'
the gypsy told Beth, her eyes narrowing as she added
shrewdly, 'Of course, that would mean you would have
to give the factory a substantial order.'

Beth's heart sank. How much exactly was a substantial
order? When the gypsy told her her heart sank even further. One hundred suites of glassware in the same pattern
was far more than she could ever hope to sell, unless...

'If I have so many could I have a mix of colours? Say
twenty-five suites of each of the four colourways?' she
asked.

The gypsy pursed her lips.

'I am not sure. I would have to check with the factory
first about that.'

'And the cost?' Beth asked her quickly. 'How much is
the glass? Do you have a price list?' she added.

The gypsy shook her head, her smile revealing the
gap in her teeth.

'How much can you afford?' she challenged Beth.

Beth paused. Haggling had never been one of her strong points—that was far more Kelly's forte than hers—but, driven by her desire to order the glassware, she named a figure per suite of glassware that allowed her some margin to bargain with.

The gypsy laughed.

'So little, and for such glass.' She shook her head. 'No,' she denied, and then she named a figure that made Beth blanch a little as she quickly worked out the cost of a total order at such figures.

'No, that is far too much,' she told the gypsy firmly, and then added, 'Perhaps I could visit the factory and speak with the manager there...'

The gypsy's eyes narrowed. Beth had the most uncomfortable impression that something she had said had amused her.

'The factory...it is very far away, a whole day...'

'A whole day.' Beth frowned.

'You can say everything you have to say to me,' the gypsy started to assure her, but Beth shook her head.

She suspected that the woman, in giving her the price, was allowing a very generous margin for herself. Common sense told Beth that had the glass been as expensive as she was quoting then it would have been sold via one of the expensive outlets she had seen on the city's main shopping streets.

As though she had guessed what she was thinking, the gypsy suddenly pulled hard on Beth's sleeve and leaned closer to her, whispering, 'The factory, it is not owned by the Czechs. It belongs to...others... You can visit it if you wish, but...' She gave a small shrug.

'I *do* wish,' Beth told her firmly.

'Very well, then I will arrange it for you. But first you have to make a show of good faith,' the woman told her.

Make a show of good faith? For a moment Beth was nonplussed, and then she realised that the woman was asking her for money. All she had on her was a small amount of currency, and parting with it under such circumstances went against everything she personally believed in, but she had, nevertheless, to do so.

With one last lingering inspection of the glassware, Beth made arrangements to meet with the gypsy again.

'Why not tomorrow?' she asked her, knowing that she was going to have to extend the length of her original visit if she did as the other woman wished.

'No. No, that is not possible. Arrangements have to be made,' the woman told Beth.

'Very well, then...' Beth wondered if she should offer to provide her own transport for the journey, but she was loath to involve Alex in what she was doing. After all, he was not going to be very pleased to discover that she was giving her business to someone else when he plainly wanted her to give it to his cousins.

However, before she could say anything, the gypsy was telling her, 'I will meet you here a week from now at seven o'clock in the morning. We will drive all day. You will see the factory and then we will drive back. You will bring with you some money...'

Some money. Beth looked at her in alarm.

It had been her intention to pay for any goods she ordered via her bank, but, rather than discuss this with the gypsy, she decided that she would leave the financial side of things until after she had reached the factory. She wasn't one hundred per cent sure she totally trusted the gypsy, and the truth was that if the glass she had shown her hadn't been so spectacularly beautiful and so very covetable Beth suspected she would not have entertained the idea of doing business via her.

In fact, Beth decided, as she walked back towards the hotel a little later, Prague was having the most decidedly odd effect—not just on her behaviour but also on the way she viewed herself.

Lust, the kind of healthy, energetic, empowering lust that other women were so cheerfully and self-confidently able to admit to, had never been an emotion Beth had expected herself to feel. She had always thought that emotionally she simply wasn't robust and self-motivated enough, that she simply didn't possess the energy or the confidence to say 'I want' about anything or anyone, and yet here she was, after less than a week here in Prague, being forced to admit to herself that not only did she want, but she wanted very powerfully and lustfully indeed. And she didn't just mean the beautiful glass.

Such knowledge was enough to stop her momentarily in mid-stride. Cautiously she dared to examine this admission a little more closely. Was her yearning to touch and explore the male beauty of Alex's body as powerful and compelling as the urge she had experienced to hold and caress the beautiful glass?

The heat that flooded her body gave her its own answer. In her hands the glass had felt cool and smooth, heavy and solidly curved, the raised rim of gilding sensuously rough against her fingertips in contrast to the smooth contours of the glass itself.

Would Alex's body feel the same? Heat exploded inside her, showering her, turning her veins heavy with liquid excitement. The sensuality of her own thoughts, so completely contradictory to anything she had experienced before, totally bemused Beth, teasing and tormenting her, enticing her to explore them further.

It was growing dark. She ought to get back to the hotel, she warned herself shakily.

As she walked past the reception desk the young man on duty called her name.

'Mr Andrews has been asking for you,' he told Beth as she approached the desk. 'He has left you a message.'

Reluctantly Beth took the sealed note he was handing her, but she didn't open it until she was in her room.

I had hoped to invite you to join my cousins and myself for dinner this evening, but unfortunately I could not make contact with you. I shall pick you up at the hotel in the morning at ten o'clock unless I hear from you to the contrary. If you wish to telephone me the number is...

Just for a moment Beth was tempted to dial the number and tell him triumphantly that she had found the glass she wanted, and without his help, but common sense warned her that this would not be a good idea. Especially since it seemed obvious that he had still not given up hope of persuading her to buy from his family, if his statement about intending to ask her to have dinner with them was anything to go by.

Had he taken someone else to meet them instead... that elegant older woman, perhaps? Determinedly Beth pushed him out of her thoughts. There were things she had to do. She was still bubbling over with excitement about what she had seen and longing to share the excitement with someone. It was too late now to ring Kelly, but she would do so tomorrow. She would have to ring her bank as well, but that could wait until after she had visited the factory. Beth wasn't sure how she was going to be able to wait.

Squeezing her eyes tightly closed, she tried to visualise the glass she had seen, but, infuriatingly, the image that formed behind her closed eyelids wasn't that of the beautiful glassware but of Alex Andrews' strong, masculine features, his compellingly unusual steel-grey eyes smouldering with a mercurial heat that made her heart flip excitedly against her chest wall and her stomach muscles contract with sensual urgency.

CHAPTER SIX

BETH WOKE UP, her body tensing as she recognised from the strength of the light filtering through her hotel bedroom curtains that she had slept beyond her normal waking-up time.

And then she started to relax as she remembered that this morning she did not have to get up early, since today she was not planning to visit any factories.

The decision she had made late last night to leave a message for Alex Andrews on his answer-machine, thanking him for his help but stating quite firmly that she now no longer needed his services and asking him to leave her a bill, had, rather oddly, not given her quite as much satisfaction as she had anticipated.

Beth frowned as she climbed out of bed and walked naked into her bathroom.

The weight she had lost in the trauma following the break-up of her relationship with Julian had now been replaced, banishing the hollow-eyed gauntness which had not suited her small curvy frame.

Prague had brought the sheen back to her hair and the glow back to her skin.

Quickly she showered and put on clean undies, then blow-dried her hair. She had just finished highlighting her naturally delicate and pale skin with blusher and applying her lipstick when she heard the room service waiter knocking.

Quickly she reached for her robe and, wrapping it tightly around her body, she went to let him in.

'Thank you, that's…' she began, and then stopped as she realised that the man pushing the trolley wasn't her normal room service waiter but Alex Andrews. Her eyes widened even further as she saw that the table wasn't set up just for one but for two.

'What are *you* doing here?' she demanded in angry confusion, instinctively pulling the robe even more tightly around her body. But as Alex set up the table Beth was treacherously aware of how glad she was that he hadn't arrived before she had had time to wash her hair and do her face; after all, why should she mind whether or not Alex saw her at her best or her worst?

She was simply reacting in a totally normal female way, she defended herself mentally. There was nothing personal in her reaction; she would have felt the same no matter who had arrived with the tray.

Would she?

Beth fought to suppress the knowledge that only yesterday, when the room service waiter had arrived, it hadn't concerned her in the least that she had had to let him in with her hair uncombed and her face still pale from sleep.

'I thought we could discuss what we are going to do today over breakfast,' Alex replied cheerfully as he pulled up a chair for her with a very professional flourish and waved her into it.

Too caught off guard to refuse, Beth automatically sat down.

'*We* are not going to do anything,' she informed him firmly. 'Didn't you get my message?'

'You don't intend to visit any more factories. Yes, I know,' Alex agreed. 'However, there is far, far more to Prague and the Republic than glass factories.'

'I'm sure there is, and I'm looking forward to discovering it and them—on my own,' Beth told him pointedly.

'I thought we'd start with a walk round the city,' Alex continued, expertly pouring Beth's coffee and then sitting down opposite her and offering her a piece of toast.

'You have no right to do this, nor to be here,' Beth told him furiously. 'I could report you to the hotel manager...'

She could, but Beth knew that she wouldn't. Someone, whether her official waiter or someone else, must have known what Alex was doing, and to report them might be to get them into trouble. Beth was far too soft-hearted to do that, and she suspected that Alex knew it.

'Why don't you want to visit any more factories?' Alex was asking her, ignoring her patently weak threat.

'Because I don't need to,' Beth told him promptly, adding, 'Not that it's any of your business...' But instead of looking suitably chastised Alex was actually looking quite stern.

'Beth, you aren't still thinking of following up that contact you made in the Square, are you? Because if you are...'

'*If* I am, then it's *my* business and no one else's,' Beth told him furiously. How dared he try to tell her what she could and could not do, and, even worse, how dared he try to make her feel as though she was a gullible little fool, incapable of making a rational or informed business decision?

'And despite what *you* seem to think I actually do know my own business and my own customers,' she continued hotly. 'I know what will and won't sell in *my* shop, and at what price, and if *you* think—'

'I'm sorry. I'm sorry,' Alex apologised remorsefully. 'I wasn't trying to imply that you don't know your own business, Beth, or your own market, but buying goods here in the Republic isn't quite like going on a buying trip at home. The Czech people themselves couldn't be more honest, but there are other forces at work here, other... problems...which have to be taken into account.

'If you really feel that this gypsy contact you've made *is* genuine, then at least allow me to come with you when you go to visit the factory...'

'Why? So that you can get the opportunity to undercut their prices and point me in the direction of your cousins' factory instead?' Beth demanded sharply, adding scornfully, 'You see, Alex, I'm not *quite* so naive as you seem to think. I'm perfectly well aware of what you're trying to do. No doubt the reason you're here today is really to try to persuade me to visit your precious cousins' business...'

Beth saw from the look on his face that her guess was right, but instead of feeling triumphant she discovered that the tiny needle-sharp sensation knowing she was right gave her actually physically hurt.

'I *had* intended to suggest that it might be worthwhile your visiting the factory, yes,' Alex agreed, his voice suddenly unfamiliarly harsh. 'But not for the less than altruistic reasons you're trying to suggest. If you must have the truth, the glass my cousins—' He stopped.

'What *is* it about you, Beth? Why is it you're so determined to suspect my motives?'

Beth pushed away her toast uneaten.

'You're a man,' she told him acidly, 'and my experience of men is that...'

There was a small, tight silence, and then Alex said harshly, 'Do go on. Your experience of men is what?'

Beth looked away from him. Something about the tight white line around his mouth was hurting her. Without knowing how it had happened she had strayed onto some very treacherous and uncertain ground indeed. What on earth had possessed her to raise a subject both so intimately personal and so volatilely dangerous?

'So, I'm to be condemned without a hearing, is that it? Sentenced for a crime I haven't even committed simply because I'm a man... Who was he, Beth?' he asked her grimly. 'A friend? A lover?'

Beth discovered that she was finding it hard to swallow. Completely unexpectedly and totally unwontedly she found that her eyes had filled with tears.

'Actually he was neither,' she told Alex shakily, and then, before she could stop herself, she was adding emotionally, 'If you must know he was the man who told me he loved me but didn't—the man who betrayed me and...'

Frantically she got up, her eyes flooding with tears, knocking over her chair in her desperate attempt to avoid crying in front of Alex and completely humiliating herself. But as she tried to run to the sanctuary of the bathroom the length of her bathrobe hampered her, and she had only taken a few steps before Alex caught up with her, bodily grabbed hold of her and swung her round to face him, his own face taut with emotion.

'Oh, Beth. Beth, please don't cry,' she heard him groan as he wrapped her in his arms. 'I'm so sorry...I didn't mean to upset you. I never...'

'I'm not upset,' Beth denied. 'I didn't love him anyway,' she told Alex truthfully, and then added less honestly, 'Men aren't worth loving...'

'No?' Alex asked her huskily.

'No,' Beth repeated firmly, but somehow or other her denial had lost a good deal of its potency. Was that perhaps because of the way Alex was cupping her face, his mouth gently caressing hers, his lips teasing the stubbornly tight line of hers, coaxing it to soften and part on a soft sigh that should have been a sharp rejection of what he was doing but somehow had become something softer and more accommodating?

As Alex continued to kiss her the most dizzying sweet sensation filled Beth.

She had the most overpowering urge to cling blissfully to Alex and melt into his arms like an old-fashioned Victorian maiden. Behind her closed eyelids she could have sworn there danced sunlit images of tulle and confetti scented with the lilies of a bridal bouquet, and the sound of a triumphant 'Wedding March' swelled and boomed and gold sunbeams formed a circle around her.

Dreamily Beth sighed, and then smiled beneath Alex's kiss, her own lips parting in happy acquiescence to the explorative thrust of his tongue.

Alex was dressed casually, in jeans and a soft shirt. Beneath her fingertips Beth could feel the fabric of that shirt, soft and warm, but the body that lay beneath it felt deliciously firm…hard, masculine, an unfamiliar and even forbidden territory that her fingers were suddenly dangerously eager to explore.

Alex made a small sound of approving pleasure as Beth's fingers rebelliously slipped between the buttons of his shirt. Her borrowed hotel robe, a 'one size fits all' garment of extremely generous proportions, was starting to slide off her shoulder, and the sensation of Alex's fingertips just brushing her bare skin sent a violent frisson of breathtaking pleasure zigzagging all down her body.

Beth wasn't used to such an explosive physical reaction to a man's touch. It made her catch her breath, her mouth rounding and her teeth accidentally closing on the fullness of Alex's bottom lip and dragging gently against it.

Alex gave a thickly audible responsive groan that shivered through her own body right down to her toes, making her curl them into the carpet. The sensual heat they were both generating was combining to melt away all Beth's inhibitions, her mouth opening eagerly to the demanding thrust of Alex's tongue.

Her robe had started to open when she had trodden on the hem during her earlier attempt to escape from the humiliation of her own tears, but Beth was totally unaware of just how much of her body it had actually exposed until she felt the warmth of Alex's hand against her breast, firmly cupping its soft weight against his palm as he slowly caressed its rounded shape with a slow, sensuous deliberation that made Beth tremble and then shudder, the rash of goosebumps raised on her skin betraying just how immediately and intensely sensitive she was to the erotic sensation of his caress.

Over Alex's shoulder she could see their entwined images in her bedroom mirror. His hand, tanned and brown, lean and muscular, in direct contrast to the pale, sheer fabric-covered globe of her breast, soft, full, rounded, compliant to his touch. Male to female, man to woman, hard against soft.

Alex was still kissing her, plundering her mouth, his free hand burrowing beneath her robe to rest just below her waist on her naked back, his fingers stroking, kneading her sensitive flesh into such a frenzy of responsiveness that she was pressing herself frantically against him, mindlessly grinding her hips into his body, desperately searching for even closer contact with his aroused hardness.

The hand caressing her breast started to stroke it

rhythmically, Alex's fingertips teasing her nipple to a stiff point beneath her gauzy bra, playing with it, flicking it with a tormenting gentleness that made Beth tremble from head to foot with hungry need.

In the mirror now their bodies were so closely entwined, so *sensuously* entwined, that they might almost already have been lovers. Beth moaned longingly, reaching out to cover Alex's hand with her own, wanting to urge him to remove the barrier of her bra. She was acting on instinct alone now, driven by a female urge programmed into her by nature itself, and, in obeying it, she had as little choice as a lemming following its preordained life path.

When Alex resisted her attempt to guide him to do what she wanted she growled her female frustration at having her need left unsatisfied beneath his kiss, making a low, keening sound that had no words but which Alex seemed immediately able to translate.

'I can't,' he told her hoarsely, his hand burning hot against her swollen breast. 'If I do, if I see you…touch you…'

His eyes flashed signals of stormy male desire, the sweetly savage bite of his teeth against the tenderness of her kiss-sensitive lips betraying how he would treat the tormenting and tormented sensitivity of her aroused nipples if she made him remove their frail protective covering. But Beth had gone beyond the safety of heeding any kind of warning.

Something—she neither knew nor cared what—had snapped the taut barrier she had wrapped around her feelings, her responses, her right to enjoy her female sexuality.

It was as though all the hurt she had experienced, all the anger, all the fear and distress, the humiliation and the pain had coalesced, exploded, burned itself out in a fierce transmuting heat that had turned her from her previously shy, inhibited, immature self into a powerfully strong and sexually motivated woman, a woman whose body demanded, expected and *intended* to have nothing less than total satisfaction of its deepest and most privately, primitively intimate sexual desires.

To her own shock, and her own fierce joy, she recognised that the Beth who had imagined the only way she could ever really enjoy sex would be in the arms of a gentle, considerate lover who would treat her as carefully as a delicately made piece of fragile glass had suddenly been replaced by a Beth who knew instinctively that what she wanted now was to enjoy sex in its rawest, purest, hottest form possible.

Like the silica at its most molten fluid form, she wanted to be taken into the creative care of an expert, an artist, a master of his craft—and of her. She wanted to watch, to be, as he poured the golden liquid form of her being into the crucible of heat that was their mutual desire. She wanted to feel the sharply passionate grate of his teeth against her tender flesh, to feel him being driven by his desire for her in the same way that Adam had been driven to eat the forbidden fruit handed to him by Eve. *She* wanted to be Alex's forbidden fruit, she recognised dazedly.

'Do it,' she commanded him tautly, dragging his hand down so that his fingers caught in the edge of her bra, revealing the soft shimmer of her naked skin and the beginnings of the wantonly dark areola of her nipple.

Her robe was fully open now, and hanging off her arms. In the mirror Beth could see her own near-naked body.

'Do it,' she repeated hypnotically, her eyes wide and dark as she stared up into Alex's.

'You don't know what…' he began, but Beth shook her head.

'Do it,' she told him a third time, holding his gaze as she let her own hand drop away from his.

She could feel his fingers trembling oh, so slightly as he splayed them across her breast, almost as though he wanted to cover her, protect her modesty, and then they tensed and curled and his thumb-tip rubbed across her tightly erect nipple, once, twice, a third time, each time lingering just a breath of time longer against the erect peak.

And then, agonisingly slowly, he very carefully peeled the fine fabric away from her breast completely.

Deep down in her throat Beth made a long, keening sound of female yearning.

In the mirror she could see the robe trailing on the floor behind her as Alex slowly released her and then very unsteadily took a step back from her.

Blindly Beth followed him.

Her body ached with need and heat, and yet the distance that Alex had put between them made her shiver with cold and loss. Instinctively she sought the warmth of his body against her, instinctively she tried to recapture it, moving closer to him, a small half-cry of protest locking her throat as her feet became caught up in the heavy folds of her robe.

As Alex reached out to help her she straightened her arms impatiently, thrusting at the cumbersome folds of the robe. Alex dropped to his knees in front of her, almost as though he intended to stop her or restrain her, but it was already too late. Already the robe had fallen back from her body.

Because her room wasn't overlooked Beth didn't fully close the drapes at night, and now the bright sunshine flooding through the gauzy nets revealed her body in all its exquisitely feminine detail. She could see herself in the mirror, and she could see Alex as well.

The hands he had put out to hold her dropped to her waist, shaping its narrow slenderness, his concentration on his exploration of her so intense that Beth scarcely dared to breathe in case she broke it.

His hands moved lower, cradling her hips. Alex leaned forward and very gently kissed her softly rounded belly, the caress of his lips the merest whisper of pleasure and promise but still more than enough to create a reaction that shuddered right through Beth's body.

Alex's head was moving upwards, his tongue-tip trailing hot darts of fire over her waist and then her ribcage. Alex's hands left her hips and his fingers encircled her towelling-clad wrists, then moved upwards to grip the sleeves of her robe as though he intended to pull it back onto her body. Instinctively Beth stiffened in rejection of what she thought he was going to do, resisting his rejection—of her. Alex lifted his head and looked into her eyes. Turbulently Beth looked back at him, a ragged breath tearing at her lungs.

She heard Alex groan, and then shockingly, excitingly, he was wrenching the robe completely free of her body and wrapping his arms possessively around her, his fingers trembling as he tugged at the fastening of her bra, his lips, his mouth, fastening eagerly over the crest of one of her breasts and tugging sensuously on it.

Beth felt faint with liquid, dizzyingly dazzling, wanton pleasure. Her hands reached out to clasp Alex's head and hold him against her body, her fingers sliding into the thick richness of his hair, tugging at it, kneading his scalp, small purring noises escaping from her throat as she moved as sensuously against him as a cat being stroked, every movement of her body against his sinuous and hypnotic.

Through half-closed eyes she saw their combined images in the mirror, images that once would have shocked and distressed her but which now merely added even greater fuel to the fire that burned through her. The sight of Alex's head against her breast, the creaminess of her skin against the darkness of his hair, the dark rigidity of her nipple demanding that it be given parity with its twin, the colour that burned Alex's face, the moist sheen she could see on her breast as he transferred his attentions from one nipple to the other—all of them combined to add to the intensity of the visual image of her own sensuality.

There was something so pagan about the whole image, about her virtual nakedness, only the sheer flimsiness of her very brief briefs a teasing barrier to Alex's hands and touch, her head thrown back in pure sensual enjoyment, her breasts full and passion-tipped, and Alex on his knees in front of her, at once both her supplicant and her master, her feminine power momentarily controlling his much stronger masculine strength. Her desire controlling his, controlling him.

She was the raw material of the beauty they could create together; he was the one who would mould it, shape it, the one who would mould and shape her. Her feelings, her thoughts, her emotions were so elemental, so intense, so powerful that Beth was held totally in thrall to them.

For the first time in her life she was tasting the full power of her womanhood, and she—Abruptly she tensed as she heard someone rattling her bedroom door warningly.

Immediately she froze, looking wildly for her robe,

but Alex was already on his feet, wrapping it round her, allowing her to flee to the sanctuary of her bathroom.

'Beth…it's all right, he's gone…you can come out now.'

Beth gnawed at her bottom lip.

In the five minutes or so it had taken the waiter to clear away their uneaten breakfast she had come back down to earth with a savage, spine-jarring, emotion-lurching and generally guilt-racked thud.

What on earth had she been doing—and why? All right, so sexually she was attracted to Alex, but that didn't mean that she had to act like a hormone-driven teenager, for heaven's sake. A hormone-driven teenager or a frustrated, sexually unsatisfied twenty-four-year-old woman.

Beth wasn't sure which image of herself she liked the least. Which image… Her face burned as she caught sight of herself in the bathroom mirror and her thoughts strayed betrayingly to those other images she had recently seen of herself.

'Beth,' Alex was repeating. 'It's okay, he's gone…'

She would have to go out sooner or later. She couldn't stay here all day, and anyway, why should she be the one to feel conscience-stricken and uncomfortable? she asked herself sturdily. After all, Alex had been just as carried away as she had herself, just as driven by desire and lust… But to be driven by lust was perfectly acceptable for a man, whereas…

These days it was just as acceptable for a woman, Beth told herself firmly. These days a woman no longer had to be fettered by the old shibboleths that had denied them their own sexuality and the right to express it. These days a woman did not have to convince herself that she loved a man just in order to enjoy her physical desire for his body and her own satisfaction. No, indeed… So why was she cowering here in the bathroom as though… as though she had done something to feel ashamed of? She *wasn't*…she *hadn't*…she told herself fiercely as she tugged open the bathroom door.

Determinedly she gave a businesslike glance at her watch as she told Alex crisply, with only just a hint of a tremor in her voice, 'I really think you ought to leave. I've got rather a lot I want to do today…'

Alex was frowning at her.

'I thought you said you were having a day off and that you wanted to do some sightseeing…'

Beth frowned in vexation.

'Yes. Yes, I did…I do… But…'

'It's raining now—the city should be relatively free of tourists. I suggest we start with a walk along the river. We could have lunch here in Prague, and then this afternoon…'

He stopped and gave her a look of heart-stopping intimacy. 'This afternoon we shall walk over the Charles Bridge…and then there's something special I want to show you…'

Beth opened her mouth to tell him that he was taking far too much for granted, that she didn't want his company, that she didn't want anything from him, but instead, and much to her own chagrin, she heard herself telling him, 'I…I need to get dressed. I…'

'You want me to leave.' Alex gave her a deliciously intimate smile. 'I know what you're saying,' he agreed huskily. 'If I stay here with you there's no way I'm going to be able… Tempted though I am, this is neither the time nor the place. Tempted though I am,' he repeated. He closed the distance between them and murmured against her lips, 'And believe me, Bethany, I am very, very tempted. Oh, yes, I am very tempted...'

Beth told herself that she was trying to resist him, and that the only reason she'd opened her mouth was to tell him to stop, but unfortunately he seemed to mistake her actions, and the next thing she knew he was kissing her with a renewal of the passion he had shown earlier. But this time he didn't take it any further. This time he released her and stepped back from her, gently pressing his fingers to his own mouth and then touching them lightly to hers before telling her huskily, 'I'll come back for you in half an hour.'

CHAPTER SEVEN

BETH FLICKED THE droplets of rain off her jacket and stared across the mist-shrouded vista in front of her. She and Alex were looking along the river, its bridges, so clearly depicted in so many tourist postcards, now barely discernible. The artists who normally thronged the streets selling their work to the tourists had already packed away their sketches, only an enterprising umbrella seller standing his ground.

'My, I never expected it to rain, not after how bright it was this morning!' Beth heard an American voice exclaim. She still had no real idea just why she had allowed Alex to persuade her to come with him. It had certainly not been her intention when she'd woken up this morning. A pink glow of self-consciousness coloured her face as her senses told her exactly why she might have changed her mind. Of course, her decision had nothing to do with that most unfortunate incident in her bedroom earlier this morning. Nothing whatsoever. That had been a mistake…a…a…

'Look,' Alex told her, taking hold of her arm and directing her attention to the hillside to their left. As he did so Alex drew Beth closer to him. It was just because the heavy drenching rain was making her feel damp and chilly that she felt this desire to nestle closer to him, Beth assured herself. That was all… It was simply a basic human need for warmth that was causing her to accept the warmth of his protective arm and the even greater warmth of his body.

They had lunch in a small traditional restaurant where the patron obviously knew Alex and welcomed him enthusiastically. But to Beth's consternation the man seemed to be under the misapprehension that Beth was Alex's girlfriend.

'There will be a big wedding here in Prague…yes?' he said jovially to Alex. 'We have many fine churches here,' he told Beth.

'Why did you let him think that?' Beth asked Alex later, when they had left the restaurant.

'Why did I let him think what?' Alex teased her, pretending not to understand.

Beth flashed him an indignant look.

'You know what I mean,' she accused him. '*Why* did you let him think that we are…?'

'What? A couple…lovers…? Is it so very far from the truth?' Alex asked her meaningfully.

'We hardly know one another,' Beth protested. Why was he doing this…pretending to genuinely care about her? She could understand him trying to flirt with her in order to secure her business, both for himself and for his family, but to try to pretend that there was more to what he was doing than mere flirtation…

'I want to go back to the hotel,' she told him curtly. 'There are things I have to do…'

'Not yet,' Alex denied, taking hold of her arm before she could stop him and drawing her in the direction of the river.

Up ahead of them Beth could see the ancient span of the Charles Bridge.

Awed by its antiquity, and her own awareness of all that it must have witnessed and withstood, Beth allowed him to guide her towards it. There was something about it, a stalwartness, a sombreness, that struck an unexpected chord within her.

'My grandfather once told me that always, in his darkest moments, he thought of this bridge and all that it and his people had endured,' Alex told her quietly.

His quiet, soft-voiced comment, so very much in tune with her own unspoken thoughts, shocked her a little. They weren't supposed to be so emotionally in accord; they shouldn't be able to pick up on each other's thoughts.

In an attempt to distance herself from what she was feeling, Beth said quickly, 'Tell me more about your grandfather.'

Alex was smiling at her. A smile that rocked her heart. Fiercely she reminded herself of all the reasons why she could not allow herself to respond to him.

Whilst Alex was talking to her about his grandfather the rain started to come down even more heavily.

'Quick, down here,' he broke off to instruct her, taking hold of her hand and hurrying her towards a small alcove set protectively into the last span of the bridge.

Without thinking, Beth automatically followed him. In the shelter it provided them with she could see Alex looking searchingly at her. Her heart started to beat far too fast.

'Beth, I know it's probably too soon to tell you this, but I think I'm falling in…' He stopped and looked down into her eyes. 'It's crazy, I know, but I've fallen in love with you,' he groaned.

'*No!*' Immediately Beth panicked. 'No, that's not possible,' she denied. 'I don't want to hear this, Alex…'

Inside she felt as though she was being torn apart. Did

he really think she was foolish enough, desperate enough, vulnerable enough to fall for his lies?

Beth was slightly more familiar with the city now, and she knew from the direction they were taking that they were walking back to the hotel. It was still raining—heavily—but even though she told herself that it would be a relief to be free of Alex there was still an uncomfortable heaviness around her heart.

The after-effects of her lunch and the distinctive and disturbing ache she was still suffering after this morning's interrupted lovemaking, Beth assured herself stoically. That was all. There was no emotional base to what she was feeling. How could there be? She felt nothing emotional for Alex at all... If she had wanted him... needed him...been *aroused* by him, then that had simply been a sexual wanting, a sexual needing, a sexual arousal. There had been nothing emotional about it. Nothing... Men didn't have the power to affect her emotionally any more. She didn't like them...didn't trust them... She was far better off on her own, using them in the way that they used her sex.

They had reached the hotel. Beth was just about to hurry towards the main entrance when Alex caught hold of her wrist.

'No, this way,' he instructed her, moving off in the direction of the car park and tugging her with him.

'Where are we going? Where are you taking me?' Beth asked as Alex unlocked the door of his hire car, refusing to release her until he had carefully tucked her into the passenger seat.

'Wait and see. It's a surprise,' he told her teasingly as he slid into the driver's seat next to her and started the engine.

A surprise.

Beth looked suspiciously at him.

'This isn't just a ploy to get me to visit your cousins' business, is it?' she accused him. 'Because if it is...'

She stopped as she saw that Alex was frowning at her.

'No, it isn't a ploy,' he denied. 'Although why...*what* is it that makes you so mistrustful of me, Beth? Is it this man, the one who hurt you?'

'He didn't hurt me,' Beth denied. 'I never loved him. I just... From the moment I arrived here you've done nothing but flatter me and flirt with me...'

'And that makes me someone you can't trust?' Alex asked her quietly.

Something about the way he was looking at her made Beth feel slightly ashamed.

'I don't want to talk about it, Alex. Where are we going? I don't...'

'Wait and see,' he repeated, and then added softly, 'Tell me about yourself, Beth.'

'There isn't anything to tell,' she protested shakily. 'I'm not someone who's either interesting or exciting.'

'You are to me,' Alex assured her with a soft emphasis that made the tiny hairs on her skin lift in sensual awareness.

Beth hadn't intended to do what he asked, but somehow or other she discovered that she was, albeit a little reluctantly at first.

'Your family sounds very much like my own,' Alex interrupted her at one point. 'My mother was always very conscious of the fact that she had no family of her own in England. The Czech people are very extended-family-conscious.'

They had left the city now, and were climbing through the hills—not that Beth could see much of them because of the heavy black clouds. The rain was causing rivulets of water to run down the surface of the road, carrying with them bits of debris. In the distance she could hear thunder which, although it didn't exactly terrify her, was not something she enjoyed.

'The weather is a lot more severe than was forecast,' Alex commented frowningly at one point, when he had had to drop the car down to a low gear to drive through a deep pool of water which had collected in the dip in the road.

'Perhaps we should turn back,' Beth suggested uneasily. She still had no idea where they were going, but they were well into the hills now, and the villages they were driving through were small, little more than clusters of houses, many of them unoccupied. Alex had explained to her that most people owned houses in the villages but because they worked in the city were only able to use them for weekends and holidays.

They were climbing higher now, through a grey, mist-enshrouded landscape that made Beth shiver a little involuntarily. Where on earth was Alex taking her?

'You're looking apprehensive. There's no need,' he reassured her, and then added wryly, 'You're safe with me, Beth, but has it occurred to you that you might not have been had you agreed to accompany your gypsy friends to wherever it was they claimed they were going to take you?'

Beth bit her lip and looked studiedly out of the car window. Alex seemed to think that she had given up her plans to go and visit the glass factory, but she hadn't... not that she intended to tell him that—or anything else about her intentions. Why should she?

'Not much further now,' he told her as he changed down a gear for the steep hill they were climbing.

Beth gasped, instinctively clinging onto her seat as they crested the mist-shrouded hill and then abruptly started to drop straight down, the road in front of them almost perpendicular, she was sure. At the bottom they had to ford what amounted to a racing stream of swirling water.

Alex grimaced when he saw her expression as she looked out of the car window.

'It's the rain,' he told her. 'This culvert makes a natural channel for it. In the old days there was actually a river here, but it was diverted.

'No questions,' he warned Beth as she started to open her mouth. 'Please close your eyes. We're almost there.'

Almost where...?

Beth was just about to object when a sudden ferocious clap of thunder made her close them instinctively. The intensity with which the rain was drumming down on the car roof suddenly seemed to treble as they started to climb again. Beth could see the jagged flashes of lightning behind her closed eyelids, but the ferocity of the storm which was raging around them made her feel too apprehensive to open her eyes.

'Where *are* we going?' Beth protested, unable to keep the betraying tremor out of her voice.

'It's a surprise,' she heard Alex repeating to her. 'Have you still got your eyes closed?'

Obediently Beth nodded, then gasped as the car rattled noisily over what sounded like a wooden bridge and started to climb a steep hillside, before levelling out, crunching over gravel and then coming to a halt.

'You can open them now,' she heard Alex saying softly in her ear, his voice sending delicious little shivers of sensation, like subtle harbingers of pleasure to come, along her sensitive nerve-endings.

Quickly Beth opened her eyes, and then widened them in stunned awe as she took in the splendour of her surroundings.

'Where on earth are we?' she whispered a little hesitantly. 'It looks like a castle...'

'That's exactly what it is,' Alex replied promptly.

Stunned, Beth stared at the creamy white walls in front of her, with their small slit windows and their dome-capped turrets. Too solidly built to be the fairy-tale castle of a little girl's fantasies, this one was built much more on the lines of an awesome stronghold. A curtain wall surrounded the courtyard they were in, and as Beth swivelled round she could see the steep incline they had climbed to reach the plateau area of the courtyard. In front of them a flight of stone steps curled away around the side of the building, and two huge arched wooden doors were ominously closed in front of them.

'What are we doing here? What...what is this place?' Beth asked.

'Want to take a closer look?' Alex invited her, opening his own car door.

Bemused, Beth nodded.

The air outside was colder than she had expected, and wetter. The rain she had heard beating down on the car roof during the drive had intensified in severity, striking her exposed face and legs so hard it almost hurt.

The mountainside the castle was built on was so high that it was actually above the mist. On a clear day the view must be awesome, Beth acknowledged. Right now she felt almost intimidated by the savagery of the lashing rain and the noise of the thunder rumbling in the distance.

'Quick...this way,' Alex told her, sheltering her in the curve of his arm as he hurried her towards the massive double doors. Once they reached them Beth saw that a small door was cut into them, which Alex unlocked with a key he produced from his jacket pocket.

Once through the door and out of the rain Beth saw that they were in a huge stone-flagged hall, with a fireplace along one wall that was almost the size of her sitting room at home. If anything the air inside the hall was even colder than outside it.

'I hadn't realised the weather was going to be quite so bad as this when I planned this trip,' Alex told her ruefully as he led the way to the back of the hall and into a narrow passage.

As she followed him up a dark flight of stone stairs Beth felt almost as though she had strayed into an *Alice in Wonderland* setting.

The stairs turned and twisted, illuminated by the light from heavy wrought-iron fittings, flickering hazardously as though threatening to go out at any second, and then suddenly they were stepping onto a large wood-floored landing area, with larger, more graceful windows and an intricate design set into the parquet of the floor.

'This is the more modern part of the castle. It was built on in 1760 by I forget which ancestor. My aunt gets quite severely cross with me for not being able to remember all the details of our family history. I suspect she thinks I don't pay attention when she's relating it to me.'

'Your aunt...your family owns *this*?' Beth gasped. He had already told her about the family's castle, of course, but she had not expected anything so grand!

'It's not so unusual—not here,' Alex told her easily. 'There are families who, after the repatriation of property following on from the Velvet Revolution, now own a handful of such places. Fortunately for us we only ever owned this one. I say fortunately because the cost of maintaining such homes can be prohibitive, as you can imagine.

'In my family's case we were fortunate in that much of the original furniture had been left *in situ*, and the castle had been lived in by a government official—or rather a succession of them—rather than simply left empty. Some of the more valuable pieces have gone, of course, and the paintings—family portraits in the main.

'As with many others of its type, the renovations to the original castle were done at the height of the influence of the Hapsburgs; there is a very strong Viennese influence in the decor of the state apartments. Let me show you.'

Still trying to take in the fact that this place, this castle, belonged to Alex's family, Beth followed him in bemusement as he led the way through a succession of rooms that made Beth feel as though she had stepped back in time. Although she was familiar with the style and decor of many of the great houses at home, the intricately lavish rococo plasterwork which decorated the walls and ceilings of the rooms she walked through made her gasp a little in wonderment.

In one room, a salon of elegant proportions, she couldn't help staring in delight at the soft watery green of the paintwork. Mirrors alternating with pastoral scenes decorated the walls, and hanging from the centre of the ceiling was the most magnificent chandelier she had ever seen.

'Ah, yes, that was how the family originally came to own the castle in the first place,' Alex told her ruefully. 'They made chandeliers for the Hapsburg court.'

'Does your family actually live here?' Beth asked him in an awed whisper.

'When they *are* here, yes. Although the state rooms are only used on formal occasions. The whole family comes and goes pretty much at will, although during the working week my cousins and my aunt stay in Prague, where they own a large apartment. This is the drawing room the family uses,' Alex informed her, taking her through into another elegantly proportioned room which, whilst still magnificent, was less heavily decorated than the rooms she had just seen—and more comfortably furnished.

'Are any members of your family here now?' Beth asked him curiously.

Alex shook his head, frowning as he saw the way she shivered and then going over to the fire which was made up in the grate. Kneeling down to remove a box of matches from a pretty covered box, he lit the fire.

'No. My aunt would have been here, but there was a burglary at the factory recently. Some antique glass was stolen—my aunt is very distressed. She blames herself. My cousins, her sons, have been urging her for some time to have a more up-to-date burglar and security system fitted at the factory as the collection of antique glassware they have there is quite unique. They have samples of the kind of glass they make going back right to the late 1600s—but my aunt, who is very much a traditionalist and a matriarch of the old school, wanted to wait until their current night-watchman, who is approaching retirement, had actually left.

'She told my cousins that it would offend Peter's pride if they were to install a security system whilst he was still there, and she didn't want to hurt him by doing so. Now she says that because of her stubbornness not only has a priceless collection of glass been stolen, but, even worse, Peter is in hospital with concussion, having been hit on the head by the gang who broke in.'

'Oh, no!' Beth couldn't help exclaiming in distress

as she listened to him. 'Will he...the night-watchman...
be all right?'

'We hope so. But until she knows that he has recovered my aunt refuses to leave the city.'

'Does she know you've brought me here...to her
home? Will she mind?'

Alex shook his head.

'It was her suggestion that I do so. She is immensely
proud of our family tradition and of this place.'

'Yes, I'm sure she is,' Beth agreed.

The heat from the fire was beginning to warm her
chilled body, but she still winced as lightning tore a jagged line right through the thick greyness of the mist outside. There was a loud clap of thunder and then almost
immediately another flash of lightning.

'Don't worry, we're safe in here,' Alex comforted her,
adding more prosaically, 'Are you hungry?'

Beth discovered a little to her own surprise that she
was, and nodded.

'You stay here, then,' Alex instructed her. 'I shan't
be long.'

He was gone about fifteen minutes, long enough for
Beth to be curious enough to wander around the room
studying the family photographs decorating the highly
polished surfaces of the heavy wooden furniture.

In one of them an unexpectedly familiar face stared
back at her. Picking it up, she studied it.

She was still holding it a few seconds later when Alex
returned, carrying what looked like a large picnic hamper.

'Is this your aunt?' she asked him, holding the photograph she had been studying out to him.

'Yes. It is,' he confirmed, smiling at her. 'How did
you guess?'

Beth said nothing. She wasn't going to tell him that she had known because she'd recognised the woman as the same one she had seen him with in the hotel in Prague, and then at the opera, and she certainly wasn't going to tell him just what assumptions she had made about the two of them. It had never occurred to her that the elegant and obviously expensively dressed woman might be a member of Alex's family, and not a rich tourist for whom he was working.

'Food,' Alex informed her as he put the hamper down. 'I'll just—' He broke off as the thunder crashed again and all the lights suddenly went out.

Cursing, Alex told her ruefully, 'I should have guessed this might happen. Fortunately my aunt always keeps a supply of candles to hand in every room. The electricity supply here is notorious for its unreliability, and these storms don't exactly help.' As he spoke he was pulling open the drawers in a pretty sofa table and setting candles in a couple of heavy silver candelabra on the mantelpiece above the fire.

'We'll have to picnic in here, I'm afraid,' he told Beth as he placed one on the table behind the sofa. Outside it had suddenly gone very dark, the wind driving the rain so hard at the windows that Beth could hear the fierce sound it made.

'Perhaps we ought to make our way back to Prague,' she suggested nervously, remembering how hazardous their journey to the castle had been.

But Alex seemed to misunderstand the cause of her apprehension, coming to stand close to her as he asked her softly, 'What is it you're afraid of, Beth? Not me?'

'No, of course not,' she denied, and then, for some reason she couldn't understand herself, she discovered that she couldn't quite bring herself to look at him, and the feeling that was curling up right through her body had far more to do with a dangerous sense of forbidden excitement than with any kind of fear.

There was something undeniably erotic about being here alone with him in this timeless place, and the lack of the modern amenity of electric light, the softness of the fire and candlelight, only served to highlight the sensation that filled her that she might have been transported back in time, to a time when for a young woman to be alone with a young man had been a very, very dangerous thing indeed.

'No, not you,' she said a little breathlessly.

'Then this, perhaps,' Alex suggested, closing the distance between them and taking her in his arms and kissing her, gently at first, almost reverently, and then far more passionately as she swayed closer to him and her heartbeat picked up and echoed the fierce rhythm of the driving rain and her own equally stormy driving inner yearning.

'We should go back,' she protested shakily when Alex released her mouth.

'We can't, it's too late,' he told her, and Beth knew that he wasn't really talking about their actual journey from the castle. 'We *can't* go back, Beth,' he reiterated as he touched her mouth with his fingertips and then traced its trembling shape with his finger. 'Not now…'

'I thought we were going to eat,' Beth reminded him. Her lips felt dry, clumsy, reluctant to form the words, reluctant to do *anything* that would increase the sensual pressure of Alex's fingertips against her lower lip but equally reluctant to deny herself the pleasure of it.

'You're…hungry…?'

The smouldering look which accompanied his comment, the way his gaze dropped from her face to her body, made Beth's heart race.

'I... I...'

'You're right. We *should* eat,' Alex agreed tenderly, reluctantly releasing her. 'Come and sit down by the fire.'

He pulled a chair up for her and Beth allowed him to guide her into it. She wasn't used to being treated so protectively, to being so *cherished*. One part of her loved it, another feared and suspected it. She didn't dare allow herself to fall into the trap of believing that any of this was real, that Alex's treatment of her, his tenderness towards her were genuine. They weren't. She mustn't allow herself to forget that he was simply using her, and that all she felt for him was, quite simply, a healthy physical female desire. She must *not* allow her thoughts or emotions to become clouded by the romanticism of the situation.

Alex picked up the hamper and carried it over to put it down on the floor between them.

'Come and sit down here,' he told her, dragging a couple of soft cushions off the sofa and piling them up against one of the chairs. 'It will be warmer. The chair will protect your back from the draught...'

Obediently Beth did as he suggested. There was something dangerously sybaritic about being here like this with him. The heat from the fire was slowly relaxing her tense muscles whilst the candlelight spread soft, sensuous shadows across the darkening room. Outside the light was already fading, the afternoon giving way to early evening as the storm clouds continued to darken the sky.

'Where did you get this?' Beth asked Alex as he opened the hamper.

'The hotel,' he informed her promptly. 'It's all cold, I'm afraid...'

Beth could have told him that for some reason she was

no longer really all that interested in food, but a self-protective instinct made her refrain from doing so. If she did Alex might be tempted to ask just what more compelling appetite had taken its place, and she was very much afraid that she might be tempted to tell him.

'Chicken?' Alex asked her, holding out a tender portion towards her.

Uncertainly Beth looked at it.

'It's good,' Alex encouraged her, taking a bite out of it and then offering it to her, commanding her softly, 'Bite.'

Unable to drag her gaze away from his, Beth did as he instructed, nibbling delicately on the chicken and then tensing as Alex reached out his free hand to push a stray lock of her hair off her face, his fingers just brushing against her mouth as he did so.

There was something almost shockingly sensual about what they were doing, about being fed by him like this, about knowing his fingers were so close to her mouth as he held the chicken and she bit into it, and the temptation to eat the meat with a deliberately erotic female show of the hunger she felt for him was something that Beth had to fight to control.

'Enjoy it,' Alex said softly to her, as though he knew what she was thinking—and feeling. 'An appetite for food is like an appetite for love…meant to be savoured and enjoyed—indulged! That's how I want to make love with you,' he told her rawly. 'Slowly and thoroughly, with every touch, every caress a feast of pleasure and indulgence.'

She was, Beth suddenly discovered, trembling so hard that Alex must be able to see and feel it.

Had Alex brought her here on purpose, to make love to her, to seduce her? If he had…*if* he had, he couldn't have chosen a more romantic setting, Beth acknowledged as Alex threw what was left of the piece of chicken on the fire. Whilst it sizzled in the heat he removed a bottle of wine from the hamper and uncorked it, pouring it into two glasses.

'To us,' he told Beth, handing her one of them and raising his own in a toast.

It was red and full-bodied, and it hit Beth's empty stomach in a warm rich wave that heated her blood, raising her temperature and lowering her resistance.

Having taken another gulp of it, she put down her glass and automatically ran her tongue-tip over her lips. In the firelight she saw Alex's eyes darken fiercely. He held out his own glass to her and told her softly, 'Drink.'

As she bent her head and took a sip he watched her, and then very deliberately and very slowly he turned the glass round, so that the place where she had drunk was facing him, and then equally deliberately he raised the glass to his own mouth, drinking from exactly the same spot she had drunk from. It was a simple enough gesture, and also a very explicit one. Beth could feel her heat, the response, the awareness, surge through her body in a jagged sensation as fierce and primitive as the lightning outside.

'It's *you* I'm thirsting for…hungry for…' Alex told her rawly.

He put down his glass and reached for her, cupping her face as he had done earlier in the day and covering her mouth with his own, his thumb probing the softness of her lower lip, his tongue sliding into the access he had made for it and entwining softly with hers.

And the heat engulfing Beth had nothing whatsoever to do with the fire, nor the sweet film moistening her skin anything to do with the rain hammering down outside.

She *did* try to be strong, to cling to sanity and reason,

reminding herself mentally that it was just desire, just sex, a physical appetite—that was all it was, all *he* was. But beneath her fingertips she could feel the heavy thudding of Alex's heart, and Alex himself was urging her to free his body from the restrictive captivity of his clothes, guiding her to buttons and fastenings which, with his help, seemed to come free with almost miraculous speed.

In the firelight his body possessed a magnificence that seemed to echo the feudal ancestry of the castle. He might have been some powerful lord and she a helpless victim of his fiery passion for her, of their *mutually* fiery passion for one another, Beth amended dizzily as she recognised how eager she was for Alex to return the favour she had done him and help her to become free of her own clothes.

Unlike her, though, Alex seemed to need no extra assistance. Beth shivered on the spasm of sharp expectation that gripped her when Alex's hands cupped her naked breasts, her nipples surging excitedly against his palms.

Hot, drenching shudders of excitement raced through her body. Alex was the furnace to which the raw molten material of her desire was drawn.

Slowly Alex removed her clothes, his gaze drinking in the sight of her naked, firelight-washed body. Beth felt as wanton and wild as though she were some long-ago earthy and elemental woman, sure and knowing in her awareness of her own sexuality and desirability.

The pride, the pleasure she felt in her own body as Alex sensuously absorbed the sight, the touch, the scent of her, watching her, stroking his hands over her skin as he shaped her, breathing in what he told her was the unforgettably precious sweet Beth-scent of her, totally banished any self-consciousness or doubt she might have felt.

Here, in the shadowed darkness of this fortress castle

which had, over the centuries, seen all the worst and all the best of every human passion, it seemed to Beth everything she felt about herself and about Alex was reduced to its purest and most basic components.

She was a woman; he was a man. She wanted him, ached for him, needed him, and she could see the corresponding intensity of his need for her both in his body and in his eyes.

He might have been her lover returning to her from the heat of battle, their coming together a fierce celebration of the fact that he was still alive; she might have been the virgin bride of the lord of this domain, giving herself to him in a solemn rite of passage.

Before them, in this place, there must have been so many, many earlier lovers, and Beth could almost feel the echoes of their loving echoing the heavy thud of her own heart.

'Have you any idea how much I've wanted to do this?' Alex groaned as he took hold of her hand, placing it palm to palm against his own, lacing his fingers with hers and then lifting their clasped hands to his mouth whilst he kissed her ring finger.

Against her will Beth felt her own emotional reaction to what he was doing. This was the embodiment of her most private romantic dreams. *This* was how she had always imagined that a lover, her *chosen* lover, would cherish and desire her. A lover who would be both humble and held in thrall to the intensity of his desire for her and yet, too, the master of it, and of her.

'I fell in love with you the first time I saw you,' Alex was telling her huskily.

Love at first sight.

Beth's heart gave a dizzying lurch. It must be the wine

that was making her so dangerously tempted to believe him, that was making her *want* to believe him.

'We hardly know one another,' she protested in a whisper.

'I know I want you,' Alex returned. 'I know I love you. I know that your body quivers with pleasure when I touch it so.'

His fingertips trailed liquid fire down her breastbone and over her belly before curling and tugging erotically, gently, on the soft tangle of curls below. As he released them Beth exhaled a long, shaky sigh that ended in a sharp gasp as his fingertip moved lower, finding the delicate cleft of the soft flesh that protected her intimacy. Like the petals of a flower opening to the sure touch of a nectar-seeking bee her body started to respond to his touch.

'And I certainly know what you're doing to me.' Alex's voice groaned thickly in her ear. 'Feel it, Beth,' he begged her. 'Feel me!'

A little hesitantly at first, but then with growing confidence, Beth spread her hands across his chest, closing her eyes in sensual pleasure as she absorbed the silken heat of his skin. Almost of their own volition her hands moved downwards, beyond the taut arch of Alex's ribcage and over the male flatness of his belly, so masculinely different from hers with its soft curves and sweetly feminine flesh. Very gently, as though just to reassure herself that she hadn't imagined it, Beth moved her hands upwards again, resting her fingertips on the solid rectangle of muscle that formed the male shape of Alex's tough, firm stomach. He wasn't overly muscular, a gym freak whose muscular development was too exaggerated to be truly desirable; he was just right, Beth acknowledged inwardly—perfect...

She hadn't realised she had said the soft, satisfied words of praise out loud until she heard Alex growl and tell her, 'You know traditionally what happens when you praise someone like that, don't you…?'

'Mmm…it makes their head swell,' Beth murmured back absently, and then realised, from what Alex was doing with her hand as he took it and placed it very deliberately and very intimately on his own body, just exactly what he'd meant.

'Mmm…and mine is getting very swollen,' he told her emphatically, although he scarcely needed to make any verbal emphasis of what was now patently obvious to her.

Beneath her fingertips the reality of his body, his maleness, his arousal, made her own flesh quiver excitedly. She wanted him…so much…wanted him…needed him…had to have him…

'Soon…soon…' Alex whispered to her, as though he recognised just what she was feeling.

He kissed her mouth, and then her breasts, gently releasing himself from her hands as he eased her down on the cushions beside the fire. Arching over her naked body in the firelight, he seemed to Beth to be the embodiment of male sexuality, of man himself. He kissed her belly and her muscles quivered, her body quickening as his hands swept downwards, parting her thighs.

Beth had a small mole high up on the inside of one thigh. She saw Alex looking at it, her body tensing as he bent his head and slowly kissed it. Deep inside, the secret female heart of her turned liquid with longing. Very gently Alex reached out to the soft flesh that protected her sex. Beth felt the breath leak painfully from her lungs. Carefully at first, and then more strongly, Alex began to touch her. Excitement exploded through Beth's body as it began to respond rhythmically to Alex's erotic caresses. When his lips and then his tongue started to follow the same path as his fingers Beth moaned a femininely protective protest, but her body's hunger was far, far stronger than any social conditioning or preconceived ideas of female modesty. Nature had already preordained, preprogrammed her body's reaction to what Alex was doing to it.

Beth gasped under the weight of the feelings gathering and coalescing inside her. It was like the climb up towards the highest, most savagely exciting, most dangerous ride she had ever gone on in her whole life. Inexorably she was being pushed towards the top, the summit, her mind and her body tight in panic at the thought of the terrifying freefall into eternity that would come once that summit was crested, even whilst she knew there was nothing she could do to stop it, nothing she *should* do to stop it, urged on as she was by something stronger by far than any mere act of mental will on her part.

Somewhere, someone was moaning: a frantic, keening sound of need that was almost primitive in its intensity. But Beth didn't realise that she was listening to herself until she heard Alex talking to her, soothing her, promising her in between the hot kisses he was pressing all over her naked body that soon he would satisfy her, soon he would fill her, soon he would give them both what they so desperately yearned for.

As he reached her breasts she could feel his hardness pressing down against her body. Her hips writhed hungrily against him, her whole body quickening as he sucked and then bit softly at her nipples. Beth cried out, but not in pain—unless her longing for him could be classed as such. Her whole body trembled, her hips lifting, her legs wrapping possessively around him as Alex stroked her body into eager acceptance of his.

He felt so good, so strong…so right, with her muscles clinging lovingly to him, drawing him deeper and deeper into the soft, welcoming heat of her body.

She heard him groan and cry out a protest that he couldn't wait any longer, that she was too sweet, too hot, too responsive for him to hold back, and then his carefully slow thrusts became an urgent fast-paced rhythm that took him deeper and deeper inside her, carrying them both to the edge of the vortex and then spectacularly carrying Beth right over and beyond it, to a place where the whole world, the whole universe dissolved in a physical and emotional display of pyrotechnics that she felt could have rivalled the birth of the world itself.

Now Beth felt she knew what drove and inspired the world's greatest artists; now she discovered, quite simply, she just *knew*.

Alex was holding her in his arms, his heart thudding wildly against hers; her breath was just beginning to slow down, and she wept a little with emotion as his body slid smoothly from her and he held her tightly and kissed her.

'Now do you understand just why I love you so much?' he demanded thickly as he kissed her again, more slowly and lingeringly.

'This really is the most wonderful fairy-tale place,' Beth told Alex dreamily. 'It has such a…a special atmosphere…'

'Mmm…it certainly has,' Alex agreed, with such a meaningful look at her that Beth could feel her face starting to burn a little.

'The antiques alone…' She started to babble a little self-consciously, all too well aware that Alex's prime focus of interest right now was not the castle or its wonderful furniture, but her…

'Well, if it's antiques you like I shall have to take you

to see my aunt's apartment in Prague. It's the family's main home and I'd like to take you there, Beth, introduce you to my family. And besides, there's something—'

He stopped. Something in his voice made Beth look a little uncertainly at him, some sense of foreboding, of a shadow about to be cast over her blissful haze of happiness.

'My aunt has some of the most wonderful examples of antique crystal in the apartment, and I'm sure she'd be only too pleased to arrange for you to visit the factory and—'

'No!'

Beth froze, suddenly wary, suspicion and anger replacing the sensual languor that had had her relaxing into Alex's arms. Now she pulled away from him, all her doubts about him surging back. Julian, too, had used her vulnerability after the kisses they had shared to his own advantage, but Julian had at least stopped at mere kisses. Alex...

'No?'

Alex, too, had withdrawn slightly, and was now frowning. 'But the glass you said you liked in the gift shop is—'

'Impossibly expensive,' Beth snapped sharply at him. 'And besides, I've sourced my own supply at my own price and—'

'You mean the gypsies?' Alex challenged her, his voice now just as sharply critical as her own had been. 'I thought we'd agreed that you weren't going to pursue that...'

Beth tightened her lips in silence and looked away from him, busying herself re-dressing.

'Beth,' Alex said warningly.

'No,' she told him shortly. '*I* agreed nothing. *You* said...'

'So you still intend...' He drew in a swift breath. 'Beth, it's far too dangerous...far too...' He shook his head. 'Believe me, they're leading you on, deceiving you. This factory they've told you about, this mythical source of wonderful glass, is just that. It has to be.

'Look,' he told her softly, leaning towards her and taking hold of her wrists, shaking them gently as though to underline his point, 'there are only a handful of factories that make such glass. I know because my cousins own one of them. It demands a special technique, a special skill...it's...'

'Please let me go,' Beth demanded with stiff formality, her eyes burning with anger and pride as he reluctantly did so. Very deliberately she rubbed her wrists where he had held them, even though in reality they did not actually hurt.

She could see, though, from the dark surge of colour that burned his skin, that he was aware of what she was silently implying, and that she had touched a small raw nerve.

Good! He deserved it.

'I know exactly what you're trying to do, Alex,' she told him crisply. 'I've been there before, you see. Been lied to and deceived by a man who simply wanted to use me for his own ends. I'm not so much of a fool, you know. This is what all this...' she waved her hand around the room and tossed her head scornfully in his direction '...has been all about. You deliberately targeted me, flirted with me...came on to me for the benefit you thought it would bring to your cousins' business, the order you thought you could get. No doubt I'm not your first victim and I doubt that I shall be your last. But where I differ from the others is that *I* saw through you right from the start. You thought you were deceiving me, using me, but in reality I was the one using you.'

'What?'

Beth stood up determinedly as she finished speaking and quickly fastened the rest of her clothes. As he stared at her Alex, too, scrambled to his feet but, oddly, his nudity, instead of rendering him foolish as it might have done another man, only served to remind Beth of exactly how she had felt in his arms, of exactly how he had felt inside her body. Angrily she tried to deny her own inner reaction, to deny what she was feeling emotionally.

'Beth, you couldn't be more wrong,' Alex told her vehemently, 'and I can't understand why you should think...' He gave a short, unamused laugh. 'Believe me, the last thing I would ever do is pimp for business for my cousins. They hardly need it; they have virtually full order books for years to come, if you wish to know...'

Beth smiled loftily and disbelievingly at him.

'That's easy to say now,' she told him cynically. 'You don't fool me, Alex. I've been caught that way before.'

'Beth, you're wrong,' Alex protested stubbornly. 'I love you.' His voice softened and then roughened slightly. 'And I believe that you love me...from the way you loved me just now... If that wasn't love, then just exactly what was it?' He reached out and touched a fingertip to her swollen lips.

'That wasn't love, it was just lust—just sex, that's all,' Beth interrupted him scornfully.

'Just sex?'

'Just sex,' Beth confirmed firmly. Why was the look in his eyes making something hurt so much deep inside her chest? He didn't really care about her. She'd be a fool if she started believing that he did. He was another Julian, just out for what he could get.

'I know exactly what's going on, Alex,' she told him coolly. 'Your cousins pay you to put as much new business their way as you can.' She gave a small shrug. 'I can't blame you for trying to push me into buying from them, I suppose, but what I *can* do is make it plain to you that it's a ploy I'm simply not going to fall for. I may have been a gullible little fool in the past, but I'm not any more.'

'I understand,' Alex told her gently. 'Another man has hurt you badly. I'd like to kill him for it, but more than that I'd like to take the pain away for you, Beth. I'd like to love you whole and happy again. Do you still love him?'

'Julian Cox?' Beth looked scathing. 'No, the man I *thought* I loved, the man I thought loved me, never really existed. Julian was like you. He just wanted what he could get out of me financially. Fortunately for me, though, unlike you, he wasn't prepared to use sex to get it.'

'You weren't lovers?' Alex asked her swiftly.

'You and I aren't *lovers*,' Beth couldn't resist telling him. 'We just had sex. And, no, Julian and I didn't have sex. I suppose part of the reason I wanted you was because I was just quite simply sexually frustrated,' she told Alex carelessly, with a small dismissive shrug, before adding musingly, 'Perhaps I should give your cousins a small order after all. You were very…thorough…'

Beth knew that she was behaving outrageously, but something was driving her on, forcing her to do so. Some protective, deep-rooted instinct for self-preservation was warning her that she must use every means she could to keep Alex at bay emotionally, to make sure that there was an unbridgeable distance between them.

'My God, if I thought you actually meant that—' Alex swore savagely.

'I do mean it,' Beth fibbed, tilting her head defiantly.

'So you *don't* love me?' Alex demanded quietly.

'No. No, I don't love you,' Beth agreed in a slightly tremulous voice.

There was a long, deathly silence and then Alex said bleakly, 'I see...'

He started to get dressed, and without looking at her he continued, 'In that case I'd better drive you back to Prague.'

'Yes, I think that would be a good idea,' Beth agreed.

CHAPTER EIGHT

'WHAT ARE YOU looking at?'

Alex didn't move as his mother raised herself up on her tiptoes and looked over his shoulder at the photograph he was studying. Her face became sad and shadowed as she recognised it.

'You still feel the same way about her.'

It was a statement, not a question, and Alex simply nodded as he replaced the photograph he had taken of Beth in Prague back in his wallet.

'Oh, Alex, I'm so sorry,' his mother sympathised.

'Not half so sorry as I am,' Alex told her dryly.

Alex's mother had heard the full story about her son's meeting with Beth in Prague and the events that had followed it from Alex himself, after he had returned home to England to take up a new appointment as the Chair of Modern History at a local university. It was a prestigious appointment, and one she felt her cherished only child entirely merited, but it had soon become plain to her that Alex was far from happy. When questioned he had grimly explained to her that he had fallen in love with a girl who had not returned his feelings, a statement which had aroused all his mother's protective maternal instincts. How could *any* woman not love her *wonderful* son?

In any other circumstances Alex would have been

amused by her reaction. His mother was neither possessive nor clinging, quite the opposite, and she had taught him to value his independence as she and his father valued theirs. Loving someone meant allowing them the right to choose their own way of life, she had always told him. One thing Alex had not told her, though, was that he and Beth had been lovers—or rather, as Beth had so clinically put it, had had sex. That was something that was far too private to be discussed with anyone. The truth was that Beth might only have had sex with him, but he had quite definitely made love with her. Made love, and put love, his heart and soul, his whole self, into every kiss, every touch, every caress he had given her.

Even now he could hardly believe the accusations she had made against him. The day after he had left her at the hotel following their return from the castle he had gone to see her, only to discover that she had checked out of the hotel without leaving a forwarding address.

It had been some time before he had been able to return home, and he had lost count of the number of occasions he had been tempted to get in his car and drive to Rye-on-Averton to see her, to demand an explanation…to beg for a second chance. But on each occasion his pride and his self-respect had stopped him. If she didn't love him then he had no right to try and compel her to accept him. But how could she have responded to him the way she had if she did not love him?

'Lucy Withers' daughter is back from Greece. She really is the most pretty girl. I saw her the other night when I called round to see Lucy. Do you remember the way she used to follow you around?'

Alex shook his head.

'Nice try, Ma, but I'm afraid it isn't going to work.

You can't stop a haemorrhaging artery with a sticking plaster,' he told her grimly.

'Why don't you go and see Beth...talk to her...?' his mother urged him softly.

Alex shook his head.

'There wouldn't be any point.'

He couldn't tell her that to do so would, in his eyes at least, be tantamount to forcing himself on Beth, and besides, he didn't think he could face the look in her eyes when she told him she didn't want him. He still woke up in the night, his body tensing in denial as he relived the first time. To go from the heights he had believed they had both reached to the depths of despair he had felt when she had told him that she didn't love him had been too much to endure at one gulp.

'Well, you know best,' his mother told him, and then added, 'Oh, I nearly forgot to tell you—your aunt telephoned. The authorities have released the stolen glassware back to them at long last. You know they were told that it had been recovered but the police wouldn't tell them anything else?'

Alex nodded.

'Well, it turns out that it had been stolen on the orders of a gang of criminals who were using it as bait to draw in unwary foreign buyers. They promised them glass of a similar quality as a means of getting their hands on foreign currency, but in reality fulfilled the orders they took with the very poorest quality, cheap stuff. The whole thing only came to light when customers started complaining to their own embassies about the orders they had received— 'Alex! *Alex!* Where on earth are you going?' his mother demanded as Alex suddenly started to stride towards the door.

'Alex,' she protested, but her son wasn't listening.

His mind working overtime, Alex hurried out to his car. As he swung his powerful BMW into the main stream of traffic his thoughts were busy.

Supposing Beth *had* been caught in this scam his mother had just described to him?

He didn't live very far away from his parents—less than fifteen minutes' drive. He soon pulled into the driveway to the large Edwardian mansion where he owned a handsome ground-floor apartment.

'Alex, it's beautiful!' his mother had exclaimed the first time he had shown it to her. 'But it's far too large for a single man.' She had looked hopefully at him, but he had shaken his head.

'I like my home comforts and my own space,' he had told her, but what he had *not* told her was that when he had been viewing the apartment what had clinched the quick sale for him had been the resemblance of the drawing room to the salon at the castle where he and Beth had made love.

There had been many times since he had bought it when he had looked into the flickering flames of the fire and wondered if he was crazy to torment himself the way he was doing…many, many times when he had had his hand on the receiver to dial the number of a builder to come and take the fireplace out. And then he had looked into the flames and remembered the way he had seen the firelight flickering shadows on Beth's body what seemed now like a lifetime ago, and he just hadn't been able to make the call.

There was no need for him to pack anything—Rye-on-Averton wasn't that far away.

Half an hour later, as he swung his big car out onto the motorway slip road, it was as though he had already driven the route before, and in his thoughts he already had.

This wasn't mere indulgence of his own needs and feelings, he assured himself as the powerful car ate up the miles. This was a duty, an almost sacred charge. An act of responsibility, an act of faith…an act of love.

White-faced, Beth replaced her telephone receiver. She had spent most of the morning on the telephone, and the call she had just received from the Board of Trade had confirmed what she had already begun to fear. The factory…her factory…simply did not exist. She had been conned…cheated…

Beth sat down on the floor of the storeroom and covered her face with her hands. What on earth was she going to do? It was bad enough that she had wasted all this time reliving what had happened in Prague with Alex, reminding herself of…of things she just did not want to remember: the silent drive back to Prague, her decision the moment she reached the hotel to find somewhere else to stay, just in case Alex refused to accept what she had told him and just in case she weakened… just in case her emotions weren't as uninvolved as she had claimed…

Then there had been her visit to the factory with the gypsy: the peculiar silence of the factory itself, the ramshackle untidiness of it, the overgrown car park, and then the oddly sumptuous office, with its dirty faded wallpaper and its completely contrasting heavily locked cabinets filled with that beautiful glass.

Beth winced as she remembered how nearly she had backed out of giving them an order when she had been told just how much glass she would have to take.

'That's far too much,' she had protested. 'I can't afford to buy so much.'

In the end they had agreed that she could divide the

order into the four different colours of glass, but she had still needed to go back to her new hotel and ring home, to persuade her bank manager to increase her overdraft facility.

'I can't increase it to that level,' he had protested. 'The business doesn't merit it. You don't have the security.'

Beth had thought frantically.

'I have some security,' she had told him, and it was true; she'd had the shares her grandfather had given her for her twenty-first birthday and an insurance policy that was supposed to be the basis for her pension. In the end her bank manager had agreed to lend her the money, secured by these assets.

She had returned home from Prague, jubilant at having succeeded in securing the order—and on her own terms. But her jubilation had been short-lived—rootless, really—and underneath it there had been a vast subterranean cavern of pain and loss which she had fought valiantly but hopelessly to deny.

'It was just lust—just sex, that's all,' she had told Alex, but she had lied... Oh, how she had lied...to herself as well as to him. The tears on her face when she woke from her longing dreams of him and for him told her that much.

'I love you,' he had told her, but she knew he hadn't meant it.

'I don't love you,' she had said, and she certainly hadn't meant that.

How was it possible for her to have fallen in love with him after all she had done to try to protect herself, all she had told herself...warned herself...? Beth had no idea, and in the weeks following her return she had been too exhausted by the pain of keeping her feelings at bay, too driven by the fear of what was happening to her, to look too deeply into the whys and wherefores of what had hap-

pened. It was enough, more than enough, just to know
that it had. To know it and to bitterly, bitterly wish that
she did not.

The only thing that had kept her going had been the
thought of her glass, her precious, wonderful glass, and
now, like the love Alex had claimed he felt for her, that
too had revealed itself to be false and worthless.

Her telephone rang and she tensed. Twice since her
return home she had received calls from Prague. On one
occasion it had been the hotel, telephoning about a scarf
she had left behind, and the second time it had been an
anonymous caller who had rung off when she'd answered
the phone.

'Alex, Alex,' she had cried out frantically, but she had
been simply crying into silence.

'Beth, it's Dee...' her landlady announced at the other
end of the line. 'Is it unpacked yet? Can I come round?'

Immediately Beth panicked.

'No. No...'

'Is something wrong?'

Beth bit her lip. Dee was too quick, too intelligent to
be fobbed off with a lie.

'Well, actually, yes...there is,' she admitted. 'The
order isn't—'

'They've sent you the wrong order?' Dee interrupted
before Beth could finish. 'You must get in touch with
them immediately, Beth, and insist that they ship the
correct one, at their own expense and express. Tell them
that if they don't you'll be submitting a claim to them for
loss of business. Did you stipulate on your contract that
the order had to be delivered in time for your Christmas
market? I know they've already delayed delivery several times.'

'I...I have to go, Dee,' Beth fibbed. 'There's another call coming through.'

What on earth was she going to do? How was she going to explain to Kelly, her partner, that because of her...her stupidity...they were probably going to have to close the shop? How could they keep it open when they didn't have anything to sell? How could they continue to pay their overheads when they had no money? She had already received one letter from the bank, reminding her that they were expecting her overdraft to be repaid just as soon as Christmas was over.

There was no way she was going to be able to do that now. She knew, of course, that Brough, Kelly's husband, was an extremely wealthy man, and no doubt he would be prepared to help them out, but her pride wouldn't allow her to be a party to that. And besides, Brough was essentially a businessman, and Beth was under no illusions about what he was likely to think of her business capabilities once he knew what had happened.

Was she *never* going to get a thing right? Was she *always* going to be taken for a fool...was she always going to *be* a fool?

It was all too much...much too much. Beth bowed her head. She couldn't cry. She was beyond that—way, way beyond the easy relief of tears—and besides, she had cried so many times since her return from Prague.

Only now, when she had reached the very bottom of her personal hell, could she truly admit to herself just how deeply she had fallen in love with Alex...how much she missed him...ached for him...

Alex found Beth's shop without any difficulty. It was, after all, on the main shopping street of the small town. He parked his car and got out, walking towards the elegant three-storey building and pausing to study the attractively set out window for a few seconds. There was no sign of anyone inside the shop, although the sign had been turned to 'open'. He hesitated for a few seconds, and then pushed open the door.

Beth heard the shop doorbell ring and called through the half-open storeroom door, 'I'll be with you in a second.'

Beth—Beth was here. Alex closed the shop door and swiftly turned, striding towards the open stockroom door.

Beth was just getting to her feet as he walked in. The blood left her face as she saw him, and for a moment she actually thought that she was going to faint.

'Alex...you...what...what are you doing here?' she whispered painfully, her eyes huge with the intensity of her shock.

Alex hardly dared to look at her.

The moment he had heard her voice, never mind seen her, he had been filled with such a need, such a hunger that he'd had to clench his hands into fists and stuff them into his pockets to prevent himself from taking hold of her.

As she saw the way Alex was avoiding looking at her, focusing instead on the untidy disarray of the half-unpacked packing cases in the storeroom, Beth knew immediately why he had come. The breathtaking cruelty of it stabbed right through her.

She saw him look at the crude unsaleable items of her order which she had already unpacked, and then, for the first time, he looked directly at her, with an expression in his eyes which she immediately interpreted as a mixture of distaste and pity.

Immediately her hackles rose defensively. Immediately she knew exactly what he was doing, that he had come to crow over her, to mock and taunt her, to tell her 'I told you so'. The fact that her thought processes might be a little illogical didn't occur to her; her emotions were far too aroused and overwrought for any kind of analytical thought.

'You *knew*, didn't you? Didn't you?' she challenged him bitterly. 'You've come to laugh at me...to *gloat*...'

'Beth, you're wrong...'

'Yes, I am,' she agreed emotionally. 'I'm always wrong. Always... I was wrong about Julian. I thought *he* loved me. I was wrong about you. I thought...I thought that at least you'd have the decency not to...' She stopped and swallowed, and then added wretchedly, 'And I was wrong about the glass as well.' Her head lifted proudly.

'Well, then, go ahead, say it... "I told you so..."' Her mouth twisted in a pitiful facsimile of a smile. 'At least I won't be making the same mistake a second time...'

Somehow she managed to force back the tears she could feel threatening her composure.

One look at the semi-unpacked crates and what they contained had confirmed Alex's very worst fears. The order she had received was wholly worthless, totally unsaleable. He ached for her as he compared what she had received to the glass produced by his cousins: fine, first-quality, beautiful stemware that richly echoed all the tradition and purity of the antique designs they still faithfully adhered to. Copies, yes, but beautiful ones, expensive ones, Alex acknowledged, as he remembered how awed his mother had been the first time she had visited Prague and the family business.

'They sell their glassware all over the world. Japan, America, the Gulf States. It is beautiful, Alex, but, oh, it's so expensive. Your cousins gave me these,' she had added reverently, unpacking the set of a dozen wine glasses which had been the family's gift to her.

'Are you insured against…this kind of risk?' Alex asked Beth gently, but he already knew the answer and didn't need the brief shake of her head to tell him that she wasn't. Compassion and love filled his eyes. He looked away from her.

'The Czech authorities have tracked down the criminals who organised this. Ultimately there will be a court case…perhaps there may even be some form of compensation for…for you…' he suggested.

Beth looked briefly at him.

'Don't treat me like a child, Alex. Of course there won't be any compensation. Why should I be compensated for being a fool? And even if there was…it would be too little too late,' she added hollowly.

'What do you mean?' Alex pounced.

'I…I don't mean anything,' Beth denied quickly, but she could tell that he didn't believe her.

'Beth, are you there?'

Beth tensed as she heard Dee's voice.

'I thought I'd come down. You didn't sound very happy when I spoke to you on the phone. If there's a problem with this glass… Oh!'

Dee stopped speaking as she walked into the storeroom and realised that Beth wasn't alone—and then she saw the glass.

Beth winced as she saw Dee's horrified expression.

'What on earth…?' Dee began, and then stopped. 'I'm sorry, Beth,' she apologised, 'but…'

Alex acted quickly. His mind had been working overtime and he had come to an impulsive and probably very unwise decision but he simply couldn't bear to see the shame and pain in his darling Beth's eyes.

'Yes, you're quite right,' he told Beth, as much to her confusion as Dee's. 'The order will have to be replaced.'

'It most certainly will,' Dee agreed swiftly, turning to Alex with, 'And in time for the Christmas market.'

'Dee...' Beth began, knowing that she would have to tell Dee the truth—that not only was Alex not responsible for her order, but also that there was no way he could correct the mistake she herself had made. Not in time for the Christmas market and, in fact, not ever. She would also have to tell Dee that she was going to have to terminate her lease, but that was something that would have to wait until after she had spoken to Kelly—and the bank.

Right now, what she wanted more than anything else was to close her eyes and transport herself back to a time before she had gone to Prague, before she had ever met Alex, before she had ever known Julian...before...

'If you'll excuse us,' Alex was saying affably but firmly to Dee, 'I think this is something Beth and I need to discuss in private.'

'Beth?' Dee began questioningly, and Beth nodded. What other option did she really have?

'Er...yes...it's all right... I'll be fine,' she reassured Dee, knowing what the other woman was thinking.

Just as soon as Beth had heard the shop door close behind Dee she turned on Alex and demanded tiredly, 'What did you say that for, about the order being replaced? You know it isn't true.'

Her voice cracked as the real emotion generating her anger surfaced and betrayed her.

'Beth. Beth, please don't,' Alex begged her, feeling her pain as though it was his own and aching to make things right for her. 'Look, is there somewhere we can go to talk in private?' he asked her.

'I don't want to talk to you. There isn't anything more

you can say,' Beth told him bitterly. 'You've done what you came to do…had your gloat. You should be satisfied with that.'

But Alex shook his head.

'You've got it wrong. That isn't why I'm here. Look, why don't I close the shop and we can talk in here and…?'

'No, not here,' Beth denied, shivering slightly as she looked round at the packing cases. She couldn't bear to spend another minute in here with them, with the evidence of her stupidity.

'I live upstairs…it's this way…'

'Let's lock the shop door first,' Alex suggested gently. Beth's face burned. She should have been the one to think of that. Where was her sense of responsibility, her maturity, her…? She tensed as Alex came back.

'I've put the "closed" sign up and locked the door,' he told her.

Silently Beth led the way to the rear door; just as silently Alex followed her.

Why had Alex said that to Dee about the glassware being replaced when they both knew that was impossible? What on earth was Dee going to think when Beth had to tell her that Alex had lied and that she had let him?

Once they were in her sitting room Beth stood defensively behind one of the chairs, indicating to Alex that he should take a seat in the other one.

'Beth, I promise you that I didn't come here to gloat,' he told her, ignoring the chair and coming instead to stand in front of her.

'Then why did you come?' Beth demanded. He was standing far too close to her, the chair between them no defence at all to the way her body was reacting to him, and certainly no defence against the emotional bombardment his presence was inflicting on her senses.

Even without closing her eyes she was sharply, shockingly aware of just how he would look without his clothes, of just how he would feel…smell…be…

A small keening noise bubbled in her throat. Frantically she fought to suppress it.

'I came because…because…I wanted to warn you just in case you hadn't actually paid for the glass already,' Alex prevaricated. It was, after all, partially true. That was certainly what had urged him into action, even if the real reasons for what he had done were far more complex and personal.

'How…how did you know, anyway…about…about the glass?'

She was, Beth discovered, finding it very difficult to concentrate on what she was trying to say. Alex's proximity was distracting and dizzying her. It would be so easy just to reach out and touch him. All she had to do was to lean forward a little and raise her hand and then she would…she could… Despairingly she moistened her dry lips with the tip of her tongue.

Hurriedly Alex looked away from her. If she kept on touching her mouth like that there was no way he was going to be able to stop himself from taking hold of her.

He tried to concentrate on what she was asking him.

'I…er…my mother told me. The glass you were originally shown was stolen from my cousins. The thieves were using it to lure unsuspecting buyers into placing orders for what they believed would be good-quality reproduction glassware like the items they had been shown—items which were, in fact, genuine antiques—and I—'

'So it wasn't just me…I wasn't the only…?'

'The only one? No, not by a long chalk,' Alex reassured her.

'The only fool,' Beth had been about to say, and she was sure that was what Alex must privately consider her to be. Now that he had told her she couldn't understand how she had ever believed the glassware she had been shown was modern. Perhaps she had believed it because she had *wanted* to believe it.

'Your cousins must be pleased to have recovered their antiques,' Beth told Alex tonelessly.

'Yes, especially my aunt. She felt the most responsible because she was the one who had resisted installing a new alarm system.'

'Did the night-watchman recover from his injuries?' Beth asked Alex suddenly, remembering how he had told her about the burglary the day he had taken her to see the castle.

'Yes. Yes, he did,' Alex confirmed, looking surprised that she had remembered such a small detail of their conversation. Beth looked away from him. She could recall virtually everything he had ever said to her, and everything he had ever done.

'Are you...are you back in England permanently now?'

'Yes...yes, I had my year out and now I've accepted a Chair at Lexminster, lecturing in Modern History.'

Beth stared at him white-faced. There was no mistaking the reality of what he was telling her, nor its truth. She might have doubted him originally when he had told her he was a university lecturer, but now, listening to the calm way he was discussing his career, she knew he had spoken the truth. She was the one who had been guilty of deceit, not him—she had wilfully deceived herself about her real feelings for him, her real reason for feeling those feelings. A sharp pain twisted through her heart. She could just imagine how attractive his female students would find him, how easily they would probably fall in love with him…as easily as she herself had done.

'Beth, about this glass. Let me speak to my family,' he began, but Beth shook her head quickly.

'I know what you're trying to do but it's no good,' she informed him tersely. 'I just don't have the money to place another order, Alex—not with your cousins, not with anyone. In fact—' she lifted her head and looked proudly at him '—when you arrived I was just about to get in touch with my partner to tell her that we're going to have to close the business down. I owe the bank too much to continue.

'Why aren't you telling me that it serves me right, that I should have listened to you in the first place?' Beth asked him painfully in the silence that followed her disclosure.

'Oh, Beth…'

Tenderly Alex closed the distance between them, reaching past the chair to take her in his arms and cradle her against his body, whispering soft words of endearment in her ear, kissing the top of her head and then her closed eyelids, her cheekbones, the tip of her nose… her lips…

'Alex… No…no…'

Frantically Beth tore herself out of his arms.

'I want you to go. I want you to go *now*,' she told him shakily.

'Beth,' Alex protested, but Beth didn't dare allow herself to listen to him.

'Very well. If you won't leave then I shall have to,' she told him, starting to hurry towards the door.

'Beth, Beth, it's all right. I'll go. I'm going,' Alex told her soothingly.

Beth didn't look at him as she heard him walking past

her towards the door. It hurt so much more to know he was leaving her life this time. Before, in Prague, she had been so angry that that had protected her to some extent from the reality of her pain. The knowledge of how she really felt about him had only come later, after the heat of her anger had died. But now she had no anger to protect her. Now there was no barrier between her and the pain.

Impulsively she hurried to her sitting-room window. Alex was just getting into his car, and Beth's eyes widened as she realised how expensive and up-market it was. Oddly, despite his casual clothes, the car seemed to suit him. In fact, Beth recognised, on a fresh stab of pain, Alex was carrying about him a very distinctive air of authority. Even in Prague she had been aware that he was quite a bit older and more mature than the majority of the young students taking their gap year out between finishing university and finding a job, but now, seeing him on her own home ground, she was struck by how easily he would fit into the same mould as Kelly's Brough and Anna's even more formidably successful husband Ward.

Alex was starting his car. Beth leaned closer to the window, yearning for one last glimpse of him. As though he sensed that she was watching him he looked back towards the window where she was standing. Immediately Beth drew away from it, pain drowning out all the voices of rationality that tried to tell her that she had done the right thing, that all he had really come for had been to taunt her and gloat over her, that he had lied to her when he had claimed to be concerned.

Half an hour later Beth was just on her way back down to the shop when she caught sight of the wedding invitation she had placed on the sitting-room mantelpiece. Dee's cousin Harry was marrying Brough's sister Eve

the week before Christmas, and Beth had been invited
to the ceremony.

A wedding. The celebration of two people's love for
one another.

Betrayingly Beth's eyes filled with acidly hot tears.

'I fell in love with you the first time I saw you,' Alex
had told her, but of course he hadn't meant it. Of course
he had lied to her.

She had known that then. She knew it now. So why
was she crying?

CHAPTER NINE

BETH SAT STARING into space, nursing a mug of coffee. She had just closed the shop for the day. It was almost a week since she had received her Czech order, and five days since she had seen Alex. Five days, three hours and…she glanced at the kitchen clock…eighteen minutes.

Kelly was away now with Brough, and Beth wanted to wait until after she had returned home before she told her the bad news about the business. She still had to speak with the bank manager as well. She got up wearily.

She was tired of explaining to eager customers that there had been a mistake with the Czech order and that the glass hadn't arrived. She had repacked the cases, but of course there was no point in trying to return them to an empty factory.

A car boot sale might be her best chance of getting rid of them—provided she was prepared to pay people to take the stuff, she decided with grimly bitter humour.

After washing her mug she went back downstairs to the shop. Some of the Christmas novelties she had ordered earlier in the year at a trade fair had arrived and had to be unpacked. Although pretty enough in their way, they could not possibly compare with what she had hoped to be displaying.

She had *some* good stock to sell—items she had

bought prior to her visit to Prague. Ordinarily Beth had
a good eye for colour, and a very definite flair for the
placement of things. In the window she had a display of
fluted iridescent pinky-gold fine glass candle-holders
and stemmed dishes, on one of which she had piled high
shimmering pastel glass sweets. It looked very effective,
and she had seen several people stop for a closer look.

Admiring it as she walked past their small cubbyhole
of an office, she could hear the fax clattering. She grimaced to herself as she went to see what was happening. It was probably a message from her mother. Beth
was going home to spend Christmas with her family and
her mother was constantly sending her shopping lists of
things she wanted Beth to buy on her behalf.

Absently Beth glanced at the machine, and then
tensed, quickly re-reading the message it was printing.

The Glass Factory, Prague, to Ms Bethany Russell.
Re your order.
We have pleasure to confirm that your order for
four dozen each of our special Venetian cut-glass
stemware in colours ruby, madonna, emerald and
gold is now completed and will be despatched immediately, air freight, to arrive Manchester, England...

Beth ripped the paper out of the machine, her hands
shaking. What was going on? She hadn't ordered any
glass. How could she? She couldn't afford to.

She reached for the fax machine, her eyes on the number printed on the message she had just received, and
then she stopped.

'Beth...?'

She hurried out of the office as she heard Dee's voice, the fax still in her hand.

'Have you heard anything about your glass yet?' Dee asked her, and then, glancing at the fax message, added, 'Oh, yes, I can see you have…they're sending you a fresh order. Well, I should think so too. When will it arrive? I'll come with you to the airport to collect it, if you like.'

'Dee, I haven't—'

'You're going to need to get it unpacked and on display as soon as it arrives. I'll come and give you a hand.

'Oh, and by the way, you know that man who was here when I came in the other day? Why didn't you tell me who he was…'

'Who he was…?' Beth repeated dully. 'I…'

'Mmm…I had to go over to Lexminster at the weekend— an old friend of my father's lives there, and of course I was at university there myself. He used to be a professor at the university and still attends some of the functions. He insisted on my accompanying him to a drinks party at one of the colleges and your friend was there.'

'Alex?' Beth questioned her. 'Alex was there?'

'Mmm…he was explaining to me about his family connections with Prague, and he did say, too, that he had told them how imperative it was that you got your order just as quickly as possible.'

'Dee, please…' Beth began. She would have to tell Dee the truth.

'I can't stay, I'm afraid.' Dee overrode her. 'I only popped in to see how you were. I've got a meeting in less than an hour. We'll go out for supper next week, but remember to ring me as soon as your order arrives…'

As she got in her car to drive away Dee was conscious of an unfamiliar heat burning her face. She glanced in

her driving mirror, anxious to see if she looked as uncomfortably self-conscious as she felt. As a young teenager she had endured the misery of a particularly painful
blush which it had taken her a lot of effort to learn to
control.

In fact, those who knew her now would no doubt be
surprised to learn just how shy and awkward she had felt
as a young girl.

All that was behind her now. Her father's death had
propelled her into adulthood with a speed and a force that
had left its mark on her almost as much as losing him had.
The pain and anguish of those dark days still sometimes
haunted her, no matter how hard she tried not to let them.

Going back to her old university hadn't helped, and
the relief she had experienced at seeing even a vaguely
familiar face at the cocktail party she had so reluctantly
agreed to attend had negated her normal sense of curiosity, so that she hadn't really asked very many questions
of Alex Andrews, although she had noted how keen he
had been to talk about Beth.

It had been her father's old friend who had brought up
the subject of Julian Cox, though, asking, 'Do you see
anything of that Cox fellow these days?' and then shaking his head before opining, 'He was a bad lot, if you ask
me. Your father...'

Anxious not to reactivate painful memories for either
of them, Dee had quickly tried to change the subject, but
Alex Andrews, who had been standing with them at the
time, had frowned and joined the conversation, asking
her, 'Julian Cox? That would be the man who Beth...?'

'Yes. Yes...' Dee had confirmed quickly. If she had to
talk about Julian, she would much rather the conversation centred on Beth's relationship with him rather than
her own or her father's. She knew that people thought

of her as being cool and controlled. Outwardly maybe she was. But inside—no one knew just how difficult she found it sometimes not to give way to her emotions, not to betray her real feelings.

'He hurt her very badly,' Alex had said curtly.

'Yes, he did,' Dee had agreed. 'We...her friends... thought at one point that...' She'd paused and shaken her head. 'That was one of the reasons we encouraged her to go to Prague. We thought it might help to take her mind off Julian. As it happens, though, her feelings weren't as deeply involved as either we or she had feared. I think once Beth realised just what kind of man he was she recognised how worthless he was, and how impossible it was for her to really care about him.

'She obviously spoke to you about him,' she had added curiously.

'She told me that because of him she found it impossible to trust any man...not in those words, perhaps, but that was certainly the message she wanted to give me.'

'Julian is an expert at destroying people's trust,' Dee had told him, looking away as she did so so that he wouldn't see the shadow darkening her eyes.

They had gone their separate ways shortly after that. There had been several old colleagues her father's friend had wanted to talk with, and Dee had good-naturedly accompanied him, joining in their conversations even though there hadn't been one of them under seventy years of age and the people and events they were discussing had had little relevance for her.

Mind you, in many ways it was just as well that she hadn't needed to concentrate too hard on what was being said. That had left her free to keep a weather eye on the room, strategically placing herself so that she had a clear view of the entrance. She hadn't wanted to be caught off guard by the arrival of…of…anyone—Sternly now, Dee reminded herself that she had an important meeting to attend, and that she needed to keep her wits about her if she was to keep the two warring factions on her action committee from falling out with one another.

A little ruefully she reflected on how something so therapeutic and 'green' as planting a new grove of English trees on a piece of land recently bought in a joint enterprise between the local council and one of her charities could arouse such warrior-like feelings amongst her committee members. Her father would have known exactly how to handle the situation, of course, and it was at times like these that she missed him the most. Chatting with his contemporaries, she had been so sharply aware of her loss, and not just of the father she had loved so much. Had he lived, what might she have been now? A wife…a mother…?

Dee swallowed quickly. She could still become a mother if that was her ambition. These days one did not even need to have a lover to achieve the ambition, never mind a partner. But she had been brought up by a sole parent herself, and, much as she had loved her father, much as he had loved her, she had missed not having a mother.

How often as a young girl had she dreamed of being part of a large family of brothers and sisters, and two parents? She had had her aunts and uncles and her cousins, it was true, but…

Her agents had still not been able to find out what had happened to Julian after he had disappeared to Singapore.

Dee moved uncomfortably in her seat. The cocktail party had reawakened old memories, old heartache and pain, old wounds which had healed with a dangerously thin and fragile new skin.

* * *

Alex smiled warmly as he heard his aunt's voice on the other end of the telephone line.

'How are you?'

'Tired,' his aunt told him wryly. 'It's meant hard work, getting this important order together for you.'

Beth was just about to close up the shop for the night when she saw the delivery van pull up outside, followed by a highly polished chauffeur-driven black Mercedes.

It had been raining during the afternoon and the pavements were wet, glistening under the light from the Christmas decorations which the Corporation's workmen had been putting up and which they were currently testing, prior to the formal switching-on ceremony the following weekend.

On the counter in front of her Beth had a list of customers she intended to ring during the evening. They were the customers who had expressed an interest in the new glass. She had not, as yet, told them that it wasn't going to be available.

The van driver was heading towards her door. Uncertainly Beth watched him, her uncertainty turning to shock as she saw the woman climbing out of the rear of the elegant Mercedes and recognised her instantly.

It was Alex's aunt, the woman she had seen him with in Prague, looking, if anything, even more soignée and elegant now than she had done then. The exquisite tailoring of her charcoal-grey suit made Beth sigh in soft envy. If she had only added a picture hat and a small toy dog on a lead she could have posed for a Dior advertisement of the fifties. Very few women of her own generation could boast of having such a lovely neat waist, Beth acknowledged as Alex's aunt waited for the van driver to open the shop door and then stand back, allowing Alex's aunt to sweep through.

'This is very good,' she told Beth without preamble. 'Alex told me that you had a good eye and I can see that he is right. That is a very pretty display of pieces you have in your window, although perhaps you might just redirect the spotlight on them a little. If you have some ladders I could perhaps show you…'

Beth was too bemused to feel affronted, and besides, she had come to very much the same decision herself only this afternoon.

'I have brought you your glass,' she added, and then said more severely, 'I hope you understand that we do this only as the very greatest favour because it is for family. It has been very expensive to pay the workpeople to work extra and push your order through. I have a rich—a very rich—oil sheikh who right at this moment has had to be told that his chandelier is not quite ready. This is not something I would normally like to do, but Alex was most insistent, and when a man is so much in love…'

She gave a graceful shrug of her shoulders.

'I have come here with it myself since we do not normally sell our glassware to enterprises such as yours. We sell, normally, by personal recommendation, direct to our customers. That is our…our speciality. We do not…how would you say?…make so much that it can be sold as in a supermarket.' She gave another dismissive shrug. 'That is not our way. We are unique and…exclusive.'

'Yes, you may put them here,' she instructed the van driver, who was wheeling in a large container. 'But carefully, carefully…

'Oh, yes, I thank you. I nearly forgot…' She thanked the chauffeur as he followed the van driver in and handed her a large rectangular gift-wrapped package.

'This is for you,' she told Beth, to Beth's astonishment. 'You will not open it yet. That is not permitted. You will open it with Alex—he will have one too—when you are together. It is a gift of betrothal—a tradition in our family.'

Betrothal!

Beth stared at her. Alex's aunt was so very much larger than life, so totally compelling that Beth felt completely overwhelmed by her. By rights she ought to be telling her that there was no way she could accept the order she had just brought. She just couldn't afford it. And she should also tell her that she resented Alex's high-handed attitude in giving his family an order on her behalf without consulting her in the first place. And as for his aunt's comment about a betrothal...

'It is also very much a tradition that the men of our family fall in love at first sight. My husband, who was also my second cousin, fell in love with me just by seeing my photograph. One glimpse, that was all it took, and then he was on his way to my parents' home to beg me to be his wife. We were together as man and wife for just two years and then he was killed...murdered...'

Beth gave a small convulsive shiver as she saw the look in the older woman's eyes.

'I still feel the pain of his loss today. It has been my life's work to do with the factory what he would have wished to be done. One of my greatest sorrows is that he did not live to see our family reunited. Alex is very much like him. He loves you. You are very lucky to have the love of such a man,' she told Beth firmly.

Beth simply had no idea what on earth to say to her, much less how to tell her that she had got it all wrong, that Alex most certainly did not love her.

'This is good,' she informed the van driver, who had

now brought in what Beth sincerely hoped was the last
packing case. There were six of them in all, filling her
small shop, and she dreaded to think what the cost of their
contents must be. Quite definitely much, much more than
she could afford, with her empty bank account and her
burdensome overdraft.

'I really don't think…' she began faintly. But trying to stop Alex's aunt was like trying to stop the awesome magnificence of some grandly rolling river at full
flood—impossible!

'You will please remove the covering,' Alex's aunt was
instructing the van driver, waving one elegantly manicured hand in the direction of the boxes.

Beth didn't dare look at him. This was an egalitarian
age, an age of equality in which, Beth suspected, the last
time a man had removed something from its packing for
her had been when her father had opened her last baby-
hood Easter egg. But to her astonishment, far from reacting with the surly resentment she had expected to Alex's
aunt's request, the van driver immediately, enthusiastically complied. Beth acknowledged the uneasy suspicion
crowding her already log-jammed thoughts: he must have
been promised an extremely generous tip indeed.

'No. No more,' Alex's aunt commanded, once the lids
were removed and the van driver was about to delve into
the polystyrene chips surrounding the contents.

'First we must have champagne,' she told Beth firmly.
'I have brought some with me and we shall drink it from
proper glasses. It is a small ritual I always insist on when
we hand over a completed order…a superstition we have
that it is bad luck not to do so.'

'Er… I…' Beth had some pretty champagne flutes
made of the same glass and in the same style as her new
window display. Quickly she went to get them, reflect-

ing ruefully that it would be far more appropriate to be using Waterford crystal—only her personal finances did not run to such luxuries.

Although Alex's aunt did raise her eyebrows a little at the glasses Beth produced, to Beth's relief she did not raise any objections.

This whole situation was completely surreal, Beth decided dizzily as Alex's aunt uncorked the champagne with a deftness that left Beth in awe. The van driver and the chauffeur had been dismissed, and only the two of them were left in the shop.

'You will open this first box,' Beth was instructed as Alex's aunt removed the top package from the nearest packing case.

Obediently Beth did as she was told, her fingers trembling slightly as she eased the carefully wrapped glass out of a box of six.

The theatricality with which Alex's aunt was surrounding the whole event was impossibly dramatic. Beth could just imagine the chaos it would cause if she were to react to every delivery they received like this. But once the glass was free of its covering, and she could see it properly, any irritation she had felt at Alex's aunt's high-handedness was banished.

A soft breath of pure, awed appreciation slid from Beth's parted lips as she drank in the beauty of the glass she was cradling. The shop's lighting made every cut facet sparkle and shimmer with the rich cranberry colour of the goblet-shaped bowl, its stem clear and pure and worked with the most intricate design of trailing ivy and grapes.

Here was a reproduction Venetian glass of truly outstanding authenticity, a fruitful marriage of ancient and modern. Wonderingly Beth ran her fingertips over it. It was, quite simply, one of the most beautiful glasses she had ever seen, if anything even better and richer than the original antique she had been shown by the gypsy.

'It is good…yes?' Alex's aunt was saying, her voice softer and more gentle as she recognised what Beth was feeling.

Beth looked up at her and saw in her eyes the same love that she herself always felt for a thing of such out-standing beauty.

'It is very good,' she agreed simply, blinking back the emotional tears that had filled her eyes.

'Ah, yes, now I see why Alex has chosen you,' she heard his aunt telling her. 'Now I see that you are one of us. This is my own design, adapted from an original, of course. I think that the vine and the grapes are a truly authentic touch for a glass designed for wine. My cousins feel it is perhaps a little too modern, but I have brought for you also some much more traditional baroque designs. You will love them all.'

'I *will* love them all,' Beth confirmed shakily, 'but I cannot possibly keep them. I can't afford…'

'I have to go. I am to have dinner with Alex's parents this evening…'

'Please,' Beth begged her. 'I cannot accept this order. I must ask you to take it away.' As she saw the look of incomprehension darken Alex's aunt's eyes, Beth spread her hands helplessly and told her shakily, 'I would love to keep it, but I simply cannot afford to pay for such an order…'

'Did I not explain?' the older woman asked her, frowning. 'There is to be no question of payment.' She added firmly, 'This is a gift.'

'A gift!' Beth stared at her, the colour leaving her face, her chin lifting as pride stiffened her body. 'That is very generous of you but I simply could not accept. For you to give me such a gift is...'

'Oh, but it is not from me. I am a businesswoman,' she told Beth sturdily. 'Not even to my own family would I make such a gesture. My finest glass—*and* my order books and workforce totally disrupted to do it. No...it is *Alex* who makes the gift to you. I told him that he must love you very much indeed. I know he is not poor—his grandfather was a wealthy man, who prospered here in his adoptive country—but Alex is an academic who will never earn himself a fortune. But who can set a price on love? Although at first I was inclined to tell him that what he asked for was impossible, when he explained to me that without this order you would lose your business, which you love so very much, I could see that your pain would be his and I gave in to the sentimental side of my nature. I am sorry, but I really must go. And remember, you are not to open my gift to you until you are together with Alex. You and he will know the right time...'

The glass was a gift from Alex. *Alex* had paid for all of this... As Alex's aunt left the shop and headed for her Mercedes Beth stared around herself.

It was impossible for her to accept, of course. Even more so now that she knew Alex had paid for everything out of his own pocket.

Her heart started to race and thud erratically as she dwelt on the implications of what he had done.

His aunt had seemed to assume that their feelings for one another were an acknowledged and established thing. Had Alex told her that? 'He loves you,' she had told Beth. 'It is very much a tradition that the men of our family fall in love at first sight.'

What if she was right? What if Alex *had*, as he had claimed, fallen in love with her...? She had been wrong about his motivation in trying to dissuade her from buying via the gypsies; she knew that now. What if she had been wrong in other ways as well? What if…?

The doorbell rang, alerting her to the fact that she was no longer alone. As she turned round she started to smile in welcome relief as she saw that her visitor was her godmother, Anna.

'My goodness, this looks very exciting!' Anna exclaimed curiously as she closed the shop door behind her. 'Ward and I were just on our way back from Yorkshire and I saw that the shop lights were on so I got him to drop me off.'

Anna and her husband Ward were looking for a new house in the area, and in the meantime they were spending their time between Ward's house in Yorkshire and Anna's existing home in Rye-on-Averton.

'Come and sit down,' Beth advised her godmother affectionately as she saw the way Anna was rubbing her side. She and Ward were expecting their first baby and Beth looked a little enviously at her, noting how well pregnancy suited her. Of course, it helped having a husband who idolised and adored you, and who thought you were the cleverest person in the whole world simply because you were carrying his child.

'That's what happens when you get to be first-time parents at our age,' Anna laughed whenever people remarked on how thrilled Ward was about their coming baby.

'Of course I'm pleased,' Ward had announced promptly once in Beth's hearing when someone had raised the subject. 'But no matter how much I shall love our daughter or our son, once he or she arrives, I couldn't possibly love them anywhere near as much as I do Anna…'

For a normally slightly dour man it had been an extremely open and emotional thing to say, and at the time she had heard it Beth hadn't been able to help reflecting on how wonderful it must be to know that one was so deeply and sincerely loved. She had gone home that night and had wept a little in the lonely secrecy of her bed, still denying to herself that Alex had meant anything to her.

'Your order has arrived, then,' Anna commented, and then caught her breath on a sharp exclamation of pleasure as she saw the glass that Beth had already unpacked.

'Oh, Beth, it's beautiful,' she half whispered in awe. 'I must confess when you told us about it I couldn't imagine...I *didn't* imagine just how wonderful it would actually be. This is exquisite...'

'Exquisite, expensive and not actually my order,' Beth told her ruefully.

'Oh?'

'It's a long story,' Beth protested, shaking her head a little in denial of the questioning look she could see in her godmother's eyes.

'I've got time—plenty of time,' Anna assured her.

It would be a relief to tell someone exactly what had happened, Beth admitted, especially if that someone was her loving, gently non-judgemental godmother.

'Well, it's like this...' she began.

'And so you see,' Beth concluded, when she had finished explaining to Anna just what had happened, 'there's no way I can keep the glass, nor accept such an expensive present...'

'Not even from the man you love?' Anna suggested gently.

Beth flushed, shaking her head.

'*Especially* not from the man I love,' she objected. 'I

just don't know what I'm going to do, Anna, how I'm going to explain…'

'Well, I can't give you any advice other than to tell you to follow your heart, to listen *with* your heart and your emotions.'

'But I can't just tell him that I love him. I can't say that I lied…that I want him…that I…'

'Why not?' Anna asked her mildly. 'You've told *me*!'

CHAPTER TEN

WHY NOT INDEED?

Beth gnawed on her bottom lip. Anna had gone and she was on her own; the shop was locked and she had made herself a meal which she had been totally unable to eat. It was now just gone seven o'clock. She had Alex's address and his telephone number because they were written on the delivery note that came with the glass. All she had to do was pick up the phone and dial.

And then what? Tell him, I love you, Alex. I was wrong about you, about everything, and now I can tell you that I've loved you all the time. Now I can allow myself to admit that I love you? Would he believe her? And even if he did how would he feel about the paucity of her gesture, her *love*, when compared with the rich generosity of his? It wasn't that she loved him any less than he did her; that was impossible. Her love was just as deep, just as committed...just as intense. It was just that her previous experience had made her wary of giving too much too soon, and meeting him had in one sense come too soon on top of her realisation of Julian's perfidy.

At least Alex would never be able to accuse her of using him as...

She started to dial his number and then stopped. Perhaps tomorrow, after she had had time to think properly, to rehearse what she needed to say…or maybe… She had taken the gift-wrapped box his aunt had given her upstairs, and her attention was caught by it. She went over to it and picked it up. It was heavy. 'You will open it with Alex…when you are together,' she had told Beth.

Suddenly a very daring and dangerous plan occurred to her. Without giving herself time to change her mind, Beth picked up the box and grabbed her coat and her car keys.

Lexminster wasn't that far away—a two-hour drive, maybe even less at this time of night.

Alex picked up some papers he had brought home to work on. His mother had telephoned earlier, inviting him over for dinner.

'Your aunt will be here, but only for the one night; she's flying on to New York tomorrow…'

Alex had been tempted, but he had already endured one very stern lecture from her on his foolhardiness and stubborn persistence in persuading her to give priority to his order for Beth. When would she receive it? he wondered. His aunt had promised, albeit reluctantly, that she would have it in time for the Christmas market.

He wasn't quite sure how Beth would react when she *did* receive it. It wasn't entirely impossible that she would send it back to him in a million broken pieces, but he suspected that it might be that she couldn't bring herself to destroy something which he knew already she would find irresistibly beautiful.

He had made himself a meal earlier but had not really felt like eating it. God, but he ached for Beth. Somehow, and he didn't know quite how yet, he was going to find a way to convince her that he loved her, that he was genuine and that she loved him—because Alex was convinced that she did. She might claim that all they had shared had been sex, but Alex knew her, and she simply wasn't that kind of woman. Her emotions ran too deep and too strong for her to divorce herself from them like that. She could not have responded to him the way she had without feeling something for him. He was convinced of it.

He frowned as he heard his doorbell ring. He wasn't really in the mood for company. He got up and walked from his living room into the hallway and opened the front door.

'Beth!'

Beth stood nervously in the doorway, her nervousness increased by the shock she could see in Alex's eyes and hear in his voice.

'I...' She took a step backwards and looked wildly over her shoulder, as though about to flee.

Immediately Alex reached for her wrist, drawing her gently but firmly inside and closing the door behind her.

Beneath his grasp her wrist-bones felt heart-wrenchingly fragile. Under her free arm she was clutching a large rectangular parcel against her body.

'A present...for me...?' he asked teasingly, trying to lighten her tension.

'No, actually it's for me...from your aunt,' Beth told him in a disjointed, almost staccato little burst of speech. 'She said you would have one too and that we had to open them together. Alex, why did you do...why did you send me the glass? You must know that I can't accept it...'

To her own consternation her eyes filled with tears. Whilst she was talking Alex had been urging her along his hallway and was now ushering her into a beautifully proportioned room which, in some obscure way, reminded her of the drawing room in the castle. Her face started to burn, her heart thumping at the memories she was evoking.

'Come and sit down and we'll talk about it,' Alex suggested, relieving her of her coat and guiding her towards a softly upholstered and very deep sofa.

A little unsteadily Beth sank into it. In addition to relieving her of her coat Alex had also relieved her of the cumbersome parcel.

When he returned he was carrying two glasses.

'It's brandy,' he told her. 'Drink it; it will help you to relax a bit…'

Dutifully Beth took a sip and then pulled a face.

'I've already had champagne with your aunt,' she told him as she put her glass down. 'Perhaps the two don't mix. Alex…I can't accept your gift. It's wonderful…the glass is beautiful, even more beautiful than I could have imagined, but why…why did you do it?' she asked him, abandoning the reasoned, rational argument she had prepared and doing instead what Anna had urged her to do and responding only to her emotions.

'Didn't my aunt tell you?' Alex asked her ruefully. He hadn't thought that his aunt would hand Beth's glass over to her in person, but then realistically he should perhaps have guessed that it was the kind of thing she would do. She was extremely picky about whom she allowed to have her precious glass, and, of course, Alex's own admissions to her had aroused her curiosity about Beth to an even greater intensity.

Beth hesitated, unable to look at him.

'She said…she said it was because you loved me,' she told him huskily. She could feel Alex looking at her, and her own gaze was drawn to his, her face flushing as she saw the look in his eyes.

'And did you believe her?' he asked her quietly.

Beth bit her lip.

'I...' She felt as though she was drowning, losing control, fighting to prevent herself from being swept under by the force of her own emotions, afraid of their power—and yet at the same time a part of her was longing to give in, to give up, to let someone else carry the burden of her loving for her.

'I...I wanted to,' she admitted truthfully.

'Why...because you wanted to have more sex with me?' Alex couldn't resist probing, a little unkindly.

Beth reacted as though he had actually physically hurt her, her breath leaking from her lungs, her face draining of colour, even her hand going out as though to ward off an actual blow.

'Oh, Beth...my love, my precious, precious love, I'm sorry,' Alex apologised remorsefully. 'I didn't mean—'

'No. No...it's all right. I know I deserved it,' Beth interrupted him jerkily. 'I shouldn't have come here.' She tried to get up, desperate to escape before she completed her own humiliation by bursting into tears. She had got it all wrong. Alex didn't love her at all. His aunt had got it all wrong.

'What you deserve is to be cherished and loved, adored, worshipped,' Alex was telling her extravagantly.

'Alex,' she protested.

'How could you *possibly* think I didn't mean it?' Alex overrode her protest tenderly. 'Have you any idea how much I've missed you, how many times I've been tempted to come and find you, capture you, kidnap you, bear you off with me to my lair as one of my ancestors might have done?'

'I can't imagine you ever displaying such caveman-like tactics,' Beth told him ruefully. 'You...'

'No? Watch me,' Alex mock-threatened her, and then,

before she could speak, he was reaching for her, wrapping her in his arms, kissing her with a passion that broke through all her resistance.

She tried to speak, to protest…plead for time and explanations, but her words were lost, silenced beneath the hungry pressure of his mouth that only relaxed when she made a tiny sound. Whilst he was kissing her he dropped his arms to his sides, sliding his fingers between hers so that they were standing body to body, arm to arm, only their heads, their lips moving. Her own body was trembling with increasing intensity as she reacted to his closeness. Her body was betraying her far more than any words, Beth knew.

'"Just sex" could never feel like this,' Alex whispered thickly against her mouth. '"Just sex" could never make me want you the way I do, and it could never make you respond to me the way you are.'

'Alex, I got it all wrong,' Beth told him guiltily. 'I totally misjudged you and I misjudged my own feelings as well, totally and wilfully. I thought—'

'I know what you *thought*,' Alex interrupted her. 'But what is more interesting right now is what you *felt*…what you are feeling… Or shall I discover for myself?'

She was wearing a soft buttoned cardigan, and as Alex started to trace the vee of flesh it exposed Beth's whole body began to quiver. Her desire for him drenched her, flooded her, melted her; she was reaching eagerly for him long before he had finished unbuttoning her cardigan, and touching him long, long before his hands had started to cup her naked breasts, stroking them, his fingers plucking delicately at her tight nipples.

'Tell me you love me,' he demanded thickly against her breast as he slid to his knees in front of her.

'I love you… I love you… I… Oh, Alex, Alex,'

Beth gasped, torn between shock and fierce arousal as he pulled off her skirt and slid his hands up under her briefs to cup the rounded shape of her buttocks whilst his tongue-tip rimmed her navel. She knew what would happen next, what she *wanted* to happen next. Just thinking about how it had felt to have his breath, his mouth, his tongue against that part of her body made her shudder from head to foot in explosive yearning.

They made love quickly and fiercely, like two starving people attacking a banquet, their appetites too hungry to be easily sated and yet their stomachs too shrunken by deprivation for the endurance required to eat their leisurely fill.

All they could manage was a taste here, a mouthful there, a gulp of love's rich, raw wine before they were both crying out in their need for completion. It came swiftly, hotly, rawly almost, Beth acknowledged as she lay panting and light-headed in Alex's arms.

Later, when he carried her to bed, she protested, 'I can't…I've got to go home. It's late—the shop…'

'You can. I am now your home. The shop can wait… we can't…'

This time they did their personal sensual banquet full justice, eating appreciatively of every course, true connoisseurs of what was set before them.

'What do you suppose is in the parcel?' Beth asked Alex drowsily just before she finally fell asleep in his arms.

'We shall have to wait and see. Remember we can't open them until I have mine.'

'Mmm… Alex, have I told you how much I love you?'

'Many times,' Alex assured her gently, knowing just why she asked.

'I never really loved Julian Cox, you know,' Beth assured him. 'It was just… I wanted to be in love with him…I wanted to believe him…'

'Forget him. He doesn't matter to us,' Alex told her.

Beth gave a soft sigh of contented pleasure. She loved it that Alex felt so secure with her, that he could accept her honest admission that she had made a mistake.

'I always knew you were plotting to make me have your aunt's glass,' she teased him lovingly as she reached out to trace the shape of his mouth with her fingertip.

As he nipped and nibbled at her probing finger Alex replied. 'No, you're wrong,' he denied, and then he said softly, 'What I've been plotting ever since I first saw you is to get you so that I can do this…'

As he rolled her over on top of him Beth protested, torn between excitement and laughter.

'Alex, we can't…not again…'

'Oh, yes, we can,' he assured her. 'Oh, yes, we can!'

EPILOGUE

'WELL, SHALL WE open them, then?' Alex asked Beth provocatively.

It was Christmas Eve and they were in Alex's apartment. They were due to spend Christmas Day with Alex's parents and Boxing Day with her own. Tonight, though, they were spending on their own. On her ring finger was the flawlessly cut diamond Alex had just given her. They had chosen it together the previous week and now, as she reached out her hands towards him to take the mysterious parcel his aunt had left with her, it caught the light, flooding the space around them with prisms of colour.

They were going to get married in the spring, here in England, and then they were going to fly to Prague for a very special family celebration which would be held at the castle.

'Another family tradition?' Beth had teased Alex when he had first mentioned it to her.

'Not exactly, but I know it would mean a lot to the family…'

'And to me,' Beth had told him seriously, her eyes full of love.

Now, as they both unwrapped their parcels, she couldn't help reflecting how very, very lucky she was. It chilled her blood to think how easily she might not have met Alex at all.

Inside the wrapping paper was a cardboard box. Quickly she unfastened it and reached inside, and then waited. Alex was watching her, his own box still unopened.

'We have to open them together,' she reminded him sternly, and then, as she saw his face, she accused him, 'You know what it is, don't you?'

'It's a family tradition,' Alex replied, his expression mock-injured.

'Oh, you,' Beth protested, reaching inside her box, the laughter in her eyes stilled as she removed its contents.

It was a lustre, just like the one she had first seen in the hotel gift shop but even more beautiful.

'Oh, Alex,' she whispered as she studied it. 'Oh, Alex, it's beautiful…'

'*They* are beautiful,' Alex corrected her, removing his own from its packaging and putting it next to hers. 'A perfect pair…like us,' he added as he bent his head to kiss her.

'A perfect pair…' Beth sighed in blissful happiness. 'Oh, Alex,' she whispered.

'Oh, Beth,' Alex whispered back, and then added engagingly, 'Do you think we might just check that it isn't just sex…one more time…?'

'It's only eight o'clock. Far too early for bed yet,' Beth protested, but her eyes were shining and there was no reluctance whatsoever in her expression as she clung lovingly to him…quite the opposite.

A perfect pair. Oh, yes, indeed… Oh, yes… Yes… Yes…

'Mmm…'

* * * * *

In memory of Dagmar Digrinová
whose enthusiasm and love
for her country inspired
this book.

THE MARRIAGE
RESOLUTION

CHAPTER ONE

DEE LAWSON PAUSED in mid-step to admire the pink and yellow stripes of the flowers in their massed corporation bed in Rye-on-Averton's town square.

She had just been to have coffee with her friend Kelly. Beth, Kelly's friend and business partner in the pretty crystal and china gift shop the two girls ran in the town—a property which they rented from Dee herself—had also been there, along with Anna, Beth's godmother. Anna's pregnancy was very well advanced, and she had laughed a little breathlessly as her baby kicked when his or her mother reached for another biscuit.

With Beth's wedding to Alex only weeks away Dee suspected that it wouldn't be very long before Beth too was blissfully anticipating the prospect of becoming a mother.

Strange to think that so little time ago motherhood had been the last thing on any of their minds.

Dee's eyes clouded a little. But, no, that wasn't quite true, was it. Motherhood, babies, children, a family were subjects which had always been close to her *own* heart, even if those feelings, that *yearning*, had in recent years become something of a closet desire for her, a sadness for what might have been had things been different.

She wasn't too old for motherhood, though, not at

thirty-one—Anna was older than her—and plenty of women in their thirties, conscious of the urgent tick of their biological clocks, were making the decision not to waste any more time but to commit themselves to motherhood even without a committed relationship with their baby's father.

Had she wanted to do so, Dee knew *she* could have quite easily and clinically arranged to conceive, even to the point of choosing the biological details of the male donor who would be the father of her child. But, strong though her maternal instincts were, Dee's own experience of losing her mother shortly after she was born meant that, despite the caring love she had received from her father, for her own child she wanted the extra-special sense of security and belonging that came from being a child surrounded by and brought up with the love of both its parents, for it and for each other. And that was something that was just not possible...not for her...not any more... Once, a long time ago, she had believed...dreamed...

But that had been before Julian Cox had wormed his way into her life, corrupting her happiness, destroying her security.

Julian Cox!

Her full lips twisted distastefully.

It was typical of the man that he had cunningly managed to escape the legal retribution which must surely have been his had he remained within the reach of European law. Where was he now? Dee wondered. She had tried through the considerable network of contacts at her disposal to find him. The last time there had been a firm sighting of him had been last year, in Singapore.

Julian Cox.

He had caused so much destruction, so much unhappiness in other people's lives, those people he had deceived and cheated via his fraudulent investment scams, people like Beth, and Kelly's husband Brough's sister Eve, vulnerable women whom he'd tried to convince that he loved purely so that he could benefit financially. Luckily both of them had ultimately seen through him and had found happiness elsewhere. For her things were not so simple. For her...

Dee stopped and glanced towards the elegant three-storey Georgian building from which the builders' scaffolding had just been removed, revealing it in all its refurbished splendour.

When she had originally bought it, the building had been in danger of having to be demolished, and it had taken every bit of Dee's considerable skill to persuade not just the planners but the architect and the builders she had hired that it could be saved, and not just saved but returned to its original splendour.

All the time and effort she had put into achieving its restoration had been well worthwhile, just for that wonderful moment when at a special ceremony the county's Lord Lieutenant had declared it officially 'open' and she had seen the name she had had recarved and gilded above the doorway illuminated by the strategically placed lighting she had had installed.

'Lawson House'.

And on the wall there was an elegant and discreet scrolled plaque, explaining to those who read it that the money to purchase and renovate the house had been provided posthumously by her father in his memory. And it was in his memory that its upper storey was going to be employed as office accommodation for the special charities which Dee maintained and headed, whilst the lower ground floor was to be used as a specially equipped social area for people of all ages with special needs, a meeting place, a café, a reading room—all those things and more.

And above its handsome marble fireplace she had placed a specially commissioned portrait of her father, which the artist had created from Dee's own photographs.

'I wish I could have known him. He must have been the most wonderful man,' Kelly had once commented warmly when Dee had been talking to her about her father.

'He was,' Dee had confirmed.

Her father had had the kind of analytical brain that had enabled him to make a fortune out of trading stocks and shares. With that fortune he had philanthropically set about discreetly helping his fellow men. It was from him that Dee had inherited her own desire to help others, and it was in his name that she continued the uniquely personal local charity which he had established.

And it wasn't just his desire to help his fellow men that Dee had inherited from her father. She had also inherited his shrewd financial acumen. Her father's wealth had made her financially independent and secure for the rest of her life. Dee did not need to earn a living, and so, instead, she had turned her attention and her skills to the thing that had been closest to her father's heart after his love for her.

As the financial brain behind all the charities her father had established, as well as their chairperson, Dee had made sure that the charities' assets were secure and profitable—and, just as important, that their money was invested not just profitably but sensitively so far as not taking advantage of other people was concerned.

All in all, Dee knew that she had a lot to be grateful for. The friendship which had sprung up between her and the two younger women, Beth and Kelly, who rented the shop premises from her, and Anna, too, had added a very welcome and heart-warming extra strand to her life. Dee was part of a large extended family that had its roots in the area's farming community and which went back for many generations; she had the pleasure of knowing that she had faithfully adhered to all the principles her father had taught her, and that her father himself was remembered and lauded by his fellow citizens.

A lot to be grateful for, yes, but she still couldn't help thinking about when... But, no, she wasn't going to dwell on that—not today—not any day, she informed herself firmly. Just because seeing Anna's pregnant state and Beth and Kelly's happiness had made her so sharply conscious of the void which existed in her own life that did not mean...

Above her head the sky was a vivid spring blue decorated with fluffy white clouds whipped along by the breeze. The Easter eggs which had filled shop windows in recent weeks had been removed to make way for flowers and posters advertising the town's special May Day celebration, which had its roots in the ancient May Day Fair which had originally been held in the town in medieval times.

There would be a procession of floats, sponsored in the main these days by corporate bodies, a funfair in the town square, a bonfire and fireworks, and, since she was on the committee planning and co-ordinating the whole affair, Dee knew that she was going to be busy.

Amusingly, she had been shown an old document recently, listing the rules which applied to anyone bringing sheep, cattle or other livestock into the town on May Day. The modern-day equivalent was making rules for the extra volume of traffic the Fair caused.

Babies were still on Dee's mind when she eventually got home. A second cousin on her mother's side had recently had twins, and Dee made a mental note to buy them something special. She had heard on the family grapevine that she was going to be asked to be their godmother. It was a wonderful compliment, Dee knew, but, oh, how it made her heart ache. Just the mere act of holding those precious little bundles of love would make her whole body ache so!

In an effort to give her mind a different and more appropriate turn of direction, she decided that she ought to do some work. Strength of will and the ability to follow through on one's personal plans were, her father had always told her, very positive assets, and to be admired. Perhaps they were, but over the years Dee had become slightly cynically aware that so far as the male sex was concerned a strong-minded woman was often someone to be feared rather than admired, and resented rather than loved.

Dee switched on her computer, telling herself firmly that it was silly to pursue such unprofitable thoughts. But it was true, a rebellious part of her brain insisted on continuing, that men liked women who were illogical, women who were vulnerable, women who were feminine and needed them to help and protect them. *She* was not like that, at least not outwardly. For a start she was tall—elegantly so, her female friends often told her enviously. Her body was slim and supple, she enjoyed walking and swimming—and dancing—and she was always the first one her younger nieces and nephews wanted to join in their energetic games whenever there was a family get-together.

She wore her thick honey-coloured straight hair long, primarily because she found it easier to manage that way, often coiling it up in the nape of her neck in a style

which complemented her classically elegant bone structure. Whilst she had been at university she had been
approached in the street by the owner of an up-market
model agency who had told her that she had all the potential to become a model, but Dee had simply laughed
at her, totally unaware of the dramatic impact of her
timeless elegance.

Over the years, if anything that impact had height-
ened, rather than lessened, and although Dee herself was
unaware of it she was now a woman whom others paused
to glance at discreetly a second time in the street. The
reason so many men appeared to be intimidated by her
was not, as she herself imagined, her strength of will, but
in actual fact the way she looked. That look combined
with the classically stylish clothes she tended to favour
meant that in most men's eyes Dee was a woman they
considered to be out of their league.

Dee frowned as she studied the screen in front of her.
One of the new small charities she had taken under her
wing was not attracting the kind of public support it
needed. She would have to see if there was some way they
could give it a higher profile. Somewhere for teenagers
to meet, listen to their music and dance might not have
the appeal of helping to provide for the more obviously
needy, but it was still a cause which, in Dee's opinion,
was very deserving.

Perhaps she should speak to Peter Macauley about
it. Her father's old friend and her own retired university
tutor shared her father's philanthropic beliefs and ideals. A bachelor, and wealthy, having inherited family
money, he had already asked Dee to be one of the ex-
ecutors of his will because he knew that she would see
that his wishes and bequests were carried out just as he
would want them to be. He was on the main committee

appointed by her father to control the funds he had bequested to finance his charities.

Thinking of Peter Macauley caused Dee to pause in what she was doing. He was not recovering from the operation he had had some months ago as quickly as he should have been, and the last time Dee had driven to Lexminster to see him she had been upset to see how frail he was looking.

He had lived in the university town all his adult life, and Dee knew how strenuously he would resist any attempt on her part to cajole him into moving to Rye-on-Averton, where she could keep a closer eye on him, never mind how he would react to any suggestion that he should move *in* with her. But the four-storey house he occupied in the shelter of the town's ancient university was far too large for him to manage, especially with its steep flights of stairs. He had friends in the town, but, like him, they were in the main elderly. Lexminster wasn't very far away, a couple of hours' drive, that was all…

It had been Dee's first choice of university, since it had offered the courses she'd wanted to take, and, more importantly, had meant that she wouldn't have to move too far away from her father. In those days the new motorway which now linked the university town to Rye had not been built, and the drive had taken closer on four hours than two, which had meant that she had had to live in student digs rather than commute from home.

Those days… How long ago those words made it seem, and yet, in actual fact, it had only been a mere ten years. Ten years…a different life, a lifetime away in terms of the girl she had been and the woman she was now. Ten years. It was also ten years since her father's unexpected death.

Her father's death. Dee knew how surprised those who

considered themselves to be her closest friends would be if they knew just how profoundly and deeply she still felt the pain of losing her father. The pain—and the guilt?

Abruptly she switched off her computer and got up.

Seeing Anna had done more than reawaken her own secret longing for a child. It had brought into focus things she would far rather not dwell on. What was the point? What was the point in dwelling on past heartaches, past heart*breaks*? There wasn't one. No, she would be far better employed doing something productive. Absently—betrayingly—she touched the bare flesh of her ring finger, slightly thinner at its base than the others. Other things—such as what?

Such as driving over to Lexminster and visiting Peter, she told herself firmly. It *was* a couple of weeks since she had last seen him, and she tried to get over at least once a fortnight, making her visits seem spur-of-the-moment and accidental, or prompted by the need for his advice on some aspect of her charity work so as to ensure that his sense of pride wasn't hurt and that he didn't guess how anxious she had become about his failing health.

Her sleek car, all discreet elegance, just as discreetly elegant as she was herself, ate up the motorway miles to Lexminster, the journey so familiar to her that Dee was free to allow her thoughts to drift a little.

How excited she had been the first time she had driven into the town as a new student, excited, nervous, and unhappy too, at leaving her father.

She could still vividly remember that day, the warm, mellow late-September sunshine turning the town's ancient stone buildings a honey-gold. She had parked her little second-hand car—an eighteenth-birthday present from her father—with such care and pride. Her father might have been an extremely wealthy man, but he had taught her that love and loyalty were more important than money, that the truly worthwhile things in life could never be bought.

She had spent her first few weeks at university living in hall and then moved into a small terraced property, which she had co-bought with her father and shared with two other female students. She could still remember how firm her father had been as he'd gone over the figures she had prepared to show him the benefits of him helping her to buy the cottage. He had known all the time, of course, the benefits of doing so, but he had made her sell the idea to him, and she had had to work too, to provide her share of the small mortgage payments. Those had been good years: the best years of her life—and the worst. To have gone from the heights she had known to the depths she had plummeted to so shockingly had had the kind of effect on her that no doubt today would have been classed as highly traumatic. And she had suffered not one but two equally devastating blows, each of which...

The town was busy; it was filled with tourists as well as students. All that now remained of the fortified castle around which the town had been built were certain sections of carefully preserved walls and one solitary tower, an intensely cold and damp place that had made Dee shiver not just with cold but with the weight of its history on the only occasion on which she had visited it.

Economics had been her subject at university, and one which she had originally chosen to equip her to work with her father. But there had always co-existed within her, alongside her acutely financially perceptive brain, a strong streak of idealism—also inherited from her parents—and even before she had finished her first university term she had known that once she had obtained her degree her first choice of career would be one which involved her in using her talents to help those in need. A year's work in the field, physically assisting on an aid programme in one of the Third World countries, and then progressing to an administrative post where her skills could be best employed, had been Dee's career plan. Now, the closest she got to helping with Third World aid programmes was via the donations she made to their charities.

Her father's untimely death had made it impossible for her to carry on with her own plans—for more than one reason. Early on, in the days when she had dutifully taken over the control of his business affairs, there had been a spate of television programmes focusing on the work of some of the large Third World aid organisations. She had watched them with a mixture of anguish and envy, searching the lean, tanned faces hungrily, starving for the sight of a certain familiar face. She had never seen him, which was perhaps just as well. If she had…

Dee bit her bottom lip. What on earth was she doing? Her thoughts already knew that that was a strictly cordoned-off and prohibited area of her past, an area they were simply not allowed to stray into. What was the point? Faced with a choice, a decision, she had made the only one she could make. She could still remember the nightmare journey she had made back to Rye-on-Averton after the policeman had broken the news to her of her father's death—'a tragic accident,' he had called it, awkwardly. He had only been young himself, perhaps a couple of years older than her, his eyes avoiding hers as she'd opened the door to his knock and he'd asked if she was Andrea Lawson.

'Yes,' she had answered, puzzled at first, assuming that he was calling about some minor misdemeanour such as a parking fine.

It had only been when he'd mentioned her father's name that she had started to feel that cold flooding of icy dread rising numbingly through her body.

He had driven her back to Rye. The family doctor had already identified her father's body, so she had been spared that horrendous task, but of course there had been questions, talk, gossip, and despite the mainly solicitous concern of everyone who'd spoken with her Dee had been angrily conscious of her own shocking secret fear.

Abruptly Dee's thoughts skidded to a halt. She could feel the anger and tension building up inside her body. Carefully she took a deep breath and started to release it, and then just as carefully slid her car into a convenient parking spot.

Now that the initial agonising sharpness of losing her father had eased Dee wanted to do something beyond renovating Lawson House to commemorate his name and what he had done for his town. As yet she was not quite sure what format this commemoration would take, but what she did know was that it would be something that would highlight her father's generosity and add an even deeper lustre to his already golden reputation. He had been such a proud man, proud in the very best sense of the word, and it had hurt him unbearably, immeasurably, when...

She was, Dee discovered, starting to grind her teeth. Automatically she took another deep breath and then got out of her car.

In the wake of the arrival of the town's new motorway bypass there had also arrived new modern industry. Locally, the town was getting a reputation as the county's equivalent to America's silicone valley. The terrace of sturdy early Victorian four-storey houses where Peter lived had become a highly covetable and expensive resi-

dential area for the young, thrusting executive types who
had moved into the area via working in the new electron-
ics industries, and in a row of shiny and immaculately
painted front doors Peter's immediately stuck out as the
only shabby and slightly peeling one.

Dee raised the knocker and rapped loudly twice. Peter
was slightly deaf, and she knew that it would take him
several minutes to reach the door, but to her surprise
she had barely released the knocker when the door was
pulled open. Automatically she stepped inside and began,
'Goodness, Peter, that was quick. I didn't expect—'

'Peter's upstairs—in bed—he collapsed earlier.'

Even without its harshly disapproving tone the familiarity of the male voice, so very, very little changed despite the ten-year gap since she had last heard it, would
have been more than enough to stop her dead in her
tracks.

'Hugo…what…what are *you* doing *here*?'

As she heard the trembling stammer in her own voice
Dee cursed herself mentally. Damn! Damn! Did she *have*
to act like an awestruck seventeen-year-old? Did she have
to betray…?

She stopped speaking as Hugo started to shake his
head warningly at her. He pushed open the old-fashioned
front-parlour door and indicated that she was to go in.

Obediently Dee did so. She was still in shock, still
grappling to come to terms with his unexpected presence. It was years since she had last seen him.

When they had first met he had been a graduate whilst
she had still been a first year student. He had been working towards his Ph.D., a tall, quixotically romantic figure
with whom all her fellow female students had seemed to
be more than half in love. Even in a crowd as diverse and
individual as his peers had been, Hugo had immediately

stood out—literally so. At six foot three he had easily been one of the tallest and, it had to be said, one of the best-looking men on the campus, so strikingly and malely attractive that he would have automatically merited a second and a third look from any woman, even without his signature mane of shoulder-length thick dark hair.

Add to the attributes of his height and male physique—tautly muscled from playing several sports—the additional allure of shockingly sensual aquamarine eyes and a mouth with the kind of bottom lip that just automatically made a woman know how good it would be to be kissed by him, and it was no wonder that Hugo had been the openly discussed subject of nearly every female undergraduate's not-so-secret fantasies.

Dee had quite literally run into him as he was rushing to one of Peter's meetings one day.

Dee, who had heard about Hugo from the female grapevine, and who had glimpsed him to heart-stopping effect in and around the campus, had been astounded to discover that Hugo was a leading activist in Peter's small army of idealists and helpers.

'What do you mean, what am I doing here?' Hugo was challenging her now curtly. 'Peter and I go back a long way and—'

'Yes, yes, I know that,' Dee acknowledged. 'I just thought...'

She was in shock; she knew that. Her body felt icy cold, and yet at the same time as sticky and uncomfortable as though she was drenched in perspiration. Her heart was hammering frantically to a disjointed and dangerously discordant rhythm, and she suspected that she was actually in danger of hyperventilating as she tried to force some air into her tense lungs.

'You just thought what?' Hugo demanded tauntingly. 'That I was still carrying a torch for you? That I just couldn't go on living without you any longer…that my feelings for you, my love for you, was so strong that I just had to come looking for you…?'

Dee blenched beneath the witheringly sardonic tone of his voice. Was it really unbearably cold in this room or was it her…? She could feel herself starting to tremble. Only inwardly and invisibly at first, and then with increasing intensity until…

'How are your husband and your daughter?' Hugo asked her with obvious indifference. 'She must be…how old now…nine…?'

Dee stared at him. Her *husband*…her *daughter*… What husband…what daughter…?

Someone was knocking on Peter's front door.

'That will be the doctor,' Hugo announced before she could gather her confused thoughts and correct his misapprehensions.

'The doctor…?'

'Yes, Peter is very poorly. Excuse me, I'll go and let her in.'

Her! Peter's normal doctor wasn't a woman!

As she stood to one side a very attractive, cold-eyed brunette walked through the door towards Hugo, saying, 'Ah, Mr Montpelier. I'm Dr Jane Harper; we spoke on the phone.'

'We certainly did,' Hugo agreed, with far more warmth in his voice than there had been when he'd spoken to her, Dee noticed, digesting the unwanted recognition that knowledge brought as uncomfortably as though it had been a particularly unwelcome piece of food.

'Please, come this way,' Hugo was inviting the doctor, and she was smiling at him as though…

Angrily Dee swallowed down her own unpalatable thoughts.

CHAPTER TWO

PETER WAS VERY POORLY. She had known he wasn't well, of course, and had been getting increasingly concerned about him, but to hear Hugo describing him as 'very poorly' had come as an unpleasant shock to her. Anxiously Dee followed Hugo down the narrow hallway. She had seen the female appreciation in the other woman's eyes as Hugo had let her in, even if it had been quickly masked by her professionalism as she'd asked quickly after her patient.

She herself was quite obviously an unwanted third, Dee recognised as Hugo outlined Peter's symptoms to the doctor and she listened intently to him, positioning herself so that Dee was blocked out of Hugo's line of vision. Not that she minded that. She was still trying to come to terms with the shock of his totally unexpected presence.

The last time she had seen him he had been a rangy young man dressed in tee shirt and jeans, his wild mane of hair curling youthfully round his face. Initially his reputation as something of a rebel had caused Dee's father to be a little bit disapproving of him, but even her father could not have found fault with the appearance he presented now, Dee acknowledged as his absorption with the doctor gave her the opportunity to study him surreptitiously. The tee shirt and jeans had been exchanged for a smartly tailored business suit, and the dark hair was no longer shoulder-length but clipped neatly to his head, but the bone structure was still the same, and so were the aquamarine eyes and that dangerously sexy mouth. Dee's heart gave a dangerous little flutter—and that was something else which did not appear to have changed either!

Anxious to distract herself, as well as concerned for Peter, she started to walk towards the stairs.

'Where are you going?' Hugo demanded, breaking off his quiet conversation with the doctor.

'I thought I'd go up and see Peter...' Dee began, but immediately both the doctor and Hugo began to shake their heads in denial.

Feeling thoroughly chastised, Dee tried to conceal her chagrin.

'I'd better go up and see him,' the doctor was saying to Hugo.

'Yes. I'll come with you,' he agreed.

Both of them were totally ignoring Dee. To suffer such ignominy was a totally unfamiliar experience for her, and not one she was enjoying, but there was no way she intended to leave—not until she had discovered how Peter was.

It was ten minutes before the doctor and Hugo came back downstairs, and Dee's anxiety for Peter overcame her outraged pride enough for her to ask quickly as they walked into the room, 'How is he? What's wrong with him? Will...?'

'He's got a weak heart and he's been overdoing things,' the doctor told her matter-of-factly. 'Trying to move some books, apparently. He really shouldn't be living on his own, not at his age. He ought to be living in some kind of sheltered accommodation since he doesn't appear to have any family, and in view of his recent operation.'

'Oh, no, that would be the last thing he would want…' Dee began to protest. but the doctor was already turning away from her.

'He was fortunate that you were here when he collapsed and that you knew what to do,' she said warmly to Hugo. 'If he'd continued to try to lift those books…' She stopped, and Dee told herself sternly that she was being unfair in thinking that what Hugo had done was quite simply what any person with any sense would have done, and scarcely seemed to warrant his elevation to the rank of a super-hero as the doctor seemed to suggest.

'I'll make some arrangements with the social services for some home help for him,' the doctor told Hugo, once again totally excluding Dee from the conversation.

'Oh,' she added, suddenly turning to glance dismissively at Dee. 'He wants to see you…'

'I told him you were here,' Hugo informed her briefly as Dee hurried towards the door.

Was she being unkind in suspecting that the doctor wanted to have Hugo to herself? And if she did what business was it of hers? Dee thought as she hurried upstairs.

Peter looked very small and frail lying there in bed, the sunshine pouring through the open windows highlighting the thin boniness of his hands.

'Peter!' Dee exclaimed warmly as she sat down beside him and reached for one of his hands, holding it tightly.

'Dee, Hugo said you were here… Now, you're not to worry,' Peter told her before she could say anything. 'Hugo is just fussing. I just felt a little bit short of breath, that's all. There was no need for him to call the doctor…

'Dee…' Suddenly he looked very fretful and worried. 'You won't let them send me…anywhere…will you? I want to stay here. This is my home. I don't want…'

Dee could see how upset he was getting.

'Peter, it's all right. You're not going anywhere,' Dee tried to reassure him.

'The doctor was saying that I ought to be in a home,' Peter told her anxiously. 'I know. I heard her…she…'

He was starting to get even more upset, increasing Dee's concern for him.

'Peter, don't worry…' She started to comfort him, but as she did so the bedroom door opened and Hugo came hurrying in, glowering at her as he strode protectively to Peter's side.

'What have you been saying to him?' he demanded acerbically. 'You're upsetting him…'

She was upsetting him? Of all the nerve.

'Peter, it's all right,' she promised her father's old friend gently, deliberately ignoring Hugo—not an easy feat with a man the size Hugo was, and even less easy when one took into account his overpowering sexual charisma. 'The only home I would ever allow you to move into would be mine, and that's a promise…'

Out of the corner of her eye Dee could see the way Hugo's mouth was tightening.

What was he doing here anyway? She had had no idea that Peter still had any contact with him. He had certainly never mentioned Hugo to her.

'I don't want to go anywhere; I want to stay here,' Peter was complaining fretfully, plucking agitatedly at the bedcover as he did so. Dee's tender heart ached for him. He looked so vulnerable and afraid, and she knew, in her heart of hearts, that for his own sake he ought not to be left to live on his own. Somehow she would have to find a way to persuade him to come to live with her, but he would, she knew, miss his university friends, the old colleagues he still kept in touch with.

'And staying here's exactly what you shall do—at least

so long as I have any say in the matter,' Hugo told him firmly.

Dee glowered at him. It was all very well for Hugo to make promises that were impossible to keep. And as for him having any say in the matter…!

But before she could say anything, to her astonishment she heard Peter demanding in a shaky voice, 'You are going to stay here, then, are you, Hugo? I know we talked about it, but…'

'I'm staying,' Hugo agreed, but although he said the words gently the look in his eyes as he looked across the bed at her made Dee feel more as though he was making a threat against *her* than a promise to Peter. What on earth was going on? What was Hugo doing here? There were so many questions she wanted—*needed*—to ask Peter, but it was obvious that he was simply not well enough to answer her—and that knowledge raised other concerns for Dee.

Peter shared with her the legal responsibility for administering the charities her father had established, and, whilst technically and practically speaking the work involved was done by Dee, via her offices in Rye-on-Averton, so far as legally rubber-stamping any decisions was concerned Peter was her co-signatory, and his authority was a legal requirement that had to be adhered to. He, of course, had the right to nominate another person to take over that responsibility for him, and Dee had always assumed that, when the time came, they would discuss who would take on that duty. Now it seemed it could well be a discussion she was going to have to have with him rather earlier than she had expected.

Peter was a gentleman of the old school, with the old-fashioned belief that women—'ladies'—needed a strong male presence in their lives to lean on, and Dee knew that he secretly deplored the fact that she had never married and had no husband to 'protect' her. She suspected too that he had never totally approved of the licence and authority her father had left to her so far as his financial interests went, and she often wondered a little ruefully what Peter would have thought had he known that her father had appointed him as a co-trustee for Peter's benefit and protection rather than for hers.

'His ideas, his ideals are more than praiseworthy,' her father had once told her, adding with a sad shake of his head, 'But...'

Dee had known what her father meant, and very tactfully and caringly over the years she had ensured that Peter's pride was never hurt by the realisation that her father had considered him to be not quite as financially astute as he himself believed he was.

In less than a week's time Dee was due to chair the AGM of their main committee. There were certain changes she wished to make in the focus and operation of her father's local charity, and she had been subtly lobbying Peter and the other members of the committee to this end.

Her main aim was to focus the benefit of the revenue the charity earned, from public donation and the endowments her father had made to it, not on its present recipients but instead on the growing number of local young people Dee felt were desperately in need of their help. Her fellow committee members, people of her father's generation in the main, would, she knew, take some convincing. Conservative, and in many ways old-fashioned, they were not going to be easy to convince that the young people they saw as brash and even sometimes dangerous were desperately insecure and equally desperately in need of their help and support. But Dee was determined to do it, and as a first step towards this she needed to en-list Peter's support and co-operation as her co-signatory.

She had already made overtures to him, suggesting that it was time for them to consider changing things, but it would be a slow process to thoroughly convince him, as she well knew, and she had sensed that he was already a little bit alarmed by her desire to make changes.

Peter had fallen asleep. Quietly Dee stood up and started to move towards the bedroom door, but Hugo got there first, not just holding it open for her but following her through and down the stairs.

'There's really no need for you to stay here with Peter,' Dee began firmly once they were both downstairs. 'I could—'

'You could what? Move him into your own home? What about your own family, Dee...your husband and child? Or is it children now? No, Peter will be much more comfortable where he is. After all, if you'd genuinely wanted him there you'd have taken steps to encourage him to live with you before now, instead of waiting until he's practically at death's door...'

Death's door! Dee's heart gave a frightened bound.

'I *did* try to persuade him,' she defended herself, ignoring Hugo's comment about her non-existent husband and family in the urgency of her desire to protect herself from his criticisms. 'You don't understand...

Peter's very proud. His friends, his whole life is here in Lexminster...'

'You heard what the doctor said,' Hugo continued inexorably. 'He's too old and frail to be living in a house like this. All those stairs alone, never mind—'

'It's his *home*,' Dee repeated, and reminded him quickly, 'And you heard what he said about wanting to stay here...'

'I heard a frightened old man worrying that he was going to be bundled out of the way to live amongst strangers,' Hugo agreed. 'At least that's one problem we don't have to deal with in Third World countries. Their people venerate and honour their old. We can certainly learn from them in that respect.'

Third World countries. It had always been Hugo's dream to work with and for the people in such countries, but a quick discreet look at his hands—lean, strong, but not particularly tanned, his nails immaculate—did not suggest that he had spent the last ten years digging wells and latrines, as they had both planned to do once they left university.

How idealistic they had both been then, and how furiously angry Hugo had been with her when she had told him that she had changed her mind, and that it was her duty to take over her father's responsibilities.

'You mean that money matters more to you than people?' he had demanded.

Fighting to hide her tears, Dee had shaken her head. 'No!'

'Then prove it...come with me...'

'I can't. Hugo, please try to understand.'

She had pleaded with him, but he had refused to listen to her.

'Look, if I'm going to stay here with Peter there are one or two things I need to do, including collecting my stuff from my hotel. Can you stay here?'

The sound of Hugo's curt voice brought Dee abruptly back to the present.

'Can you stay here with him until I get back?'

Tempted though she was to refuse—after all, why should she do anything to help Hugo Montpelier?—her concern for Peter was too strong to allow her to give in to the temptation.

'Yes, I can stay,' she agreed.

'I'll be as quick as I can,' Hugo told her, glancing frowningly at his watch. A plain, sturdy-looking one, Dee noticed, but she also noticed that it was a rather exclusive make as well. His clothes looked expensive too, even if very discreetly so. But then there had always seemed to be money in Hugo's background, much of it tied up in land, even if he had preferred to make his own way in his university days. His grandmother had come from a prosperous business family, and she had married into the lower levels of the aristocracy.

In Hugo's family, as in her own, there had been a tradition of helping others, but Hugo had dismissed his grandfather's 'good works' as patronage of the worst kind.

'People should be helped to be independent, not dependent, encouraged and educated to stand free and proud...'

He had spoken so stirringly of his beliefs...his plans.

Dee longed to reiterate that he had no need to concern himself with Peter, that *she* would take full responsibility for his welfare, but she sensed that he would enjoy dismissing her offer of help. She had seen the dislike and the contempt darkening his eyes as he'd looked at her, and she had seen too the way his mouth had curled as he had openly studied her as she crossed Peter's bedroom floor.

What had he seen in her to arouse that contempt? Did he perhaps think the length of her honey-blonde hair was too youthful for a woman in her thirties? Did he find her caramel-coloured trousers with their matching long coat dull and plain, perhaps, compared with the clothes of the no doubt very youthful and very attractive women *he* probably spent his time with? Did it amuse him to see the way the soft cream cashmere of her sweater discreetly concealed the soft swell of her breasts when he had good reason to know just how full and firm they actually were?

What did it matter *what* Hugo thought? Dee derided herself as he turned away from her and strode towards the door. After all, he had made it plain enough just how little he cared about *her* thoughts or her feelings. She shivered a little, as though the room had suddenly gone very cold.

Ten minutes after Hugo had left Dee heard Peter coughing upstairs. Anxiously she hurried up to his room, but to her relief as she opened his bedroom door she saw that he was sitting up in bed, smiling reassuringly at her, his colour much warmer and healthier than it had been when she had seen him earlier.

'Where's Hugo?' he asked Dee as she returned his smile.

'He's gone to collect his things,' she answered him. It hurt a little to recognise how eager he was to have the other man's company—and, it seemed, in preference to her own.

'How are you feeling?' she asked him. 'Would you like a drink…or something to eat?'

'I'm feeling fine, and, yes, a cup of tea would be very welcome, Dee.' He thanked her.

It didn't take her very long to make it, and she carried the tray upstairs to Peter. In addition to his tea she had made him some delicately cut little sandwiches, as well as buttering two of the home-made scones she had brought with her for him. She knew he had a weakness for them, and couldn't help smiling at the enthusiasm he exhibited when he saw them.

'I didn't realise that you and Hugo had kept in touch,' she commented carefully when she was pouring his tea. He had insisted that he didn't either need or want to go back to sleep.

'Mmm… Well, to be honest, we hadn't…didn't. But then I happened to run into him a few months ago quite by chance. He was here in Lexminster on business and we were both guests at the same drinks do. I wasn't sure it was him at first…but then he came over and introduced himself.'

'Mmm…he has changed,' Dee agreed, bending her head over the teapot as she poured her own tea and hoping that her voice wasn't giving her away. *She* would have recognised Hugo anywhere—there were some things that were just too personal ever to be changed. The aura that surrounded a person's body, which one knew instinctively once one had been permitted within their most intimate personal space, their scent, as highly individual as their fingerprints, and even the way they breathed. These were things that could not be changed.

'What's he actually doing these days?' she enquired as carelessly as she could.

'Hasn't he told you? He's the chief executive in charge of a very special United Nations aid programme. As I understand it, from what he's told me, their plan is to educate and help the people they're dealing with to become self-sufficient and to combat the ravages of the years of drought their land has suffered. He's very enthusiastic about a new crop they're still working on, which, if it's successful, will help to provide nearly forty per cent of the people's protein requirements.'

'That *is* ambitious,' Dee acknowledged.

'Ambitious and expensive,' Peter agreed. 'The crop is still very much in the early experimental stages. The whole scheme involves huge amounts of international funding and support, and one of Hugo's responsibilities is to lobby politicians for those funds. He was saying that he'd much prefer to be working in the field, but as I reminded him he always did have a first-class brain. At one time I even thought he might continue with his studies and make a career in academics himself, but he was always such a firebrand…'

A firebrand. Dee had thought of him more as a knight in shining armour, rescuing not distressed damsels but others less fortunate than himself and with far more important needs. Being romantic and idealistic herself, it had seemed to her that Hugo had met every one of her impossibly high ideals and criteria, morally…emotionally…and sexually… Oh, yes, quite definitely sexually! Her virginal reluctance to commit herself physically to a man had been totally and completely swept away by the passion that Hugo had aroused in her. Utterly, totally and completely. She hadn't so much as timidly crossed her virginal Rubicon as flung herself headlong and eagerly into its tumultuous erotic flood!

'You should talk with him, Dee,' Peter was continuing enthusiastically. 'He's got some very good ideas.'

'Mmm… I hardly think learning to grow our own protein is a particularly urgent consideration for the residents of Rye,' Dee couldn't resist pointing out a little dryly.

It irked her a little to be told she should crouch eagerly at Hugo's feet, as though he were some sort of master and she his pupil. In fact, it irked her rather more than just a little, she admitted. She might not have completed her degree course—her father's death had put an end to that—and she had certainly not been able to go on to obtain her doctorate, but what she had learned both from her father and through her own 'hands-on' experience had more than equipped her to deal proficiently and, she believed, even creatively with the complexities and demands of her own work. So far as she was concerned she certainly did not need Hugo's advice or instruction on how to manage her business.

'You've got a definite flair for finance,' her father had told her approvingly, and Dee knew without being immodest that he had been quite right.

She also knew she had a reputation locally for being not just astute but also extremely shrewd. Her father, on the other hand, had been almost too ready to trust in other people's honesty, to believe that they were as genuine and philanthropic as he himself had been, which was why…

'Dee, you aren't listening to me,' Peter was complaining tetchily.

'Oh, Peter, I'm sorry,' Dee apologised soothingly.

'I was just saying about Hugo, and about how you would be well-advised to seek his advice. I know your father was very proud of you, Dee, and that he meant it for the best when he left you in charge of his business affairs, but personally I've always felt that it's a very heavy burden for you to carry. If you'd married it might have been different. A woman needs a man to lean on,' Peter opined.

Dee forced herself not to protest. Peter meant well, she reminded herself. It was just that he was so out of step with modern times. It didn't help, of course, that he had never married, and so had never had a wife or daughter of his own.

'By the way, did you ever find out what had happened to that Julian Cox character?' Peter asked her.

Immediately Dee froze.

'Julian Cox? No…why do you ask?' Warily she waited for his response.

'No reason; it was just that Hugo and I were talking over old times and I remembered how badly your father was taken in by Cox. That was before we knew the truth about him, of course. Your father confessed to me—'

'My father barely knew Julian,' Dee denied fiercely. 'And he certainly had no need to confess anything to anyone!'

'Maybe not, but they were on a couple of charity committees together. I remember your father being very impressed by some of Julian's ideas for raising money,' Peter insisted stubbornly. 'It was such a tragedy, your father dying when he did. To lose his life like that, and in such a senseless accident…'

Dee's mouth had gone dry. She always hated talking about her father's death. As Peter was saying, it had been a tragic, senseless way to die.

'Hugo said as much himself…'

Dee felt as though her heart might stop beating.

'You were discussing my father's death with Hugo?'

The sharp, shocked tone of her voice caused Peter to look uncertainly at her.

'Hugo brought it up. We were talking about your father's charity work.'

Dee tried to force herself to relax. Her heart was thudding heavily as anxiety-induced adrenalin was released into her bloodstream.

'I'm a little bit concerned about this bee you've got in your bonnet about these young people, Dee,' Peter was saying now, a little bit reprovingly. 'I'm not sure that your father would have approved of what you're trying to do. Being philanthropic is all very well, but these youngsters…' He paused and cocked his head. 'I applaud your concern for them, but, my dear, I really don't think I can agree that we should fund the kind of thing you've got in mind.'

Dee's heart started to sink. She had always known it

would be difficult to convince Peter to support what she wanted to do, and the last thing she wanted to do now was to upset him by arguing with him. She had no idea how serious his condition might be, and she suspected that any attempt on her part to find out would be met with strong opposition from Dr Jane Harper. If it were Hugo, now, who wanted to know…! She was being unfair, Dee warned herself mentally—unfair and immature. But that didn't mean that she wasn't right!

'What exactly *is* Hugo doing in Lexminster?' she asked Peter, trying to give his thoughts a new direction.

'It's business,' Peter told her vaguely.

'Business?' Dee raised her eyebrows. 'I thought you said his work involved lobbying politicians for international support for his aid programme.'

'Yes. It does,' Peter agreed. 'But Lexminster University has access to certain foundation funds which have been donated over the years to be used as the university sees fit.'

'For charitable causes,' Dee agreed. She knew all about such foundations.

'Hugo hopes to get the university to agree to donate all or part of them to his aid programme.'

'But *I* thought they were supposed to be used to benefit university scholars' projects.'

'Hugo *was* a university scholar,' Peter reminded her simply. Yes, he had been, and Peter was on the committee that dealt with the disbursement of those funds, as Dee already knew. She started to frown. Was Hugo's desire to move in with Peter and take care of him as altruistic as it had initially seemed? The Hugo she had known would certainly never have stooped to such tactics. But then the Hugo she had known would never have worn a Savile Row suit, nor a subtly expensive and discreet cologne that smelled of fresh mountain air just warmed by a hint of citrus.

Dee was becoming increasingly alarmed at the thought of leaving Peter on his own with Hugo, but she sensed that it wouldn't be wise to express her doubts. From what Peter had already said to her it was obvious that for him Hugo could do no wrong.

Dee was frowning over this unpalatable knowledge when she heard someone knocking on the front door.

'That will be Hugo!' Peter exclaimed with evident pleasure. 'You'd better go and let him in.'

Yes, and no doubt lie prone in the hallway so that he could wipe his boots on her, Dee decided acidly as she got up off the bed.

CHAPTER THREE

'How's Peter?' Hugo asked Dee tersely as she opened the door to him.

'He seems a lot better, although I'm sure that Dr Jane Harper would be delighted to give you a much more professional opinion if you wanted one,' Dee responded wryly, forcing herself not to wince as Hugo's glance swept her from head to foot with open dislike.

'It's odd how one's memory can play tricks on one. I had a distinct memory of you being an intelligent woman, Dee.'

'Well, I'm certainly intelligent enough to wonder what it is that makes *you* so anxious to help Peter.'

As Dee stressed the word 'you' she could see the anger flashing like lightning in Hugo's eyes. It gave her an odd, sharp stab of pain-tipped pleasure to know that she had drawn such a reaction from him, even whilst she had to force herself to blot out of her memory the knowledge that once there had been a time when that lightning look had been born of the urgency of his desire *for* her, instead of the urgency of his ire *against* her.

'I am anxious to help him, as you put it, because it concerns me that he should so obviously be on his own,' Hugo replied pointedly.

'He isn't on his own; he's got me,' Dee protested fiercely.

Immediately Hugo's eyebrows rose.

'Oh…? He told me that the last time he had seen you was over two weeks ago.'

Angrily Dee frowned.

'I try to see him as often as I can, but—'

'Other people have a prior claim on your time?' Hugo suggested. 'Be honest, Dee, *you* couldn't have moved in here to take care of him, could you?'

'He could have come to Rye with me,' Dee protested, without answering his question. 'And if you hadn't been here he would have.'

'He would? Yes, I'm sure he would. But would that have been what he really wanted? He wants to stay here, Dee. This is his home. His books, his things, his memories…his *life*…are all here.'

'Maybe, but you can't stay with him for ever, can you, Hugo? And what's going to happen to him once you've gone?'

'Since, for the foreseeable future, I'm going to be based in the UK, there's nothing to stop me from making my home here in Lexminster if I choose to do so. It's convenient for the airport and—'

'You're planning to live *permanently* in Lexminster…?'

Dee couldn't help her consternation from showing in her voice, and she knew that Hugo had recognised it from the look he gave her.

'What's wrong?' he taunted her. 'Don't you *like* the thought of me living here?'

'No, I don't,' Dee told him truthfully, too driven by the way he was goading her and the shock of what he had just told her to be cautious or careful. 'I don't like it at all.'

'Oh, and why not, I wonder? Or can I guess? Could it have something to do with this...?'

And then, before she could guess what he intended to do, he had dropped the hold-all he was carrying and pinned her back against the wall, his hands hard and strong on her body as he held her arms, his body so close to her own that she could feel its fierce male heat engulfing her.

Once, being held like this by him would have thrilled and excited her, her awareness of the danger he was inciting only heightening her intense desire for him. The sex between them had been so passionately explosive that for years after he had gone she had still dreamed about it...and about him, waking up drenched in perspiration, longing for him, aching for him; and now, like a faint reflection of those feelings, she could feel her body starting to shudder and her nipples starting to harden beneath the practical protection of her jumper.

'Cashmere... Do you know how many Third World people the cost of this would feed...?' she heard Hugo murmuring contemptuously as his fingers touched the soft fabric of her sleeve. His mouth was only centimetres from her own, and Dee knew that merely to breathe would bring it even closer, but she still couldn't resist the urge to verbally defend herself. After all, it wasn't as if he was any less expensively dressed.

'It was a present,' she told him angrily. 'From a friend.'

'A friend...' Hugo's eyebrows rose. 'A *friend*, and not your husband?'

'I don't *have* a husband,' Dee gritted furiously.

'No husband!'

Something hot and dangerous flared in his eyes and Dee started to panic, but it was too late. The damage had already been done, the tinder lit.

'No husband,' Hugo repeated thickly. 'What did he do, Dee? Refuse to play the game your way…just like I did…?'

'No. I—'

Dee gave a gasp and then made a small shocked sound as the pressure of Hugo's mouth on her own prevented her from saying *anything* else.

It had been so long since she had been kissed like this. So long since she had been kissed at all. So long since she had felt… Hungrily her mouth opened under Hugo's, and equally hungrily her hands reached for him.

She was reacting to him as though she was starving for him…dying for him, Dee recognised as she fought to control the primeval flood of her own desire. Her reaction to him must be something to do with all her dredging up of the past, she decided dizzily. It couldn't be because she still wanted him, not after all these years… Years when she had been willingly and easily celibate…years when the *last* thing she had ever imagined herself doing was something like this. He was kissing her properly now, releasing her arms to cup her face.

Dee gave a gasping moan beneath her breath as his tongue traced the shape of her lips. If he kept on kissing her like this… Beneath her sweater she could feel the taut ache in her breasts—an ache that was already spreading wantonly even deeper through her body.

Against her mouth Hugo was saying tauntingly, 'No husband, you say. Well, it certainly shows.'

Immediately Dee came to her senses. Angrily she pushed him away, managing to lever herself off the wall as she did so.

'I've heard the rumours about women of a certain age, with their biological clocks ticking away, but…'

'But you prefer them slightly younger…around Dr

Jane's age, no doubt,' was the only reply that Dee's shaking lips could frame.

She was totally stunned by her own behaviour, her own reaction, her own feelings. What on earth had she thought she was doing? She felt as though she had been subjected to a whirlwind which had sprung up out of nowhere, leaving her…devastated.

'What I prefer is…my business,' he told her quietly, and then, whilst she was still trying to pull herself together, he demanded curtly, 'How long have you been divorced?'

'Divorced!' Dee stared at him. 'I'm *not* divorced,' she told him weakly. She saw the look on his face and then added angrily, 'I'm not divorced because I have *never* been married.'

'Not married? But I was told… I heard…' He was frowning at her. 'I heard that you'd married your cousin and that you had a daughter…'

Dee thought quickly. Two of her cousins *had* married, and they *did* have a daughter of nine now, but she didn't tell Hugo so, simply shrugging instead, and informing him dismissively, 'Well, I'm afraid you heard wrong. That's what listening to gossip does for you,' she added pointedly. 'I'm not married, I don't have a daughter, and I'm most certainly not a victim of my biological clock.' Two truths—one fib. But she was determined that Hugo wasn't going to know that!

'You wanted children so much. I can remember that that was one of the things we used to argue about. I wanted us to wait until we'd had a few years together before we started a family, but you were insistent that you wanted a baby almost straight away, just as soon as we were married.'

As he spoke automatically Dee reached for the bare

place on her ring finger which had once carried his special ring—a family heirloom he had given her to mark their commitment to one another.

'So that's two things we still have in common,' she said. 'Neither of us is married and neither of us has children.'

'Three things, in fact, when you count…' He was looking at her mouth, Dee recognised, and beneath her sweater the ache in her breasts became an open yearning pulse.

'Three…?' she managed to question croakily, ignoring the savage tug of her own newly awakened sexuality.

'Mmm…both of us are involved in fundraising for charitable organisations. I'd better go up and see Peter,' he added calmly.

'Er, yes…I…' She was behaving as foolishly as though she were still the teenage girl he had knocked off her bicycle as he'd come flying round the corner on his way to one of Peter's meetings—a meeting he had never actually attended. By the time he had picked her up and carefully checked her over for bruises or any other damage, and then insisted on taking her for a restorative cup of coffee, Peter's meeting had been over—but their love affair had just been beginning.

Half an hour later Dee had said goodbye to Peter and was on her way back home. The dazzling sun shining through her windscreen was making her head start to ache—or was her headache being caused by something far more personal?

She still couldn't believe she had reacted the way she had to Hugo's kiss. It was just so totally foreign to her nature to allow herself to get so out of control, never mind to exhibit such naked sexual hunger… How Hugo must have been laughing at her, enjoying her self-inflicted humiliation, enjoying her eager desire for him…her need…

Groaning under her breath, Dee suddenly realised that she was almost in danger of overtaking a car which was in the outside lane of the motorway whilst she was on the inside one, and quickly she took her foot off the accelerator.

She shouldn't be thinking about Hugo. By rights what she ought to be concentrating on was the problems Peter's continuing ill health could cause her professionally. Perhaps now was the time to tactfully find a way of persuading him to relinquish his role on the committee, but there was no way she would want to broach such a subject with him if it was going to adversely affect his health. Just exactly what *was* wrong with him she would have to find out, but she suspected that the only way she was going to be able to do that was through Hugo.

It galled her pride to even think of having to ask for Hugo's assistance, but the work of the charity was far too important for her to let her own pride stand in its way— for her father's sake.

Her father. Dee could feel her eyes start to sting with tears, hot and acid, too painful to be allowed to fall.

'Oh, Dad,' she whispered under her breath.

'Accidental death,' the coroner had pronounced gravely at the inquest, and even then Dee had not cried. She had wanted to…needed to…but she had been too afraid to do so, afraid that even now someone might still stand up and say the word she had so dreaded to hear—'suicide.' No one had said it openly to her, or even hinted at it in her presence, but she had heard it nonetheless in her nightmares, whispered malevolently on the fetid breath of envy that could so easily have destroyed her father's reputation and everything he had worked so proudly for.

Suicide. The taking of his own life because he had been too afraid…too ashamed…

Suicide. But it had *not* been. He had *not* taken his own life…he had *not* destroyed his own reputation even if Julian Cox had. Julian Cox…

The floodgates were open now, and the memories could not be held back any longer. Impatiently Dee drove up the slip road and off the motorway, anxious to be safely at home before she was swept under in their powerful undertow.

Julian Cox, her father, and most of all Hugo; those were the ghosts who inhabited her past, the ghosts she had fought so strenuously to hold at bay. Julian Cox, her father, Hugo…and the saddest and most forlorn ghost of them all: the ghost of the love she and Hugo had once shared.

She could feel her tears now, as sharp and painful as splintered shards of glass, burning her eyes, but she must not let them fall yet, not until she was safely in the privacy of her own home.

Hugo… Hugo… Why…why had he come back…?

The sun was still shining, its evening rays casting a warm mellow golden glow over her driveway and home as Dee brought her car to a halt in front of the house where she had been brought up. But she was oblivious to the tranquil serenity of her surroundings as she got out of the car and headed for the house.

Once inside, she hurried into the elegant drawing room which she only really used when she was entertaining, tugging open the doors to the drinks cabinet and searching inside it for something—anything—that would help to blot out the emotional pain she was feeling. Something—*anything*—that would act as a protective buffer between her and the thoughts she did not want, the feelings she did not want, the *past* she didn't want.

Her fingers curled round the cool glass of a bottle. Whisky. It had been her father's favourite but very rare bedtime treat.

Through the tears still blurring her eyes Dee looked at the bottle, and then very carefully and very slowly she replaced it in the cabinet and closed the doors. Squaring her shoulders, she walked firmly out of the room and headed for the kitchen.

As she shrugged off her coat and reached for the kettle she closed her eyes. Her father had been a man of such strong principles and such great pride, and in no area of his life had he had more pride than in his love for his daughter. He had been a quiet, gentle man, reserved in many ways, but Dee had never, ever doubted that he loved her.

After the death of her mother, when she had been so very young, he had brought her up on his own, declining to take the advice of his many female relatives and either hire someone to look after her or, once she was old enough, send her away to boarding-school. Perhaps the way he had brought her up *had* been a little old fashioned, perhaps she *had*, as one of her aunts had once criticised, become a small adult whilst she was still a child, perhaps she *had*, through her father, developed too strong a sense of duty and too weak a capacity to have fun, but she had been a happy child, a much loved child; she had never doubted that.

Yes, there had been times when she had longed almost passionately for her mother, when she had wondered, especially as she had matured, just how different she might have been had she had the benefit of a maternal womanly influence. And, yes, there had perhaps been times when she had felt that her father's standards were almost impossibly high, when she had felt that he was a little too remote, when she had longed a little rebelliously for her life to possess more fun and less responsibility, less duty.

The kettle was boiling. Dee made herself a cup of coffee, carrying the mug with her as she walked from the kitchen into her study.

On her desk were the notes she had made on the scheme she was hoping to persuade Peter to lend his support to. It *was* ambitious; she knew that. Foolhardy, she knew others might say, although she preferred to use the words 'innovative' and 'adventurous.'

Whilst, technically, she and Peter had charge of the finances of the foundation her father had established before his death, morally she felt obliged to take into account the views of the other committee members, especially since part of the charity's income came from public donations.

What Dee really wanted to do with the money was to establish workshops where local youngsters could learn a proper trade. She couldn't lay claim to her idea being original. Anna's husband, the millionaire philanthropist Ward Hunter, had already done something similar in the northern town where he had been brought up.

There had been a time when Ward and Dee had been at loggerheads, due to a misunderstanding between them, but now they got on extremely well together, respecting one another's financial acumen and moral strengths.

Ward had already promised to give Dee all the help she needed in setting up her workshops, but, of course, Ward could not convince the foundation's committee to support her.

She had already found an almost perfect site for her venture: a large, empty late-Victorian villa on the outskirts of the town, with plenty of land and, even better, a large range of outbuildings.

Ward's apprentices learned their trades in a similar environment, but Dee, her maternal streak coming to the fore, also wanted to convert rooms in the main house into small bedsits for her young trainees.

It was, she knew, a very ambitious scheme, and to show her own belief in it she had decided that she would make a large—a very large—private financial contribution towards it.

Once it was finished it would bear her father's name— a further tribute to him—a personal tribute from her to him.

Only the previous week, when she and Anna had been talking about Anna's coming baby, Anna had asked her gently if she had ever thought of marrying and having a family herself. Anna, gentle, kind, compassionate, was not the sort to pry, but Dee had been able to guess what she was thinking. They had been looking at the beautiful delicate layette, the little hand-embroidered items which Anna had bought for her baby, and Dee knew that her own envy had shown as she'd gently touched the tiny little garments.

She had smiled painfully, shaken her head and told Anna wryly that she was far too bossy and set in her ways for any man to want to put up with her. Of course Anna had demurred, but she had seen that Dee hadn't wanted to pursue the subject.

How could she have? How could she have said to Anna that deep within her own tender, vulnerable heart she knew that there was no way she could marry a man she did not love totally? No way she could marry a man she could not commit herself to utterly and completely, no way she could marry a man she could not trust utterly and completely. Only a man to whom she could tell her most secret hopes—and her most secret fears—and to whom she could reveal her inner self totally. And such a man, quite simply, did not exist.

There was no one, could be no one, to whom Dee could ever tell her deepest, darkest fears, to whom she could ever reveal her deepest and darkest secret. How could she, when the secret was not really her own, when to reveal the fear that had haunted her for so long would mean a potential betrayal of the man to whom she owed the deepest bond of loyalty there was—her father?

Once she had told someone else, *anyone* else, about the fear that lay over her life like a dark bruising shadow, once she had shared her fear, her doubt with someone else, it would be like opening Pandora's box. It would be like... Dee started to shiver.

'Sometimes I think you love your father more than you love me,' Hugo had once told her almost accusingly, when she had explained to him that she had to go home for the weekend to see her father.

'Not more,' she had reassured him. 'He's my father,' she had tried to explain.

Hugo had a different relationship with his parents than she'd had with her father. For a start he had two of them, a father *and* a mother, and he had siblings, an older brother and two sisters. And, in the tradition of the British upper classes, he had been sent away to boarding-school, and so, to him, the closeness which had existed between Dee and her father—their mutual dependence on one another, the loyalty and love she'd felt for him—had been hard for him to comprehend.

Hugo...

Dee wrapped her hands defensively around her coffee mug, giving up any attempt now to pretend that she was going to work. It had been such a shock to see him again, but nothing like as much of a shock as it had been when he had kissed her. And yet Hugo and kisses were linked inescapably together in her mind, her memories. The one impossible to detach from the other.

Hugo and kisses...

Dee sat back in her chair and let her mind drift...

CHAPTER FOUR

'Mmm… Just imagine what it would be like to be kissed by that…' Dee's companion murmured appreciatively as she rolled her eyes and cast a slumberously eager glance in Hugo's direction.

'Don't you mean him?' Dee corrected her primly, affecting not to be impressed by the picture of stunning male sensuality that Hugo made, taut muscles rippling down his back and arms as he pulled powerfully on the oars of the boat he was helping to crew.

'Mmm…what I wouldn't give for an hour on my own with him,' her fellow student breathed excitedly, ignoring Dee's disapproving shake of her head.

'Oh, come on,' she protested when Dee refused to relent. 'You can't pretend that you can't see how scrumptiously sexy he is.'

'He's very good-looking,' Dee conceded sedately.

'Good-looking! He's a hundred, million, zillion times more than just good-looking,' Mandy breathed blissfully. 'He's just a living, breathing, walking, talking hunk. He's… Oh, no, he's looking at us. He's looking at us,' she whispered frantically to Dee. 'Dee, he's looking at us…'

'No, he's not; he's squinting because the sun's in his eyes,' Dee corrected her, but for some reason her own heart had given a funny little throb as Hugo had turned his head and appeared to look over in their direction. She knew perfectly well what her companion had meant when she'd tried to find the words to describe Hugo's sexual appeal.

'Lord, but I think I'd die if he ever actually spoke to me. I mean, Hugo Montpelier. *The* man...*the* hunk... *the* dreamboat. He could have any girl he wanted, but he doesn't sleep around and he doesn't have a steady. One of the third years actually tried to ask him out, but he said that he didn't have time and that he was too busy. He's quite definitely hetero, though, no doubt about *that*. One of the girls taking Modern Languages told me that she'd managed to get a snog with him at one of last term's parties and that it was just to die for. She said she practically felt she might have an orgasm there and then, on the spot...'

Dee looked away. Her own sex drive was healthy enough, but her upbringing had been slightly old-fashioned. She had had dates, kissed boys, that kind of thing, and she knew that when she fell in love there would be no holding back from her, but she knew too that her passionate nature meant that she would only feel safe and secure giving herself completely in a relationship if she knew that her feelings were returned. Casual sexual experimentation, playful dabbling in the shallow waters of sexual curiosity were not for her. She was made for the deep, dangerous ocean, the primitive, primal life force of a sexuality that commanded and demanded total commitment from both sides—total commitment and total love.

But that did not mean that she was totally immune to the powerful aura of Hugo Montpelier's strongly male sexuality. He wore it like a banner, proudly and fiercely, and yet at the same time he wore it like a shield, protectively and defensively. Dee had heard all the gossip and speculation about him, the excited girl-chat that went on in the hyped-up, female-hormone-drenched atmosphere of their first-year halls. She had listened to the fevered and feverish uninhibited fantasies of her peers, which ranged from the foolishly idiotic to the frankly obscene.

Less than two months into her first term at university, she might still physically be a virgin but mentally her sexual knowledge had been expanded in a way that quite frankly had left her feeling slightly shocked.

One of the fantasies she had heard expressed regarding Hugo was whether he could last long enough to fully satisfy an excited pair of girls who had graphically described just what they would like to do with him if they had him in bed with them, and just what they would like him to do with them.

'Didn't you know? It's every man's special fantasy,' one girl had purred when she had seen Dee's shocked expression. 'And I should know,' she had added tellingly, grinning at Dee. 'Ask my twin sister. There isn't a man alive who doesn't think that he's got what it takes to satisfy two women at the same time.'

'Nor a woman alive who doesn't *know* that he hasn't,' another girl had muttered sardonically to Dee as she'd overheard the other girl's remark.

Three-in-a-bed romps might be what were in the minds of some of the girls who drooled over Hugo, but so far it seemed that none of them had managed to persuade him to join them. He had been seen escorting one girl, but she had simply turned out to be a friend of a friend and already virtually engaged, and he had been seen at a drinks party escorting the daughter of one of the university's Chairs, but she had since gone to America to finish her education.

'So it's open season on him,' one girl had declared

gleefully. 'And don't forget, whoever gets him, we all want a full report…'

Dee had left at that point. She wasn't a prude but… But what? But the images the others' comments had conjured up in her brain were far too private to be acknowledged, never mind shared. Not that Hugo was likely to ask her out. She suspected that she simply wouldn't be his type. He was so popular, so sought after, that no doubt when he did date a girl he would choose one who…who what? Who would make no bones about the fact that she was quite happy to jump into bed with him and have sex with him simply for sex's sake? Whilst she, Dee… No, they would have nothing in common.

Three days later, as though fate had overheard her and decided to teach her a lesson, she found out just how wrong her judgement had been.

There she was, riding her hired bicycle across the cobbles, struggling to control it, when Hugo came racing round the side of the building, the full weight of his body hitting her sideways on.

Neither she nor the cycle had stood any chance. He was six feet three and a sportsman, she was five feet nine and slim, the cycle was nearly twenty years old and rheumaticky; the result was inevitable. Regrettably the cycle, venerably ancient though it was, was left to fend for itself whilst Hugo went to Dee's rescue.

She was picked up, carefully dusted off, and even more carefully inspected for damage, and all the time Hugo was apologising to her in his deep rough voice that made her feel rather as if a cat was licking her skin with its rough tongue. But his hands as he touched her were anything but rough; he was so careful and tender with her. Her shirt, a neatly buttoned-up affair, had a rip in it and her jeans had dirt stains down one side. The combs had fallen out of her hair and there was a nasty patch of grazing on her index and middle fingers, where they had come into contact with the gravel, but otherwise she was all right—as Dee gravely assured Hugo.

'Thank goodness for that,' he said in relief. 'For a moment I thought I might really have hurt you.'

'It was an accident,' Dee felt bound to point out. It was very chivalrous of him to shoulder all the blame, especially when both of them knew that she shouldn't really have been cycling where she had.

'Look, I was on my way to a meeting, but would you let me buy you a coffee? You never know,' he told her gravely, 'you could be suffering from shock.'

There was no 'could be' about it, Dee admitted inwardly, though her shock wasn't caused by her fall but by the fact that he had actually offered to buy her a coffee, which must mean...

'You *have* hurt yourself,' she heard Hugo saying tersely as he suddenly caught sight of her fingers.

'Oh, my hand—that's nothing,' Dee denied, trying to tuck her grazed fingers out of sight behind her back just in case he decided that their gravel-pitted state meant that she wasn't fit to be seen in a coffee shop.

'Nothing...let me see.'

Before she could stop him he had taken hold of her hand and was gravely inspecting it. Dee wasn't small, and her hands were elegantly long and fine-boned, although when compared with Hugo's they suddenly looked almost deliciously frail and feminine.

Her heart tripping excitedly against her ribs, Dee watched as he carefully brushed away the bits of gravel adhering to her skin.

'This should really be cleaned,' he told her gravely. 'I've got rid of all the gravel, but...'

'It's fine,' Dee started to say, and then stopped, unable to speak, unable to draw breath, unable to do anything as Hugo lifted her fingers to his mouth and slowly and carefully started to suck on them.

Dee felt as though she was going to faint. The sensation was just so unbelievable, the warmth, the wetness, the slow, rhythmic sucking movement of his mouth.

She tried to protest, and managed to make a sound that came out like a small whimper, the merest breath, more easily recognisable as one of intense appreciation than one of protest.

Much later Hugo told her that he hadn't initially meant his action to be sexual. He had simply been genuinely concerned about the state of her hand and had reacted promptly and very much in the fashion of his own practical, prosaic country-bred mother, who had, when he was a small child, often 'cured' small childhood cut fingers and bruises with a cleansing maternal lick.

'All mother animals do it,' he told Dee simply.

'Yes,' she agreed, doe-eyed, 'but you weren't…you aren't my mother.'

'No,' he conceded, 'I'm not your mother.' And then he gently continued with what he had been doing, which was peeling her pretty lace bra away from the fullness of her breasts so that he could expose the dark pink crests to his ardent gaze and even more ardent mouth…

Although the area of the campus they were in when the accident happened was normally a busy one, today, for some unaccountable reason, no one else seemed to be around and they were, to all intents and purposes, alone, so that there was no one else to hear the small anguished sound of shocked virginal pleasure that Dee made, nor the totally male, all-male, all-possessive look that Hugo gave her in response. His gesture might not have begun nor been intended as sexually erotic, but by the time he slowly relinquished her fingers neither of them was in any doubt as to what it was or how it was affecting them—nor what it portended. Peter's meeting—their shared destination—was forgotten.

Dee walked at Hugo's side in a daze as he guided her, guarded her almost, keeping her body protectively and possessively close to his own, towards the café. Her bike he had disposed of, propped up against a wall. She would, no doubt, have to pay a hefty fine to the firm she had rented it from for the damage caused, inflicted on its ancient frame, but Dee didn't care. Quite simply she wasn't capable of caring about anything or anyone right now, and nor was Hugo.

The café Hugo chose was small and dark, smelling richly of fresh ground beans and thick with cigarette smoke. He guided her downstairs to its dimly lit cellar and to a small table tucked away in a natural alcove, his body shielding her from anyone's curious or predatory gaze.

He ordered for them both, a cappuccino for her and a coffee, plain, black and strong, for himself.

'I got used to drinking it like this last summer, when I was doing volunteer work in Africa,' he told her when their coffee arrived.

A simple enough statement, and yet it proved to be both the cornerstone and the basic foundation on which they went on to build their relationship, promoting between them a sense of shared purpose, an intimacy which Dee, with her upbringing, might have found very difficult to reach out for had they taken the route of learning about one another simply through their sexual desire for one another.

Much, much easier for her to let down her guard and

express a very natural and enthusiastic interest in his
voluntary work than to respond to him or acknowledge
her sexual awareness of him. Much easier for her to be
herself, to show herself and all the charming complexities of her delicately drawn personality through the questions he then asked her in return than if he had only been
able to communicate with her through the guarded protective response she might have made to merely sexual
overtures—which was not to say that there was no mental
or verbal communication between them; there was, very
much so. It surrounded them almost visibly and physically, crating so powerful an aura that the girl bringing
them their second and then their third cups of coffee
sighed enviously as she went back to the kitchen to tell
the girls there about the pair of besotted lovers sitting at
one of their tables.

They talked for so long that they missed Peter's meeting completely.

'I don't want to let you go,' Hugo told Dee as they
left the coffee shop and stood together on the busy street
outside. 'There's so much I want to tell you…so much I
want you to tell me. I want to know everything there is
to know about you, right from the day you were born.'

Dee laughed, flushed, and then laughed again, before
protesting, 'Oh, but that would take all night.' And then
she flushed again, but it wasn't embarrassment that was
making her skin glow so warmly. It was the way she was
feeling inside, just thinking about what it would be like
to spend the night with Hugo.

She saw that Hugo was smiling, a male glittery smile
that made her heart flip over. It made him look so dangerous, so attractive…so…so…sexy…

'So…?' he whispered.

'I…' Dee felt herself floundering, flustered and incoherent as she fought for some semblance of adult sophistication, some slick answer that would defuse the exciting tension building up between them.

But where another and more experienced girl might have teased, tongue-in-cheek—'so...persuade me'—all Dee could manage was a stammered, 'I can't... I don't...' She stopped and shook her head, and then told him with honest simplicity, 'I don't do things like that.' She saw his eyes widen before he gave her a swift, comprehensive look that rested on her mouth, her breasts, and then lower, before returning to her eyes.

'What...not ever?' he asked her gruffly.

From somewhere Dee found the courage to meet his eyes and hold his steady look.

'Not ever,' she confirmed.

'The tribe I was working with last summer have a tradition that whilst a girl has to marry a man chosen by her family she has the right to choose for herself the man who will be her first lover. It's considered the greatest honour a woman can bestow on a man, to choose him and to choose him out of love, to bestow on him her love and herself, and I happen to agree.'

Dee could feel herself starting to tremble, while her body had become taut with responsive desire.

'Of course, some of the men get a little bit impatient waiting to be chosen, and then they snatch away the girl of their choice in case she chooses someone else. They seduce her with gifts and kisses.'

His voice was dropping as he spoke to her, becoming lower and raw. Dee made a little husky sound of protest, and as her lips parted Hugo warned her thickly, '*Don't* do that. Otherwise *I* shall be the one stealing *you* away. Have dinner with me tonight,' he begged her abruptly, and then, when she hesitated, he told her, 'You needn't worry. I'm not suggesting… It will be somewhere safely public,' he told her gravely, 'for both our sakes. The way I feel about you…' He stopped and shook his head.

'In Africa a man considers himself to be very much a man, and his woman very much *his* woman, very, very responsive to *him*, and their love a sacred thing if she conceives his child the first time they make love. Here, in our so-called civilisation, things are different.

'Once you were in my arms I know that I wouldn't be able to stop myself from responding to man's most basic instinctive urge, to bury myself as deep inside you as I could, to give my seed, give our *child* the very best chance it could have of being conceived. And I know, too, that that would be the very worst thing that could happen to it and us right now… I've seen students struggling with domesticity and a baby. It doesn't work,' he told her flatly.

Dee was too shaken by his earlier comments to say anything. Deep down inside her body she could feel her *own* very basic response to *him*, and she knew that what he'd said had touched a deep cord within her.

Of course she didn't want to get pregnant. Of course she didn't. But of course she did—oh, how she did. But she couldn't…wouldn't…

'Do you understand what I'm trying to say to you?' Hugo was asking her tenderly. 'Dinner is all that I can let myself give you tonight, Dee, even though it's very far from all I *want* to give you. Very, very far. So will you, please, please have dinner with me?'

'Yes,' Dee responded simply.

After she left him she made a detour on her way back home to call at her doctor's surgery and ask for an appointment to discuss birth control. She knew she was blushing as she made her request, but the receptionist was completely matter-of-fact about the whole thing.

Dee knew that most of her fellow students were using one form of birth control or another.

'You *can't* leave it up to the men,' one of her house-sharers had commented bluntly as she had hunted in the bathroom for the small white pill she had lost as it popped out of the packet. 'After all, they are *our* bodies, and *we're* the ones who have the right to decide.'

'The right and the responsibility,' another girl had chimed in, a little bitterly. 'The two go hand in hand.'

Hand in hand... Dee looked down at where *her* hand was linked with Hugo's.

To her relief none of the others had been there when he had come to collect her.

'Nice place,' he commented as Dee closed the front door behind them. 'Must be quite pricey to rent, though, even sharing...'

'Not really...and it isn't rented. I'm actually buying it,' Dee told him casually. 'It's a good investment. Dad is helping me. I haven't made my mind up yet, but I may keep it on even when I've finished my degree course. The rental I could get will cover the mortgage and the running costs, and property prices are rising at the moment, so... In fact, I think it could be an idea to buy a few more, but to do that I'd have to ask Dad to let me break into my trust fund and I'm not sure—'

'Your trust fund?' Hugo gave her a sharp look. 'Now you're scaring me. That sounds like pretty serious money.'

Dee stopped walking to look uncertainly at him. She didn't normally speak so unguardedly to people about her personal background, but she felt so relaxed with him, and besides, he had talked about his days at public school and his own background, so she had assumed that his parents were financially well off.

Now it seemed she had been wrong.

'My family is land-rich but money-poor,' he told her dryly, correctly interpreting the questioning uncertainty in her eyes. 'They're rich in family connections and the ability to trace the family tree back to the Norman Conquest. There is money—yes—but it doesn't run to providing each of us with our own private trust funds...'

'Oh, but my father did that because without him I'd be on my own,' Dee protested, anxious to defuse what she feared was going to become a thorny issue between them.

'Yes, I can understand that,' Hugo responded gently. 'If you were mine *I* would want to protect and safeguard you too. I'm just surprised that he allowed you to come to university. From the sound of it I imagine he would have preferred to have you privately educated at home.'

Dee gave him a quick look, warily conscious of the irony beneath the seemingly sympathetic words.

'Perhaps he *is* a little bit old-fashioned,' she responded with quiet dignity, all her protective instincts coming to the fore as she sensed Hugo's unspoken criticism of the father she loved so much. 'But I would much rather have a father like that—a father I can look up to and admire... and trust, a man of...of compassion and...and honour... of integrity—than someone...'

Her voice became suspended with emotion at the thought that she and Hugo might already be on the verge of a quarrel, but immediately Hugo soothed her, gently stroking her hand as he apologised. 'I'm sorry... I shouldn't have implied... I guess I'm just jealous...' he told her whimsically. 'And not just of your trust fund...'

Of course that made her laugh, as he had intended it

236 THE MARRIAGE RESOLUTION

would, and she was secretly pleased he kept on holding her hand as they walked down the street together.

He hadn't said exactly where they were going, but Lexminster was a relatively compact city, and after the revelation about her trust fund she was reluctant to suggest that they could take her car to their destination.

Later, when she discovered the cavalier attitude Hugo had to driving-he had learned to drive in an ancient Land Rover on his grandfather's estate and further honed his 'skill' driving across the dry, mud-scarred ribbed and ridged empty riverbeds of the drought-ridden area where he had done his voluntary work—she would be glad she had not been subjected to it on their first date.

It was a late November evening, with just a warning that frost might be in the air later. The autumn had been fine and dry, and the leaves were still at the delicious stage of rustling pleasurably beneath one's feet when walked on, their scent evocative and slightly pungent on the clear air as they walked down the tree-lined main street of the city.

The restaurant Hugo had chosen was a small Italian family-run place, down a narrow side street, and Dee fell in love with it and the family who owned and ran it the moment they walked in.

They greeted Hugo like a member of the family, Luigi, the burly grey-haired patron, punching him genially on the shoulder and then wincing in mock pain and shaking his arm.

'He is built like an ox…like a bull,' he amended, with a laughing look in Dee's direction.

Of course she blushed, and of course Bella, his wife, tutted and protested that Luigi was embarrassing her, smothering Dee with warmly maternal concern and protection as she assured her that she was not to take any notice of Luigi's poor attempt at humour.

'What? You mean to say that you do *not* think of me as a bull?' Hugo teased Bella, lifting his arm and tensing his muscles in a mock display of male strength.

'Aha, it is not the size of this muscle *here* that counts,' Luigi warned him. 'Is that not so, *cara*?' he asked his outraged wife.

Dee listened to their byplay with a mixture of delight and self-consciousness. Luigi was barely her own height, and Bella was even smaller, both of them plump and round and very obviously well and happily married. So much so that it was impossible for Dee to take offence at Luigi's references to Hugo's sexual machismo. He was as proud of him as though Hugo had been his own son, as proud of Hugo's maleness as though it had been his own, and it was a simple and honest pride, with nothing offensive or prurient about it.

'She is *bella*, very *bella*,' he told Hugo approvingly, after he had subjected Dee to a thorough and very malely appreciative visual inspection, his eyes twinkling as he made this report to Hugo.

'She is indeed, and she is *my bella*,' Hugo retorted warningly.

It was the start of one of the most magical evenings of Dee's life.

She ate and drank with an appetite that was totally unfamiliar to her. Hugo, she noticed, whilst he enjoyed his food and his wine, was careful not to drink too much nor to allow her to do so, and she acknowledged that she loved his protective attitude towards her. It made her feel so…so safe, so cherished…so loved.

So loved.

There was no doubt in Dee's mind that she was in love.

She had been in love from the moment Hugo had picked her up off the gravel, she suspected, and it was the most intoxicating, the most exciting, the most life-enhancing emotion she had *ever* experienced.

It was late when they left the restaurant. The promised frost had become reality, sparkling on the ground and the trees, vaporising their breath as Dee gave a small gasp at the cold shock of it against her face.

'It's so cold,' she protested as she huddled deeper into her coat.

'Mmm… Come here, then,' Hugo told her, wrapping his arm around her as he drew her as close as he could to his own body.

Happily nestling close to him, Dee laughed when he tucked his hand into her pocket.

'Aha…all you *really* wanted to do was to keep your hand warm in my pocket,' she teased him.

'Wrong,' Hugo corrected her huskily. 'All I *really* want to do is to keep *all* of you warm in my bed, with my body…my hands and my mouth. Has anyone ever made any kind of love to you, Dee? Has anyone ever touched you…kissed you…?'

'Of course they have,' she squeaked indignantly. Just because she was a virgin that didn't mean she was *totally* sexually ignorant.

'In my last year at school I went to loads of snogging parties…'

She could see the little puffs of white air appearing from Hugo's mouth as his body gusted with laughter.

'Oh, snogging parties… That wasn't *exactly* the kind of kissing I meant. What I meant was, has anyone kissed you…intimately, caressed your body with their mouth, explored you with their hands and their tongue, made you…?'

Frantically Dee covered her ears, torn between excited shock and self-conscious chagrin that he had to explain to her so graphically just what he meant. She knew what he was describing, of course, had even wondered in her most private intimate moments just how it would feel to have a man, *her* man, make love to her in such a way, but she had never dreamed that she would walk down a public street whilst he, that man, teasingly described to her an act which she had assumed was something a man only did for a woman if she was very, very fortunate or very, very loved.

'Do I take it that that's a no?' Hugo asked her, still laughing, but Dee could hear the rusty betraying note in his voice, and she could see the way he was looking at her. She might not be sexually experienced, but she was no fool. Hugo wanted to touch her, caress her, taste her, in the way he had just described, and unless she had got it wrong he wanted to do it very, very badly indeed and very, very soon…like now, in fact. Her heart started to thud. She felt dizzy with excitement and the euphoria-inducing realisation of her own female power.

'Oh, it's going to be so good for us,' Hugo groaned as he drew her into the shadow of a convenient side street and swept her promptly and expertly into his arms. Not that Dee was attempting very much resistance, and she didn't offer any either a few seconds later, when he slipped his hands inside her coat and wrapped his arms around her body so tightly she felt she could hardly breathe. Their kiss was everything that a first kiss should be—tender, exciting, passionate, their mouths eager and hungry, their bodies urgently hungry for the feel of the other. But even though Hugo had put his hands under her coat, a little to Dee's surprise he made no attempt to do anything more than simply hold her.

'I daren't,' he told her gruffly, his voice muffled between kisses as though he could read what she was thinking. 'God knows I want to, but if I touch you now... Remember what I said to you this afternoon?'

'About...about making babies...' Dee responded shakily.

'Don't. Don't even say it,' Hugo groaned as he moved his body even closer to her own, swiftly unfastening his own coat. Dee could feel his hard arousal. Immediately her own body quickened, revealing a capacity for sexual responsiveness which she had never guessed she possessed. The nature and the intensity of the ache raging through her shocked her, and yet it excited her as well.

Her fellow students' lusty comments about sharing their beds and their bodies with Hugo slipped warningly into her mind, and instantly she was seized with such a strong surge of female determination and possessive jealousy at the thought of someone daring to try to take away her man that the primitiveness of her emotions bemused her.

'What is it...? What's wrong?' Hugo asked her. He had buttoned up her coat and was smiling tenderly down at her as his hand cupped her face, and his forefinger firmly tilted her face up to his so that he could look into her eyes.

'I was just thinking about something one of the other girls said and how jealous it was making me,' Dee responded honestly.

'What girl?' Hugo asked her, puzzled. 'There is no girl, and I promise you,' he added, his voice dropping huskily, 'I shall never give you any cause to be jealous. I would never, could never, do anything to hurt you. There is no other girl.'

'No,' Dee agreed, smiling up at him. But she still

couldn't resist murmuring mischievously, 'Still, I'm glad that *I* don't have a twin sister…'

'What?'

She laughed and shook her head, refusing to explain. There was no way she would *ever* want to share Hugo with another woman, in bed or out of it. No way at all.

CHAPTER FIVE

THEY HAD BEEN going out together for over a month before they finally made love, although Dee knew that no one who saw them together during those early weeks would have believed it.

Dee hadn't said anything about either her running into Hugo or having dinner with him to any of her friends, but within a week, in the way that these things so often had of getting out, it seemed that everyone did know.

It was only later that Hugo actually admitted that he had let it be known that she was his.

'I had to do it. Just in case anyone else started to make a play for you,' he defended himself.

Dee shook her head, but by then she was too much in love, too deeply committed to him to protest very much. Those were heady days, exciting days, frustrating days too. Her doctor had warned her that it would be several weeks before she could rely completely on the efficiency of her birth control pill to prevent an unwanted pregnancy, and Hugo had announced very firmly that there was no way he wanted them to run that risk. He also wanted there to be nothing between them the first time they made love together. 'And I mean *nothing*,' he had repeated, with heavy sensual emphasis.

Both of them had family commitments which would

take them home and away from each other over Christmas. Hugo was going north with his parents, to spend Christmas and the New Year with his grandfather.

'A huge quarrelsome gathering of our clan—quite literally,' he told Dee wryly. 'My grandfather insists that we stick to tradition, despite the fact that Montpelier House is a huge great freezing barn of a place that's impossible to heat. My parents will have a row on the journey up there because my mother won't want to go, and another on the way back because my father won't want to leave. It happens every year. My elder sister's children will cause complete havoc and chaos, and my younger sister, who doesn't have any, will get all high-minded and sanctimonious about the way she is bringing them up, insisting that she's spoiling them, and then they'll both turn on me when I tell them not to be such idiots… I promise you, it's dreadful.'

'It sounds wonderful,' Dee told him enviously. She too would be spending Christmas with her own extended family. She and her father would be visiting the farm where he had been brought up and which was now farmed by his brother. Dee's cousins would be there, and her aunts and uncles, and there was a good-sized group of them, but Dee and her father had always been a little on the outside of everything. Her father was something of an enigma to the rest of his family, and, whilst they loved him, they never seemed to feel totally at home or relaxed in his company, Dee had noticed, and that had rubbed off on her too.

'My brother has more in common with his livestock than he has with me,' her father had once commented witheringly to her after a particularly sharp exchange between the two men. There would be jokes and party games at the farm, but Dee knew that she would not be able to throw herself into it as unselfconsciously as she would have liked because she'd be conscious of the fact that her father could not do so.

The best bit of Christmas for her had always been the quiet shared hours she and her father spent alone together: the ritual attendance at church, the early-morning rising, the excitement as a child of her stocking, the comfort of the traditional cooked breakfast after their return from church, followed by the thrill of opening her proper presents. These days the present bit of Christmas was, of course, not quite so exciting, but she still enjoyed their small traditions.

Her father was a keen swimmer. As a young man he had swum for the county, and this year Dee had been thrilled to find a book in Lexminster by one of his boyhood heros, a little-known Channel swimmer, which she knew he would be delighted to have. He also had a weakness for Turkish delight, which she had also bought him, and she had saved hard for an antique snuff box to add to his extensive collection.

He would, she knew, give her a small parcel of shares—a gift and a test, for she was free to do what she wished with them, either keep them or sell them. All she had to do was use her own judgement to decide. The shares would be in unfamiliar companies: Australian mines, South American crops. Last year she had been spectacularly successful in her decision. The shares she had kept had increased their value two hundredfold. She would be hard put to it to better that this year.

She missed Hugo, as she had known she would. After all, they had been seeing each other every day, and she was so very, very much in love with him—and he with her. What she hadn't expected or been totally prepared for was the way his absence manifested itself in an actual physical ache of longing for him.

Her father guessed that something was wrong, and Dee could hear the curt note of disapproval in his voice as he demanded to know, 'What's wrong with you, Dee? I hope you haven't done anything foolish and got involved with some student...'

Hugo isn't 'some student,' Daddy, Dee wanted to protest, but something stopped her, warning her that her father wasn't quite ready yet to admit another man into her life or her heart. In the last few weeks she had become far more aware of the vulnerability of the male ego. After all, Hugo could, at times, display an unexpected vein of jealousy against her father which both touched and amused her, making her feel so protectively tender towards them both that it made her heart ache.

'He's my father and you're my...you're mine,' she had whispered reassuringly to him as she'd lain in his arms.

They had been at his flat, untidy and strewn with papers and possessions. It even smelt different from her own all-female household, Dee recognised. Although they still hadn't actually made love in the fullest sense of the words, there was very little that Hugo did not know about her body, nor her about his. It had shocked her a little to discover how easily and thoroughly he could satisfy her and she him without that final act of penetration, but that did not mean that she did not want it.

Looking lovingly up into his eyes, she had teased the thick springy curls of his hair with her fingers. She loved the way it brushed his shoulder and her own skin when he kissed and caressed it. It felt so soft and yet so strong... so vibrant...just like him. She liked to bury her face in it and breathe in its scent, *his* scent. It suited him worn that length, made him look individual, gave him all the romantic appeal of a macho Renaissance warrior knight…

They did, of course, speak to one another often over the Christmas holiday, and then, three days before they had arranged that they would go back to Lexminster, Hugo rang her.

'I can't bear it any longer,' he groaned passionately. 'I've got to see you.'

'But it's too soon. We said next Monday, and besides, you're in the north and—'

'No, I'm not, I'm here…back…'

'In Lexminster?' Dee gasped. 'But…'

'You can come to me, Dee,' he told her softly. 'Or I can come and get you… I don't mind which, but I can't spend another night without seeing you.'

He could come and get her. Dee could just imagine her father's reaction to that!

As it was it was difficult enough convincing him that she needed to return to university three days ahead of the time she had already stipulated. He was huffy and a little distant with her, and Dee knew why, even though she tried to pretend that she was not aware of his reaction. No mention was made of Hugo, and Dee cravenly hoped that there would not be…not yet…not whilst their feelings for one another were so…so overpoweringly intense. She wasn't ready yet to let anyone else into their relationship, not even someone as close as her father.

As she drove away from him, for the first time in her life Dee knew that she was actually happy to leave her father behind. She loved him dearly, of course she did, but now there was a new male focus in her life; now she was ready to step from girlhood into womanhood, from the protection of her father's arms to the excitement of

Hugo's. She had rung him to tell him that she was leaving and he was waiting for her when she arrived.

'Don't get out of the car,' he told her as he hurried down the stone steps leading to her house, where he had been sheltering from the driving rain.

'*Don't* get out? But I thought you wanted...'

'Oh, I do, I do,' he assured her wickedly, with a sabre-toothed male smile. 'But not here...'

'Not here? But...'

'I want this to be special...very, very special,' he told her huskily, and then he urged her, 'I'll drive you...'

'No, I'll drive,' Dee told him firmly. 'Where are we going?'

When he told her she gasped.

'You've booked us a room at the De Villiers Hotel—but, Hugo, that will cost a fortune.'

'No, not a room,' he contradicted her.

Dee looked at him. She knew his zany sense of humour by now.

'Not a room... What, then? A wooden seat in the grounds?' she asked warily.

'No, not that.' Hugo laughed. 'I've booked us a suite,' he told her quietly.

'A suite...' Dee squeaked. 'But Hugo, the cost...'

'Mmm...I know; I hope I'm going to be worth it,' he told her, straight-faced, making her dissolve into giggles.

The hotel wasn't very far away, just a few miles the other side of the city, a beautiful Edwardian house set in its own grounds which had been converted to a very prestigious hotel. Dee had been there once—with her father, when he had taken her out for a birthday lunch. The food, the room, the service had all been first-class, and Dee had felt truly spoiled and treasured.

It was a favourite with local brides, not for their receptions so much as for their wedding nights. Rumour had it that the discreet addition of a Jacuzzi to the bridal suite had resulted in totally blissed-out couples pronouncing fervently that they were most definitely going to come back.

At the thought of the bridal suite and its Jacuzzi Dee suddenly felt very hot, and slightly dizzy.

'You haven't…it isn't…you haven't booked the bridal suite, have you?' she asked Hugo faintly.

He laughed again.

'No, I haven't,' he reassured her, adding, tongue-in-cheek, 'We don't want everyone to know what we're going to be doing, do we?'

'You mean to say they won't?' Dee responded dryly.

He hadn't booked the bridal suite, but what he had neglected to tell her was that *all* of the hotel's four suites possessed their own Jacuzzis.

As Hugo told Dee later, he just wished he had had a camera for that unforgettable look on her face as the porter swept into the room and then opened the door to the large *en suite* bathroom with a theatrical flourish.

'How could you?' she whispered to him once the porter had gone. 'It makes me feel that we're being so…so obvious.'

'One of us certainly is,' Hugo agreed, with a rueful glance down at his own body.

Dee closed her eyes. She gave up. Just what did you do with such a man?

Hugo soon showed her, adroitly locking the door and then going over to uncork the bottle of champagne that was chilling in an ice bucket.

'I've ordered us a cold supper,' he told Dee. 'But first…' He poured her a glass of champagne and handed it to her. 'To us…' he toasted her solemnly.

A little shakily Dee lifted her glass to her lips and took a sip. Suddenly, and totally unexpectedly, alongside her excitement she could feel a definite twisting thread of shy, virginal self-consciousness, she acknowledged.

'We'll never drink all that,' she told Hugo unsteadily, looking at the large bottle.

'Not from these,' he agreed, putting down his glass. 'Shall I tell you how I intend to drink it?' he whispered as he came towards her and removed her own glass before taking her in his arms. 'I intend to pour it over your naked body and lick every droplet off you, drink every last bubble, and then I shall…'

He should have sounded ridiculous, but somehow he didn't; somehow she was reacting to what he was saying, the picture he was drawing in her mind and on her senses, with a frantic little shudder that made him groan and start to kiss her with uninhibited passion.

He had just started to unfasten her top when they heard the door. Cursing, he released her and went to open it. It was the waiter with their supper, and Dee knew that as he wheeled in the table her face was as pink as her champagne. The meal Hugo had chosen was everything that a romantic meal should be. Dee couldn't imagine how much it must have cost him. Lobster, her favourite tiny wild strawberries, hand-made chocolates, the kind he knew she had a passion for, all of it washed down by carefully chosen wine—even if Dee only sipped at hers. Hugo, she noticed, did the same.

'Satisfied?' Hugo asked her softly, when Dee had eaten the last of the chocolate truffles.

Her colour rose, but Dee still managed to meet his eyes as she told him boldly, 'No, and I shan't be until…'

'Until…?' Hugo pressed as she stopped speaking.

'Until I can feel you inside me,' she whispered on

a sudden rush, but now she couldn't quite manage to sustain that eye-to-eye contact. Not that she needed to. Hugo had already left his seat and was swooping down on her, practically lifting her off her chair as he took her in his arms.

'Oh God, Dee, you don't know what you're doing to me,' he told her rawly, and as she felt the emotion surging through his body Dee realised properly, for the first time, just what a strain the last few weeks must have been for him, and just how much control he must have been exercising over his own desires and needs.

'Come here. Come *here*,' he whispered urgently to her, even though she was already there in his arms, and his words were a soft chant of tender love as he cupped her face and started to kiss her. 'Mmm… You taste of chocolate,' he murmured appreciatively as he tasted her mouth, testing her reaction.

'And you taste of—' She started to tease back, then stopped, her eyes darkening with a passion she made no attempt to hide as she told him huskily, 'And you taste of you, Hugo, and it's the best taste in the world…the *only* taste I could ever want. You are the only man I could ever want, and I want you so badly. I want to touch you, hold you, taste you…'

She heard him groan deep down in his throat, a male purr of tormented longing. She lifted her fingers to his throat and touched it, feeling the vibration of the noise he was making against her fingertips. She loved the feel of his skin, the feel of his body. She loved it when she closed her hand, her *hands*, around him and felt the satisfying hard swell of his body as he reacted to her touch.

'Both hands?' he had teased her, the first time she had wrapped them lovingly around him.

'Mmm…but you do wonders for my ego. *One* will do, Dee…'

'One will *do*,' she had acknowledged. 'But it feels so good to hold you like this, with two…'

'I can't argue with that,' he had agreed throatily, but he had still been laughing a little at her.

He had stopped laughing, though, when she had held him still and bent her head to place a ring of shyly adoring kisses around the taut head of his erection.

Oh, yes, he had stopped laughing then.

Now, with the lights turned down low over the large, luxurious bed, Hugo undressed her slowly. They had been to bed together before, but this time, somehow, it was different…special…and the moment he stepped away from her he gave her a look so full of import that it made Dee shiver a little to read the message in his eyes. This was their night of commitment to one another, the final bridge to cross on their way to *complete* commitment, the final act which they had not yet shared.

They already knew one another's dreams and one another's hopes, they already knew what they were destined to be and to do—that together they would work for the benefit of mankind, that they would leave university to work together in the field, would marry before they left. Hugo was so idealistic—even more so, in some ways, than she was herself. He believed passionately in what he wanted to do and he was totally and utterly committed to it. To deny him the opportunity would be like cutting off one of his limbs, only worse.

'There's so much we can give them, so much we can put back into a culture, a country, that in the past we've only taken from and destroyed, and there's so much we can learn from them. They have so little in materialis-

tic terms, but they have their pride and their dignity—
their heritage.

'My father doesn't approve of what I'm planning to
do, you know, and neither does my grandfather, but it's
something I *have* to do…I couldn't live with myself if I
didn't,' he had told her passionately, and Dee had known
exactly what he meant. His idealism only made her love
him more, even whilst she knew that it would also mean
that there would always be a small part of his heart and
his emotions that did not belong totally to her.

He was very like *her* father, in that his pride in his
own beliefs ran very strongly in him. *Very* like her father.

'It's your turn,' Hugo whispered to her now, as his
tender glance caressed and reassured her. Very carefully
Dee started to undress *him*, her fingers trembling not with
nervousness but with the intensity of her suppressed and
aching longing for him.

'No, that's cheating,' she protested huskily when,
without waiting for her to finish, he leaned forward and
started to nibble the side of her neck, his hand cupping
and stroking her naked breast. Dee closed her eyes as she
felt her body's reaction, going still as she tried to stem
the fierce hot tide of it, rising not so much up through her
body as washing fiercely down through it, to that place
where the sheer pressure of it forced into life a fierce,
tumultuously beating pulse.

Hugo's lips caressed her shoulder, her collarbone, and
then moved lower, nuzzling at the soft curve of her breast
and then the taut crest of her nipple before closing over
that nipple itself. Dee made a fiercely guttural noise of
throaty excitement, her fingernails digging into Hugo's
skin, but if he felt any pain he certainly didn't show it.
However, his slow, careful suckling on her nipple did,
suddenly becoming an urgent, body-trembling erotic tug

that made Dee groan as she buried her hands in his hair
and held him passionately to her.

Somehow she was on the bed. Somehow Hugo was undressed. Somehow he had positioned her so that he could
kneel between her splayed legs as he kissed her quivering
belly. Now, with no need to control her longing for him,
Dee could respond to him as she had so much longed to
do, arching her spine and lifting herself to the tormenting
lap of his tongue as he licked at the moist slickness of her
body. There was no need for the champagne—her own
desire had covered her skin in its own sweetly scented
mist of arousal—but, wonderful though the touch of his
mouth against her body was, it wasn't what Dee really
wanted. Not now. Not this time.

'Are you sure you're ready for me? Do you want…?'
Hugo asked her hoarsely as she reached for him, wildly
begging him, eagerly demanding to feel him deep inside her.

'Oh, yes, yes…' Dee groaned longingly.

She couldn't take her eyes off him, watching him as
urgently, as hungrily as he watched her.

'I'm afraid of hurting you,' he confessed as he hesitated, but his body wasn't afraid, Dee recognised, her
eyes widening as she watched him lowering himself towards her. He looked so good, so…so ready…so—

She gave a little whimper of sound as she felt him rubbing himself slowly against her.

'That hurt?' Hugo asked her in concern.

Dee managed to laugh.

'Yes,' she told him. 'It hurts because it's not…because
I want you *inside* me…' She gave a smothered gasp as
she felt the first of the deep penetrative strokes she had
so longed for, her eyes widening as she realised how well
their bodies fitted together.

No way did the sensation she had of being filled, stretched completely, in *any* way approximate to any kind of pain, but the intensity of her pleasure was so acute that it could almost be described as a kind of special agony, a racking urgency, a pulsing, heart-jerking, driven compulsion that had her calling out Hugo's name as she clung frantically to him.

It didn't last long; both of them were too aroused, too wrought up emotionally and physically, for it to do so. Dee knew she had been virtually on the point of orgasm even before Hugo had entered her, and he had been almost as close to the edge of his own self-control.

Dee had barely felt the first quivering explosion of her own completion when Hugo cried out her name, the hot, fierce pulse of his ejaculation drenching her body with a fiercely sweet burst of pleasure.

She was, Dee discovered seconds later as she relaxed into his arms, crooning happily in delighted pleasure, making soft cooing sounds of love to Hugo as he held her.

'It will be better next time,' she heard him promising her as he smoothed back her hair and kissed her tenderly. 'I'll make it last longer and—'

'*Better*…than *that*…*impossible*!' Dee assured him blissfully.

'Oh, Dee, Dee, is it any wonder that I love you so much?' Hugo praised her adoringly. 'I should not have met you, you know. You shouldn't really have existed. I didn't *plan* for this to happen. I wasn't *going* to fall in love, and I certainly didn't want to make the kind of lifetime commitment I want to make to you to any woman until I was at least thirty.

'It's just as well that you and I share the same ideals and the same ambitions. I don't think I could have borne it if you'd been the kind of woman who expected me to stay at home and get myself the sort of job my father wants me to get. Something in the City that will make me a lot of money. I'm not going to be much of a catch as a husband, you do realise that, don't you? Our children will complain and all your friends will think that you're crazy to love me. Your father will quite definitely disapprove…'

'No, he won't,' Dee denied. 'He'll admire you for what you're doing—and it is admirable, Hugo, to want to help others. I couldn't love you so much as I do if you were any way different from the way you are, and I certainly wouldn't want to change you or the plans you've made.'

'Mmm…it's providential, isn't it, that you'll have completed your degree course just about the same time as I finish my Ph.D.? There's no way I can make time to go back to working in the field until I finish it, but once I have, once we've both completed our studies… There's so much I want to do, Dee. So very, very much…'

'Mmm…I know,' she agreed, and then added with sweet provocativeness, 'You haven't even touched the champagne, and then there's the Jacuzzi… How long have you booked the suite for?'

'Just tonight,' Hugo told her ruefully.

'*Just* tonight? You mean we've still got it for a whole twelve hours?' Dee teased him, mock wide-eyed.

'A whole twelve hours,' he agreed, but he was mumbling the words a little because Dee was kissing him.

'Then we don't have a *moment* to waste, do we?' she told him as she trailed her fingers slowly over his body.

'No, I don't suppose we do,' he agreed.

CHAPTER SIX

DEE woke up with a start. Her heart was pounding and her mouth felt dry. She had slept heavily but not refreshingly, almost as though she had been drugged, and as she lay in bed she was conscious of an unfamiliar reluctance to get up, almost a *dread* of doing so, as though by remaining where she was she could hold her apprehensions and low spirits at bay.

Unfamiliar? Not exactly. Not totally. There had been a period after her father's death, a time once the urgency of the immediate calls upon her time and attention had slackened a little, when she had experienced a similar longing to crawl away and hide somewhere safe and womb-like. She had had to fight to overcome it, to tell herself that the decisions she had made had been right and necessary, to urge herself to go on. Resolutely she threw back the bedclothes and slid her feet to the bedroom floor.

Her bedroom was her own secret, special place, somewhere that no one else was allowed to enter. Not so much because it was a private sanctuary, Dee recognised, but because of what she knew it betrayed about a deeply personal side of her nature.

The walls were painted a soft washed colour, somewhere between blue and green, and the windows were draped in gossamer folds of creamy white muslin. The

same fabric fell from the ceiling and was gathered back
softly at either side of her double bed, which, like the
chaise longue at its foot and the comfortable bedroom
chair by the window, was covered in a cream-coloured
cotton brocade. The carpet too was cream. The whole
ambience of the room was one of soft delicacy. A stranger
looking into Dee's bedroom and making a character assessment of her from it would have judged her to be soft
and ethereal, a creature of fluid, feminine moods and
feelings, a dreamy water sprite of a woman, whose sen-
sibilities were as delicate and tender as the petals of the
fresh cream flowers that filled the bowl on the pretty antique table she used as a dressing table.

As Dee showered and then dressed she acknowledged
that the cause of her sense of wanting to curl up protectively and let the world get on without her for a while
were the two completely contradictory forces lining up
against one another for battle inside her head.

On the one side was her need to persuade Peter, without either alienating him or even more importantly hurting him, that it was time for him to step down from the
foundation committee, and her knowledge that the best
way to achieve that goal would be to win Hugo's support,
to actively *court* his help and approval of her plans, whilst
on the other was her totally opposing need to have nothing whatsoever to do with him, to blot him completely
out of her thoughts, her mind, her life, her heart.

Abruptly Dee stopped brushing her hair, her body
convulsing in a small involuntary shiver.

She had fought that battle once, fought it and, she had
believed, won it, inch by painful inch, hour by agonising hour. She put down her hairbrush and stared unsee-
ingly into her mirror. She was afraid, she acknowledged
grimly. Afraid of having to re-enter the long, painful time

of darkness she had already been through once, afraid of
what might happen to her if she allowed Hugo to come
back into even the smallest corner of her life, and that
was why she had been so reluctant to face the day.

Yes, she was stronger now than the girl she had once
been, but then she had had the advantage of being motivated, driven by what she had considered to be almost
a crusade; then she had had zeal and youth on her side.
Now…

Now she still believed as firmly as she had done then
that she had made the right, the only decision, but now
the brightness of her fervour, her belief was shadowed,
obscured sometimes by her own inner images of what
might have been, the child or children she might have
had, the life, the love she might have shared.

As a young man Hugo had been, if anything, even
more fervent in his beliefs than she had been herself,
and, unlike her, he had been sharply critical of what he
had termed the selfishness of a materialistic society and
those who supported it. As an idealist, his views had
sometimes been diametrically opposed to those of her
father—or so it had seemed at times.

'What do you expect my father to do?' she had demanded angrily of him once in the middle of one of their
passionate arguments. 'Give *all* his money away…?'

'Don't be ridiculous,' Hugo had snorted angrily, in
defence of his own beliefs.

He had been equally passionate about how important it was for those involved in aid programmes to be
completely free of even the faintest breath of scandal, of
anything that could reflect badly on the cause they were
representing. Oddly enough, that had been a belief he
had actually *shared* with her father.

Perhaps because she was a woman, Dee was inclined

to take a more reasonable and compassionate view. Human beings were, after all, human, vulnerable, *fallible*.

There was no point in giving in to her present feelings. She would, she decided firmly, take the bull by the horns and drive over to Lexminster so that she could both see how Peter was and either talk with Hugo or arrange a meeting with him so that she could raise the subject of the committee with him.

Her mind made up, Dee told herself that she had made the right decision. What had happened…existed…between her and Hugo all those years ago had no relevance to her life now, and it certainly had none to his. Her best plan was simply to behave as though they had been no more than mere acquaintances, and to adopt a casually friendly but firmly distancing attitude towards him.

A very sensible decision, but one which surely did not necessitate four changes of clothes and a bedroom strewn with discarded, rejected outfits before Dee was finally ready to set out for Lexminster—over an hour later than she had originally planned.

Even so, it had been worth taking time and trouble with her appearance, she told herself stoutly as she climbed into her car. Her father had been of the old school, and had firmly believed in the importance of creating the right impression, and in taking time over her clothes she was just acting on those beliefs, Dee assured herself.

The cream dress she was wearing was simple, and the long slits which ran down both sides made it easy to move in without being in any way provocative—at least that was what Dee thought. A man, though, could have told her that there was something quite definitely very deliciously alluring about the discreetly subtle flash of long leg that her skirt revealed when she walked.

Its boat-shaped neckline was sensible—even if, regrettably, it did have an annoying tendency to slide down off one shoulder occasionally—and the little suedette pumps she was wearing with it were similarly 'sensible.' The pretty gold earrings had been a present from her father, and were therefore of sentimental importance, and if she had dashed back into the house just to add a spray of her favourite perfume and check her lipstick—so what?

As Dee drove through the town centre she noticed a small group of teenage boys standing aimlessly in the square, and she started to frown. She knew from the headmaster of the local school, who was on the board of one of her charities, that they were experiencing a growing problem with truancy amongst some of the teenage children.

Ted Richards felt, like her, that the town's teenagers needed a healthy outlet for their energies and, perhaps even more importantly, that they needed to have their growing maturity recognised and to feel that they were a valued part of their own community.

In contrast to the disquieting boredom Dee had recognised in the slouched shoulders and aimless scuffling of the youngsters, when she drove past her own offices the area outside it was busy, with the town's senior citizens making use of the comfortable facilities of the coffee shop and meeting rooms on the ground floor of the building. Only the other morning, as she had walked through the coffee shop, she had noticed that the list pinned up on the noticeboard inviting people to join one of the several trips that were being planned was very fully subscribed.

Teenagers did not always take too enthusiastically to being over-organised, especially by adults. Dee knew that, but she was still very conscious of the fact that their

welfare and their happiness was an area which needed
an awful lot of input.

Anna's husband, Ward, had certainly opened her eyes
and inspired her in that regard. Perhaps it might be worthwhile asking Ward if he would show Peter round his own
workshops, Dee mused as she left the town behind her—
always providing, of course, that Peter was well enough
for such an outing.

Peter had a very special place in Dee's heart. She never
found it boring listening to his stories of his young man-
hood, especially when those stories involved her own
father.

It was lunchtime when Dee reached Lexminster. In addition to the file she was compiling containing her plans
for Rye's teenagers, she had also placed in the boot of her
car one of her home-made pies, which were a special favourite of Peter's, as well as some other food.

She had a key for Peter's house, but, out of habit, she
automatically knocked on the door first and then, when
there was no response, fished the key out of her bag and
let herself in, calling out a little anxiously as she stepped
into the hallway,

'Peter, it's me—Dee.'

She was just about to head for the kitchen with her
groceries when, unexpectedly, the kitchen door opened.
But it wasn't Peter who opened it, and as she saw Hugo
frowning at her Dee's heart gave a dangerous flurried
series of painful little thuds.

'Oh…' Dee's hand went protectively to her throat. 'I
didn't… You…'

'I heard you knock but I was on the phone,' Hugo told
her curtly before adding, 'Peter's asleep. The doctor was
anxious that he should have some proper rest, so she has
given him a shot of something to help him sleep.' He

frowned as he looked at her disapprovingly. 'I just hope that you haven't woken him.'

To her chagrin his criticism made Dee feel as awkward and guilty as a little girl, causing her to retaliate defensively, 'Was it really necessary or wise of the doctor to drug him?'

'Drug him…what exactly are you implying?'

'I'm not implying anything,' Dee denied. 'But at Peter's age, the fact—'

'Jane is a qualified doctor, Dee, and if she thinks that some mild form of gentle sedation is called for…'

Dee's heart twisted betrayingly over Hugo's intimate use of the doctor's Christian name, and the way his voice had softened noticeably as he spoke it.

'I actually needed to talk to Peter,' she announced, deliberately changing the subject. 'But if he's been sedated…'

'You *needed* to talk to him? So this isn't just a social visit to enquire after his health, then.' Hugo pounced.

'I *am* concerned about his health, of course…'

'But obviously not concerned enough to have called in a doctor,' Hugo pointed out dryly.

Dee could feel her face starting to burn with a mixture of guilt and anger.

'I *would* have done so, but, as I explained yesterday, I haven't—'

'Had time. Yes, I know. What was it you needed to talk to Peter about?'

Dee looked sharply at him. There was no way she could bring herself to enlist Hugo's aid whilst he was being so antagonistic towards her.

'I rather think that that is Peter's and my business, don't you?' she asked him coolly.

Immediately Hugo's eyebrows rose, the look he was

giving her every bit as disdainful as the one she had just given him.

'That rather depends. You see—' He broke off as the telephone in the kitchen started to ring, excusing himself to Dee as he went to answer it.

'Yes, that's right,' she heard him saying to whoever was calling. 'No, that's no problem. I shall be staying here anyway, so you can contact me here... No, that's not a problem; there's no time limit... My work means that I can base myself virtually anywhere just so long as I have access to the conveniences of modern technology.... No...I haven't told her yet, but I intend to do so...'

Dee hadn't deliberately eavesdropped on his conversation, but it was impossible for her not to have overheard it, even though she had walked into the hall. As she heard Hugo replacing the receiver, Dee walked back towards the kitchen.

'Since I can't see or speak with Peter, there isn't much point in my staying. When he does wake up please give him my love. I've brought some food and—'

She stopped as Hugo cut her off abruptly, telling her brusquely, 'You can't go yet. There's something I have to tell you.'

Something he *had* to tell her? Whatever it was she could tell from his expression that it wasn't anything pleasant. Her heart started to thump. Had Peter said something to him about her father...about the past? But, no, Peter didn't know. She had never... But he could have guessed, had his own suspicions...and...

'What is it? Tell me...'

Dee could hear the anxiety crackling in her own voice, making it sound harsh.

'We'll go into the other room,' Hugo suggested. 'We're

right under Peter's bedroom here, and I don't want to disturb him.'

Her heart pounding in heavy sledgehammer blows, Dee followed him into the parlour.

The air in the room was stale and stuffy, and automatically she walked towards the window, skirting past Hugo and the large pieces of Victorian furniture which dominated the room.

'What is it? What do you want to say to me?' Dee repeated tensely.

Hugo was frowning, looking away from her as though… Surely he…?

'Peter and I had a long chat after you'd gone last night…'

Dee could feel the violence of the heavy hammer-blows of her heart shaking her chest. Here it was: the blow she had always dreaded. Peter had spoken to Hugo, shared with him his doubts and fears about her father. Doubts and fears which he had never voiced to her, but which, like her, had obviously haunted him.

'He was telling me that your father…'

Dee closed her eyes, willing herself not to give in to the creeping remorseless tide of fear rising up through her body in an icy-cold wave.

'My father is *dead*, Hugo,' she cried out passionately. 'All he ever wanted to do was to help other people. That was *all* he ever wanted. He never…'

She stopped, unable to go on.

And then she took a deep breath, straightening her spine, forcing herself to look Hugo in the eye as she demanded huskily, 'What did Peter tell you?'

'He said that he was concerned about your plans to alter the focus of your father's charity. He told me that he was afraid that you were allowing yourself to be swayed by your emotion, and he said, as well, that he was afraid that you would try to pressure him into supporting you.'

Dee stared at him uncomprehendingly. Peter had talked to Hugo about her father's charity and *not* about his death. He had confided to him his fear of her desire to change things, his fear that…

The relief made her feel weakly light-headed. So much so that she actually started to laugh a little shakily.

'It's all very well for you to laugh, Dee,' Hugo chided her. 'It's obvious to me what you're trying to do. You want to steamroller Peter into supporting these changes you want to make, even if that means forcing him to act against his conscience.'

Dee fought to gather her thoughts. In the initial relief of discovering that Peter had not discussed her father's death with Hugo she had overlooked the gravity of what he was telling her. Now she was becoming sharply aware of it.

'Peter had no right to discuss the charity's business with you,' she reprimanded sharply. 'The charity is a private organisation run by the main committee of which *I* am the Chairperson. How that committee operates is the business of ourselves and ourselves alone—'

'Not quite,' Hugo interrupted her quietly, 'as I'm sure the Charity Commissioners would be the first to remind you…'

At this mention of the government body responsible for overseeing the proper management and control of charities Dee's eyes widened in indignation.

'We have no call to fear the Charity Commissioners,' she told Hugo firmly. 'Far from it.'

'I wasn't suggesting that you might,' Hugo responded coolly. 'However, this might be a good point at which to remind you that all your father's charities are overseen by that committee, and that whilst you *may* be the Chairperson of it, or them, you do *not* have the right to steamroller through whatever changes you wish to make.'

'To steamroller through…' Dee gasped in fresh indignation. 'How dare you? What exactly are you trying to suggest?' she demanded. 'My father's wishes are and always have been paramount to me when it comes to my role as—'

'Are they?' Hugo interrupted her. 'Peter doesn't think so.'

Dee sighed and took a deep breath, swinging round. 'My father wanted his own charity to benefit his fellow citizens. When he initially established it there was a need in the town to help the elderly, and that is exactly what we have done, but now… Things change…and I believe that our help is needed now far more by our young people.

'But none of this has any relevance to you, nor can it be of any interest to you,' she told Hugo firmly. 'I realise that to someone like you, who is used to dealing with the needs of people and situations a world away from what we are experiencing in Rye—people to whom the meagrest ration of food makes the difference between living and dying…'

She stopped, and then told him fiercely, 'The elderly in Rye are more than adequately provided for, but our teenagers…there's nothing for them to do, nothing to occupy or interest them. Ward says…'

'Ward?' Hugo interrupted her sharply.

'Yes, Ward Hunter,' Dee replied briefly. 'Ward has already put into operation—and very successfully—the kind of scheme *I* want to help establish in Rye.'

'Peter said that he felt that you were being influenced to break away from your father's ideas,' Hugo told her critically. 'And that's why—'

'Hugo, Peter means well, but he's old-fashioned. He can't see.' Dee paused and frowned. 'I really do need to talk with him to make him understand…'

'You mean to put pressure on him to go against his own beliefs,' Hugo told her caustically. 'Well, I'm afraid that just isn't going to be possible, Dee.'

'What? Why? What's happened?' Dee demanded, her heart immediately filled with fear for her father's old friend. Was there something about his health that Hugo was concealing from her?

'Why? Because this morning Peter asked *me* to act for him as his representative on the committee, and—'

'No…' Dee denied, grabbing hold of the edge of the table as she tried to control the shock that was making her body tremble. 'No, he *can't* possibly have done that.'

'If you wish to see the formal papers then I'm sure his solicitor will be happy to send you copies.'

'His solicitor?' Dee's voice faltered. 'But…'

'How does it make you feel, Dee, to realise that Peter felt concerned enough, distressed enough, to tell me that he wanted to sign a Power of Attorney in *my* favour so that I could deal with all his affairs because he was afraid that you might pressure him into doing something he didn't feel was right?'

Dee's face drained of blood.

It wasn't just the shock of hearing that Hugo would be taking Peter's place on her committee that was making her feel so sick with despair, it was also the heart-aching knowledge that Peter had felt that he couldn't trust her. Fiercely she blinked back the shocked, shamed tears she could feel burning the back of her eyes.

'Peter has given you Power of Attorney?' Dee asked weakly. She felt very much as though she would like to sit down, but her pride wouldn't allow her to betray that kind of weakness in front of Hugo of all people. She turned away from him and faced the window whilst she fought for self-control.

It seemed doubly ironic now, in view of what Hugo had just said, that she had actually entertained the thought of asking for his help in persuading Peter to give to her the very authority he had actually given to Hugo.

'Yes, he has,' Hugo confirmed. 'And you may be very sure, Dee,' he continued sternly, 'that I shall ensure his wishes are respected and that you do not ride roughshod over them. I dare say that you and this...this Ward Hunter believe that you have the power to bring the other members of the committee round to your way of thinking, but I can promise you—'

'The decisions of the committee have nothing to do with Ward,' Dee protested defensively. 'And in fact...'

'Exactly.' Hugo pounced triumphantly, overruling her. 'I'm pleased to see that you recognise that fact, even if that recognition is somewhat belated. From what Peter has been telling me it seems to me that you've been managing your father's charity very much as though it's your own personal bank account and that you—'

'That's not true,' Dee gasped angrily. 'Even if I wanted to do that—' She stopped and swallowed hard. 'What you're suggesting is... All I'm trying to do is to help those who need it most.'

'In your judgement,' Hugo pointed out.

'Hugo, Peter means well, but he's...'

'He's what? Not capable of making his own informed decisions any more?'

'No, of course not,' Dee protested.

'I'm glad. "No, of course not," indeed,' Hugo agreed. 'He tells me that the committee are due to meet soon to discuss their plans for the next twelve months. As his legal representative I shall, of course, attend the meeting on his behalf.'

Dee gulped.

'But you *can't*.'

'Why not?' Hugo challenged her coolly.

'Well, you might not be here. You must have business to attend to…'

'I shan't be going away—at least not in the foreseeable future. As I was just confirming to Peter's bank manager on the phone, I am free to work wherever I choose, and, since Peter needs to have someone close at hand to keep an eye on him right now, it makes sense for me to move in here with him.'

Dee felt cold all over, and tired, very tired. It appalled her that she, whom everyone considered to be so strong, could feel like this.

'You don't understand; *Peter* doesn't understand,' she started to protest.

'On the contrary, I think you'll find that I understand very well,' Hugo contradicted her flatly. 'Your father might have set up and funded his charity originally, Dee, but it is *not* your plaything. You do not have sole control over it; you and your boyfriend cannot simply—'

'Ward is *not* my boyfriend,' Dee was stung into replying, her face flushing with resentment at the way Hugo was talking to her.

'No? Well, whatever his relationship with you, Peter is very concerned about the influence he seems to have over you.'

'Peter is old-fashioned, set in his ways. He is wonderful, and I love him dearly, but he can be very stubborn, very blinkered.'

'He's only one member of a committee of seven people, Dee, and if he is the only one who does not share your point of view then I cannot understand why you should be concerned...'

Dee closed her eyes.

The fact of the matter was that Peter was *not* the only one likely to express doubts about what she wanted to do.

'Look, I've got an appointment in half an hour,' Hugo told her as he glanced at his watch.

As he spoke he was holding the door open for her, as though she were some candidate for a job and he had just finished interviewing her, Dee reflected angrily. She contemplated telling him that she was not going until she had spoken to Peter, and then acknowledged that there was little point in putting herself in an even more vulnerable position than she already was.

Head held high, she marched towards the open door.

'I shall see you on Monday,' Hugo told her cordially as she stalked past him. 'I understand that the committee meeting is set for eleven a.m.?'

'Yes, it is,' Dee agreed distantly, trying not to grind her teeth with vexation as he escorted her to the front door. How could Peter have done this to her? Put her in this position?

She could feel her fury and her frustration causing a tight ball of emotion deep inside her chest. As she passed him Hugo touched her briefly on her bare arm. Immediately Dee drew back from him, as though he had branded her.

'Dee, Peter is only acting out of concern—for you and for your father. He looks upon his role on the committee as an almost sacred trust, and he—'

'And you think that *I* don't?' Dee almost spat at him, her eyes burning with the intensity of what she was feeling as her gaze locked with his.

'Dee, your father set up this charity for a specific purpose, and I feel—'

'I don't care what you feel.' Dee cut across him furiously. 'You know nothing about my father, what he wanted, what he believed. You despised him because he was wealthy and you resented him because he was my father and I loved him.'

Dee stopped, unable to go on, her voice choked with emotion.

'You're being unfair,' Hugo told her sharply. 'I certainly never despised your father.'

'You said that in your view it was impossible for someone with my father's business interests and love of making money to be truly altruistic.'

'You're taking things out of context,' Hugo said curtly. 'What I actually said was that it was impossible for anyone to be as *saintly* as you insisted your father was. You put him up on a pedestal, Dee, and I—'

'You were determined to pull him down off it,' Dee reminded him fiercely. 'You're the last person who should be on his committee, Hugo,' she told him starkly, 'and I don't think I'll ever forgive Peter for what he's done. You have no right...'

She stopped as she felt her emotions threaten to overwhelm her.

How many times in the past had they argued like this? How many times had Hugo forced her into a corner from which she had had to defend her father to him?

As she started to turn away, out of the corner of her eye Dee saw a car pulling up next to her own, and the doctor getting out. Ignoring Hugo's sharply authoritative, 'Dee, wait,' Dee walked quickly to her own car. She was literally trembling with angry emotion. She felt sick with the force of it. Shakily she set her car in motion.

CHAPTER SEVEN

THREE HOURS LATER, when she walked into her office in Rye-on-Averton, the first thing that Dee saw lying on her desk was the file she had so carefully and optimistically prepared with Ward's help, outlining her proposals for the way the charity could help the town's young people.

Her heart was still pumping fast with adrenalin. The drive home had done nothing to reduce her sense of injustice—or her anger against Hugo. She wasn't used to having her plans thwarted, to not being in total control of her life or her own decisions. But anger alone wasn't responsible for the tension that had her pacing the floor of her office with all the pent-up energy of a caged tigress.

How dared Hugo interfere in her life, her plans? How dared he tell her what she could and could not do?

Hugo knew nothing about the problems of small-town living; how could he? How would *he* feel were she to try to tell him his business? If she were to claim that…?

'Oooohhh,' Dee made an angry growl of female protest as she paced her office floor with renewed fury.

There was no point in blaming Peter; he was ill…getting old… She could just imagine how Hugo must have coaxed him to give him that Power of Attorney, Dee reflected darkly.

Perhaps it wasn't just the *university's* money Hugo was

after for the United Nations aid programme. Dee smiled grimly to herself as she gave in to the temptation to give full rein to her ignoble thoughts.

Peter was unmarried, with no family, and had a very healthy portfolio of investments—she should know; she was the one who had advised him on them. There had always been a tacit understanding between them that his money would be willed to her father's charity, but perhaps Hugo had other ideas.

Even though she knew she was allowing her anger to drive her thoughts and suspicions down extremely illogical routes, Dee refused to let go of them. Common sense told her that Hugo, even if he wasn't the scrupulously honest person she thought him to be, would not risk his reputation by doing something so potentially dangerous. Peter's money would be the merest drop in the ocean compared with the millions that Hugo would have under his control.

She looked at her desk. She was supposed to be seeing Ward this weekend, so that they could go over her proposals together for one final time.

To her consternation Dee felt the hot, painful tears of anger and disappointment filling her eyes.

Still prowling the room, she stopped her restless progression to study the large photograph of her father which she had had blown up and framed and which hung above the room's fireplace.

It was one of her favourite ones of him. In it he was just starting to smile, so that one could see the warmth in his eyes. He had been looking directly at her when the photograph had been taken—coincidentally, as it happened, by Peter—and whenever she felt really low Dee always drew strength from standing in front of it, right in his line of vision, so that she would feel again the warmth of his smile and his love.

This time, though, it wasn't totally effective. This time, knowing...remembering...how much her father had loved her could not totally ease the pain from her heart or the discord from her mind.

'You know nothing about my father...you despised him...' she had accused Hugo. It wasn't strictly true. What Hugo despised was the world he considered her father had represented: the world of money and prestige, of placing more importance on possessions than people. But her father hadn't been like that. He had been good with money, yes, and proud, very proud, but he had also been compassionate and caring, and it had hurt her more than she had ever been able to say to either of them that he and Hugo had not got on better together.

'But, Daddy, I love him,' she had told her father helplessly when he had questioned the amount of time she was spending with Hugo.

'You don't know what love is,' her father had objected. 'You're a girl still...a child...'

'That's not true. I know I love you,' Dee had defended herself firmly. 'And I'm not a child, nor even a girl now. I'm over eighteen...an adult...'

'An adult? You're a baby still,' her father had scoffed, and then added gruffly, '*My* baby...'

'Oh, Dad,' Dee whispered now, her eyes refilling with tears. She had tried so hard to bring Hugo and her father closer. Too hard, perhaps. Certainly the harder she had tried, the more both of them had become entrenched in their suspicions of one another.

'How can he claim that he loves you?' her father had demanded once. 'What plans has he made for your future? The last time I spoke to him he told me that as soon as he'd finished his Ph.D. he was planning to take himself off to some desert or other.'

'Dad, he isn't so very different from you,' she coaxed her father. 'You both have very philanthropic natures and—'

'Maybe, but I would never have left your mother or you to go traipsing off all over the world,' her father interrupted her sharply.

Dee took a deep breath, knowing that the moment she had been putting off for so long could not be put off any longer.

'Dad, Hugo won't be leaving me,' she told her father quietly.

'Not leaving you? You mean he's changed his mind... seen sense?' her father demanded.

'No. Hugo hasn't changed his mind,' Dee answered him steadily. 'He still plans to go, but...' She paused, and then looked lovingly at her father. 'I'm going to go with him, Dad...'

'You're *what*?'

She had known he wouldn't be pleased, of course. Although no firm plans had been made she knew that he had hoped she would move back home after university, and until she had met Hugo she too had assumed that that was what she would eventually do.

Her father had never tried to hold her back, nor to impose his views on her. He had been the one to encourage her to leave home and go to university, but...but he wasn't really ready, deep down in his heart, to let her go completely yet.

'This is what Hugo wants. What do you want, Dee?'

I want you and Hugo to like each other. I want to be happy. I want Hugo, she could have said, but she knew that in his present frame of mind her father's heart was closed to the needs of her own. 'This is something I want to do for myself,' she told him quietly. 'I *have* to go, Dad. I love him!'

'Well, you're over-age, and I can't stop you,' he responded curtly.

Hugo loved her, too, she knew that, but he was fiercely, passionately determined to carry out the plans he had discussed with her. If she didn't go with him Dee knew he would go on his own. That didn't mean he would stop loving her—she knew he wouldn't—but it *would* mean that there would be a large slice of his life which she could not share.

Hugo was a crusader, a man who needed to live life on a grand scale, a young man full of the passionate intensity of his youth, and if Dee felt in her heart that her own inclinations lay closer to those of her father, if she felt that she could do just as much good working to help those in need at home as she could helping those who lived in such tragically difficult circumstances, if her dreams were smaller and gentler than those of the man she loved, then she felt that they were perhaps best kept to herself.

Hugo's family had already thrown enough cold water on his dream. Hugo needed her support and her love, and *she* needed to be with him.

In years to come the time they would spend together would be something they would remember, a memory that would help to bond them together, something to tell their children.

A small smile curled Dee's mouth.

Hugo might be all crusading male eagerness where his own life was concerned, but she knew instinctively that when it came to his children, to *their* children, he would want to protect them just as fiercely as her father did her.

In many ways they were so alike, so alike and so fiercely jealous of one another. Sometimes she felt like a bone they were both determined to possess.

In another few weeks she would sit her finals. Hugo had already completed his work, and their plan was that just as soon as they could they would leave together. Hugo had already approached one of the main aid agencies, and both of them had been provisionally accepted onto a scheme they were operating in Ethiopia.

Dee had suggested that before they left they should both spend time with their respective families, but Hugo was impatient to leave just as soon as possible.

Although officially they still had separate homes, Dee now spent most of her time at Hugo's and she had her own key. Her father might logically guess that she and Hugo were lovers, but Dee was sensitive enough to know that he would not want to have such suspicions confirmed. He came from a generation when a couple's sexual life was something strictly private, and really only acceptable inside the respectable confines of a marriage. Dee knew that it was different for her and Hugo, of course. The thought of how it would feel not to have the freedom to reach out into the night and touch Hugo's naked body, not to know the special pleasure of knowing that body so well that it was almost as though, in some way, it had become hers, was simply unbearable, and not just because of the sexual frustration she would suffer. She loved Hugo so much that she wanted to be close to him in every way there was.

Emotionally, mentally, physically and of course sexually, they had no secrets from one another, no prohibited areas. Dee loved lying in bed and watching as Hugo padded around the bedroom, his naked body as splendidly magnificent as that of a male cheetah in his prime. Everything about him sang with energy and health, from the silky, sleek gleam of his skin to the thick, shiny glossiness of his hair.

It still amused—and amazed—her to see the way he could respond physically to her just because she was looking at him.

'*You're* the one who's caused it,' he would tease her as his busy perambulations about the flat became halted by the demanding urgency of his arousal. 'So now it's up to you to do something about it.'

'Such as what?' she would ask, mock innocently, all the while her fingers delicately caressing him.

'Mmm…well, that will do for a start,' he would murmur to her as he covered her mouth with his own, his weight pushing her back against the pillows.

They had been together for over two years, but the intensity of their physical desire for one another still had the power to awe and excite Dee. She only had to run her fingers teasingly along the length of Hugo's erection, or just merely circle its head and caress it playfully, for him to immediately be so responsive to her that her own body flowered into delirious response. Sometimes, in the middle of a serious discussion, she would reach across and touch him temptingly, laughing as he tried to hold on to the thread of his argument, her eyes betraying the wonderment and awe she still felt that he should love and want her so much.

They had their quarrels, of course. Both of them were strong-willed and passionate, both of them felt things very deeply, and both of them were very vocal in stating those beliefs, but the only real issue of contention which existed between them was that of Dee's father. She had introduced them to one another with loving pride—and anxiety—and soon discovered that she had been right to be anxious.

The evening had ended with her father and Hugo arguing passionately about the morality of the government in power; her father had been pro-government and Hugo anti. Torn between both of them, she had tried to placate her father, knowing how it would hurt his pride to have to acknowledge the strength of Hugo's arguments. But then later, when they had returned to Hugo's flat, Hugo had claimed that she had supported her father against him, and not just that but, even worse, she had denied her own beliefs as well.

'You know as well as I do that I was right,' Hugo had told her fiercely, for once refusing to respond to the loving little kisses she'd been pressing placatingly along his jaw. 'You've agreed with me that—'

'Dad's old-fashioned and set in his ways,' she had told Hugo. 'I didn't want to hurt him…'

'But you don't mind hurting me,' Hugo had challenged her grimly.

She had sighed and wrapped her arms lovingly around his neck.

'Does it matter which of you won the argument?'

'Yes,' Hugo had told her simply, before pointing out more acerbically, 'If it didn't you wouldn't have found it necessary to side with your father, would you?'

'I meant, does it matter to you?' Dee had countered placatingly. 'It isn't easy for Dad, you know Hugo, having to accept you into my life.'

'It isn't easy for me having to accept him into ours,' Hugo had retorted. 'One day you're going to have to choose which of us your loyalty really lies with,' he had warned her.

But Dee had crossed her fingers behind her back, tell-

ing herself that, given time, the pair of them would become better friends. And perhaps they might have done
if Hugo had been more willing to give ground to her father and listen to his advice, even if he didn't act on it, or
if her father had been able to accept that Hugo needed to
be allowed to feel that her father respected his viewpoint
even if he couldn't agree with it.

As it was, with neither of them prepared to give
ground, Dee had eventually resorted to keeping the peace
between them by keeping them apart.

Later on, when she was sitting with her father, all too
conscious of the growing male antagonism between him
and Hugo, and just about to have a final attempt at bringing her father round to the idea of her working abroad
with him, the doorbell rang. Whilst he went to open the
door Dee acknowledged that if she had to choose between
them, then she would choose Hugo. Her father was her
past…Hugo was her man, her lover, her present and her
future. Her heart sank as her father walked back into the
room accompanied by his visitor.

Her father had first introduced her to Julian Cox just
after Christmas. Although he was no more than five or
six years older than Dee, Julian dressed and behaved
more like a man of her father's age, and Dee particularly
disliked the patronising way that Julian behaved towards
her, and the disparaging references made to her status as
a student. Her father, though, refused to acknowledge any
fault or flaw in him, and constantly sang his praises to
Dee, drawing Dee's attention to his politeness and good
manners, his smart way of dressing.

Personally, Dee found him smarmy and totally unap-
pealing, but she had no wish to widen the rift developing
between her and her father by telling him so. Her father
had informed her that Julian worked as a freelance finan-

cial consultant, and, at her father's instigation, Julian had been invited to join the committees of two of the charities her father was involved with.

The two men seemed to spend a good deal of time together, and Dee acknowledged as she watched the familiar way Julian dropped into one of the sitting-room armchairs that it irked her that he should be so much at home in her father's house. Almost immediately as he sat down Julian began a conversation with her father which totally excluded Dee, eventually turning to her and apologising insincerely.

'Oh, I'm sorry, Dee...we must be boring you. Finance isn't of any interest to you students, is it? Unless you're agitating for larger grants.' He guffawed loudly at his own joke, and to Dee's irritation she could see that her father was actually smiling.

It was very tempting to tell Julian that, far from not having any interest in finance, she had managed very successfully to turn the modest investments she had begun with into a very respectable amount of money.

The two men were discussing the charity her father had begun to set up to benefit the local townspeople.

It was obvious to Dee from what was being said that Julian Cox was expecting to play a very major role in the control of the foundation's assets. Dee found this information disquieting.

'What's wrong with him?' Hugo had asked Dee when she had tried to explain her instinctive dislike of Julian to him.

'He makes the hairs on the back of my neck stand up,' was all Dee had been able to tell him.

'Dee,' Hugo had teased her, 'I thought only *I* could do that.'

'It's not the same,' Dee had objected. 'When you do

it it's because…because I love and want you, but when it's him, it's because… He makes my skin crawl, Hugo… there's something about him that I just don't like. I don't trust him…'

'Tell your father, not me,' Hugo had counselled her.

'He wouldn't listen,' Dee had admitted uncomfortably.

Hugo's eyebrows had risen, his mouth curling cynically as he'd commented, 'No…but according to you your father is a man of reason and compassion, a man who is *always* willing to listen to the views of others. Others, but not, it seems, to me or to you…'

'Hugo, that isn't fair,' Dee had protested. 'We're talking about two different things. My father—'

'Your father is jealous because you love me,' Hugo had told her flatly, 'and until you accept that fact I'm afraid you and I are never going to see eye to eye over him.'

'Now you're doing what you always complain my father does,' Dee had told him angrily. 'Now you're trying to put emotional pressure on me. Hugo, I love him…he's my *father* and I want so much for the two of you to get on well together…'

'Have you told *him* that?' Hugo had asked her wryly.

It was an argument that was destined to run and run, and of course it had.

'Have you told him yet?' Hugo asked Dee that evening.

'Yes,' she acknowledged tiredly.

'And…' Hugo prodded. 'Or can I guess?'

'He wasn't very happy,' Dee admitted.

'So, tell me something I don't already know,' Hugo drawled. 'I suppose he claimed that you would be wasting your degree and the government's money, that you'd be exposing yourself to almost certain death, that I was being a selfish so-and-so and that I should stay at home and get myself a proper job…'

His comments were so acutely right that Dee felt her eyes prick with vulnerable tears.

'Hugo, he's my father; he loves me. He's just trying—'

'To come between us?' Hugo suggested bitterly.

'He just wants to protect me,' Dee protested. 'When you…we…have children, you'll feel the same.'

'Maybe I shall, but I certainly won't put emotional pressure on them or try to control their lives for them,' Hugo told her tersely.

'Julian Cox arrived whilst I was there. It sounds as though he's trying to persuade Dad to put him on the Foundation committee.'

'So?' Hugo questioned.

'I don't trust him, Hugo. There's something about him.'

'He's not my type, I agree,' Hugo replied, 'but then I've never been into making money, so…'

'Maybe not, but that's because *you've* never needed to be,' Dee responded, with an unusual touch of asperity. 'You get an allowance, Hugo, as well as your grant. One day you'll inherit family money—even though you claim your parents aren't wealthy. My father has had to make his own way in life. He's proud of what he's achieved and so am I, and I hate it when you go all aristocratic and contemptuous about him. There's nothing wrong about being good at making money.'

'Isn't there?' Hugo asked her quietly. ' My great-great-grandfather made his from coal, from sending people deep down into the earth to dig for black gold for him. There's a plaque outside the colliery that he owned. It commemorates the deaths of twenty-nine men who were killed making my great-great-grandfather a millionaire.

He gave their widows a guinea each. It's all there in his accounts. Like your father, *he* had a good head for money. I used to dream about them sometimes, those men, and how it must have felt to die like that.'

'Hugo, don't,' Dee pleaded, white-faced. Hugo rarely talked about his family history, but Dee knew how he felt about it.

As she turned towards him Hugo cupped her face in his hand as he begged her hoarsely, 'Don't ever leave me, Dee. Don't let your father come between us. I love you more than you know. You've enriched my life, made my life better in so many ways. Without you…'

'Without me you'd still go to Ethiopia,' she told him quietly.

His eyes darkened.

'Yes,' he agreed simply, before adding harshly, 'I have to, Dee. I can't… I have to. But I shan't be going without you,' he added softly. 'Shall I?'

He was kissing her by then, and so there was no vocal reply that Dee could give other than a soft, blissful sigh as she moved closer to his body.

Later, their bodies closely entwined, Hugo leaned over her propping his head up on his elbow as he told her quietly, 'Dee, there's something I have to say to you.'

'Mmm…?' she encouraged him languorously.

It wasn't unusual for him to tease her with this kind of pronouncement, which was usually followed by a declaration of his love or an announcement that some part of her body was filling him with unquenchable desire, and so, smiling back at him, she waited happily.

'This aid work—it isn't just something I want to just do to fill in a year,' Hugo told her abruptly.

Dee sat up in bed. She knew already how strongly Hugo felt about what he wanted to do, but this was the first time he had mentioned it being more than a short-term vocation.

'I was talking to someone the other day, and they were saying how desperately they need people to take on not just work in the field but fundraising as well.'

'But you can't do both,' Dee objected practically.

'Not at the same time,' Hugo agreed. 'But there's a desperate need for people to increase everyone's awareness of how vitally important good aid programmes are, to act as ambassadors for them. Charlotte was saying that I'd be ideal for that kind of role, especially once I'd got some practical hands-on experience in the field.'

'Charlotte?' Dee queried uncertainly.

'Mmm...Charlotte Foster. You don't know her. She graduated a year ahead of me and she's been working for a children's charity. She's just come back to this country and I bumped into her the other day in town.'

Dee listened in silence.

'It will perhaps mean that I shall have to spend longer in the field than we'd planned.'

'You mean it might mean that *we* are going to have to spend longer in the field than *we* had planned,' Dee corrected him gently. She saw instantly that she had said exactly the right thing.

'I *knew* you'd understand,' Hugo exulted as he hugged her tightly. 'It will mean having to put off having a family for rather longer than we agreed.'

He shook his head and groaned.

'Charlotte was telling me that they go into the most unbelievable details before taking people on their permanent staff. There have been so many scandals involving people misusing charity money that now they check and double-check to make sure there's absolutely no chance that anyone they employ carries even the merest whiff of scandal. Charlotte told me that they've recently asked one of their executives to leave because his stepfather turned out to have been under suspicion of being involved in some kind of financial fraud. But then, of course, you can understand why they have to be so careful.'

'Mmm…' Dee agreed.

'You're wonderful. Do you know that?' Hugo told her happily. 'The ideal woman for me…the ideal wife!'

The next few days were busy ones for Hugo. His decision to make his commitment to working for an aid charity a permanent rather than a temporary one meant that, with Charlotte's encouragement, he was toing and froing from Lexminster to London, seeing people and being interviewed.

'There's so much we still need to learn,' he told Dee excitedly one afternoon, after he had returned from a briefing session with the agency Charlotte had recommended him to.

'We're finding that the people themselves actually teach us how we can best help them. Charlotte says—'

It was less than a month until Dee sat her finals. She had been studying when Hugo had rushed in, and, despite Hugo's insistence that Charlotte was simply a friend, to Dee it was quite obvious that the other woman was in love with him. Her patience snapped.

'I don't care *what* Charlotte says,' she told him sharply. 'There are other things in life, you know, Hugo, like the fact that I've got my finals in four weeks' time.'

'You'll pass them,' Hugo assured her cheerfully. 'Look, Charlotte's invited us out for a celebratory dinner tonight.'

'A celebratory dinner?' Dee queried.

'Mmm… She's pretty sure that I'm going to be offered a permanent post with the agency. Come on, you can shower first.'

'Hugo, I can't go out…not tonight,' Dee protested, indicating the books in front of her. 'I've *got* to study. Look, you go,' she told him in a gentler voice. She hated having to spoil his pleasure, but she still had to break the news to her father that they would be gone longer than they had originally planned, and that Hugo intended to make a permanent career in the aid field—which meant that they would be travelling the world for most of their married lives, Dee suspected. There was no way she could study with Hugo prowling the flat in his present electrified, excited state. She would be able to work far better if she was on her own.

'Well, if you're sure you don't mind,' Hugo said.

'Mmm…I love you,' he whispered to her half an hour later, just before he left. Smiling at him, Dee returned his kiss.

'You can show me how much later,' she teased him.

Oddly, once he had gone she found it almost impossible to settle back into her work. On impulse she went over to the telephone and dialled her father's number.

He answered almost straight away, and Dee could tell from the way he said her name that he had been hoping that she might be someone else. That alone was enough to make her frown. Her father was *never* too busy to speak to her when she phoned—in fact he was always complaining that she didn't ring often enough— and besides, some sixth sense, some daughterly awareness, made her instantly pick up that something was wrong.

'Dad—' she began urgently, but he was already cutting her off, telling her curtly,

'Dee, I have to go. I'm expecting another call…'

'Dad,' she protested, but it was too late. He had already hung up.

Dee waited ten minutes and then rang again, but the line was engaged. It was still engaged when she tried a second time and then a third.

It was now nearly ten o'clock, but, late though it was, Dee knew that she just had to see her father.

Scribbling Hugo a note, she hurried out to her car.

CHAPTER EIGHT

THE PHONE RANG abruptly on Dee's desk, breaking into her thoughts of the past. Automatically she reached for the receiver. Her caller was Ward Hunter, and after Dee had asked after Anna's health, Ward began, 'Look, I've been thinking. It might be a little unorthodox, but if you'd like me to come along and talk with your committee, explain to them how we've gone about things and—'

'Ward, I'd love you to, but I'm afraid it won't do any good. There's a problem.'

Briefly Dee outlined to him what had happened.

'You say this man has somehow persuaded Peter to give him Power of Attorney? Who is he, Dee? Is he related to Peter or—'

'He's not related to him but they are old friends,' Dee interrupted him. 'In fact, I...I actually know him myself,' she added reluctantly.

'Oh. I was just thinking that it might be worthwhile making some enquiries to see if he had put any kind of pressure on Peter to...'

'No. No, I don't think there's any question of that. He's very high up in one of the main aid agencies, Ward, and from what I know of him...' She stopped, unwilling to go on. No one in her present life knew anything about

Hugo, and that was the way she wanted things to stay. After all, what was the *point* in them knowing?

'Mmm…what I can't understand is why this Hugo, whatever his name is, has decided to oppose your plans, when anyone with any sense can see how beneficial they would be.'

'Hugo thinks he's on a moral crusade,' Dee told him wryly.

'Well, don't give up yet,' Ward encouraged her. 'Surely there's still a chance that you can persuade the rest of the committee…?'

'A very remote chance,' Dee agreed. 'A *very* remote chance.'

Five minutes after she had said goodbye to Ward the telephone rang again. This time it was Beth who was telephoning her.

'Dee, how are you?' she asked cheerfully. 'I saw you in Lexminster today. Why didn't you call and see me?'

Beth and her husband-to-be were living just outside the town in a pretty eighteenth-century farmhouse they had recently bought. Alex was the university's youngest chair. He lectured in Modern History whilst Beth still owned and ran the pretty glassware shop in Rye-on-Averton with her partner, Kelly, which she rented from Dee.

'I would have loved to but I didn't have time,' Dee fibbed.

'No, I understand. Anna mentioned that you're busy with your plans to open a workshop along the lines of Ward's. Well, if you want someone to teach your teenagers all there is to know about making glass, Alex's aunt is due over this summer, and, believe me, *no one* knows more about it than she does.'

Dutifully Dee laughed. She had met Alex's aunt, and

she knew that she was very much the matriarch of the
Czech side of Alex's family.

'Look, I was wondering if you might be free for supper on Saturday night. I know it's short notice, but Alex
is having to entertain someone—something to do with
setting up a new scholarship.'

'If this someone is a he and you're—' Dee began
firmly, but Beth anticipated her and laughed.

'He is a he, but I promise you I'm not trying to match-
make. Please, Dee.' Beth was beseeching her.

Unwillingly Dee gave in. The last thing she really felt
like doing was being sociable.

'Seven-thirty for eight, then,' Beth informed her, ringing off smartly before Dee could change her mind.

It was dark by the time Dee eventually let herself into the
house that had been her father's. It had been dark too the
night she had driven home in such anxiety, slipping her
key into the lock and hurrying into the hallway, calling
her father's name.

He hadn't answered her, and it had been a shock to
go into the kitchen and find him sitting there, immobile
and silent.

Equally shocking had been the sight of a bottle of
whisky on the table beside him and an empty glass. Her
father rarely drank, and when he did it was normally a
glass or maybe two of good wine.

'Dad...Daddy,' she pleaded anxiously, her heart plum-
meting as he turned his head to look at her and she saw
the despair in his eyes.

'Daddy, what is it? What's wrong?' she asked him,
running over to him and dropping to her knee in front of
him. They had never been physically demonstrative with

one another, but almost instinctively Dee took hold of his hands in both of hers. They were frighteningly icy cold.

'What is it…are you ill…? Dad, please…' she begged him.

'Ill…?' His voice cracked harshly over the word, sharp with bitterness and contempt. 'I *wish*… *Blind*, that's what I've been Dee, corrupted by my own pride and my vanity, my belief that I knew…' He stopped, and Dee realised that the tremors shaking her own body were coming from his. It shocked her immeasurably to see him like this, her father, who had always been so strong, so proud…

'Dad, please—*please* tell me what's wrong.'

'You shouldn't have come here. What about your finals…? Where's Hugo…?'

'He…he had to go out.'

'So he isn't here with you?'

She could see the relief in his eyes.

'At least I'm spared *that*, although it can only be a matter of time and then everyone will know.'

'Know what?' Dee demanded.

'That I've been taken in by a liar and a cheat, that I've given my trust to a thief and that he's… Gordon Simpson rang me last week,' he told her abruptly.

Gordon Simpson was the manager of the local branch of their bank, and a fellow committee member with her father on the local branches of two national charities.

'He's been going through the charity accounts with the accountant, and certain anomalies have come to light.'

'Anomalies…what, accounts mistakes, you mean?' Dee asked him, perplexed. She knew how meticulous her father was about such matters, and how annoyed with himself he would be at having made a mistake, but surely not to this extent.

'Accounting mistakes? Well, that's one way of putting

it.' He laughed bitingly. 'Creative accounting is how the gutter press prefer to refer to it—or so I'm told.'

'Creative accounting.' Dee's blood ran cold. 'You mean *fraud*?' she asked him in disbelief. 'But that's *impossible*. *You* would never—'

'No,' he agreed immediately. '*I* would never…but Julian Cox… He deceived me, Dee, took me in completely. He's cheated the charity out of a good few thousand pounds already, and all under my protective aegis. Oh, Gordon told me that no one would hold me to blame… he said he'd been as convinced of the man's honesty as I was…but that doesn't matter. *I* am still the one who was responsible for allowing him to become involved. I am still the one who vouched for him.

'Of course, I've repaid the missing money immediately, and Gordon and Jeremy, the accountant, have given me their assurance that the matter won't go any further.

'I tackled Cox immediately, and do you know what he had the gall to say to me? He told me that…he tried to blackmail me, Dee. Me! He threatened to go to the press and tell them that I'd supported him, encouraged him, unless I agreed to let him get away with it.

'Gordon and Jeremy said there was no point in pursuing him legally, and that to do so would bring the matter into the public arena and damage people's faith in the charity. They said that since I'd offered to refund the money the best thing to do was to simply keep the whole thing quiet.'

'Oh, Dad,' Dee whispered helplessly. She knew how strongly her father felt about matters of law and morality, and how much it must be hurting him to have to tell her. It wasn't just his pride that had been damaged, she knew, it was his whole sense of self, his whole belief about the importance of honesty.

Dee tried her best to comfort and reassure him, but she felt helplessly out of her depth. He was, after all, her father, and a man, and he was also of a generation that believed that it was a father's and a man's duty to shield and protect his womenfolk from anything that might cause them pain.

He had, Dee recognised, always sheltered her from the unpleasant things in life, and it frightened her to see him so vulnerable, so alarmingly unlike himself.

She spent the night at home with him. When she rang Hugo to tell him what she was doing there was no reply to her call, and, illogically, some of the anger and resentment she felt against Julian Cox she transferred to Hugo, for failing to know of her need and thus failing to meet it.

In the morning her father's air of restless anxiety made her feel equally on edge. He had someone he needed to see, he told her evasively when he came back downstairs for the breakfast she had prepared, but which neither of them ate, but when she asked him who he refused to answer her.

Since she had last seen him he had lost weight, and his face looked gaunt. Dee's heart ached for him. How could Julian Cox do this to her father?

'You haven't done anything wrong,' she told him fiercely. 'It's Julian Cox and not you.'

'Nothing wrong legally, maybe, but I still let him make a fool of me. I trusted him and, what is worse, I trusted him with other people's money. Who's going to believe that I didn't know, that I wasn't a party to what he was planning to do?'

'But Dad, *you* don't need the money.'

'*I* know that, Dee, and so do you, but how many other people are going to question my honesty? How many are going to believe there's no smoke without a fire?

'You'd better get back to Lexminster,' he told her wearily. 'You've got your finals in four weeks.'

'I've got plenty of time to study.' Dee fibbed. 'I want to stay here with you, Dad. I'll come with you to this meeting…I—'

'No.'

The sharpness of his denial shocked her. She had rarely seen him angry before, never mind so frighteningly close to losing control.

'Dad…'

'Go back to Lexminster, Dee,' he reiterated.

And so, stupidly, she did. And that was a mistake; an error of judgement; a failure to understand that she would never, ever forgive herself for.

If Julian Cox was responsible for her father's death, then she was certainly a party to that responsibility. If she had refused to go back to Lexminster, if she had stayed with him…

But she didn't… She drove back to Lexminster, desperate to see Hugo and tell him what had happened, running in fear to him, like a child denied the comfort of one strong man's protection and so running to another.

But when she reached the house Hugo wasn't there.

He had left her a note, saying that he had been called to London unexpectedly to attend another interview and that he didn't know when he would be back.

Dee wept in a mixture of anger and misery. She wanted him *there* with *her*, not pursuing some selfish, idealistic dream. She *needed* him there with her, and surely for once *her* needs came first. Was this how it was going to be for the rest of their lives? Was Hugo *always* going to be missing when she needed him? Were other people *always* going to be more important to him than her? She was too wrought up to think or reason logically;

it didn't make any difference that Hugo had no idea what was happening—it was enough that he just wasn't there.

Anxiously Dee rang her father at home. There was no reply. She tried his office, and gritted her teeth as she listened to the vague voice of the middle-aged spinster he employed as his secretary more out of pity for her than because he actually needed her help. She lived with her widowed mother and three cats, and was bullied unmercifully—both by her mother and the moggies.

'Your father—oh, dear, Andrea, I'm sorry; I have no idea... He isn't here—'

'He said he had an appointment with someone,' Dee told her, cutting across her. 'Is there anything in his diary?'

'Oh, let me look... There's a dental appointment—but, no, that's the fifteenth of next month. Just let me find the right page. Oh, yes...here we are. And it isn't the fifteenth today at all, is it? It's the sixteenth... No... he *was* to have seen that nice Mr Cox for lunch today...'

She paused as Dee made a fierce sound of disgust deep in her throat. What was loyal Miss Prudehow going to say when she learned just how un-nice 'nice Mr Cox' actually was? When she learned just what he had done to Dee's father—her employer?

Five minutes later, having extracted from her the information that she had no idea where Dee's father was, Dee replaced the receiver and redialled the number of her father's home. Still no reply. Where was he...?

It was later in the day when she knew. Early in the evening, to be exact.

The young policeman who came to give her the news looked white-faced and nervous when Dee opened the door to him. After he had asked to come in, and followed her inside the house, Dee noticed how he was unable to meet her eyes, and somehow, even before he said her father's name, she knew.

'My father?' she demanded tautly. 'Something's happened to my father...'

There had been an accident, the young policeman told her. Her father had been fishing. Quite what had happened, no one was sure. But somehow or other he had ended up in the river and got into difficulties. Somehow or other he had drowned.

Dee wanted badly to be sick. She also wanted badly to scream and cry, to deny what she was being told, but she was her father's daughter, and she could see that to give in to her own emotions would upset the poor young policeman, who looked very badly as though *he* wanted to be sick as well.

Dee had to go back with him to Rye. There were formalities to be attended to but not, thankfully, by her. She wanted to see her father, but Ralph Livesey, his friend and doctor, refused to allow her to do so.

'It isn't necessary, Dee,' he told her firmly. 'And it isn't what he would have wanted.'

'I don't understand,' she whispered, over and over again and throughout it all. 'How *could* he have drowned? He was such a good swimmer and...'

As she looked at Ralph she saw the look in his eyes, and instantly a sickening possibility hit her like a blow in the solar plexus.

'It *wasn't* an accident, was it?' she whispered sickly to him. 'It wasn't an accident.'

Her voice started to rise as shock and hysteria gripped her. 'It wasn't an accident. It was Julian Cox...he did it. He killed him...'

'Dee,' she heard Ralph Livesey saying sharply, before

turning to the policeman who was still there and telling him, 'I'm afraid she's in shock. I'll take her home with me and give her something to help her calm down.'

Once he had bundled her into his car Ralph Livesey was grimly relentless with her.

'Whatever *you* might think, Dee, so far as the rest of the world is concerned your father died in a tragic accident. I don't want to cause you any more pain. I can understand how upset you are, but for your father's sake you *have* to be strong. To make wild accusations won't bring him back, and could actually do him a lot of harm.'

'Harm? What do you mean?' Dee demanded.

'There's already some disquiet in town about…certain aspects of your father's professional relationship with Julian Cox.'

'Julian tried to deceive Daddy. He lied to him,' Dee defended her father immediately.

'I'm quite sure you're right, but unfortunately your father isn't here to defend himself, and Julian Cox is. To suggest that your father might have taken his own life will only exacerbate and fuel exactly the kind of gossip he would most want to avoid.'

'You mean that Julian is going to get away with *murdering* him?' Dee protested sickly. 'But…'

'I understand how you feel, Dee, but Cox did *not* murder your father. No one did. My guess is that he slipped off the bank whilst he was fishing. We've had a lot of rain recently, and the ground is treacherous. He lost his balance, fell into the river, probably knocking himself unconscious as he did so, and whilst he was unconscious, very tragically, he drowned.'

Dee looked at him with huge pain-filled eyes.

'I *can't* believe it was an accident,' she whimpered to him. 'Dad was a strong swimmer and—'

'It was an accident,' Ralph Livesey told her firmly.

'That is my judgement as a doctor, and I believe it is the one your father would have wished for.'

It was almost a week before Dee was able to leave Rye and return to Lexminster. There were formalities to attend to—formalities relating to her father's business affairs which, as Dee might have expected, had been left in meticulous order. Meticulous order, maybe, but someone would have to take over the business, someone would have to stand in her father's shoes. Dry-eyed, Dee had calmly made a brief list of those who might be able to do so, and then equally calmly she had put a cross through them all. There was only *one* person who could be trusted to carry on the work her father had been so dedicated to—only one person who could ensure that his memory was forever enshrined in the hearts and minds of the townspeople with all the respect and love to which he was entitled—and that one person was her.

Once she had made her decision she made it known to her father's solicitors, now hers, and all those people he had worked most closely with.

'But, Dee, whilst I applaud your desire to do this, it really isn't practical,' her father's solicitor told her. 'For one thing you've still got your finals ahead of you, and for another...'

Dee closed her eyes, and on opening them looked at him and through him.

'I'm not going back to university,' she told him distantly. How could she? How *could* she leave Rye? How could she leave her father's name and reputation unprotected and vulnerable to the likes of Julian Cox? She had made the mistake of leaving her father unprotected once, and look what had happened. She wasn't going to do it again. It never occurred to her that she might be in shock, or that her emotions might be warped and twisted by the sheer intensity of what had happened.

She had made her decision.

Hugo would have to be told, of course, but she doubted that he would care very much. If he cared he would be here with her, wouldn't he? If he cared he would have saved her father, wouldn't he? But he hadn't done. Had he?

Two days after her father's death, and the day before his funeral, she had a telephone call from Hugo.

'Dee, what on earth…? I've been ringing the house for the last two days. What are you doing in Rye?'

'I had to come home,' she told him bleakly.

'Look, I'm not going to be back for another few days. Whilst I was having my interview they told me that some-one had dropped out of one of their training programmes, and they asked me if I'd like to take his place. It will speed things up by about six weeks, since they only run these induction programmes every two months, but of course it's meant that I've had to put everything else on hold.

'They do it here in London, in-house, and they're put-ting me up with one of the guys who works for them. Dee, it's fascinating, but it makes me feel so inadequate. There's just so much to learn and know. Some of these people are still farming using methods that date back to biblical times, and…'

Still numb from the trauma of her father's death, Dee was only distantly aware of Hugo's selfish absorption in himself, and his total lack of awareness of her own need, her own pain and anger—emotions which fused together to make her feel that she had to protect her father, not just from Hugo's lack of love for him but also from his patent lack of awareness that anything was wrong with

her. And so, deliberately, she said nothing—after all, why
should she? Hugo quite obviously didn't care. Somewhere
deep inside she knew that somehow this discovery was
going to hurt her, and very badly, but right now all that
mattered was her father—not her, and most certainly not
Hugo and his precious interview!

'Hugo, I've got to go,' she interrupted him unemo-
tionally.

'Dee…? Dee…?' she heard him demanding in astonishment as she replaced the receiver.

The phone rang again almost immediately, but she
didn't answer it. She couldn't.

Tomorrow her father was to be buried, but Hugo was
more interested in the farming methods of people he
didn't even know than in her father's death and her own
pain. Her father had been right to question Hugo's love
for her. And even if he did love her as much as he had always claimed to…as much as she loved him…there was
no future for them together now, Dee recognised. How
could there be? Her place was here, in Rye. It had to be.
She owed it to her father.

Dee closed her eyes. Right now she couldn't think
about where Hugo's life and future lay. Right now all
she could think about was that Julian Cox had destroyed
her father…taken his life…and that it was down to her
to ensure that nothing else was taken from him, that his
reputation remained intact—and not just intact but re-
vered and honoured.

Hugo tried to talk her out of her decision, of course, but
she had remained obdurate. Her refusal to answer the
phone had caused him to come straight back to Lexminster, but by then Dee's resolve had hardened. All that she
allowed herself to remember of their relationship was

that Hugo had never loved her father and how important his ambition was to him—far more important than her.

'But, Dee, we love each other,' he pleaded with her, white-faced and patently unable to take in what she was telling him.

'No,' she announced, averting her face from his. 'I don't love you any more, Hugo,' she lied. 'My father was right; it would never have worked between us.'

She couldn't tell him why she had to stay. He wouldn't have understood.

A part of her ached for him to tell her that there was no way he was going to accept her decision, that there was no way he was going to let anything come between them even if it meant giving up all his own plans, but she knew, of course, that he would never do so. His plans meant too much to him—as much as her father meant to her.

'Dee, let someone else take over your father's business affairs,' Hugo pleaded with her.

'I can't,' Dee told him sharply.

'Why…what's so damned important about making a few more hundred thousand pounds?' he challenged her angrily.

Dee shook her head. She could have told him that it wasn't the money she needed to protect, it was her father's reputation—but how could she tell him that her father had taken his own life? That he had been on the brink of being branded a cheat and perhaps even worse?

It wasn't so very long ago that Hugo had been telling her just how important it was that his *own* reputation was above reproach. How would he feel at the thought of potentially being contaminated by the slur on her father's reputation via *her*? And if she was not there to protect him there was no saying what damage Julian Cox might do to the memory and the name of her father. He hadn't gone for good, Dee knew that instinctively. He would be back, and who knew what malicious rumours he might choose to spread when he did return?

'Dee...I don't understand,' Hugo was saying helplessly. 'Is there someone else? I know your father...'

'Don't talk to me about my father.' Dee responded fiercely. 'It's over, Hugo. It's over. If you can't accept that then I'm sorry... I have to go now,' she told him stiffly, standing up.

'You have to go now... Just like that... Just as though we're two mere acquaintances instead of—' he began savagely. 'You and I are lovers, Dee...we planned to marry, to raise a family. You wanted to have my child, my *children*,' he reminded her grimly, 'and now you're acting—'

'Acting!'

Dee's body quivered. Hugo mustn't suspect the truth, mustn't ever know just what it was costing her to do this, to send him away, but she had to do it. She had to do it both for her father's sake and his own.

'I've changed my mind,' she told him.

He reached for her then, and she read the purpose in his eyes even before his mouth crushed down on hers. She stood motionless in his embrace until he lifted his head, and then she told him in a dry, whispery voice, 'If you do, now, Hugo, it will be rape...'

He let her go immediately of course. She had known he would. He stormed out of the house, his face white with bitterness and anger.

She didn't cry then, and she didn't cry the following day either, when she buried her father.

She remained at the graveside for over an hour after the other mourners had gone, and when she eventually turned to leave she saw Hugo, watching her from several yards away.

He made to come over to her, but she shook her head and walked quickly in the opposite direction, balling her hands into fists in the pockets of her coat, her body stiff with a mixture of fear and rejection. She didn't dare let him see how vulnerable she felt, or how much she longed for him, how much she wanted him…how much, already, she ached for him and missed him.

It simply couldn't be. How could it? Her place wasn't with him any longer.

At Dr Livesey's insistence, after the funeral she went to stay with her father's aunt in Northumberland for several weeks. When she returned there were several notes in her post from Hugo, begging her to get in touch with him. She burned them all. And then, six weeks after her father's death, she woke up one morning like someone coming out of an anaesthetic or a long paralysis, the pain of her returning un-numbed emotions so intense that the agony of them almost made her scream.

Hugo!

Hugo! What had she *done*? Not only had she lost her father, she had sent away the man she loved, the only man she would ever love.

Hugo!

Hugo!

She dialled the number of his Lexminster flat and then, when there was no reply, she drove over to Lexminster to find him.

The shock of discovering that his flat was empty, and then of learning from a neighbour that Hugo had left for Somalia the previous day, made her reel with sick shock.

He had gone.

She had lost him.
It was over.
Now there was no going back.
Hugo!
Hugo!

CHAPTER NINE

'WARD, I'M WORRIED about Dee.'

Ward Hunter replaced the financial section of the paper he had been reading and looked across the breakfast table at his wife.

They had been married less than a year, and he marvelled that he could have managed to live so long without her. Just the sight of her pretty face on the pillow in the morning had the power to lift his heart to a degree that left him shaken with the depth of their love.

The fact that she was carrying their child only increased his awe that life should have thought him worthy of such munificence.

'You mustn't worry,' he chided her tenderly, adding a little bit more dryly, 'Especially about Dee. She's more than capable of running her own life, and running it extremely well.'

Anna gave a small sigh. Much as she loved her husband, there were some things, some signs, that only another woman could fully appreciate and understand.

Dee was very self-sufficient, very strong and independent, yes, but Anna was an extremely intuitive woman and she was concerned about her friend.

'What exactly did she say to you about there being a

problem with her plans to establish a unit like yours?'
Anna asked Ward thoughtfully.

'Not much. Just that,' Ward responded unhelpfully.
'But that won't be worrying her. Not Dee. She thrives
on having something to get her teeth into.'

'Mmm...'

Ward had a point, but Anna was still not totally reassured. She made a mental note to telephone Dee, or, even
better, to call round and see her.

Grimly Dee opened her front door and let herself into
her house. She had just spent the morning and the best
part of the afternoon going round trying to discreetly
canvass some support for her plans from the other committee members, but so far their reaction had not been
reassuring.

Only the bank manager shared her view on how important it was to make the changes she wanted to make.

As she walked into the kitchen she dropped her files
on the table. One of them contained her carefully worked
out and detailed proposals for what she wanted to do and
the other, which she had taken to discuss with her solicitor, was the original deed which had been drawn up when
her father had first instituted the charity.

His depressing but expected advice had been that there
was no loophole via which she could push through her
proposals without the support of Peter Macauley—in
other words, Hugo.

'I sympathise with what you want to do, Dee,' he had
said, 'but without the agreement of Peter's representative
on the committee, it just isn't possible.'

'I've got my own funds,' Dee had reminded him. 'If
I use them...'

'I can't possibly advise you to do that,' he had counselled her sharply. 'You're still only a young woman. You have your own future to think of. You already make a very substantial personal donation to the charity and—'

He had stopped, shaking his head, and Dee had known that he spoke the truth. It was her responsibility to manage the funds in the foundation her father had set up, and to this end, with Dee's agreement, he had placed most of his personal wealth in that foundation.

Whilst Dee had certainly been left adequately financially provided for by her father, she had not, by any means, been left the vast fortune other people thought. The fact that she was now a reasonably wealthy woman owed more to her adroit financial management of her own assets than to her inherited wealth, and Dee was pleased that it should be that way. But, like him, she preferred to donate most of the money she made to the local charity he had established, rather than amassing it for herself. But no one knew better than she did herself just what her ambitious scheme was likely to cost. There was no way she could fund it by herself—not in the immediate future.

How *could* Peter have done this to her?

She filled the kettle and went to stand by the sink, looking out into the garden as she waited for it to boil. Pointless, though, to blame poor Peter; he was only following the dictates of his conscience.

The doorbell rang. Dee was tempted to ignore it. The last thing she felt like right now was having to be sociable, but, as she hesitated, it rang again.

Squaring her shoulders, she went to answer its summons.

As she opened the front door, initially a beam of bright sunlight semi-dazzled her, so that for a moment she actually thought she must be seeing things. She blinked quickly once, and then once again, but no, she was *not* seeing things. He, Hugo, was actually standing there.

'Hugo,' she protested dizzily as he stepped towards her, but it was too late to protest or to deny him admittance because he was already standing in her hallway.

'What is it? What do you want?' she demanded sharply as she closed the door.

'I had to see you,' he responded. 'We need to talk.'

The sombreness of his voice and his expression immediately aroused Dee's anxiety.

'What is it?' she repeated as she led the way to the kitchen. 'Is it Peter? Is he worse? Is he…?'

As she opened the kitchen door and Hugo followed her inside the telephone rang in her study.

Excusing herself to Hugo, she went to answer it.

'Dee, it's me, Anna,' she heard her friend announcing as she picked up the receiver. 'I thought I'd just ring for a chat. How *are* you? Ward told me about the problems you're having with the committee—'

'Er, Anna, can I ring you back later?' Dee interrupted her quickly. 'It's just that…I'm rather busy at the moment.'

Dee didn't want to offend Anna, but she knew there was no way she could talk to her with Hugo in the house.

'Yes. Of course. I understand,' Anna agreed immediately, but Dee could sense that she was a little surprised.

Replacing the receiver, Dee hurried back to the kitchen. As she opened the door she could see Hugo standing by the table holding her file that related to the plans she had hoped to put to the committee. He was quite blatantly reading the file, and angrily Dee demanded, 'What are you doing? Those are private papers.'

'Are *these* the proposals you were planning to put to

the committee?' Hugo asked her brusquely, ignoring her angry demand.

Dee glared at him.

'Yes, as a matter of fact they are. Not that it's any business of yours.'

Abruptly she stopped, remembering too late just exactly what business it actually was of his, but it was too late now to recall her childish taunt.

A little to her surprise, though, instead of picking her up on it Hugo merely continued to frown and returned his attention to her open file.

'Your proposals call for a very radical change in direction for the charity,' Hugo told her.

Through her open study door Dee could hear her fax machine clattering.

Impatiently she looked from Hugo towards the study. The fax could be important. In some of the markets in which she had dealings a delay of only minutes in a deal could mean a financial loss of many thousands of pounds.

Turning her back on Hugo, she hurried back to her study, ripping the printed message out of the fax machine and quickly running her glance over it.

Body found in sea off Singapore identified as that of Julian Cox. Singapore authorities are investigating possibility of murder as Cox known to be a heavy gambler with large outstanding debts. Any further instructions?

The message had been sent via the agency Dee had used to try to trace the whereabouts of Julian Cox, and, although she had always known that wherever he had gone he would sooner or later return to his dishonest, cheating ways, she had not expected to receive news like this.

She closed her eyes, and then opened them again and reread the message. How ironic. How quixotic of fate—if it *was* Julian Cox—that he should be found drowned… just like her father.

Dee started to shiver, a low, agonised moan whispering dryly past her from her taut throat.

'Dee? Dee, what is it? What's wrong?'

Dee was vaguely conscious of Hugo coming into her office and taking the fax from her, but the message, coming on top of her recent mental reliving of the events leading up to her father's death, was having a dangerously traumatic effect on her. She knew that Hugo was there, she knew he had taken the fax from her and she knew too that he had read it, but even though she knew all these things somehow they were not completely real to her. What *was* real…*all* that was real…was that Julian Cox was dead: he had now gone beyond her justice, and beyond any earthly court of law's jurisdiction. The judge he now had to face…

'Cox is dead,' she heard Hugo saying. 'I didn't realise he meant so much to you. You never seemed to care very much for him.'

'*Care…*' Dee could feel something splintering sharply inside her, lacerating her so painfully, emotionally *and* mentally, that the agony of what she was experiencing made her want to scream out loud.

'Oh, yes, I *care*… I care that he cheated and deceived my father. I care that he nearly destroyed everything my father had worked to achieve. I care that he threatened him with humiliation and I care that my father trusted him and believed in him whilst he was cheating him. I care that because of him my father died…I care that he caused my father to take his own life. I care that because of him I lost *the* man—'

As Dee put her hands up to her face she discovered to her own bemusement that it was wet and that she was crying, that her hands were trembling, her body shaking violently. She was, Dee recognised distantly, dangerously close to losing control.

'Dee, what are you saying?' she could hear Hugo demanding curtly. 'Your father and Cox were partners, close friends...'

'Julian Cox was no friend to my father,' Dee denied chokily. 'He threatened him with blackmail... Oh, God... why did I let it happen? Why didn't I stay with him? If I had, Dad would still be alive today and I...'

She stopped. She would what? She would have been married to Hugo...the mother of his children...?

'I should have stayed, but I didn't...I was so selfish... I wanted to get back to you. I never dreamed that Dad would take his own life, that Julian would drive him to take his own life. He must have been so afraid, so alone. I let him down so badly.'

'Dee, your father *drowned*,' Hugo told her gently. 'It was an *accident*.'

'No... My father drowned, yes, but it *wasn't* an accident. How could it have been? He was an excellent swimmer, and why would he have gone fishing anyway? He told me that he had a meeting.'

She was shivering violently, her body icy cold but her face burning hot.

'Dee, you've had a bad shock,' she could hear Hugo telling her softly. 'Why don't you come and sit down in the kitchen and I'll make us both a hot drink? Come on. You're cold; you're shivering,' he told her when Dee started to shake her head in violent denial of what he was saying.

'I don't *want* a drink. I don't want *anything*… I just want you to go.'

It was over. At long last it was over. At long last there was no need for her to pursue Julian Cox any more. Fate had stepped in and taken over, but oddly Dee couldn't feel relieved. She couldn't in fact feel anything, only an aching, agonising awareness of how senseless, how wasteful her father's death had been. For the first time since her father's death Dee was able to admit to herself that, alongside her pain and her anger against Julian Cox, there was also a sharp thorn of anger inside her against her father—anger that he could have done what he had done without thinking how much it would hurt her, how much she would miss him…how much she loved him. She had always known how important other people's respect had been to him, how much he'd valued it—but surely not more than he'd valued her?

But he had left her, turned his back on her and her love for him, her need for him, and ended his own life. And she had been left alone to face the consequences of what he had done. Her eyes filled with fresh tears, a searing animal moan of pain escaping her lips. She was shivering, freezing cold, but suddenly she was aware of a sense of blissful warmth and comfort as Hugo crossed the small space between them and took hold of her.

'Dee, you're not well. Let me call your doctor.'

'No,' Dee protested immediately. Her doctor was still Dr Livesey, and she didn't want to see him. He had been the one who had insisted her father's death was an accident.

'Well, at least let me help you upstairs.'

Dee tried to resist. There wasn't anything wrong with her, not really. It was just the shock, the relief of knowing that it was over, that Julian Cox wasn't going to be able to taunt or torment her any longer.

There had been so many times over the years when she had longed to be able to share her feelings with someone else, when she had longed to be able to tell them what had happened, but she had never dared allow herself to give in to that temptation. It was as though in some horrible Faustian way she had struck a deal with the devil—the devil in this case being Julian Cox himself. As though by keeping her silence she was ensuring that he kept his, that he didn't attempt to besmirch her father's memory. Although logically, of course, Dee knew that he couldn't have done so without risk of exposing himself. There had been periods when he had actually lived away from Rye, no doubt practising his deceitful, dishonest ways some-where else, but he had always returned.

Now, though, he couldn't harm anyone any more. Not her father, not Beth, not anyone. It was over.

She frowned in bewilderment. She was in her bed-room, but she had no recollection of having walked up-stairs. Hugo was closing her bedroom door.

'Dee, is there someone I could ring—a friend you'd like to have here with you?' Hugo was asking her.

Immediately Dee shook her head, cringing mentally at the very thought of having to explain to anyone.

'I just want to be on my own,' she told Hugo shakily. 'I just want to be left alone.'

She felt most peculiar, oddly light-headed and so cold still. She wanted to crawl beneath the covers of her bed and lie there. She didn't want to see or speak with *anyone*.

She was only a few feet away from the bed, but for some reason as she tried to walk towards it her feet felt almost too heavy for her to lift. The bed wavered and dipped as she tried to focus on it, the floor tilting. She gave a sharp cry of protest and another softer one of shock as suddenly Hugo was next to her, supporting her, holding her.

Holding her!

Dee closed her eyes, longing flooding through her—a longing that was so intense, she could feel it in an actual physical inner pain. With her defences down, shot to pieces, the mantra she had taught herself, that Hugo belonged to her past and love was something she had learned to live without, no longer had the power to work, even if she could have remembered it.

Suddenly she was a girl again, longing for the security of her lover's arms, wanting him so much, aching for him so intensely.

'Hugo.'

As she whispered his name she wrapped her arms tightly around him, closing her eyes, ecstatically breathing in the scent of him.

'Hugo.'

She turned her head, desperately seeking his mouth with her own.

She heard him say something, her name, a plea…a sound. It didn't matter.

His hands were cupping her face, his lips, his mouth responding to the hungry passion of her own.

Once, a lifetime ago, they had kissed like this as hungrily and needfully as this, unable to take the time to draw breath properly, their hearts thudding in rapid unison, the passion between them building to such a pitch that it was almost too much to be endured.

Once, a lifetime ago, she had already experienced this need to lose herself completely in him, to be absorbed totally into him, to become somehow a part of him, so that the two of them were one indivisible whole.

Frantically Dee clung to him. She had lost him once, just as she had lost her father. Her father was lost to her for ever, but Hugo was here, alive, warm, *real*.

Passion—the kind of passion that allowed nothing to stand in its way, that swept down like an avalanche, swamped like a tidal wave, burned a path like a forest fire—gripped her, filling her, leaving no room for anything else.

She might as well have been blind, deaf and dumb for all the attention she paid to the logical warnings of her brain.

She heard Hugo groaning, and her senses recognised the sound, receiving it, registering it and interpreting it. Her hands slid feverishly down his back, past his waist, spreading against the hard masculine shape of his buttocks, pressing him into her own body just as when, long ago, that soft little groan had been a signal and an invitation for her to touch him in just that way, a sensual message from him that he wanted her to touch him, that he wanted her to show that she was responding to his desire for her and that she welcomed his arousal. So now Dee responded to it as such, trembling a little in the ferocity of her own passion as she felt the unmistakable hardening of his body.

'Dee...'

His voice was low, raw with longing, liquid with need, roughened by a soft burr of warning.

'Yes. Yes, I know,' she whispered back to him between the hungry kisses they were still exchanging.

'Undress me, Hugo,' she begged him. 'Quickly, I can't wait.'

As though to prove her point, she started to tug at her own top, moaning a little in frustration when he didn't immediately come to her aid. Hugo had never been the

kind of lover who had allowed their lovemaking to drift
into a stale routine, a familiarity that meant that he no
longer had to court her, and automatically she abandoned
her attempts to remove her own clothing and turned instead to the much more exciting task of removing his,
tugging frantically at the buttons on his shirt, muttering
little absorbed sounds of protest as her fingers refused
to work fast enough to satisfy her urgency.

'Hugo, help me,' she demanded feverishly. 'I want to
see you, *touch* you…*taste* you… Hugo…'

She gave a small gasp of satisfaction as the button
she was tussling with finally came free exposing the
upper half of his chest. Impatiently she tugged at another, and then another, so totally absorbed in her task
that she wasn't fully aware of the sudden tension that
gripped Hugo's body and the way he drew in his breath
in a swift, sharp gasp. His skin was slightly darker now
than she remembered it—his time spent in the field was
responsible for that, no doubt—and the muscles beneath
his skin were somehow more solid, heavier, stronger, just
as the silky sprinkling of dark hair she remembered as
being quite light was now thicker, different, somehow far
more dangerously masculine and exciting.

Since she was not in the habit of studying men's bodies, and since there had been no intimate relationships
in her life since Hugo had left it, she had no way of comparing him with any other man, but Dee knew instinctively that his body, at once both so familiar and yet at
the same time so pulse-racingly different, was a kind of
body that very few men of his age possessed. Wonderingly she touched the soft hair that shadowed his skin,
and then very deliberately followed the line it made down
the length of his torso.

'Dee.'

The hoarse explosive sound of protest he made shocked her into stillness. Questioningly she looked up into his eyes.

'Dee!' he said again, and then as he looked back into her eyes he stopped and groaned, closing his own eyes and then opening them again to tell her rawly, 'Come here... If you're going to torment me like that then I'm going to do a little tormenting of my own.'

His fingers were much defter on the fastenings of her clothes than hers had been with his shirt. It took him only seconds to remove her silk blouse and the bra she had been wearing under it. His hands were on the waistband of her trousers when she leaned forward and delicately started to nibble at his throat, tender little biting kisses of a type he had always loved.

As her trousers slithered to the floor his hands swept up, cupping her breasts, moulding and caressing them, the pads of his thumbs rubbing urgently over her already stiff nipples. Dee moaned his name and pressed her hot face into the curve of his shoulder, the urge to rake her fingers down the length of his back so strong that she had to fight not to give in to it.

The shock of the news of Julian's death coming so hard on the heels of the even greater shock of seeing Hugo again had totally destroyed the protective walls she had built around her feelings, leaving her achingly aware of how much she loved him, how intensely she longed for him. They were so powerfully strong that she couldn't find the words to express them. All she could do was to try to show him, smothering the hard warmth of his chest with her kisses, stroking the smooth flesh of his back, making small keening noises in her throat as he reciprocated and touched her.

Her body remembered every touch, every stroke,

every fingerprint of his hands against her; remembered
them and responded to them, her nails digging into his
skin in frantic pleasure as he lowered his head and started
to kiss the soft flesh of her breasts. Dee trembled from
head to foot, unable to understand how she had been able
to bear to give up such savagely sweet pleasure, how she
had been able to live without it and without him.

The ferocity of her need made her moan in soft frustration as she tried to press her body closer to his and felt
the thick fabric of his jeans rubbing against the softness
of her own bare skin.

'Hugo… Hugo…' she protested.

'What is it? What's wrong?' she heard Hugo asking
her thickly.

'This is wrong,' Dee responded passionately, her fingers plucking at his jeans. 'I want to feel you. *You*, Hugo.
I want to see you, touch you.' Her voice started to rise a
little as her feelings rioted out of her control. She could
see Hugo's reaction to her need in the way his eyes darkened, a dark red tide of male arousal colouring the taut
flesh of his face.

'You want me…you want this…?' she heard him demanding thickly as he reached for his belt and started
to unfasten it.

Once, long ago, as a young girl, she might have looked
modestly away. But she was a woman now, not a girl, and
Hugo was a man. *Her* man.

Her mouth was soft and red, swollen by the passion
of their shared kisses, her eyes dark and filled with open
longing as she followed the movement of his hands.
Deep down inside her own body she knew how much
she wanted him. She held her breath, her body tensing as
he removed the rest of his clothes. The very maleness of
him almost took her breath away. She had seen him like

this before, of course, but for some reason the impact of him on her now was a thousandfold more dangerous than she could ever remember it being before.

Unable to stop the long, low sound of female need that escaped from her throat, she put her fingertips to her lips.

'Don't do that,' Hugo warned her hoarsely, and then he was reaching for her hand, carrying her trembling fingers to his own mouth which he brushed softly against the sensitive pads of her fingertips. Dee felt her whole body turn wantonly liquid, and then begin to burn with shocking heat.

Very slowly and deliberately Hugo began to lick her captive fingertips, and then even more slowly to suck them. He was looking straight into her eyes, and even though she knew just what he could see in them, and how impossible it was for her to hide her reaction from him, she wanted him so much that it physically hurt—agonisingly so, so much so that she had to close her eyes against the hot burn of her pain.

'Dee. Dee…don't…don't cry…please don't cry,' she heard Hugo begging her hoarsely, dropping her hand to cup her face and reinforce the intensity of his words with suffocatingly tender kisses that inflamed her even more rather than soothed her. Unable to stop herself, she reached out and touched him, her fingers trembling a little at first as they enclosed him. His flesh felt smooth and hot, the shape and texture of him so instantly and vividly remembered that automatically she was already caressing him, stroking him firmly and possessively, knowing just how he liked her to touch him and where. This was *her* territory, *her* love, *her* man.

'Dee…'

She heard the warning in his voice but she was oblivious to it, totally lost in the fiercely sensual pleasure of caressing him.

'Dee...' Hugo warned her thickly again, when she failed to heed his warning. But Dee didn't want to listen. She could feel Hugo's hands on her body, hot and heavy, and their movement dictated the fierce pulse Dee could feel thudding against her stroking touch.

She was wearing a pair of tiny silky briefs, the merest wisp of fabric. She could feel Hugo tugging impatiently at them, but even without feeling them slither to the floor she would have known the moment she was free of them from the way Hugo suddenly sucked in his breath and the tension she could feel in his body.

He had once told her, both of them giddy, dizzy with satisfied passion, how much he loved the way the silky triangle of dark hair between her thighs so delicately hid the secret of her sex, and she had responded in kind, her eyes soft with love as she had compared the soft silkiness of her own body hair to the much thicker and more vigorous curls that surrounded his own sex. Now that contrast between them, which as a girl she had simply taken for granted, had an almost primitive effect on her senses. *Now* it made her feel intensely aware of his maleness, his potency, so much so that her body physically shook with the force of her awareness of him and of it.

'You're just the same. You haven't changed,' she heard Hugo whispering rawly to her. 'And I've never forgotten—*never.*'

Unable to stop herself, Dee felt the first of her pent-up emotional tears splash down on the hand he had lifted to touch her.

'Dee, what *is* it...? What's wrong...? Oh, Dee. Dee, don't, please, my darling. Please don't cry,' she heard

Hugo begging her as he wrapped her in his arms and picked her up.

'I'm not crying. I'm not crying,' Dee denied. 'I just want you inside me so much that it hurts, Hugo. Please don't make me wait any longer…please.'

'Dee. I can't…I haven't got—'

'You can,' Dee protested fiercely, reaching out to touch him. He was so strong, so ready for her. How could he say otherwise when she could feel how much he wanted her?

She pulled away from him and walked unsteadily towards her bed, climbing onto it and holding out her arms to him.

It seemed to take a lifetime for him to reach her, and another for him to join her, to take her in his arms and kiss her, slowly, almost reluctantly at first, and then with a hunger that was almost elemental, almost savage. But something within her responded to his urgency, something within her wanted it, she recognised, as his hand parted her thighs and his fingers found the moist readiness of her.

'No, it's not that I want. It's you,' Dee told him thickly. 'I want you, Hugo, you…'

She cried out as he entered her. It had been so long, and she wanted him so much. Her body was so exquisitely sensitive to him that each thrust of him within it filled her with an almost unbearable surge of pleasure.

She had known him like this so many, many times before, and yet this was different, Dee acknowledged. This went beyond the satisfaction of a mere physical need, beyond the mutual pleasure of reaching a sexual pinnacle.

The urge to let herself reach the climax of her pleasure was almost unbearably strong, but something made her delay it; something made her urge him to thrust even deeper inside her, as deep inside her as it was possible for him to reach, because that way...

Unable to control her longing any more, Dee cried out in abandonment. Deep within her body she could feel the hot pulse of Hugo's release, so deep within her body that she could feel her womb physically contract. A strange feeling filled her, an unfamiliar sense of giving in to fate, to a power stronger than her own.

'Hugo.'

Lovingly she traced the shape of his mouth with her fingertip.

'I never really stopped loving you, you know. I had to send you away, though, because of Dad.' Fresh tears filled her eyes.

'Dee, you can't really believe that your father took his own life,' Hugo protested as he kissed her and brushed them away. 'I know that he and I didn't see eye to eye, but there is no way, in my opinion, that he would ever have done something like that, no matter what kind of pressure he came under.'

'Is that what you really think?' Dee asked him uncertainly.

'Yes, I do,' Hugo confirmed. 'Your father was a strong man Dee, a good man. He loved you far too much to do something that would hurt you.'

'Julian Cox's deceit humbled him, Hugo. Humiliated him. He had trusted him, believed in him. For him to have discovered that Julian had been using his patronage to steal money... Dad paid it all back, of course, but...'

Dee yawned deeply.

'I feel so tired,' she complained. 'I still can't totally believe that Julian Cox is dead, or that...'

She yawned again, more deeply this time.

'Go to sleep,' Hugo told her gently, leaning over to kiss her mouth.

Obediently Dee closed her eyes.

Hugo waited until her breathing told him that she was fast asleep before easing himself out of bed. Peter was due to see the heart specialist whom the doctor had called in this evening, and Hugo had promised he would be there with him.

There hadn't been time for him to say to Dee all the things he had wanted to say. Her disclosures about her father had filled him with pain and pity. They had always been close, and he could understand how it must have hurt her to think of her father taking his own life, but despite what she had told him Hugo felt sure that his death had been a genuine accident.

It was strange how things worked out. He had come here today, driven by an impulse, a *need* so strong that no amount of logic had been able to prevent him from responding to it. Even though every bit of common sense he possessed had told him that he was a fool to even think of approaching Dee and telling her how he felt, asking her if there was any way she was prepared to give the love they had once shared a second chance, he had still felt compelled to do so.

What had actually happened between them was nothing short of miraculous. Dee still loved him. He was older now, and wiser too, and he could recognise that, much as he had loved Dee as a young man, there *had* been a certain selfishness in him, a certain single-mindedness which had driven him to pursue his own goals, his own dreams, and to expect Dee to make them hers.

Things were different now. It hadn't taken him very long to discover that without Dee his ambitions, his dreams had become curiously unfulfilling. There had been the satisfaction of knowing that what he was doing was for the benefit of others, but there had also been the loneliness of living his life on his own. Not that he hadn't had plenty of discreet and sometimes not so discreet offers of female companionship and love, but no other woman could possibly measure up to Dee.

He had told himself that, in choosing to put her love for her father above her love for him, Dee had been the one who was the loser, but when he had received the news that she was married and expecting a child he had known just which of them was the one to suffer the most.

If he hadn't been given that mistaken bit of gossip would he have acted differently? he mused as he dressed and quietly went downstairs, letting himself out of the house.

He would let Dee sleep off the trauma of the day and then, once Peter had seen the specialist, he would ring her, invite her out for dinner, take her somewhere discreet and romantic where he could...

Humming to himself, he unlocked his car.

Oh, yes, if he hadn't thought she was married and out of reach, he suspected that he would have come back sooner. Much sooner. And if he had...

Immediately his imagination conjured up an image of two children: a boy with his mother's eyes and a girl.

Oh, yes, he still loved her...had never stopped loving her...and right now—before he reversed his car out of her drive he glanced up towards Dee's bedroom window—right now the temptation to go back into the house and stay with her was so strong that... But he owed it to Peter to be with him.

Peter.

He grimaced ruefully to himself. Peter had rather misled him with his anxiety over Dee's proposals, and he could see that he was going to have to have a talk with him.

Dee!

He didn't dare start thinking about her, Hugo recognised. Not now. Not whilst he was driving.

CHAPTER TEN

DEE woke up abruptly from the dream she had been having. In it she had been walking with her father along the river. He had been holding her hand, just as he had done when she had been a little girl, smiling at her as he'd paused and pointed a shoal of minnows out to her as they swam busily in the reeds. The water had been so clear she had been able to see the bottom of the river.

Further out from the bank, though, the water had been much deeper, and suddenly she had felt afraid, drawing back, gripping her father's hand tighter, but he had laughed at her, telling her that there was nothing to be afraid of and that he loved her.

There were tears on her face, Dee recognised, but they were tears of love. As she sat up she noticed a piece of paper lying on the empty pillow beside her.

Uncertainly she picked it up, her heart thumping heavily as she recognised Hugo's handwriting.

'I love you', he had written.

I love you.

Dee closed her eyes. Hugo loved her and Hugo had told her that he didn't believe her father had taken his own life. She slid out of bed and padded over to her bedroom window. It was almost dusk, and Hugo's car had gone from her drive. She had no idea where he had gone, or why, but Dee knew instinctively that he would come back.

'I love you', he had written, and coming from Hugo those words meant exactly that. He loved her.

Her body ached in odd, unfamiliar and yet somehow very familiar little ways and places. She could still smell Hugo's scent on her skin, and if she closed her eyes she could almost feel the touch of him beneath her fingertips. She had no idea what lay ahead of them.

Hugo could, he had told her during their argument at Peter's, live virtually wherever he chose. His role within the aid programme was no longer one that required him to work out in the field. *Her* work demanded that she live here in Rye-on-Averton, but if the committee refused to sanction the changes she wanted to make to the charity she wasn't sure that she wanted to remain involved in it. Her father's charity could be carried on without her direct involvement, and without her fearing any damage to her father's name. She had no responsibility, no duty to keep her in Rye now. She could move, live wherever she wished, go with Hugo wherever *he* wished. *If* that was what he wished.

'I love you', he had written. Not, I want you, I need you…with me always…as my partner, my wife, the mother of my children.

Children. Dee touched her stomach. Did Hugo know, as she had known, had he felt as she had felt, that fierce pulse, that fusion, that heartbeat of time which had created a new life…their child? Or was it just a woman's thing, a woman's special secret knowledge, that awareness that her own body was no longer exclusively her own?

Hugo's child conceived within her. Her father would have loved to have had grandchildren.

Her father.

Dee closed her eyes and then opened them again. Was Hugo right, or had he simply been trying to comfort her?

She went to the bathroom and showered quickly. There was something she had to do. Somewhere she had to go.

'Well, now that Mr Stewart has been able to put Peter's mind at rest, he certainly won't need to be so dependent on you,' Jane told Hugo briskly.

They were in the kitchen of Peter's house. The specialist had left, having examined Peter thoroughly and then declared that he was extraordinarily fit for a man of his age and likely to live at least another ten years. But the doctor had lingered on after he had gone.

'He feels very vulnerable and alone,' Hugo told her.

'Mmm… Well, you mustn't allow him to become too dependent on you, you know. After all, you have a right to a life of your own,' she added, with a coy look, before continuing, 'Speaking of which, I was wondering if you'd like to have dinner with me one evening.'

Hugo smiled gently at her.

'It's very kind of you, but I'm afraid I can't…'

Couldn't and certainly didn't want to. The only woman he wanted to be with was Dee—the only woman he had ever wanted to be with, the only woman he would ever want to be with.

It had been his pride that had prevented him from pleading with her to change her mind all those years ago when she had told him it was over between them, and if he had known then just *why* she had said it… But she had taken good care that he shouldn't know.

It was later than he had hoped before he could leave. Peter had wanted to talk over the specialist's comments, and Hugo hadn't had the heart to cut him short or show any impatience.

'You're going out? But it's late,' Peter protested when Hugo explained.

There was no reply to the brief phone call he made before he left Peter's, and he assumed that Dee must still be asleep. But when he pulled into the driveway of her house he saw that her car was missing and he started to frown.

He hadn't said, of course, that he would come back that evening, but somehow he had assumed that… That what? That she would be there waiting for him with open arms…?

He grimaced ruefully as he felt his body's reaction to his thoughts.

He could stay here in his car and wait for her to return, but suddenly Hugo thought he knew where she might have gone. It was an instinct, a gut feeling, with nothing logical or practical to back it up, but nevertheless he set his car in motion, driving through the town.

A dozen or more teenagers were sitting on the benches in the town square, obviously at a loose end. Dee's report had surprised him, and made him feel rather ashamed of the judgements he had made.

As he drove through the town he could see his destination ahead of him—or rather its spire.

The first time she had brought him to Rye-on-Averton, Dee had pointed out the pretty parish church to him. Her parents had been married there, she had told him, and she'd hoped she would be. Many generations of her family were buried in its graveyard, including her father.

As he drove into the close that led to the church he saw Dee's parked car. Sometimes it paid to listen to one's instincts.

* * *

The graveyard was quiet and shadowy, but it was a pleasantly peaceful place rather than a threatening one, Dee acknowledged. She had never been here at night before, although she had visited it many, many times during the day, especially in the early days after her father's death, with the rawness of her own heartache. Now the scars were softer. She touched her father's headstone and traced the words carved there.

'*Was* I wrong, Dad?' she asked him huskily. 'Was it really an accident after all? It hurt me so much to think that you'd deliberately left me,' she told him conversationally. 'To feel that your pride and other people's respect for you were more important to you than my love. I hated Julian Cox for what he'd done, and sometimes I almost felt as though I hated you as well.

'Hugo says you would never have taken your own life. Never have hurt me by doing such a thing. You were always so quick to criticise him, and he you, but I knew it was just because both of you loved me. I hated having to choose between you, but how could I go with Hugo, leaving you to face the fear which had driven you to your death on your own? I had to stay...I had to protect your reputation from any harm that Julian Cox might do to it.'

'Dee...'

She froze, and then swung round as she recognised Hugo's voice.

'Hugo...what are you doing here? How did you know...?'

'I just knew,' he told her gently as he came towards her, stopping just a few feet away from her.

'I had to come here,' she told him simply. 'I had to... to talk to Dad...to ask him...to—'

'Dee, why *didn't* you tell me what you feared?' Hugo interrupted her softly. 'Surely you could have trusted me.'

'I could have trusted you, yes,' Dee agreed quietly, 'but I couldn't burden you with my…my doubts, Hugo. You'd already told me how important it was that you had an unblemished reputation. For me to tell you that I thought my father might have taken his own life, that he could have become embroiled in a sordid fraud case… I couldn't do it to you. I…I couldn't expose my father to *you*, and I couldn't expose *your* reputation to…'

'And besides…' Dee looked away from him '…I felt that I wasn't important enough to you…that your plans, your ideals mattered more, and I was afraid…I was afraid of committing myself completely to you, Hugo, because I feared that you wouldn't commit yourself completely to me.'

'So you told me you didn't love me any more. Was it true, Dee?'

Dee shook her head.

'No. Never,' she told him in a raw whisper. 'I wanted you to come back. I wanted to tell you that I'd changed my mind. But you never did…'

'No?' Hugo gave her a wry look. 'I managed to last six months in the field without you and then I had to come back, but when I did I heard that you'd got married, that you and your husband were expecting a child.'

'It wasn't true,' Dee told him, shaking her head. 'My cousin married, but…'

'Perhaps I should have asked more questions…probed more deeply. But I was so shocked, so bitterly hurt that… I think I hated you then, Dee,' Hugo told her gruffly. 'There's never been anyone else for me…no one ever came close to making me feel the way you did…do…'

'No, it's been the same for me. I…I wanted a family… a child…children…so desperately at times, Hugo, that I almost contemplated… But…' She paused. 'In the end

I just couldn't. I couldn't bear my child to have any father but you.'

She looked down at the gravestone.

'Do you *really* think it was an accident?'

'Yes, I do. A tragic, senseless, wasteful accident—but still an accident, Dee.'

'An accident...' Dee touched the stone tenderly and then, lifting her fingertips to her mouth, she kissed them softly and then touched them to the stone.

'Goodbye, Papa,' she said softly, using the pet name she had had for her father as a little girl. 'May you rest in peace.

'I think maybe you're right,' she told Hugo, her eyes brilliant with unshed tears as she added huskily, 'I hope that you are right.'

'I am right,' Hugo promised her, and he held out his hands to her and commanded, 'Come here. I've missed you so much, Dee, wanted you so much—so much more than I've ever allowed myself to know. But today, holding you...touching you... I couldn't endure to lose you again. I don't know how I've endured these years without you.'

Dee stood up and let him take her hands in his and draw her towards him. The warmth of his hands wrapped around her own filled her with the most intense sense of peace, of release, and somehow, as she went to him, Dee suddenly knew that he was right, that her father hadn't taken his own life.

With that knowledge came a lifting of her heart, her spirits, that made her feel almost light-headed, buoyant, filled with such a sense of joy and love that the intensity of her emotions seemed to make the air around her sing. Like a weight slipping from her shoulders and from her heart she could feel all the animosity she'd had, all the anger, all the bitterness she had felt towards Julian Cox leaving her like ice melting in the warmth of the sun. There was no room in her heart any more for such dark and painful feelings, because now it was overflowing with the joy of rediscovering the love she shared with Hugo.

'Let's go home,' Hugo suggested simply.

'Home!'

Dee gave him a whimsical smile as she let him guide her back to where their cars were parked.

'And where exactly might that be?'

They had reached the edge of the graveyard, and as he led her through it and onto the road outside Hugo turned her towards him and told her as he bent his head to kiss her, 'Home for me is where *you* are, Dee. *Wherever* you are.'

He followed her back to her house, parking his car behind hers, taking the key from her trembling fingers to unlock the door and then kicking it shut behind him before taking her in his arms and kissing her.

'How did you know where I was?' she asked him when he released her.

'I don't know…I just did. I had planned to take you out somewhere special for dinner. It's a bit late for that now.'

'Mmm…' Dee agreed, and then added teasingly, 'It looks like you'll have to think of some other way to satisfy my…hunger…'

'Oh…I thought I'd already done that,' Hugo responded just as teasingly, adding suggestively, 'But of course, if that wasn't enough…'

'Hugo!' Dee exclaimed. 'What about Peter? He—'

'Peter's going to be fine. That was why I went back.' Quickly he explained to her about the specialist's visit.

'Which reminds me—these proposals of yours…'

Dee tensed. Surely they weren't going to quarrel so soon?

'I'm not prepared to change my mind about them, Hugo,' she warned him quickly. 'Not even for you. I know how Peter and the others feel, but I truly believe that there is a genuine need—'

'I agree.'

Dee stared at him. 'You do?'

'Mmm…and from what I've read of your proposals I have to admit that I can't really understand just *why* Peter is so opposed to them.'

Dee sighed. 'Neither can I—not really. But he is getting old, and he's very set in his ways.'

'I'll try and talk to him,' Hugo promised her. 'Unfortunately, morally, if nothing else, whilst I'm acting as his Power of Attorney I have to vote as he would wish to have done.'

'I understand that,' Dee assured him gravely.

'I have to *vote* as he would have done, but that doesn't mean that I can't make my own assessment of the situation and try to persuade him accordingly,' he told her.

'I thought you'd have enough to do lobbying the university authorities without lobbying Peter on my behalf,' Dee told him ruefully. 'Is it really fair, though, Hugo, to try to persuade the university to use funds that are meant to be used for the benefit of scholars' charitable work to help finance aid programmes, no matter how deserving they might be?'

Hugo gave her an astonished look.

'Is *that* what you think I'd do? You're wrong. The reason I want to speak with the university authorities is to try to persuade them to introduce a vocational course for students to educate them about the way we work and

the way they can help us. We need young, keen, innovative brains to come up with solutions to the problems
we're constantly facing—but right now what I need most
of all is you.'

'Me…?' Dee looked at him mock innocently.

'Mmm… You,' Hugo repeated.

This time they made love slowly and tenderly, luxuriat-
ing in every touch, every kiss, sharing their joy at their
mutual discovery of each remembered pleasure and adding new ones to them.

'You're even more beautiful now as a woman than you
were as a girl,' Hugo told Dee as he stroked his fingertips along the soft warm curves of her body.

'And *you* are even more dangerously sexy,' Dee told
him, glaring mock angrily at him as he threw back his
head and laughed. 'You don't believe me? Ask Dr Jane
Harper,' she challenged him.

'Who's Dr Jane Harper?' Hugo demanded huskily as
he bent his head to tease the erect nipple he had just
been stroking.

Dee closed her eyes and gave a soft moan of liquid
pleasure.

'I felt so *jealous* of her,' she admitted.

'Not nearly so jealous as I was over your supposed
husband,' Hugo assured her, his voice suddenly stark
with pain as he told her, 'You don't know what that did
to me, Dee, how close I came to—' He stopped. 'But I
told myself there were still people who needed me, even
if *you* were no longer one of them. Life has to go on. Your
father knew that too, Dee.'

'Yes,' she agreed quietly. 'I believe he did.'

It was easy to let go of the past and all the pain it contained now that Hugo was here with her, holding her, loving her. She was never going to let him go again. *Never*.

Their guests had gone and Beth was stacking the dishwasher whilst Alex washed the crystal glasses which had been a gift to them from his family in Prague.

'Wasn't that the most extraordinary thing with Dee and Hugo?' Beth asked him conversationally.

'Dee and Hugo…what do you mean? What was extraordinary about them?' Alex replied, frowning. 'I admit that the fact that they already knew one another was a coincidence…'

'Oh, Alex! Surely you *must* have seen…noticed…?' Beth demanded.

'Seen *what*? They hardly spoke to one another all evening,' Alex protested.

Beth rolled her eyes.

'They didn't *need* to speak. You could practically feel the air palpitating around them.'

'Palpitating?' Alex gave an amused snort of derision. 'Hearts palpitate, Beth. Air—'

'Yes… Yes, exactly.' Beth pounced before he could finish. 'And *their* hearts were palpitating all right. There's something going on between those two,' she pronounced darkly. 'Heavens, the way they were *looking* at one another—I almost expected the air between them to self-ignite…'

Alex gave a theatrical sigh.

'Look, I don't want to dampen your hopes. I know that you, and Anna and Kelly for that matter, are so blissfully pleased with yourselves for being lucky enough to find such wonderful men, but— Ouch!' Alex protested as Beth threw a dishcloth at him.

'*We* were lucky, huh?'

'Beth, where are you going?' Alex asked her as she suddenly turned and walked towards the kitchen door.

'I'm going to ring Anna…in private…'

'You don't think that Beth guessed, do you?' Dee asked Hugo anxiously as she snuggled into his arms beneath the warmth of her duvet. 'She gave me a *very* knowing look when she said goodnight.'

'Well, if she *has* guessed it wasn't my fault,' Hugo responded virtuously. '*I* wasn't the one playing footsie under the table—and very suggestively too, I might add.'

'I've already told you that was an accident,' Dee protested. 'I'd lost my shoe…'

'Mmm, and I nearly lost *my* self-control. Anyway, what does it matter if she did guess?'

'You *know* we said that we wouldn't go public until after the committee meeting. If I'd known when she originally invited me to dinner that Alex's duty invite was you, I—'

'You mean *you* said we wouldn't go public…'

'We don't want the other members of the committee to think that—'

'That what?' Hugo teased her. 'That I'm so desperately in love with you that you used your wicked wiles to get me to vote in your favour?'

'Certainly not. I would never do anything like that,' Dee protested indignantly.

'No…? Are you sure?' Hugo wheedled coaxingly as he slid his hand over the curve of her hip.

'Mmm…I thought *I* was supposed to be the one doing the seducing,' Dee murmured huskily.

'Mmm. Well, perhaps I'm trying to use *my* wicked wiles on *you*.'

'What for?' Dee asked him softly as she opened her mouth to his kiss. 'I've already given in to you...'

'Mmm...you have, haven't you?' Hugo agreed. 'And pretty soon everyone's going to know that you have, *aren't* they?' he asked her, gently patting her stomach.

'Hugo,' Dee objected. 'How did you know?' she asked him. 'It's far too soon yet, and...'

'I know for exactly the same reason that *you* know,' Hugo told her. 'What we shared was just too powerful, too strong, too intense for us not to have created a new life together.'

'We can't be sure...' Dee warned him. 'Not yet.' But Hugo could see the hope in her eyes, and his heart melted with love for her.

'You'll have to marry me now,' he told her.

'Yes, but not until after the committee meeting,' Dee told him teasingly.

'Not until after the committee meeting,' Hugo agreed.

'And so, in conclusion, I would like to reiterate that in my view this committee has a moral obligation to the original founder of the charity to follow in his footsteps and apply charitable help to that section of the community where it is most needed. As this report in front of you proves quite conclusively, it is needed nowhere more than in the relief of the deprivation that is being suffered by the town's young people.

'To give them not just a sense of self-worth, nor even a future to look forward to, but positive and concrete proof of their town's faith and belief in them would surely be a fitting tribute to the spirit of everything that your founder stood for. By helping those young people we are *investing* in the future. Not just *their* future, but the future of our own descendants as well. To deny them the opportunity to become responsible citizens would, in my view, be a grave moral indictment of us as human beings.

'To take on a task of the magnitude of this one is a very bold and courageous step, there is no doubt about that, but I believe it is one we are capable of making. The question is, do you believe it?'

Dee gasped as Hugo sat down to a standing ovation from the whole committee.

He had completely surprised her when he had asked the committee if he might address them, not as Peter's representative but as a private individual.

Although somewhat surprised, they had agreed. Hugo's reputation had gone before him and Dee had seen how impressed they were by him.

Now, as he sat down, her eyes filled with proud tears. Here, in the shape of the words her husband-to-be, her lover, the father of her child, their child, their children, had just uttered, she had heard the vindication of everything that her father had hoped and worked for.

Hugo had put her case so well, turning it on its head so that instead of pleading with the committee to have compassion for the young of the town he had actually made them feel that they were *already* the compassionate, wise, comprehending people they must prove themselves to be.

As she looked around her she could almost sense her father's presence and his approval, his *love*. Ignoring the amazed looks of the other members of the committee, she went over to Hugo and kissed him.

'I love you,' she told him huskily. 'I love you so much.'

There was no doubt about the way the committee would vote; she could see it in their faces. Rye's young people would have their new centre and meeting place.

They would learn proper trades, they would thrive and grow, and the town would thrive with them.

Tonight she was hosting a very special dinner party. Those who had been invited thought it was being given to celebrate her birthday, and that was what she wanted them to believe—Kelly and Brough, Anna and Ward, Beth and Alex.

She looked down at the diamond ring glittering on her left hand. Hugo had given it to her this morning…in bed.

Like the ring on her finger, her life had come full circle, bringing her back to the place she most wanted to be, the person she most wanted to be with. And tonight, at dinner, she would introduce Hugo to her friends as her husband-to-be, her lover. The shadows Julian Cox had thrown over her life had gone for ever. Hugo had banished them with the warmth of his love.

'Stop looking at me like that,' he warned her in a whisper against her ear as he bent his head towards her. 'Otherwise…'

The votes had been cast and the result was a resounding yes.

Dee was still looking at Hugo and whispered softly, 'Most definitely, yes.'

EPILOGUE

THE BELLS GAVE tongue, a burst of joyous, almost triumphant sound, as Dee and Hugo emerged from the church into the sunshine outside.

'Why is it that women cry at weddings?' Brough demanded as he, Ward and Alex exchanged very male looks with one another while their respective partners, to a woman, viewed the bride and groom through a happy film of tears.

'It's because we're so happy, of course,' Kelly answered him truthfully.

'So very, very happy,' Anna concurred softly as the three women looked tenderly at one another.

This morning, before the service, as the three of them had bustled about Dee's bedroom helping her to get ready, Dee had suddenly commanded them all to stop, and opened the bottle of champagne in an ice-bucket next to her dressing table, pouring four glasses.

'To love and happiness,' she had proposed, raising her glass, and then, as the other three had joined her in her toast, she had added with a wicked, very Dee-like smile, 'And to the man who is in many ways the author of the happiness we have all found in this last year or so.' Whilst the others had hesitated, her smile had deepened, and she'd enlightened them. 'Julian Cox. Without him *none* of us would have met our wonderful, perfect partners.'

'You want to *toast* Julian Cox?' Anna had marvelled softly. 'Oh, Dee...'

'Why not?' Dee challenged her gently. 'There isn't room in my life any more for negative, destructive feelings, Anna... I don't need them...'

'Dee's right,' Kelly had confirmed. 'Julian might have cast a horribly grey and threatening cloud over all our lives in one way or another, but it quite definitely turned out to be a cloud with a silver lining.'

'Well, then, perhaps we should make our toast to hidden silver linings,' Beth had suggested.

Between them they had finished the bottle of champagne, but, watching Dee now, Anna knew that it wasn't the champagne that was responsible for the glow of happiness on her face, that open look of love with which she was regarding Hugo. The bells were still pealing, the rose petals making a silver and pink moving cloud around the bridal couple, and Dee looked radiant in her wedding gown of antique cream lace. Anna, Beth and Kelly, her three supporters-cum-attendants, were dressed in similarly elegantly styled gowns of toning cream raw silk, trimmed with the most beautiful matt dull gold cummerbunds fastened with huge soft bows at the back. The little bridesmaids, in contrast, were in the same colour combination, but their dresses were pure fairy tale—masses of cream silk voile over matt gold underskirts.

The photographers coaxed everyone together for a final photograph outside the church. That over, Dee turned to whisper something to her new husband. After giving her a tender kiss, Hugo detached himself from her and came over to where the other six were standing.

'Can you start getting everyone organised to leave for

the wedding breakfast?' he asked Anna. 'Dee and I have something we want to do before we leave, so if you could cover for us for a few minutes…?'

'No problem,' Anna assured him, and she and the others started to discreetly get the guests moving.

'Do you think he knows?' Dee asked Hugo quietly as she leaned her head against his shoulder and looked down at her father's grave. She had just placed her bridal flowers on it, and as Hugo's arm tightened around her a happy tear splashed down onto the cream blooms.

'I don't know,' Hugo told her softly. 'But what I *do* know is how much, how very much, I love you, Dee…' He could feel her trembling as he kissed her. 'Come on,' he told her firmly. 'You and I have got a wedding breakfast to attend.'

'You and I?' Dee questioned, smiling at him. 'Don't you meant the three of us…?' As she turned towards him in profile it was possible to see what the elegant shaping of her gown had kept modestly concealed: the ripening shape of her body.

'The three of us,' Hugo echoed huskily, whilst outside the church the final flurry of rose petals sank gently onto the earth.

* * * * *

REQUEST YOUR
FREE BOOKS!

2 FREE NOVELS PLUS
2 FREE GIFTS!

YES! Please send me 2 FREE Harlequin Presents® novels and my 2 FREE gifts (gifts are worth about $10). After receiving them, if I don't wish to receive any more books, I can return the shipping statement marked "cancel." If I don't cancel, I will receive 6 brand-new novels every month and be billed just $4.30 per book in the U.S. or $4.99 per book in Canada. That's a saving of at least 14% off the cover price! It's quite a bargain! Shipping and handling is just 50¢ per book in the U.S. and 75¢ per book in Canada.* I understand that accepting the 2 free books and gifts places me under no obligation to buy anything. I can always return a shipment and cancel at any time. Even if I never buy another book, the two free books and gifts are mine to keep forever.

106/306 HDN FVRK

Name   (PLEASE PRINT)

Address   Apt. #

City   State/Prov.   Zip/Postal Code

Signature (if under 18, a parent or guardian must sign)

Mail to the **Harlequin® Reader Service:**
IN U.S.A.: P.O. Box 1867, Buffalo, NY 14240-1867
IN CANADA: P.O. Box 609, Fort Erie, Ontario L2A 5X3

Are you a current subscriber to Harlequin Presents books
and want to receive the larger-print edition?
Call 1-800-873-8635 or visit www.ReaderService.com.

* Terms and prices subject to change without notice. Prices do not include applicable taxes. Sales tax applicable in N.Y. Canadian residents will be charged applicable taxes. Offer not valid in Quebec. This offer is limited to one order per household. Not valid for current subscribers to Harlequin Presents books. All orders subject to credit approval. Credit or debit balances in a customer's account(s) may be offset by any other outstanding balance owed by or to the customer. Please allow 4 to 6 weeks for delivery. Offer available while quantities last.

Your Privacy—The Harlequin® Reader Service is committed to protecting your privacy. Our Privacy Policy is available online at www.ReaderService.com or upon request from the Harlequin Reader Service.

We make a portion of our mailing list available to reputable third parties that offer products we believe may interest you. If you prefer that we not exchange your name with third parties, or if you wish to clarify or modify your communication preferences, please visit us at www.ReaderService.com/consumerschoice or write to us at Harlequin Reader Service Preference Service, P.O. Box 9062, Buffalo, NY 14269. Include your complete name and address.

Love the Harlequin book you just read?

Your opinion matters.

Review this book on your favorite
book site, review site, blog or your own
social media properties and share
your opinion with other readers!

In Buckshot Hills, Texas, a sexy doctor meets his match in the least likely woman—a beautiful cowgirl looking to reinvent herself....

Enjoy a sneak peek from USA TODAY *bestselling author Judy Duarte's new Harlequin® Special Edition® story,* TAMMY AND THE DOCTOR *,the first book in Byrds of a Feather, a brand-new miniseries launching in March 2013!*

***

Before she could comment or press Tex for more details, a couple of light knocks sounded at the door.

Her grandfather shifted in his bed, then grimaced. "Who is it?"

"Mike Sanchez."

Doc? Tammy's heart dropped to the pit of her stomach with a thud, then thumped and pumped its way back up where it belonged.

"Come on in," Tex said.

Thank goodness her grandfather had issued the invitation, because she couldn't have squawked out a single word.

As Doc entered the room, looking even more handsome than he had yesterday, Tammy struggled to remain cool and calm.

And it wasn't just her heartbeat going wacky. Her feminine hormones had begun to pump in a way they'd never pumped before.

"Good morning," Doc said, his gaze landing first on Tex, then on Tammy.

As he approached the bed, he continued to look at Tammy,

his head cocked slightly.

"What's the matter?" she asked.

"I'm sorry. It's just that your eyes are an interesting shade of blue. I'm sure you hear that all the time."

"Not really." And not from anyone who'd ever mattered. In truth, they were a fairly common color—like the sky or bluebonnets or whatever. "I've always thought of them as run-of-the-mill blue."

"There's nothing ordinary about it. In fact, it's a pretty shade."

The compliment set her heart on end. But before she could think of just the perfect response, he said, "If you don't mind stepping out of the room, I'd like to examine your grandfather."

Of course she minded leaving. She wanted to stay in the same room with Doc for the rest of her natural-born days. But she understood her grandfather's need for privacy.

"Of course." Apparently it was going to take more than simply batting her eyes to woo him, but there was no way Tammy would be able to pull off a makeover by herself. Maybe she could ask her beautiful cousins for help?

She had no idea what to say the next time she ran into them. But somehow, by hook or by crook, she'd have to think of something.

Because she was going to risk untold humiliation and embarrassment by begging them to turn a cowgirl into a lady!

***

*Look for TAMMY AND THE DOCTOR from
Harlequin® Special Edition® available March 2013*

SPECIAL EDITION

Life, Love and Family

Coming in March 2013 from fan-favorite author

KATHLEEN EAGLE

Cowboy Jack McKenzie has a checkered past, but when rancher's daughter Lily reluctantly visits her father, he wants more than anything to show that he's a reformed man. Has she made up her mind too early that this would be a short stay at the ranch?

Look for *One Less Lonely Cowboy* next month from Kathleen Eagle.

Available March 2013 from Harlequin Special Edition wherever books are sold.

HARLEQUIN®

A *Romance* FOR EVERY MOOD™

Stay up-to-date on all your
romance-reading news with the
Harlequin Shopping Guide,
featuring bestselling authors, exciting new
miniseries, books to watch and more!

The newest issue will be delivered right to you
with our compliments! There are 4 each year.

Signing up is easy.

EMAIL

ShoppingGuide@Harlequin.ca

WRITE TO US

HARLEQUIN BOOKS
Attention: Customer Service Department
P.O. Box 9057, Buffalo, NY 14269-9057

OR PHONE

1-800-873-8635 in the United States
1-888-343-9777 in Canada

Please allow 4-6 weeks for delivery of the first issue by mail.

HSGSIGNUP

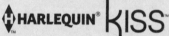